To: L

The Mill Children

Suzanne Marshall

The Mill Children

Suzanne Marshall

© Suzanne Marshall

Published by Suzanne Marshall

January 2009

Third reprint September 2009

Available from: hilldene1@aol.com or
Telephone: 01944 710880
£7.99 plus £1 postage

ISBN 978-0-9558909-0-1

Prepared and printed by:
York Publishing Services Ltd
64 Hallfield Road
Layerthorpe
York YO31 7ZQ
Tel: 01904 431213
Website: www.yps-publishing.co.uk

Acknowledgements

Thanks are due to my husband Steve, for his balanced judgement and tireless support; to Bob Jackman, chairman and tutor of Scarborough Writers' Society whose pleasure in teaching inspired me to start, continue and finish this novel and who gave so generously of his time to review each chapter; and to his wife Mary, an avid reader, for her insightful comments.

About the Author

Suzanne Marshall grew up in Scarborough and took pleasure in writing from an early age. A career in nursing followed by marriage and the business of raising a family in Brussels, Saudi Arabia, Sussex and York never quite extinguished this urge. Encouraged by writer's groups over the years, she produced poems, plays, short stories and articles and in the process discovered her forte – researching and writing historical novels.

The Mill Children was inspired by a history lesson on a wet afternoon at Skellfield Hall, the school she attended, formerly a stately home, which features so vividly throughout this book. Now settled near Scarborough, she is currently working on a sequel.

Chapter One

It was the hour of five on a winter's morning. The distant toll of a factory bell echoed across the valley, striking wakefulness and dread wherever it was heard. For the army of child slaves, compelled to work amongst the ceaseless whirring of a million hissing wheels, another day had begun. Tiny footprints in the snow showed where some had hurried and others had fallen behind sobbing, aware that the lash of the whip awaited them. One such child fell with a piteous cry and lay in her winding sheet too weak to rise, her blood congealing fast in the bitter cold. Fate hung in the balance as a carriage approached. Had the horse not stumbled on the early morning ice and the coachman not paused to examine his charge, a life might have been spared but, as it was, the pale distorted limbs were soon covered with a blanket of soft white flakes and the coach passed by. Another nameless child had found its final rest.

The deep and narrow lane down which the wind howled was a good two miles from the mill and the occupants of the coach noticed that the throng of children grew as they approached it. In the comparative warmth of their leather cab, Mr Wood turned an earnest face to his comrade.

1

'This, Mr Oastler, is what I want you to see. In London you campaign for the abolition of slavery abroad, yet here in Yorkshire, within sight of your own home, the cruelties that are practised in our mills leave me sleepless at night. These children are hired for a pittance, sir, not bought like the negroes. They are not even cared for as a beast that is valued for its worth, simply worked and discarded when they wear out or die.'

Richard Oastler MP scanned the bleak landscape outside and looked at the shuffling tide of ragged humanity converging on the huge, five-storey woollen mill. He shifted uneasily in his seat. Had he not seen these buildings grow, with their chimneys like soulless steeples stark against the sky, from the comfort of his own mansion? High on the hill, safe from the billowing smog that often obscured the town, he had not given a thought to the problems attendant on the new age of steam. He saw for the first time the price these infants, some as young as five, some barefoot, were paying for the pace of change. The hideous, prematurely aged faces of the young convinced him that here was a kind of slavery on his own doorstep.

A group of three, clinging together against the cold, shrank away from the iron-rimmed wheels of the cab. On an impulse, Oastler struck the roof hard with the tip of his cane. When the coach stopped he called out to them.

'Come here, boy! Don't be afraid. I wish to talk to you.' The tallest of the group plainly was afraid but, used to obedience, stepped forward and stood with head bowed.

'What's your name, boy?'

'William, sir.'

'Speak up, boy, William who?'

The lad, through shortness of breath, seemed unable to raise his voice and reluctant to be delayed.

'William Cartwright, sir.'

'Tell me, William,' Oastler continued, softening his tone, 'do you fear a beating if you are late?'

'Yes sir, not just me, sir, but my sister and cousin too.' He indicated the shivering ten-year old girl, who clung whimpering to his threadbare clothes, and the slightly taller youth behind. He had thick dark hair and seemed the fittest of the three.

Oastler turned to his friend as he opened the cab door and beckoned them in.

'I shall not be a cause of their punishment today.'

All three hesitated, wide-eyed, uncertain. This had never happened before. Then as one they scrambled inside and sat huddled together in the corner, savouring the shelter and warmth of the coach.

Mr Wood leant forward, his generally retiring nature overcome with the genuine compassion he felt.

'See the state of their limbs, sir, and the curve of their spines. They grow up, if they grow up at all, as cripples after working in the mill. Fourteen hours a day, sometimes more, often standing or stooping beneath the dangerous cogs with the fly in the ball of the hand and a mere thirty minutes to rest at noon. The machines are relentless. If the children don't keep up or they fall asleep the overseers beat them.' He ran a silk handkerchief across his brow and adjusted his top hat before continuing softly.

'I have been reading the bible, sir, and in every passage I find my own condemnation. I cannot allow you to leave me without a pledge that you will use your influence to remove these cruelties from our factory system.'

Oastler, an elegant gentleman who devoted his energies to the stewardship of Fixby Hall where he currently lived, enjoyed responsibility. But he was still at thirty-one a young man fired with ambition and a great gift for oratory. He saw poverty every day. It was part of life but these three children bore witness to Mr Wood's words and he was deeply moved. He turned to the eldest boy once more, whose scant hair hung in strands round an almost skeletal face.

'At what age did you first go to work in the mill?'

The lad cast his eyes down. Had he ever known another life?

'When I was turned five, sir.'

'What age are you now, William?'

'Fifteen.'

'What hours of labour do you work at this time?'

There was a pause as the boy struggled to lip-read what he could no longer hear.

'From six in the morning until eight at night, sir.'

4

'With what intervals for refreshment and rest?'

Mr Wood, seeing him hesitate again, intervened.

'Forty minutes at noon, sometimes only thirty, and what little they take with them is soon covered in dust and fit only for pigs,' he added vehemently.

Oastler smoothed his soft kid gloves thoughtfully.

'And when trade is brisk, what are your hours?'

'From five in the morning until nine at night.'

'How far do you live from the mill? One, two miles?' William nodded, pointing back down the road to the village.

'Is there any time allowed to get your breakfast in the mill?' All three children fixed hollow eyes on Oastler and shook their heads in unison. He continued. 'What is your business in the mill?' Again there was a pause so that the MP rephrased the question more simply. 'I mean, what do you do?'

'I am a doffer, sir.'

'Do you consider doffing a laborious employment? Is it hard work?'

'Aye.'

'Explain what it is you have to do.'

William, keen to understand and please this evidently important gentleman, lifted a thin gnarled arm to demonstrate.

'When the frames are full, they must be changed. We must take the flyers off and the full bobbins and carry them to the roller and then put empty ones on and set the frame going again.'

'Does that keep you constantly on your feet?'

'Aye. There are so many frames and they run so quick. We cannot stop for anything.' A consumptive cough wracked the boy's lean chest and Oastler instinctively covered his mouth.

'Suppose you flagged a little. Suppose you got behind. What would they do?'

'They would strap us,' he wheezed.

'Are they in the habit of strapping those who are last in doffing?' All three nodded again, sensing this man could be trusted. 'Constantly?'

'Aye sir. The little 'uns too.'

Oastler turned his gaze towards the girl with matted flaxen hair. She reminded him of a small bird, crouched motionless against the hand of its captor.

'Girls as well as boys?'

'Aye.'

'What is your name, my dear?' he enquired gently.

'Beth,' she whispered, then with a hint of pride and an imperceptible lift of her chin, 'Beth Cartwright.'

'Do they beat you severely too?'

For answer she drew back the sleeves of her calico smock. The second boy, more guarded and thoughtful than the other two and more sturdily built, exposed an unhealed wound on her shoulder. Oastler examined it with horror and muttered a word to his friend before turning his attention to him.

'And you are Beth's cousin, are you not?'

'Aye. I'm Jack Cartwright, sir.'

'How long have you worked in the mill?' A shadow slid over the boy's brooding face before he answered.

'Since last year, sir. Since they sent me away from London to live here with William and Beth. Their mother died of the fever a month since so we're alone now.' He touched the leather-buttoned seats of the cab, lost for a moment in the past.

'My father had one of these. I used to help him with the horses on the rank. Then one day...' The dark eyes misted over. 'One day a runaway horse knocked him down. The wagon crushed him. I never saw him again.'

Mr Wood drew his silk handkerchief a second time and blew his nose fiercely.

'Ah, the sadness of it,' he sighed. 'Soon the boy will be crippled like the rest.'

The coach was fast approaching the mill and Oastler, making best use of the purpose of their trip, continued his questions.

'During these long hours of labour, can you always be punctual? How do you awake?' He was addressing William again now who shivered and shook his head.

'I used to be lifted out of bed, sometimes asleep, by my mother. Now I must wake the others. We dare not be late.'

'But if you are late, you are beaten?'

'Aye, sir. Most often beaten. Sometimes not paid and that is worse for then we don't eat.'

'In your mill, is chastisement towards the latter

7

part of the day always going on?' Jack, whose hearing was as yet unaffected, responded quietly.

'Aye. Always.'

The three were distracted now by the toll of the bell overhead and their bony fingers clawed for release at the heavy upholstered door. Oastler opened it and watched them dart off through the snow like frightened animals until they became lost in the multitude of children converging on the blackened factory walls. There was just enough moon to leave the scene etched on his mind ~~and~~ he would never forget it. He looked gravely at his friend and extended a firm hand.

'You have my word,' he said, 'that I shall not rest until I have done what I can for these unfortunate souls.'

Dialogue appalling Illerode
children don't recognise
Class its ment.

Chapter Two

It was hard to say who was the weaker, William or Beth as, bent against the wind, the three collapsed in a drift of snow close to the factory door. The huge bolts were not yet drawn to allow admittance so they had time to gaze back at the receding carriage and ponder their strange experience. They were not to know then that their plight would inspire the young man within it and sow the first seeds of reform for the factory workers. One day, that early winter morning in 1830 would be remembered. For now, however, and for seventeen long years to come, nothing but fate could change their wretched lives.

The sound of iron grating in the lock sent a stir through the ragged crowd. The porter, a giant of a man hand picked for the job, cracked a whip above the frail bodies that surged around him.

'Be gone to your work, you worthless brats,' he goaded, wiping the sweat of the furnace from his brow. The furnace in the bowels of the factory kept the mighty steam engines turning and thus the spinners and weavers in the great halls above relentlessly at their tasks.

It was a long climb to the fourth floor where the Cartwrights' only comfort was in being able to catch sight of each other as they laboured along their rows of yarn. Jack dragged his cousin up the last flight before pausing on the landing to let him gain breath. William felt hot to the touch. Beth sank onto the top step, her little head nodding from want of sleep.

'Does he have the fever, Jack?' she whispered, her eyes suddenly wide as saucers at the memory of her mother's recent death. William, hearing the heartbreak in her voice, straightened himself and took her hand. His quiet words of comfort were lost as he opened the workroom door. The noise within was deafening, defying conversation until nightfall when the wheels and gears that towered above choked to a halt once more.

Beth retched at the stench of gas and oil and hurried to take up her position on a spinning mule. Soon hundreds of labouring lungs would foul the air further as they gasped for breath in the rising clouds of dust. The overseer, a weasel-faced man who enjoyed his power, cuffed William and Jack as they passed down the vast hall to station themselves at other machines. This was only morning. By noon his strap would be out to keep the little ones awake. He disliked Jack. The lad stared at him without flinching when the whip fell on his bare flesh and would not be cowed as the others were. He must make an example of him soon he thought, mindful of the baton he kept for this purpose. Tomorrow he would bring it and then he would teach the creature who was boss. He passed on down the aisle between row after row of cranking machines with the thought uppermost in his mind.

Jack watched him go with relief. He had not been long enough in the mill to accept the horrors that he saw around him. Some tried to escape. He had seen them dragged back to the manager's lodge, locked up for days, starved and beaten and then returned to the mill too sick and maimed to walk twenty yards. No one that he knew had ever got away.

The whirling spindles were gathering speed now, keeping him constantly at his task, but his mind was free, not yet deadened by the years of toil that the others had suffered. As his fingers moved deftly, replacing the reels and piecing together the broken threads, his thoughts slipped back over the last few months. So much had happened since his aunt had died. One tragedy heaped on another or so it seemed. At first he had turned to William, his elder by four years, to fill the great loss of his own father's death but his cousin was sick and his strength was failing. Already they struggled to pay the rent for the draughty room that served as their home. If they failed, it was only a matter of time before the workhouse claimed them. He shuddered at the sight of the children labouring beside him who were contracted to the mill from the blackened building across the yard and who knew no other life but to respond to the machines and the will of their masters. His lips moved in a silent resolve that whatever happened, this fate should not befall them.

The overseer's lash fell sharply on his shoulders prompting a quick intake of breath but he looked up, defiant as ever, into the venomous face.

'There be no talking in here, you lazy cur,' the man mouthed above the roar of the spinning mules. He raised an arm to strike again but was distracted by a sudden commotion further down the hall. A small girl, flattened against the floor to collect fragments of wool, had lost a clump of hair in the moving cogs. Jack turned away as she was dragged out by her crooked legs to whimper quietly in the corner. When he looked again, thankful at least that it was not Beth, blood had begun seeping from her scalp onto the dirty sacking piled against the wall. Such sights were not uncommon, in fact he had seen young limbs torn from their sockets and flesh sliced from bone as the day wore on and tiredness took its toll but his stomach still heaved with revulsion. He rubbed his sore eyes and gripped the fly firmly once more. He must stay awake. The moving metal parts had no guards to protect the unwary.

At noon the signal was given for a thirty-minute break and, like puppets whose strings had suddenly been cut, the children sank where they were, more interested in sleep than their meagre portions of bread. Jack shuffled along the line of machines to find Beth, already insensible, curled up like a kitten against a stack of wool. There was no sign of William so Jack, too, lay down to sleep.

All too soon they were summoned by threats to return to their work and the long day continued. Back and forth, back and forth, bending and stretching up and down their rows till the pain in their twisted bones could only be endured by their greater fear of the whip.

At last, the whirling spindles slowed then ceased. Outside, the clatter of hoof beats rang through the night air as wheels rumbled over icy cobbles. Draught animals strained against the whip, cab drivers in search of a fare shouted and beckoned above the tumult, dogs barked and doors banged as the townsfolk bid each other goodnight. Fine ladies in fur coats stepped hurriedly into carriages to avoid the ragged hoards that poured from the factory gate.

William, supported by two of his friends, was amongst them. He had seen Jack carrying Beth like a broken doll across his shoulders and knew that for her sake he would hurry on home. The youth next to him placed a hand on his arm.

'Can you walk on your own?' he asked with brotherly concern.

William glanced up at the hollow eyes that mirrored his own and forced a lopsided smile.

'Aye,' he murmured, knowing already they would not meet again. He wanted to call after him, to say something more but his throat was too dry. His fever was worse. He limped down the steps, oblivious to the cold and the fierce pangs of hunger that usually plagued him. He turned down the street and stumbled forward, using the iron rails for support. At times his frail body folded, forcing him to stop and wait for the will to continue. He was so tired, so very tired. His legs felt as weak as a new born lamb's yet instinctively they carried him on. He was almost home when the moon, racing between clouds, plunged him suddenly into darkness. A cat streaked from the shadows causing him first to stumble then to fall heavily on the frozen ground. Moments later a figure emerged from a terraced house, gathered the boy in his arms and carried him gently to a small back room.

By the light of a single candle, Jack struggled to save his cousin's life. He chafed the bloodless hands and hugged the stiffening ribs as if, by doing so, he could reanimate the cold flesh.

'Don't leave us, William,' he pleaded. His usual bravado had gone. Instead he was a young boy wanting the comfort of his mother's arms or his father's reassuring voice. But there was no-one in the damp and draughty room except an exhausted Beth asleep in the corner – no sound except the wind rattling against a broken pane.

He shuddered, half from cold, half from fear as he drew the candle close to William's feeble breath. He was fading fast.

'Don't leave us alone,' he cried again, staring around him at the grotesque shadows dancing on the flagstoned floor. When he looked again William's eyes were open and fixed upon his own. His parched lips moved.

'Come closer, Jack,' he whispered, reaching for his cousin's hand. 'Don't be afraid. I am not sorry to leave this life.' He paused, breathing rapidly now, then as if vehemence gave him strength, he continued.

'They'll come and take you when I am gone – to the workhouse or the mill. Don't wait for that.' He lifted his head with an effort. 'You must leave here.

14

You are still strong, Jack. Take Beth away. Her future rests with you.'

He dropped back, his energy spent, and Jack knew when the candle burned steadily against the chalk white skin that he was dead. He shed no tears. He wanted to scream but found that his throat was too tight. From the opposite recess he heard a muffled sob and turned to see Beth stifling her grief in the folds of her dead mother's dress. Eventually, her sad questioning face peered up at him and he answered it by taking her outstretched palm and drawing her close. He didn't feel strong but William had told him what to do.

By the time dawn broke he had thrown off the mantle of childhood and a new resolve had taken its place. Outside, virginal snow covered the landscape, stretching into low cloud over the hills. It was Sunday and Jack could see the devout already making their way along the track that led down by the beck to the church. He would take Beth away while the villagers were at prayer, he decided, before word got round of his cousin's death and before the parish officers could decide on their fate. Nothing could be worse than their present life and his mind was quite focused now on the challenge ahead.

William lay at peace beneath a threadbare cloth and a wreath of twisted ivy that Beth had made. Jack gathered a skillet, a soup pan, two earthenware mugs and a knife together with all the warm cloth he could find and packed them in an old sack. On the top he placed a tinder box that belonged to his father, a possession he treasured as much for the memories it contained as for its practical use.

'Must we leave William now?' Beth sobbed, stemming her tears with the wool blanket Jack had wrapped round her.

Jack nodded as he swung the sack across his shoulders and took her firmly by the hand.

'Aye, we must. There's nothing for us here.' He looked at the tracks in the snow. They would head for the church so that their footprints would be lost amongst the others. The bell had stopped ringing and the doors would be closed now. No one would see them as they slipped down to the beck and walked upstream along its pebbled bank. With luck, by the time they reached the woods, the snow would have covered their trail and not even the dogs would be able to trace them.

Apart from a pig snuffling in the gutter and an old man bent over a shepherd's crook, whom Jack knew to be almost blind, they followed this plan without encountering a soul. It was with strangely mixed emotions that they paused on the brow of the city hill to look back – Beth at the cluster of buildings on the village street where her parents, grandparents and siblings had lived and died – and Jack beyond at the blackened outline of the mill towering through grey smog like an evil fortress in a fairy tale. But up here they breathed in the clean fresh air of the new morning and felt the slight warmth of the sun against their faces as the snow began to melt. Up here there was hope and even through her tears, Beth could sense it. A robin chirping on a nearby tree with its head cocked quaintly to one side made her laugh in spite of her sorrow so that Jack, hearing her, laughed too and felt heartened. He adjusted the blanket round her thin neck

'You'll see. Jack will look after you. Jack can do anything,' he declared, with the optimism of youth. Then bundling her in front of him and stopping only to adjust his knapsack, he strode firmly after her. He had made a big decision for a young boy of eleven, one perhaps that he could only have made in a moment of despair, but there was no going back.

Beth remained resolute too as they picked their way through a wonderland of trees transformed by snow. It was only when the wide unfamiliar landscape of the moor stretched ahead that she began to flag. The wind sighed over the barren hills and made her shiver with cold rather than excitement now. As afternoon gave way to evening, she trotted soberly at Jack's side, becoming more and more aware of her aching legs and empty stomach. At last, it was evident she could go no further.

'Can't we stop for a while?' she pleaded as she sank to the ground to rub her blistered toes. 'My feet won't take me no further tonight.'

Jack paused, leaning on his stick, and looked up at the veiled spectre-like sun. It glanced through a gossamer of thin cloud. He calculated that they had less than an hour before nightfall but where, he wondered, would they find a place to sleep? Here there were no dark backyards to sneak into or tarpaulins to climb under as there would be in the city. In fact there was nothing, not a hedge or a haystack or a building of any kind. They would have to go on while there was light enough to see and before the frost returned.

'Come on, Beth,' he coaxed, 'you must keep going till the sun goes down. Then you can have your bread and sleep for as long as you like.'

The fresh air and cold wind had whipped colour into her cheeks and her soft honey-coloured eyes shone slightly as she struggled to her feet. She mustn't let him down.

'We'll head east, away from the sun,' Jack explained, slipping an arm round her tiny frame. 'One day perhaps we'll reach the sea. You've never seen the sea, Beth, have you?'

He was a great story teller and his skill came in useful now, taking Beth's thoughts away from her painful feet to lands of adventure peopled by heroes he liked to call Jack. He was engrossed in such a tale when he stopped in mid sentence. Ahead of them, nestled in a fold of the hills was a small farm. Outside a man was forking hay from a wagon into a pasture where moorland sheep were gathered. It was their best and only hope of shelter but a copse surrounded the scene and snow still clung to the thin covering of turf. Their footprints would be seen if they approached. Jack narrowed his eyes against the last rays of the sun, scouring the area until he spotted them – an outcrop of rocks on the hillside behind. He pointed them out to Beth.

'That's where we'll go,' he urged, pushing her onward again. 'From there we may find a way to the barn.' Beth rubbed her chilled hands and drew her blanket tighter around her. Down there on the farm, the sunset had cast a veil of pink gauze over the white roofs. It looked warm and inviting.

'I'd like that, Jack,' she agreed, stumbling gamely through the heath.

It was dark and the man had left his sheep to munch quietly under the trees when they crept towards the rugged stone walls of the barn. They paused, holding their breath, as his dog lingered, sniffing the strengthening breeze before following his master to the farmhouse door. It was harder to find entry than Jack had expected. At last however, a broken slat slid away and they tumbled inside.

'There must be a loft,' Jack whispered, exploring the walls for the rungs of a ladder. But Beth was already prostrate. He ate his portion of bread, covered her gently with a dry woollen cloth from his sack, then settled himself on a bed of straw. As his eyes closed, he felt sure he saw William smiling his lopsided smile but he wasn't afraid. William was with him just as his father was and they were telling him what to do.

Long sentences and flowery speech

Chapter Three

With no factory bell to rouse them, the two slept blissfully, well beyond the hour that Jack had intended. A scuffle in the rafters was the first sound he heard, followed by a high pitched screech, then a scattering of feathers and falling eggs as a tawny hen made an unsuccessful bid for escape. The reason was soon clear. A fox had slipped through the broken slat and now carried the bird limp in its jaws down the rickety stair. Jack leapt from his pallet of straw, surprising the animal to such an extent that it dropped its twitching prey at his feet and fled. The commotion woke Beth, who sat up, pale-faced and stiff, rubbing her eyes.

'Look! Eggs, Jack. Some have cracked but they haven't all broken. We can keep them, can't we?' She gathered five or six that had landed nearby and cradled them like jewels in the palm of her hand. Jack was cold. He needed food and drink to function more clearly but apart from Beth's morsel of bread they had neither. He thought of the gibbet he had seen once in London and of the body that had swayed for days in the wind before dropping, shrunken and grotesque, to the ground.

'That, lad,' his father had warned him, as he reined in the coach to emphasise his point, 'is what happens to those who are tempted to steal.' He had never forgotten the image or the fear it evoked. Yet Beth must have food, and where else would he find it?

'Aye, we'll keep the eggs. They'll not miss those – but the hen we'll leave,' he decided. He took out the pan from his sack, lined it with twigs and hay and stowed the cracked shells carefully inside, then, on an impulse, scooped up what he could of the yolks that were seeping through the straw.

'There,' he said firmly, handing her one of the earthenware mugs. 'Dip your bread in that. We must keep walking today and it'll make you strong.'

They were about to set off on their journey again when voices echoed across the yard outside.

'Quick Beth, in here.'

They had just time to conceal themselves in an old wooden butt near the door. By luck more than judgement, it swung fully open on its creaking hinge, completely obscuring their hiding place. Even the dog ran straight on by to stand barking instead over the mangled remains of the hen. Crunching footsteps followed.

'As like as not, they'll be in a barn somewhere. Either that or perishing as they deserve.' Jack recognised the guttural tones of the parish official and curled up closer to Beth's trembling form.

'Left that poor dying brother, they did – and on the Sabbath too. I shall not spare the rod when I find them, Mr Roberts, I can tell you that.' He lunged at the straw with a pitchfork as the farmer, not given to talk, picked up the hen by its severed neck.

'Stealing chickens too, I shouldn't wonder,' the official added, glancing at it. 'They'll be in here somewhere, I'll guarantee that.' He continued to probe with vicious thrusts, both down in the stalls and finally up in the loft. By the time he returned, the farmer had located the broken slat and Jack could just distinguish his slow, measured voice.

'This was no children, Mr Cruickshank. This was a fox. And this was a rogue hen that never would roost in the hut. Now if they had slept in here – you tell me – would they have left a prize like this?' Muttering under his breath, Mr Cruickshank looked at the plump savaged bird, then headed brusquely back to the yard.

'Bring me my horse, Mr Roberts. I'll not waste your time or mine. I've other places to go. There's a coin for your trouble.' He paused before continuing. 'I'll see you're rewarded if you bring me news. He's a strong lad and the girl has deft hands. We need them in the mill, Mr Roberts, and I'll see the poor-house brings 'em up right. All they need is the firm hand of a god–fearing man. I bid you good day.'

Minutes passed before their heavy boots could no longer be heard and Jack and Beth dared emerge. Outside, the sky was platinum grey and the sheep, sensing a storm, still clung to the shelter of the trees and the dwindling bundles of hay. Beth wanted to cling to the farmstead too and especially to the kitten that struggled to escape from the folds of her calico smock, hissing and spitting with outstretched claws. But Jack was adamant. They must leave at once before someone returned. He was proved right, too. As they darted from rock to rock up the hillside, the farmer did return with his tools to mend the broken slat.

'See, Beth, I was right, was I not? It's like my stories,' he grinned. 'Jack always gets away.' He chuckled with satisfaction. Beth shook her head firmly, however.

'You may have been right Jack' she said in her precise, childish voice, 'but I think it was this. It's lucky, I know it is.' She produced a locket, her only personal possession, which contained a swatch of her mother's hair.

'Well, maybe,' Jack conceded, humouring her. 'At least we're still free but we must keep to the moor and away from the road.'

Buoyed by their belief in a better life, they stumbled through black heather and patches of snow against a wind which came in increasing gusts, content for the present to simply put miles between themselves and their past. The adrenaline that had carried them through the previous day was tempered now by reality. Even Jack fell silent as he led the way eastward, further each hour from the only shelter they knew. But his step was still firm and the regular tug on his young cousin's arm had lost none of its resolve. He skirted the whitened bones of an old ram that obstructed their path. Better to die with pride out here, he thought, than to suffer injustice at the hands of unscrupulous men. He glanced at Beth. Her small face was almost hidden within the folds of her woollen wrap. He could just see her eyes, fixed on the ground, deep in thought like his own. Her breathing became laboured as the moorland track took an upward turn and the air became thin and sharp.

'Jack?'

'Aye?'

'Where do you suppose William is now?'

Jack paused, searching to find words that would bring her comfort. The truth was, he didn't know. He had wanted to know once when his mother had died but he had asked too many questions and the priest had told him he was a wicked boy. Now he kept his thoughts to himself and let others believe what they wished. But he wouldn't lie.

'Where do you believe he is, Beth?'

'He's with Mam. I just know he is. Anyway, I've asked God to make sure,' she added peeping briefly up at her cousin for reassurance.

'I'm glad you believe that,' he replied simply, giving her a hug.

The wiry heath that had torn at their ankles and sapped their strength was replaced by weathered rock and turf as the barren Pennines rose before them. This was a bleak, inhospitable place but Jack had learnt from the men at the mill that the rich vale of York lay beyond. As afternoon gave way to evening, however, their fortunes took a turn for the worse. The snow, which had held off all day, began to fall imperceptibly at first, soft flakes on a silent landscape. Then the wind gained pace and transformed them into needles of ice. Jack pointed to a gully in the fold of two hills. They could travel no further in the face of this storm. It would have to suffice. With more bravado than he felt, he urged Beth on.

'We'll find shelter down there. Hurry! Hurry!' he roared above the gale. They stumbled and slithered over gritstone and granite until they sank with chattering teeth against the west side of a rock. Here at least the wind could not wreak its vengeance against them. Huddled together around their sack, they could do nothing more than wait for change. Jack's spirits sank as the temperature dropped and the daylight waned. Doubts assailed him for the first time and he turned his head away from Beth to hide his trembling lips. There was a lump in his throat that always came when he restrained a tear. She mustn't see that he was scared. She depended on him now. Perhaps they should have stuck to the road instead of striking out boldly across the hills. Wanting space for himself and time to think, he got up, instructing Beth to stay where she was.

'I'll not be long. I'll just take a look,' he told her. The wind caught at his clothes again, blowing them hither and thither like the sails of a ship leaving harbour.

'Don't get lost, Jack,' Beth's muffled voice beseeched him. He felt his way round the rock to gain a view of the gully that ran between the shards of weathered stone. It was fast filling up with snow and the path to the east that they might have followed was scarcely visible at all. He stared into the white void, listening to the awesome sound of the elements sighing eerily over the land. At first he thought he imagined it – the urgent rhythm of a horse's hooves. No flesh and blood rider would gallop so fast in conditions like these. But, screwing up his face against the storm's blast, he looked again and felt his heart leap. This was no apparition but the pounding black outline of a riderless horse. The saddle had slipped beneath its flanks and the animal had been panicked into headlong flight. As the crazed eyes drew near, Jack seized the moment, that second in time that would change their lives. He had already leapt into the gully when he caught Beth's words from above.

'Don't, Jack, think of your poor papa!' And he did think of him as he stood steady and firm with arms outstretched. He thought of him too as the sheering hooves plunged into thick snow, lost their footing and spun high into the air, leaving the horse winded and prostrate, inches from where he stood. He bent quickly to grasp the broken reins, then instinctively spoke in a low calm voice.

'Whoa there, lass, whoa there,' he murmured, stroking the trembling limbs and feeling with sure hands each fetlock in turn. Sensing his experience, the animal lay still. 'Aye, you'll be fine lass,' he continued, 'you'll be fine, just fine.' A smile of triumph lit up his face and he held his shoulders square – no longer a frightened child but strong and brave once more.

When the girth was released, the mare snorted with relief and struggled to her feet. Jack adjusted the saddle behind her withers then ducked beneath to tighten the canvas straps. He stroked her nose thoughtfully as Beth scrambled down a bank to join him.

'Is it our horse now?' she asked, gazing in wonder at the huge black beast that seemed to submit to Jack's control.

'Nay, we'll have to go on,' he told her, 'or we'll lose her tracks. Somewhere out there a man may be hurt.' He hitched their sack to a strap on the pummel then lifted Beth's squealing figure high above his head. 'You shall ride in front and I behind,' he decided. 'You needn't be afraid – we shall just walk on till darkness falls.' With a born horseman's ease he was soon in the saddle, gathering the reins and pressing his ragged heels against the mare's warm ribs. The two of them, wrapped against the blizzard in a length of cloth, swayed as her long stride carried them east along a path that was vanishing fast. The hoof prints had sunk deep in the snow and could still just be seen as the last light left the sky. Jack had fixed his attention on a small cluster of trees ahead where they might find shelter when Beth called out to him suddenly.

'There, there he is. I can see a boot! D'you suppose he's dead?'

The mare pulled up of her own accord and sniffed with pricked ears at the inert form as Jack leapt to the ground and scooped away snow with his frozen hands. Tracing the contours of a well-built figure of above average height, his fingers swiftly uncovered first soft leather boots, then breeches, fawn jacket and white stock. The cape of a heavy riding-cloak had wrapped itself round the stranger's face. Jack swept it aside to reveal a young man with fine regular features, an aquiline nose and deep forehead across which fell an unruly shock of damp blonde hair. Undoubtedly a gentleman – but was he alive? He chafed the pale marble skin, shouted loud into his ear and pinched the lobe hard. There was a slight movement of the long fine lashes but the eyes remained closed.

'Is he dead?' Beth repeated looking down in awe. She still sat motionless in the saddle, too scared to dismount.

'No, he's not dead. But he soon will be if we don't get him warm.' He cast around, pondering what to do. The trees were too far away but his glance returned to a mound in the snow nearby. As he struggled towards it against the wind, something firm underfoot caught his leg – the same object, perhaps, that had struck the mare and unseated her rider. But what he discovered when he tugged it out gave him hope. It was a broken panel from a wattle pen – the sort the shepherds used to segregate sheep.

'Wait here, Beth!' He was gone dragging it behind him before her protests reached his ears. Shelter was all that mattered now and his instincts proved right. There beneath the drift were the other three sides of the wattle pen and he could even feel straw beneath the snow. Shaking with cold, he mustered his strength to form a roof with the fourth broken panel then set about clearing a space within. He brought Beth first, leaving her to get warm as best she could while he secured the mare to a flimsy post. It was almost dark when he turned his attention back to the man and he did not pause to examine him again. Precious minutes passed as he dragged him across the white expanse. Finally under cover and safe from the wind, he let go of his charge and collapsed.

By the time Jack's aching lungs had recovered, Beth had overcome her awe, undone the stranger's stiff cravat and wrapped his body in a woollen sheet.

'The tinder-box, Jack – you could make a fire,' she suggested as she unpacked the items in their threadbare sack. He shook his head.

'Too wet, everything's too wet.'

'You could try,' she insisted, picturing the soft orange lick of the flames. 'We could use the straw that you put in our pan to cover the eggs.'

The thought hadn't occurred to him but she was right. He got up without a word, cut a small square in the ground close by and arranged the fragments of chaff in a lightly stacked pile. It worked. His old tinder box worked.

'Quick, Beth. Look for straw and pieces of wattle.'

His mind was alert again as the small glow grew bigger. He scooped snow into the pan and warmed it over the precious heat, thawing his fingers with glee in the process. The mare, standing with her tail against the storm and head lowered, moved closer and Jack noticed for the first time a small bag on the saddle. He pointed it out to Beth. Reaching bravely up, she detached the package before hurrying back to continue her vigil. Jack tipped the contents onto the ground. There was a bottle of strange gold liquid which made him wrinkle his nose in disgust then on an impulse taste on his tongue. It felt warm. He had smelt it once on his father's breath on a bitter night and it had made his cheeks glow. Perhaps it would do the same for this man.

'Try some on his lips,' he instructed Beth, as he turned his attention back to the fire and set out the mugs to warm. When the water boiled, he would cook the eggs. What a feast they would have, he thought, willing the flames to burn on his meagre supply of broken twigs. He was watching them bubble gently when he heard a muffled cough, followed by a groan and Beth's excited voice.

'He's moving, Jack. He's waking up!'

They peered down, slightly apprehensive now, as the lashes parted and striking blue eyes gazed back at them. He had a kind face, Beth decided, basing her judgement on the humorous curl of his lips when he saw them. But the illusion was soon gone. He struggled to sit up and failing, fell back frustrated, clutching his leg.

'Give me the brandy,' he demanded, ignoring them both. He seemed used to waking up in strange situations and made no enquiries about who they were or where he was. Checking the bottle against the light of the fire, he took another draught, then sighed, though whether from pain or pleasure they couldn't tell.

'We found you in the snow, sir,' Jack ventured to explain. 'Out cold you was on the ground, sir.'

'So I am saved by a shepherd boy,' the stranger mused slowly, 'and a moorland waif,' he added, glancing at Beth with a sardonic grin. 'My, but you're an ugly, half-starved little thing. Help me sit up, will you.' His face creased as Beth strained her thin arms to lever him forward and position their sack behind his body.

'Take a sip of this, sir. It's water but at least it's hot.'

The blue eyes swivelled round.

'Add some brandy, boy. I've broken my leg. What's your name?'

'Jack, sir. Jack Cartwright.'

'Well Jack.' He paused to savour the heat from the fluid then drained the mug and wiped his mouth on a ruffled cuff. When he continued, his speech was slurred. 'Well, Jack. I want you to listen. When the storm clears you must follow the track east to the crossroads, then turn north past the oaks and keep to the stream. Lady will know the way after that. Just give her her head. You must bring help. D'you understand?'

Jack nodded earnestly. 'What if the storm doesn't clear, sir,' he started to say but already the lids had closed. He shook him but the only response was a gentle snore. Resigned, he crept closer to the dwindling flames.

'It's best he sleeps,' he told Beth as he handed her a soft-boiled egg from the pan and placed the remaining twigs on the fire. They ate noisily, sucking their fingers with murmurs of delight as the wind continued to roar overhead. Anyone venturing out there tonight would soon lose their way in the swirling snow. They would bed down till morning and hope the storm passed.

In fact the storm did pass in the early hours but a heavy frost replaced it. The sky so impenetrable before was now studded with stars and a full moon embraced a strangely silent world. Jack woke from a fitful sleep to rub his frozen hands and feet. There was no more comfort to be gained from the fire – its embers were long dead and (in any case) he had run out of fuel to revive it. He peered outside where even the mare was pawing at the snow and stamping her feet, evidently keen to be on the move. Perhaps now was the time – perhaps he should go. But he didn't like the thought of leaving Beth. Suppose something went wrong and she was taken away? Suppose the man died while he was gone? He couldn't be sure how long it would take to return.

At that point an idea formed in his mind and he began to brush the snow from their wattle roof and to search the corners for pieces of rope. The chill of the night had disturbed Beth, too, and she sat hunched and miserable in the shadows, too cold to speak when Jack stepped inside to outline his plan. She watched with chattering teeth as he undid the corners of the wattle pen, took two lengths of rope and attached them to the stirrups on either side of the mare. The other two ends he tied firmly to the wattle frame that had served as their roof.

'It'll work. You'll see. Pack up quick, Beth.' The stranger didn't stir as they splinted his leg, swaddled him in cloth and rolled him onto their makeshift sleigh. Jack flicked the reins against Lady's neck but already she seemed to know what to do.

'Good lass,' he encouraged as she plodded forward through the frozen snow. 'You've been in the traces before, I can tell.' Behind them, beneath the pale moon, her master lay still as the strange contraption slid over the snow. His future and theirs now lay in her steady homeward stride.

Chapter Four

For what remained of the night, the mare trudged on with head held low and heavy against the bit. Her ears were laid disconsolately back but she pricked them forward when they passed a signpost and turned down a path that ran crisp and straight between an avenue of trees. Oak trees, as the gentleman had said. Her pace quickened again when a river, running high and fast, adjoined the road. Jack, glancing anxiously back at the still form bumping over the rutted track, reined her in.

'Steady there, Lady,' he soothed. But her nostrils were in the wind, sensing home was near, and he had no doubt now that she would take them there. They were heading north, he noted, as a pink dawn seeped through gauze in the early morning sky. Soon it was haemorrhaging colour over a distant spire and over the water that babbled nearby.

Jack and Beth hugged each other close to keep warm and watched as the Vale of York, flat and serene, unfolded before them. A sleepy sandstone village was just visible ahead.

'Suppose someone sees us? What will we do?' Beth echoed Jack's thoughts and he tensed in the saddle, turning again to look at the strange spectacle behind them and the face of the stranger, paler than ever in the growing light. He had not moved since the journey began apart from the involuntary bobbing of his head to the movement of the sleigh.

'Hold on,' Jack murmured, 'Hold on.' He released his grip on the reins, allowing the mare to increase her stride. The road followed a high stone wall, old and covered in lichen, and overhung by beech and walnut and rhododendron boughs. He could not see what lay beyond until they drew level with a slate-roofed lodge. It guarded the entrance to an imposing park and the name Skellfield Hall beneath a coat of arms was engraved on a large stone plaque. When the mare began to turn between the iron gates, both Jack and Beth at first restrained her, but she tugged against the bit and showed a flash of will that wouldn't be denied.

'It's her home!' Jack exclaimed. 'A gentleman's home. This must be where she is stabled.' With mixed feelings of awe and unease, they fixed their eyes on the mansion ahead – a rectangular Georgian building with fine stone columns and a flight of steps leading up to a heavy oak door. Surrounding the sweeping drive were balustrades, sunken gardens and hedges of yew and to the right, an archway leading to a courtyard behind. Set in front, in the frozen splendour of the parkland, a lake shone like a gem under the first rays of the sun

Jack sat speechless in the saddle. How would they be received at such a fine house? Had he done the right thing? His thoughts were interrupted as they approached the arch by a servant girl carrying two pails of milk. She stopped short in her tracks and stood transfixed, staring at them. As the sleigh drew level, she dropped her buckets in the snow and put her hands to her mouth.

'Saints preserve us! It's young master Henry!' she cried, gathering her skirts and running back to the kitchens to raise the alarm. By the time Lady drew up at her stable door, the maid had returned with all the staff she could find and quick hands were unleashing the stretcher and bearing it indoors.

'Where shall we take him, Mr Scott?' a flustered footman called, as the butler, impeccably dressed in spite of the hour, appeared on the scene. His ex-military training came into play as he snapped out his response.

'To the house-keeper's sitting room, my lad. The coals are still hot in there. Florrie, light the fire in master Henry's room and put a warming pan in the bed. Off you go, girl, and be quick about it. Sarah, tell Mr Bellmore to alert the master. And someone tell Tom to saddle a horse and be ready to ride to the doctor's house.'

The commotion subsided and Jack and Beth were left alone in the courtyard, near to exhaustion after their night in the storm. No one had told them what they should do. Several minutes passed before they slid, stiff and shivering, to the ground. On an impulse, Jack lifted the latch on the nearest stall. The fresh straw inside was enticement enough.

'Watch out, Beth,' he warned, as the mare brushed past to forage for food in the empty trough. 'Find a place in the corner to keep yourself warm.'

With the saddle removed, he used a bundle of straw to rub the horse down, feeling, as he did so, the circulation returning to his own frozen limbs. He had almost finished when he heard running feet on the cobbles outside and a half-dressed youth appeared at the door.

'Now then, what's you doing with Lady?' he demanded. 'No one comes in here 'cept me and old Tom. No one, see?'

Jack stared wearily at the mop of unruly red hair and the flushed red face, then turned back to his task.

'She needs a rug and a hot bran mash, if you're her lad' he said firmly, ignoring the threatening stance of the taller boy, 'and she needs it fast.'

'Now look here!' The youth edged nearer, picking up a rake and wielding it like a weapon between his muscular arms. They were never to know what might have happened next as the dairymaid returned with a message from the house.

'Joe Garner,' she scolded. 'Not you, fighting again!' She turned her round plump face to Jack then stared with outright contempt at Beth who was shaking uncontrollably beneath her wet and dirty rags. 'Cook says you're to come to the kitchen, so you best follow me.' Exercising her authority with relish over those she perceived to be more lowly than herself, she swept across the courtyard towards the servants' block, leaving the two to struggle with their sack behind. A scullery maid, scrubbing a flagstoned floor, paused to gawp as they passed through her domain. Beyond, the kitchen beckoned with its comforting smell of freshly baked bread. As the doors opened before them and they stepped into the warmth, Jack and Beth could only wonder at the scene inside. Word had got round of their strange arrival and the staff had gathered to glean what they could. They nudged and muttered amongst themselves until an ample woman hurried in, adjusting her hair beneath a lacy cap.

'Out! Out of my kitchen!' she ordered, shooing the maids before her with small fat hands. 'You two – come and sit here near the range. Take off those clothes and put on these clean ones. You can't talk to the master like that and or even Mr Scott for that matter. It wouldn't do at all.' She brooked no resistance.

Jack ducked away from her flannels and towels but Beth gave herself up to the woman's care, her face wreathed in ecstasy. She could think of no greater pleasure in the world than the heat of the water against her skin and the glow that she felt sitting next to the oven door. All she wanted now was sleep but it was evident their presence would soon be required.

Mrs Bullen, for so she was called, then filled two bowls with porridge from a cauldron on the hob.

'That will bring back your strength,' she observed, standing back with hands on hips to watch the pair scoop up the steaming food, a distant maternal memory perhaps provoking a tear. Jack bolted his portion like a starving dog then wiped his mouth under her disapproving eye on the sleeve of his wrap. All the same, she gave him a little more before turning to the housekeeper who had just entered the room – a sombre, rather gaunt lady with an air of quiet authority. She wore a long, tightly-buttoned dress, tailored right up to the neck so that her face seemed disembodied. Beth stole a glance at her from beneath her lowered lashes and leant closer to the range. She wanted to stay in this haven of warmth with its shelves of shining copper pans and rows of utensils and she didn't want to leave the kindly Mrs Bullen. But the cook was a practical woman too and she wafted her hands in a gesture of dismissal.

'Off you go. The master wants to see you. Mrs Buchanan will show you the way.'

The housekeeper nodded silently and ushered them out. They followed her barefoot along a stone passage until it gave way to an ante-room with a black and white marble floor. She indicated that they should wait on a small wooden bench near the study door then disappeared about her own business. Jack and Beth looked up in wonder at an ornate gallery and beyond to the fine domed window above. Occasionally, a passing maid or footman, aware of the unfolding drama, peered down at them and whispered. An early morning draft whistled suddenly beneath the door and as it slipped off its latch their attention was drawn to the voices within. Jack put a finger to his lips and tilted his head to catch the words.

'I shouldn't have listened to you, Lizzy,' a man's voice was saying. 'I should have insisted. Give him time you said, he'll come round. If he'd married Lady Jane last year, this would never have happened. The boy's gone off the rails, thanks to your indulgence. I should never have allowed it. A spell in the cavalry! That's what he should have had!'

A female voice remonstrated with him.

'I understand you're upset, dear, and who knows you may be right. But he doesn't love Jane and you can't change that.'

'Love! What's that got to do with it in our position? She's a fine girl – an ideal match – and a family would have taken his mind off wenches and ale. Why, he'll finish up a wastrel like that brother of mine, mark my words, he will. Our only son and heir.'

At that point a maid bearing a silver tray and china cups hurried towards the study, preceded by Mrs Buchanan, who knocked loudly on the door.

'Come in,' the man responded and Jack caught a glimpse of freshly burning coals in the iron grate. Soon he and Beth were summoned too and stood hesitant on the threshold of a room lined to the ceiling with leather books.

'Come in, come in,' a distinguished figure with sleek silver hair repeated, pacing impatiently in front of the fire. He adjusted the belt of his velvet dressing gown.

'I'm Sir George Cunningham and this is my wife, Lady Elizabeth.' He indicated the lady seated by his side with pale blonde hair tied loosely over her left shoulder. She too had left her bed chamber in a hurry and wore only a cream robe. 'I gather we have you two to thank for our son's safe return, he continued, 'and we do so most sincerely. But I want you to tell us exactly what happened.'

Jack cleared his throat nervously but related their night in the storm without his usual embellishments. The adventure had been quite extraordinary enough. When asked why they had been out in such weather he hesitated, a fact that didn't go unnoticed by the sharp blue eyes of the master.

'I was going to the coast to find a job on a whale ship, sir.' He added on an impulse 'it's a fair wage, I believe.'

'Good. Good for you,' Sir George replied, turning to Mrs Buchanan. 'See to it, will you, that they are rested and nourished before they go on. Perhaps you could find them some decent shoes.' The interview seemed to be over and Jack felt dismayed. He had no real hope of finding a ship and, even if he did, what would happen to Beth.

'Please, sir,' he pleaded, 'I was brought up with horses. I could work in the yard. I could do anything, sir. And Beth here, there's no one better with a needle and thread.'

'My dear fellow, d'you suppose I can employ every soul that passes my gate. Why you're barely adult. And your cousin there is as weak as a kitten. What good would she be to me?'

Lady Elizabeth glanced at Beth, shifted slightly in her chair but, aware of her husband's mood, judged it best to say nothing.

'We'd work hard for a few pence, sir, really we would.'

But it was no good. The housekeeper intervened,

pushing them bodily out of the room and closing the door on her master. Jack's mind was racing. He had nothing to lose. In a trice he had broken from her grip, re-entered the room and addressed himself to Sir George once more.

'Please, sir, we'll do anything at all for a bed and a bowl of porridge. We ran away from the mill, see, and they'll put us in the work-house if they find us now.'

'That's enough, boy, leave us please.' He turned to the window, preoccupied now like his wife by the sound of a horse's hooves. The doctor was here at last. Jack crept away, submitting to the sharp cuff he received from Mrs Buchanan and the look of reproach from Beth. Eventually they were taken to an attic room with a row of iron beds that were usually kept for visiting staff. There they slept till the late afternoon. Beth woke first, stretched, rubbed her eyes and smiled at Jack's dark tousled head still snug beneath the linen sheets. Standing on tiptoe at the small end window, she could see the lake as flat and smooth as a mirror and the park glistening beneath a fresh fall of snow. What a magical place this was, but there was no work for them here she thought, sadly. Soon they must move on to an uncertain future.

Thoughts of that future were dispelled, however, when the housekeeper escorted them downstairs once more to the noise and hubbub of the servants' hall. A long rectangular table had been set for the evening meal and Jack and Beth watched bemused as footmen in smart green livery claimed their

Maids don't have linen sheets

seats in order of rank amongst the various grades of household staff. Last of all, Joe Garner hurried sheepishly in and took his place at the bottom end. Over the scraping of chairs, after grace had been said, the butler called down to him.

'Move up, Joe. Make room for our visitors, would you.' The lad's face reddened with indignation but seeing that this freed him from the lowliest position, he settled himself closer to the plump pink figure of an indifferent maid. As bowls of meat broth and bread were passed round the assembly, Mr Scott continued.

'You will all be relieved, I am sure, to hear that Master Henry is comfortable tonight. Thanks to the good Lord and these two young people, his leg should heal with patience and care.' He peered at Jack and Beth. 'When you go on your way tomorrow, you leave with our very best wishes and, I understand, a new pair of shoes for each of you.'

No more was said on the matter and as the meal got noisily underway, few noticed the housekeeper respond to the master's bell. When she returned, she stood for a moment with hands clasped, then stooped to whisper in the butler's ear. Voices dropped away and attention turned to her expressionless face.

'I see,' Mr Scott responded slowly, stroking his chin and clearing his throat to make a wider announcement. 'It seems that some of your duties will change. Master Henry will be confined to his room for many weeks. Maria, you will leave the laundry to attend to his needs and Paul,' he turned to the footman on his left, 'you will make yourself available too.' His eyes settled on Jack, whose interest was focused on what might soon be his last bowl of soup. 'Now, young man, you told the master you were good with horses, so he is giving you the chance to prove that's so. You'll sleep in the attic above the yard. Joe will find you a bed and you'll work for old Tom. Is that what you want?'

Jack, struck dumb with surprise and a mouthful of Mrs Bullen's freshly baked bread, could only nod vigorously as Mr Scott continued.

'And you, Beth, will take Maria's place in the laundry tomorrow. She can share a room with you, Annie, on the top floor.' The scullery maid started to protest but, ignored as usual, confided instead in the equally outraged Joe.

Beneath the table, Beth searched for Jack's hand and held it tight in a gesture of trust and gratitude. She raised her small chin above her empty pewter plate, straightened her back and spoke for the first time with clarity and strength.

'Thank you, sir. The master won't be sorry. We'll work hard. You'll see. You'll all see.'

From her place further down the table, Mrs Bullen gazed at the child's elated face and hid a secret tear.

Chapter Five

Beth untied her fine blonde hair, shook her head and lay back in the long grass. A warm breeze rippled pleasantly across her face. She smiled and stretched, savouring the sun's healing rays through her crisp linen dress. Moments like this were precious. For most of the week she was up at dawn, carrying pails of water up three flights of stairs. Then she had all the fires to lay, brass to clean, silver to polish and, after each meal, the crockery to wash and sewing to do. The chores seemed never-ending so that she was seldom in her bed before midnight.

Yet she felt content. Her body had developed a woman's curves after a full six years of nourishing food. She gazed through sleepy, half-closed eyes at the cathedral of dancing beech leaves above. She was perfectly at peace. So much so that she didn't hear Jack loping towards her until his voice interrupted her thoughts.

'Can't stop today, Beth,' he said when he caught his breath. 'My time off has been changed. Well, look at me. What do you think?' he grinned, sweeping his arms low in a lavish bow. Beth, resting on her elbows, shielded her eyes against the sun. At seventeen Jack had grown into a fine-looking youth with a physique made strong by harrowing the soil and harvesting the land. It was his care of the horses however that had impressed old Tom.

'Well?' he challenged.

'You're a footman!. You're a footman at last,' Beth exclaimed, struggling to recognise the familiar, light-hearted cousin she knew beneath the new gold-buttoned jacket.

'You look quite the gentleman – quite the gentleman, and me still just a kitchen maid! Turn around. Let me see.' She examined the fit of his smart, green livery as he watched her, amused.

'Aye, I'm a footman and I'm to take Sir George into York tomorrow. Maybe, I'll even be staying the night.' His eyes danced with excitement but Beth's face was downcast. After all, there would be no more meetings on her afternoon off.

'You'll be a lady's maid soon, you'll see.' His voice lacked conviction, knowing that the chances were very remote, but to his surprise she had ideas of her own.

'I'd like to be a cook one day,' she said as she watched a swan glide into view on the lake. 'I can make jam already.'

'Tell you what,' Jack continued, seeking to cheer her, 'you've always wanted a garden. I'll dig you a small patch down by the river beneath the trees. No one will know except you and me. It'll be our secret. But you can't go near the boathouse – it's all locked up and you're not allowed. Joe told me. He told me someone drowned there once.'

Beth watched the swan dip its head beneath the calm blue surface of the lake, then drift behind the island out of sight. Her thoughts were in turmoil. Life would be different in future. They had both grown up and the childhood bond that had held them close must be severed if Jack was to prosper. She too must find her own way forward. But the garden would be something tangible, a memorial to their past, something they could share.

'I'd love that, Jack,' she said simply.

After he had gone, bounding like a deer through the parkland towards the stable yard, she lay for a while trying to regain a sense of peace. But it was no good. She felt listless now and carrying her shoes and her summer bonnet, she wandered towards the edge of the lake. The island in particular drew her eye. Something was causing small movements in the reeds, but whatever it was, was just out of sight.

At first she leant forward, then tiptoed through the water to gain a better view. She had just time to see them – eight tiny cygnets on a large bed of twigs – before she heard the ominous beat of wings. At the far end of the lake, a swan was airborne and heading towards her to defend its young. Beth didn't hesitate. She gathered her skirts, splashed back to the bank and fled down the well-worn path to the house with the bird in angry pursuit. When she dared to glance back it was approaching fast.

Shielding her face with her hands and crying out in alarm, she ran blindly on. The impact, when it came, stunned her. She found herself face down on the grass but moments passed before the truth dawned. It was not a swan that pinioned her to the ground but the powerful arms of a stranger whose weight was squeezing the breath from her body. Images from the past, images she wanted to forget, flooded into her confused thoughts and she struggled savagely as the swan circled overhead.

'Steady on, there,' a familiar voice rebuked her. He examined a finger. 'You little tigress! You've almost drawn blood.'

Beth turned wild-eyed towards him.

'Well, if it isn't the moorland waif,' he continued, dusting himself down in a leisurely fashion before extending an arm to help her get up.

'Master Henry,' Beth stammered, 'I didn't know you was here at the house. I won't bother you no more.'

'Back from the Grand Tour, my dear – to the delights of home,' he added with a mischievous wink. Recoiling visibly, Beth covered her dishevelled hair with a bonnet now spattered in mud. Henry looked her over with a connoisseur's eye. 'Skellfield suits you,' he observed. 'There's flesh on your bones and a bloom in your cheeks – but you'll never be pretty. Well, good day, my dear. Don't go near the swans when they're nesting again. I might not be there to save you next time.'

Swinging a smart cane stick, he strode on his way leaving Beth to trudge back with her mind in a whirl. She had appeared ungrateful, she supposed, but six years hadn't erased the ghosts of her past. How could he know how damaged she had been by the unspeakable acts she had witnessed in the mill? She hurried towards the servants' quarters, ignoring Joe's greeting as she crossed the yard, eager only to resume her work. Work occupied her mind and blocked out the pain and the awful scene that haunted her still.

But the incident had revived it and even behind the door of her attic room it wouldn't go away. The stench of the man, the vice-like grip of his gnarled hands as she struggled to escape, the coarse texture of the sacking on the factory floor against her young skin. She could see and feel it all again. His crooked teeth approaching hers, the press of his loins, the ugly fumbling with his belt, the violation, finally, that she had no power to prevent. And afterwards, the hellish incessant roar of the machines as she lay torn and bleeding before the whip forced her back to her place on the loom.

She had never told anyone, not even Jack. Had she confided in William, he would only have risked his frail life to avenge her. So the secret was hers alone – a secret that gnawed at her soul and blighted her path to womanhood. Already she rejected the gauche attempts of the servant boys to steal a kiss or catch her eye in church. Instead of girlish gossip, she sought solitude in the peaceful rolling acres of the park. Only Jack was to be trusted in her private world; only he gave her confidence in the servant's hall when ribald remarks made her cheeks burn and her eyes prick with unseen tears.

But Jack would be away much more often now, escorting the family to other fine houses and to meetings in York. A smile briefly transformed her.

He had done well. Of course she could still rely on Mrs Bullen's fiercely protective support. The older woman's faith in her had never wavered and had been justified by her willingness to work and her hunger to learn.

Hearing Annie's heavy, flat-footed tread on the stairs, Beth hastily smoothed her skirt and secured her windblown hair. It was true she was not pretty, she thought without regret, wiping a smudge of soil from her cheek. In the small, cracked mirror that Jack had retrieved from a household bin, the face that looked back at her was pleasant but plain, the honey-coloured eyes, which might have been her best feature, emotionally dulled and remote.

She turned towards the door as Annie burst in and flung herself with her usual abandon onto the bed alongside her own. The two of them shared the small, windowless room which was furnished sparsely with a chest of drawers, a number of hooks and a large china jug and bowl. The scullery maid kicked off her shoes and rubbed a painful corn on her toe.

'My, I've just seen your Jack, crossing the yard. Smiled at me, he did. As pleased as punch he was. And Joe. Joe looked as sour as yesterday's milk! No coachman's uniform for him. Tell you what,' she added, her dark eyes gleaming, 'I'll let Joe walk you back from church, if you'll kind of arrange for me and Jack – well you know.'

Beth did know. She also knew Annie's graceless ways would not impress Jack. He was popular with the staff, even with the family upstairs, and his story-telling powers had become renowned. At Christmas and Easter, even on dark winter nights, he was often called upon to entertain. But after one or two youthful liaisons had ended in tears, at least for the maids concerned, he had steered clear of romance. He enjoyed good company, a beer and a light-hearted rapport with friends but his heart and his head were focused on work. That, after all, was where freedom lay.

'Forget about Jack,' Beth soothed, intent on diplomacy. 'Joe's been good to you and he'll need a kind word at dinner tonight. Besides, it's mutton stew – you know you like that. And afterwards cheese with pickle that I made myself,' she added, knowing food was the key to Annie's spirits. 'Come on, my friend, or we'll be late.'

Chapter Six

Life did change over the next few weeks. A mature Jack emerged, one not so given to youthful exuberance but more to restraint and reflection. He had confidences he must keep now, Beth supposed, and it wouldn't do to disclose his master's business. But he didn't forget the promise he had made. One day as she scrupulously polished the copper pans, he slipped into the kitchen and drew her aside.

'It's ready,' he whispered. 'The garden, remember? Meet me after church and I'll show you where.' He was gone before Annie could catch his eye.

Beth paused, wiping her brow with the cuff of her starched linen dress. More often than not she was busy on Sunday, paring potatoes and plucking the birds for the visiting guests. Surely he knew that Lady Jane Harrington was due to arrive? She pictured the stylish barouche with its matching bays sweeping down the drive, Jack lowering the footplate and stepping smartly back as the tall brunette stepped gracefully down.

She had glimpsed the scene some weeks before as she placed scented roses on a marble stand. The visits were more frequent now. Once again the maids hurried upstairs with sachets of lavender to hang in the closets and large bouquets of hand-picked flowers. Had Master Henry chosen them himself, she wondered. Was this refined lady to be his wife? The servants' hall was rife with gossip and predictions of a marriage the following spring. She turned back to the table with its daunting array of unpolished pans. If she finished her chores, she thought, returning a gleaming skillet to its hook on the wall, she might still slip away after church the next day.

It was past midnight before she sank into bed with reddened hands and an aching back. She was asleep before Annie's snores had reached their peak and barely stirred until the knock on the door at dawn aroused them. She laboured alongside a yawning Annie to carry pails of water up flights of stairs, then hurried back down to prepare for the guests. Finally, after a snatched breakfast, Mrs Bullen dismissed them.

'Off you go – but mind you put on your Sunday best.'

Church was a formal occasion. Sir George and his wife, with Henry and the two married sisters who joined them, occupied the family pews at the front. Parishioners filled the seats behind while the back was reserved for the household staff, all of whom were expected to attend.

Beth took a seat at the end of a row and knelt for a while in thought rather than prayer. It was a moment of peace and a time for reflection which her duties seldom allowed. A time not just to mourn the family she had lost but to count her blessings too.

The organist raised his hands as the gentry approached, then, as though at a signal, brought them down with a flourish onto the keys. The resulting jubilant chords shattered the quiet air. Beth's eyes flew open. She had been far away in a childhood meadow where beehives and bird song were as sweet and familiar as her mother's voice. Startled, her hands flew up, dislodging her hat and sending the prayer book she clasped to her chest spinning out of her grasp and into the aisle. She could only stare at the scattered pages and the broken spine as disapproving glances turned her way. The procession drew to a halt. Beneath her misshapen hat, she watched, mortified, as Henry stooped to pick up the pieces and replace them in her lap.

'Clumsy girl,' she heard Lady Jane comment as she reclaimed Henry's arm. 'I mean it's not as though these people can read,' she added dismissively.

A hint of a wink as he passed on by did nothing to relieve Beth's total dismay. The incident would be remembered when her work was reviewed at the end of the year and her hopes of promotion would surely be dashed. Embarrassed and saddened, she sang in a flat, wavering voice the hymns that through repetition she had learned to love. She would escape to the kitchen as soon as she could, she decided, where at least she was valued for what she could do.

But Jack would have none of it.

'We'll visit old Tom's grave,' he whispered, when they gathered in the sun outside the church. 'Then we'll slip out at the back while they're all walking home.'

Reluctantly at first, Beth allowed herself to be led down lichen-covered steps to a mossy path. Bordered on either side by rhododendrons, it was known as the belt and it encircled the whole estate. Here, in the spring, she had gazed in wonder at the sea of harebells beneath the mighty oaks and chestnut trees that grew undisturbed near the river's edge.

As the sound of running water grew louder, the path became a thread through a jungle of overgrown weeds and brambles which tore at their clothes. The boathouse lay beyond, obscured almost entirely by emerald green ivy and honeysuckle leaves. Beth drew back, unwilling to risk any further censure.

'Come! We're almost there,' Jack urged and, as he spoke, the foliage fell away to reveal a small glade. Beth was entranced. Light dappled the soil which had been worked to a fine tilth and foxgloves and flowers already hummed with bees.

'Well, do you like it?' Jack grinned.

Her eyes shone in response, her misery banished at least for the present.

'I shall collect seeds from the flower heads,' she declared, 'and cuttings from the shrubs. And the stones over there – I shall use those too. Oh, it will be beautiful, Jack, you'll see!'

'It's our secret, Beth. No one comes down here because the river runs fast and it's already claimed another man's life. You'll be safe enough if you stay away. You must promise me that.'

'Aye, I promise – and I love our garden, Jack.' She gave him a spontaneous hug and a kiss on the cheek which surprised and pleased him. She was learning to show her emotions again.

The two of them laughed as they darted through pathways back to the house, Jack to the stables and Beth to change out of her Sunday best. Crisp and clean in a smock, she hurried down the marble passage to the kitchen door. There would be words of reproach but life had its pleasures too, she reflected. She would look them all in the eye and simply get on with her work.

Chapter Seven

The excitement woke Jack early. He could hear the horses stirring in the stalls beneath the thin wooden floor of his room. His mind, already alert, sifted through all the things Tom had taught him over the past six years: Tom, the man of quiet dignity who saw in a mill boy the son he was denied and whose legacy Jack would always remember. He had died just a month before. The loss of such a fine horseman had saddened the household but Sir George had listened to his final advice.

So here he was, for the time being at least, coachman to the master of Skellfield Hall. His eyes lingered with pride on the smart green livery hanging on the door but he was under no illusions. The fine suiting would be no substitute for experience when he was out on the road today with four in hand and twenty miles of dry, rutted track ahead. There was no threat of floods or storms as there would be in winter but a partridge flying out of a hedge could alarm a spirited horse – and one bad move could end his career.

It would be his first trip into York as driver rather than groom. Now he, rather than Tom, must remember the route through the busy, cobbled streets to the old George Inn where his master pursued his interest in politics and steam trains with the city's new breed of enterprising men.

The stable clock in the courtyard chimed the hour – five as he had guessed – and he was off his straw mattress and thumping the neighbouring doors before it had ceased. Joe shared now with another youth and was not best pleased that Jack had a room of his own. He grumbled in response to the wake-up call but nevertheless spread a cold wet cloth over his florid face to ward off an all too familiar headache from last night's ale.

'Make it sharp, Joe. The coach must be ready for seven o'clock and I'll need the lads to harness the team.'

A shriek of protest came from inside the room and Jack smiled as he went back to pull on his working clothes. Some other poor wretch would have to put up with Joe's bullying ways. He bounded downstairs, rolling up his sleeves and paused, as he always did, to stroke the muzzle of his favourite mare.

'Not today, Lady – you've earned a rest. I'm taking the four young blades today.' He glanced at the bays tossing their heads and stamping the ground as he passed on by to measure their feed. By the time the clock chimed six, the yard echoed with the clatter of hooves, the clink of chains, even bawdy catcalls as Annie delivered hot water for the men. Ignoring them, she sidled round a door to speak to Jack.

'Mrs Bullen says not to forget your breakfast

and when you come up, Beth's packed you some cheese and cake for the trip. Will you buy me some chocolate in York, Jack?' she added in a whisper. 'They say it's the latest thing and I ain't never had none.' She grinned at him, revealing imperfect teeth but whether he heard, she couldn't be sure because of the grinding of wheels on cobble as a crested coach emerged from the mews. It was a splendid sight in the early morning sun and Jack cast a critical eye over every detail, even bending his tall, square frame to examine the soft leather seats inside. He checked the lamps and, with an old piece of cloth, gave all the brass fittings a final buff.

'Right, lads. Let's have the team in their traces now.' Again, every detail of the harness and carriage pole were checked and rechecked and the horses hooves given an extra polish. Satisfied at last, Jack turned on his heel and went in to change. Well before seven, he drew the four bays to a halt at the foot of the steps outside the Hall. They chafed gently at the bit as Sir George walked past a footman to run a discerning hand over their flanks.

'You'll need a shilling and sixpence for the toll-gate, Cartwright, and I trust you know the way when we get to York? Past the fever hospital, through Bootham and St Leonard's Place to the George in Coney Street. You will stable the horses there till the evening. Is that clear?'

'Aye, sir,' Jack responded, tipping his hat before setting it more firmly over his thick dark hair. At last they were off, clattering briskly down the drive. Already he felt his tension ease. The sun was rising on a summer morning, giving the landscape a charm of its own, and his spirits were high. Was there anything more pleasant than bowling between the hedgerows on the top of a fine coach? Life had not many things better than this, he decided.

His confidence was transferred to the horses. He watched their ears flicker back and forth to his every command and smiled proudly, remembering the battered London Hackney cab that had taught him his trade. No gentleman would have travelled in that, for fear the last dandy had wiped his shoes on the seat, or worse, that it harboured disease. But true horsemanship, he acknowledged, he had learned from old Tom and he had a strong sense now that life was his for the taking, that something good lay ahead.

Towards midday, he saw the fever hospital on his left and shortly after, the distant spire of the Minster, which grew in magnitude as the horses trotted on until it towered above them. He allowed himself a wistful glance at the stone walls of St Peters, the school, he had been told, Master Henry had attended. Then he followed the elegant curve of St Leonard's Place, a new wide road built to allow carriages to pass with ease.

A pauper begging barefoot on the corner caught his eye but the flicker of comradeship they might once have shared was gone. The lad's cold stare reminded Jack that his smart green livery had closed a door on his past. Oddly disconcerted, he looked away and smiled instead at a flower girl whose sidelong glance suggested she had more to offer than blooms. Ahead, the approach to Coney Street narrowed.

'Steady there,' he called, throwing his weight against the reins of the lead horses and slowing them to a walk amid the noise and jostle of people and wagons and dogs. Sensing the familiar, they turned with ears pricked under the great arch of the post house. There a groom stepped forward to hold them so that Jack could let down the step for Sir George.

'Well done, Cartwright. I have business here, but have the horses ready at seven tonight. I shall be staying in Monkgate. You may consider this afternoon your own. Get to know York, lad, but don't be late back.'

'No, sir. Thank you, sir,' Jack replied as the patron ushered his master into the oak-walled rooms of the Inn. Once in the yard, stable hands surged forward and Jack had to be content with watching the men as he ate Beth's cheese on a wedge of bread. Their expertise soon impressed him, however, and he turned his attention to the street outside. To left and right, small shops offered everything from cakes and candies to mutton, hats and shoes but there would be time for that later. Right now he was ready for a pint of ale.

Opposite the George a rival staging company, The Black Swan, echoed with the constant arrival of flagging horses and the lively departure of fresh ones. He watched fascinated for a while before pushing open the tavern door. Inside, the smell of leather, horses and alcohol dominated a dark, gas-lit room that housed a mass of noisy humanity. He chose a seat in the corner from where he could see rather than be seen, exchanged a coin for a tankard of the local brew and settled back to absorb the city scene.

There was talk of trains and railways and of how these might bring coal to York, and thus factories to compete with the towns in the west. Jack supped his beer faster till the colour rose in his cheeks. More factories. More children to suffer as he and Beth had done. He looked around at his fellow men. Had they no idea of the human cost? Next to him, a man with a fresh complexion caught his eye and leant forward.

'I see you're a coachman too,' he observed. 'Mark my words. Those rail men, Hudson and the like, they'll be the death of us. A station in Tanner Row, lines planned to Leeds and Derby and London. Aye, the York and North Midland Railway Company – there's no stopping them now. A few more years and the stages will feel the wind of change, you mark my words.'

He returned to his glass of porter, expecting a response, but Jack was still incensed by life's injustice. He swirled his ale and stared angrily into its depth.

'I haven't always been a coachman. When my father died I was sent to work in the mills.'

The man looked up with renewed interest, his face flushed but still genial.

'Did you now?' he said slowly. 'There's been a deal of talk in the north about the mills. Talk as how the children are treated like slaves, working fourteen, sometimes sixteen hours a day.'

It was Jack's turn to lean forward in earnest.

'Talk? What sort of talk?'

The coachman scratched his grey beard thoughtfully.

'Well, it started a year or two back when a man called Oastler came to town. Richard Oastler. The Factory King, they call him. He stayed there at the George across the way. People came from all over the county that day and it rained like the devil. I saw him as a matter of fact from this very place. I saw him gallop off to the Knavesmire to rally the crowds. What a spectacle it was when they came through the gates. Thousands of them. Thousands there were. To show their support for the The Ten Hours Bill.'

Jack ordered two ales, took off his hat and moved a seat closer. He didn't want to miss a word this man said.

'The Ten Hours Bill? Tell me about it, if you would.'

'Why, thank you, lad. I'll not say no to one for the road. But you've surely heard of the Sadler Report? They say the poor man died from the effort of it all. Eighty seven witnesses but the law didn't change and nor has it since. I doubt they'll ever get the ten hour day in the mills.'

Jack could hardly contain his excitement.

'And this man Oastler. Does he still fight for the cause?'

'Aye, I believe he does. Even went to see the Prime

Minister, Wellington, in London once but the great man is afraid of people power. He'd use force if he had to, to put them down.' He drew a finger sharply across his throat and laughed. 'It's my belief that parliament lives in fear of the guillotine.'

'D'you recall what he looked like, this Richard Oastler?' Jack persisted. 'Was he tall, dark, somewhat like myself?'

'Aye, that's right lad, somewhat like yourself and a smart man by any standards.'

Jack seized the coachman's hand and shook it hard.

'Thank you, my friend, thank you,' he said as he got up to leave. In the sunshine outside he took a deep breath. Was it possible? Had the man he last saw with Beth and William on that winter's morning six years before become the champion of the mill children's cause?

Chapter Eight

Jack tiptoed across the scrubbed kitchen floor towards Mrs Bullen's ample figure. She was muttering to herself as she gathered ingredients from the shelves above to combine in her large metal bowl.

'Something tasty?' he joked, peering over her shoulder and stretching his arms round her corseted waist. He waited with a grin for her usual rebuff.

'Jack Cartwright!' She turned to beam at him, her floured hands fluttering with delight. 'No one but you has done that since my poor Walter died. You'll make some lass happy one of these days,' she added with a sigh and a mischievous wink. Jack watched her face as he pulled a small brown bag from his pocket.

'It's cocoa. I got it from a grocer in Walmgate and it cost a fair penny, I can tell you. A treat for you and Annie and Beth.'

'Cocoa! Why that's my favourite drink but we shan't sup it without you. Come to my sitting room after lunch. Beth and Annie could do with some cheer. Worn out they are, cleaning up after all that carousing last night. I'm not surprised Master

Henry disappeared when Sir George came back.' She bustled towards the pantry, shaking her head. 'He and those feckless friends of his.' An hour later, relaxing after the demands of feeding the household, Mrs Bullen retired to her small sitting room with a tray of steaming mugs. 'There you are, girls. Your first sip of cocoa. A rare treat that is.'

Beth sipped slowly at first, unsure of her taste for such pleasures. But as the sweet flavour melted on her tongue and trickled down her throat, her eyes softened and she smiled across at Jack.

'Tell us all about it. Tell us about your trip to York.'

In due course, Jack told them about his extraordinary conversation with the coachman in the inn. Mrs Bullen listened intently too as she savoured her cocoa. When he had finished, her eyes narrowed.

'I wouldn't go talking too much about reformers, lad. Not in this house. Sir George – he wouldn't like it. He's a good master but he don't want no talk of change. Why, they don't know what that might lead to.'

Beth drained her mug and stared into the bottom as though through it she could see the past.

'I remember Mr Oastler – if that was he. I remember his eyes most. Kind eyes they were, you could tell, and he listened to us, he really listened.' She mused silently for a moment. 'Not a day goes by that I don't think of that hateful mill and those poor suffering souls. When I'm scrubbing floors I think of them. When I'm polishing brass, I hear their cries.

Scrubbing

66

If this man can help them,' she added with sudden passion, 'I swear I too would join the march and for pity's sake cry out for change.'

Mrs Bullen, always one to hide her emotions behind practical acts, collected the mugs briskly.

'Why, lass, you dwell too much on the past. You need some fresh air on that pale face of yours. Take a walk but don't let the family see you, or my old soft heart will get me dismissed. As for the rest of you, back to your work.'

Beth knew exactly where she would go. Down by the river, the soil had responded to her nimble hands and she lost no time in seeking out the path that would lead her safely through the tangle of thorns. The garden, when she reached it, was bathed in the warmth of the afternoon sun. She sank into the chair that Jack had fashioned from a fallen log, and sighed with delight. This beautiful sanctuary with its heady scents and jewel-like colours was hers alone. No one was likely to discover her here.

It wasn't long, however, as she prodded and peered at tender young plants, before her peace was disturbed. Laughter echoed through the trees and a quick glimpse confirmed that it was Lady Elizabeth walking arm in arm with Henry's sister, Nell. The younger girl had spotted the track and, keen to explore, was chiding her mother for holding back.

'Why can't we go down to the river, Mama? It's years now since Uncle Edward died. See here – someone's been using this little track.'

Beth gathered her skirts in alarm, casting around for a way of escape. She mustn't be seen, for Mrs

Bullen's sake, and certainly not on prohibited land. Fleeing towards the river, she crept along its mossy bank towards the shroud of foliage on the boathouse walls, quite forgetting her promise to Jack. Her tiny shoes sank in the mud and soon her bonnet with its white satin bow lay crumpled beside them. Aghast at her bedraggled state, she clutched at the lock on the boat house door. To her surprise it gave way and she stumbled inside just in time.

'Saints preserve us,' she whispered, echoing Annie's favourite phrase, as Lady Elizabeth and her daughter Nell turned back to a more expedient path.

'Saints preserve us indeed.' Startled, Beth turned to scan the darkness for the man who possessed that deep sardonic voice. Of course she knew who it was. She could just make out his long back, reclining against the timbers of the jetty.

'Master Henry,' she stammered, uncertain how either would explain their presence.

'That's right, my dear. Master Henry it is,' he responded, quite unfazed. 'Oh dear, oh dear, not another crumpled hat. What is it this time? Another swan?'

Beth, lost for words, seized at the excuse.

'Yes, yes,' she nodded firmly, feeling the colour rise in her cheeks. 'I'm afraid of swans. I've always been afraid of swans. My mother knew I was frightened of swans.' She was talking too much.

'Come closer, let me see you,' he demanded, 'but mind where you tread.' He leaned forward to look at her wide startled eyes. 'You're lying, aren't you?' he said shortly. 'There are no swans down here.' Beth nodded her head just as firmly, relieved to be free of her falsehood. Nervously twisting the ribbons of her bonnet, she felt close to tears. She would have to tell him the truth about her garden she decided but, to her surprise, he didn't ask her why she was there.

'Well, it seems we both have our secrets, my dear.' He sank back against the wall and reached deep into the shadows. 'This is mine,' he added, almost to himself, as he drew out a flask and caressed its silver casing. 'The family curse. Uncle Eddie knew all about that.' There was bitterness in his voice as he gulped the liquor with obvious distaste, then defiantly drained the contents. The effect was soon evident. Sensing that his interest in her had waned, Beth slid silently back towards the door. She had almost reached it when her foot caught the edge of a rotting board.

'Wait!' It was an order and she paused with her hand on the latch. 'Wait. I need someone to talk to. Come and sit down.'

'Please, sir, I have my work to do. I should go now.' His unpredictable state alarmed her and she had no wish to encourage his clandestine drinking – a subject which was giving rise to gossip lately and was obviously why he was in the boathouse alone.

He folded his arms and laughed, enjoying her discomfiture.

'I am your master, am I not? Your work will wait. Tell me what your life is like. Is it better than mine,

no gentlemen would confide in a maid

d'you suppose?' He needed distraction from his mental pain and the gulf between them intrigued him.

Beth hesitated before responding cautiously.

'I am happy here. I have friends and good food and no one whips me no more. But I dare say I work harder than you would care to.'

'Ah, work again. That's what I lack, is it?' He talked freely knowing that she was of no consequence and too afraid to be judgemental. 'Well, I dare say you're right. I should have joined the cavalry like my celebrated father,' he added with a hint of cynicism. 'My leg put an end to that, you know. No battles for me. I must be kept safe to run the estate. My God, how it bores me.'

Perceiving no way to escape, Beth settled herself on an upturned hull. There were jetties built into the walls of the boathouse and an inlet of water between which gave no indication of the current beneath. She was careful to sit on the opposite side from where, in the shade, she felt safe and free to observe. He was the strangest of men, she decided, but she had to admit the most handsome too, with a fineness of feature that would always betray his privileged class. His striking blue eyes swivelled suddenly towards her to fix like search lights on her anxious face.

'Don't you think so?' he demanded, unnerving her further. Beth hadn't been listening. She had been looking at the high sweep of his brow and the way his blonde hair fell carelessly across it. At the lean cut of his cheeks and the firmly chiselled jaw that reminded her of a statue she had seen once in her youth.

'I don't think nothing, sir,' she mumbled, resolving to listen in future.

But it was too late, his mood had changed.

'What do you mean, you don't think nothing?' he growled. 'Do you have no thoughts at all in that plain head of yours? Is it stuffed full of cotton and straw and notions of work?' Stung by his rudeness and with her nerves as tight as a bow, Beth's usual reserve fell away.

'Aye, I have thoughts, sir,' she cried across the divide. 'Thoughts that you could never know, for all your high learning. Thoughts about being hungry and cold and having no shoes, of my mother dying of fever with no medicine to save her and William, poor William, begging us to leave him without even a grave. Aye, I have thoughts.' Tears welled in her eyes and she paused, swallowing hard to keep them at bay.

'That's better, that's better,' Henry encouraged, watching her quite intently now. 'Some anger at last from my moorland waif. But there's more, isn't there? Something has maimed you. A man perhaps? Against your will?'

Beth leapt to her feet. No one had probed that wound before and she wasn't going to suffer Henry's insults now.

'Yes, I thought so. That's your secret, my dear,' he called as she fled, tearing her underskirts in her haste.

Deprived of an audience, his smile soon faded.

He cursed softly until his hand located the familiar curves of a bottle in the stern of a boat.

Chapter Nine

It was Saturday, not quite noon, and Jack had made good time. Sir George had dismissed him, and the horses were settled in a mews behind Lord Mayor's Walk. His step quickened. Times like this were few when he could explore the narrow streets of York and breathe again the scents and stenches of the market place, just as he remembered them in London in his youth. He would go past the stalls of freshly slaughtered meat in the Shambles, on to Walmgate to buy cocoa from Mary Tuke's shop, then across Castle Mills bridge and back through Tower Street and Goodramgate. It was more than his job was worth to be late but as long as the horses were rested and waiting when his master required them at five o'clock, he had nothing to fear.

There seemed to be an unusually large throng approaching the bar at Monkgate. Almost a carnival atmosphere prevailed. Jack decided to bide his time and avoid the crush by eating Beth's cake and cheese on the grassy slopes beneath the walls. He flung himself down and unbuttoned his livery in response to the growing heat of the sun and the total absence of clouds or a breeze. A perfect summer day. He would have an ale in a hostelry later, he decided, anticipating the taste on his parched throat and the pleasure of convivial company.

He thought of Beth as he ate his lunch and felt briefly guilty. Life had drawn them apart through no fault of their own, like two parallel lines that could never be broken but no longer crossed paths. She had evaded his glance across the table last night and had seemed quieter of late but he hadn't found time to draw her aside. Was he too obsessed with his own progress now?

'You going to watch too, sir?' Jack squinted sideways at a peasant who was scraping dung from his clogs on the turf nearby.

'Watch what, good fellow?' he responded, sitting up abruptly and re-buttoning his jacket.

'Why, the hangings. Haven't you heard? Two felons and a gypsy for the high jump today. Should be a good show.' He distorted his face to portray a strangled corpse and laughed. It seemed to Jack that he was slightly crazed but he knew how such spectacles could affect his fellow man. He had once seen a wretch ride in a cart on his own coffin with a noose round his neck from Newgate to the gallows and he had no wish to repeat the experience. Not wishing to talk to the depraved stranger, he leapt to his feet and allowed himself to be swept between the stone ramparts into the city within.

Amongst so many, he soon became hostage to the crowd in the network of streets. When these widened into a concourse nearer the centre, the swell of humanity grew to such an extent that he feared the weakest would be trampled – a fear born of tragedies he had heard talk of in the past.

Whilst he struggled to maintain his own balance, his concern focused on a slender loose-limbed girl in a cape the colour of rose-hips who was being tossed like flotsam on the ebb and flow of a tide. A kerchief, secured at the nape in the style of a gypsy, restrained an abundance of nut-brown hair. Fearing she would fall, Jack attempted to reach her but, when he did so, let his hand fall rather too hard on the profusion of curls. She turned like a wild creature to stare at him with such clear blue eyes that he forgot, for once, his clever repartee and was aware of nothing else. He knew instantly that it was one of those moments; a moment like the night in the storm that, for better or worse, would change his life.

She, however, engrossed in some private sorrow, shrank into the crowd. Jack was bewildered. Why had she seemed so familiar? She was a gypsy, he felt sure, but her fine features were not those of a Romany. He had seen no trace of tears yet grief had been etched on her face. Then the answer came to him. She was not here to watch this loathsome performance but to mourn the death of one of her kind.

He followed, in spite of himself, across the open ground in front of the debtor's prison to where he knew those condemned were brought from their cells to die. The atmosphere sickened him but still he pursued the girl closer and yet closer to the gallows. There, young thieves had gathered to profit from revellers and mourners alike. A roar went up as a castle door opened and rose to a crescendo as the doomed men mounted the scaffold with hands pinioned to their chests in an attitude of prayer. The two felons gazed, mute with shock, at the sea of baying faces and the bier nearby. Soon it would convey their bodies away with dangling heads and broken necks.

In contrast the third man stood tall against his aggressors, with shoulders squared. His dark eyes swept over the assembly, silencing with their strange brilliance those who returned his stare, until they came to rest on the girl in red. At pains to point her out, he turned aside to speak to the priest. The old man nodded in response but searched in vain for a letter he had placed in the folds of his cassock.

'Pa!' the girl called but her voice was drowned by the chaos around her. In despair, she pressed a locket in the shape of a heart against her lips then held it aloft for her father to see. In a trice, a ruffian had snatched it and ducked away with a true dodger's skill. He hadn't reckoned however on a streetwise lad whose speed equalled his own and whose strength soon compelled him to release his prize. He made good his escape as Jack, clutching the pendant, waded back to the barrier where weeping relatives were stretching out arms to their loved ones. It was too late, however. Distraught at her loss, the girl had fled from the horror to come.

On the scaffold, the final brief prayers had been said. Jack's attention was only drawn back from his futile search by the arresting voice of the dark-eyed man.

'You sir, you must take the letter.' He indicated a package that the priest had at last retrieved from his garments. Jack shook his head and backed away.

'No. Not I. I can't read,' he protested.

'It is my final wish,' the gypsy repeated firmly. 'You must take it and trust me. I know many things. Take it before I die and I shall go in peace.'

Jack felt, not for the first time, that events were beyond his control. He could not refuse. He accepted the letter from the flustered priest and stood in silence, a reluctant witness, as white hoods were placed on the victim's heads. The executioner, reprieved from a sentence of death himself to perform his brutal task, stank of liquor as he moved amongst the men. He walked unsteadily as he checked the knots on each short length of rope. Finally, he pulled the bolt and released the trap.

At that point Jack gagged and did not wait to see what would follow. He knew all too well how long condemned men could take to expire – sometimes half an hour, unless a merciful friend pulled hard on their thrashing limbs from below. Was he alone in feeling revulsion, he wondered, as he forced his way out of the jeering mob to be violently sick in the gutter? A lean dog sniffed his ankles. Barefoot children played hopscotch in the shade. Life went on. Yet in spite of its horrors, today there was a strange new fire in his soul. He looked up at the strip of blue beyond the roofs. Somewhere under that midsummer sky was a girl with nut-brown hair and eyes the colour of bluebells in spring.

Chapter Ten

Beth paused by the drawing room door on her way upstairs. The fire that normally roared in the grate was spluttering beneath a feeble column of smoke. It was Annie's job to see that the room was warm in the morning and Mrs Buchanan would not be well pleased. Her friend would be spared a scolding, Beth reasoned, if she could revive it before the family emerged. Setting down her pail in the stairwell and darting quickly through the heavy two-leaved doors, she reached for the bellows that stood to the side of the marble hearth. Soon the coals glowed and, replacing the instrument, she was about to slip away when the clatter of hooves outside and the chance of catching a glimpse of Jack, enticed her towards the open window.

But it was not him and she withdrew sharply as a woodman with a wagon of logs gave her a sly wink. Her thoughts returned to the brushing of floors, the beating of carpets and the unmade beds that awaited upstairs. This elegant room with its cabinets of carved oak, its corniced ceiling and life-sized pictures of kings and dukes was not her domain.

No sooner had she tiptoed forward, however, than she heard footsteps in the hall. Instinctively, she shrank back behind the folds of the crimson drapes, though quite why she had done so instead of walking boldly out she couldn't explain – unless it was the glimpse of Henry Cunningham's distinctive blonde hair and the memory of her last encounter. He picked up a letter from a silver tray and strolled preoccupied towards the light. Beth scarcely dared to breathe as she watched him break the seal with a swift movement of his long, fine fingers. His profile hardened as he read then, cursing softly, he crushed the missive in the palm of one hand, strode back towards the fire and hurled it into the leaping flames.

Beth closed her eyes with relief and drew air into her lungs. Surely now he would leave and allow her to escape unseen. He stood for an age with his hands on the mantel piece and his eyes fixed on the burning logs. Would he never go, she wondered, risking a glance at his broad, well-suited shoulders and his long lean muscular limbs. To her dismay, he moved instead towards a decanter of port on the dresser and filled a crystal goblet up to the brim. Her dismay turned to horror as Sir George's voice and that of his wife echoed on the stairs. They entered the room together.

'Don't you think it's a little too early for that, Henry?' he said evenly, looking his son in the eye but containing his irritation. Henry skirted round him, holding his glass high, to escort his mother to her favourite chair. His smile as he leant over her dispelled any words of reproach. How easily he could charm this gentle woman and how much he enjoyed being the object of her favour. He turned back to his father, standing square, matching strength for strength. In many ways they were very alike despite the erect figure of the older man and the slight swagger of the young buck. Henry had challenged him from a young age however, resentful of any authority – a result, Sir George would say, of his mother's spoiling nature.

'I suggest you put that down, Henry,' his father repeated firmly. 'We need to have a talk and now seems as good a time as any.'

Behind the curtain, Beth froze. What should she do? She had no wish to be party to this private conversation. But the moment had passed when she could curtsy and excuse herself from the room. The family had settled in the damask chairs near the fire and Henry, defiant as always, examined the contents of his glass.

'It is never too early for the fruit of the vine,' he announced airily. 'Why, I declare it puts a spring in my step.'

Sir George interwove his fingers and looked at his son thoughtfully.

'Yes, well it's the spring in your step that is causing concern. Cavorting with your friends into the early hours when I am away does not endear you to the servants, my boy, and I cannot allow it to go on. Your conduct has not been what I expect.'

Henry stared at the ornate cream and gold coving overhead then glanced at Lady Elizabeth whose own eyes remained downcast.

'Indeed, I know exactly what you expect, father.'

Sir George continued, determined at last to take action against his wayward son.

'At your mother's request, I have given you time – too much time, it would seem. You've been on two Grand tours, at considerable cost to myself, I might add, but who did you choose to consort with in Paris and Venice and Rome? Certainly not the cream of society who might have brought benefits to our family name. And your stay in the Highlands was disastrous. There can't be an ale-house in Scotland that doesn't know my son is a wastrel.' He paused, unmoved, as his wife, stifling a sob in a lace handkerchief, fled from the room. Then his knuckles whitened in anger on the arms of his chair.

Henry, sensing a line was about to be drawn, set his empty goblet down.

'You have no sense of purpose or direction,' Sir George continued. Therefore I shall make the rules from now on. You will marry Lady Jane before April is out next year or seek your fortune elsewhere.' He got up, to Beth's great relief, to follow his wife.

Henry rose too.

'Lady Jane informed me by letter this morning that her mother is encouraging her to marry John Dunne.'

'Then it is in your interests, my lad, to see that she doesn't,' Sir George growled back as he turned on his heel.

The silence was suddenly palpable. The pollen

from a bouquet of flowers was threatening to make Beth sneeze. In an effort to avert it, she clutched her nose, making the curtain twitch enough to draw attention to her hiding place. She held her breath as firm footsteps approached and swept the drape aside. The shock of being discovered released a succession of sneezes.

'I meant no harm ...... Achoo! ...... honest, Master Henry, I meant no harm ...Achoo! Achoo! I can e...ex....'

'Explain?' Henry added helpfully. 'A swan again, was it?' He nodded gravely, plainly enjoying the diversion from his own unhappy state of affairs, then threw back his head and laughed till a tear escaped and he had to pause to wipe it away. 'Ah, little Beth – you're a tonic,' he smiled. On an impulse, he swept her tiny frame against his broad silk waistcoat and twirled her round until her senses quite left her. He stopped just as suddenly.

'I forgot, you don't like that, do you? Put it down to the wine. I meant no harm, honest,' he mimicked with a captivating grin. He was gone from the room a moment later, leaving Beth to smooth her dress and calm herself as best she could. She picked up her mop and pail from the stairwell in a daze and walked with sober dignity up the first flight of stairs. By the time she reached the second, a giggle refused to be quelled. On the third, a glorious surge of laughter rose from the depths of her body to echo beneath the sunlit domes above.

Annie appeared from a doorway, her face streaked with soot.

82

'Whatever's the matter, Beth? I ain't never heard you laugh like that before. Was something funny?'

Chapter Eleven

The steady rhythm of Lady's hooves echoed on the parched earth. Ahead, a stream meandered between the Howardian hills, cutting a swathe through the rich tapestry of the Harringtons' estate. Lady Jane's ancestral home was a noble sight indeed, Henry thought. It was easy to see why his father sought an alliance with such distinguished blood.

He leant back in the saddle and allowed his slightly trembling hands to relax the reins, until the canter became a trot and the trot an ambling walk. The mare headed towards the water and he made no attempt to stop her, nor to prevent her wading in the shallows to satisfy her thirst. His thoughts were on the task that lay ahead – the great sacrifice that he was about to make to please the one person he loved – his mother. Her health was failing and seeing at last the truth of her husband's words, she had beseeched him not to leave but to mend his ways and carry out his father's wishes.

A movement on the far side of the stream caught his eye but not feeling his usual ebullient self without a flask in his pocket, he kept quite still. A young woman with a kerchief tied at the nape was gathering hazel and elder and strips of willow. The hazel rods would be whittled into pegs and the willow into baskets to hawk up at the hall, just as her kind did at Mrs Bullen's kitchen door. Nearby, a kettle hung on a tripod over a slowly burning fire, and a black and white cob dozed in the sun at the end of a long rope. Somewhere beneath the trees, he could just make out a four-wheeled potters cart with a heavy canvas roof on a bowed wood frame.

The girl moved nimbly about her chores, aware of a human presence as gypsies always are, but choosing to keep herself to herself. Henry pondered for a moment on what it would be like to live a wandering life, to be free of constraint and have only oneself to consider. His reverie ended with a deep sigh as he hauled Lady's head from the water and dug her sharply in the ribs. The mare responded with a sudden burst of speed which Henry didn't check until she slithered to a halt in the courtyard of Brampton Hall.

'My dear fellow, what a delightful surprise,' gushed the mistress of the house, ushering him into their finest room. 'I must send word at once to tell Jane you are here.'

'Ah yes,' Henry said, adopting his smoothest tone. 'She wrote to me, you know. And what I have to say cannot be delayed.' He took a deep breath. 'In truth, Lady Clarissa, I have come to ask for your daughter's hand in marriage. Should she accept me, I would be honoured indeed.'

'Is that so?' Lady Clarissa murmured, tilting her head and fixing him with an unblinking beady stare. 'Of course,' she added slowly, 'there would have to be no more of this, shall we say, youthful behaviour of yours. You do understand. We have our daughter's reputation to think of. However...' she clasping her hands in eager anticipation. 'I'm sure the influence of such a well-bred and strong-minded young woman is just what you need.'

It was discreetly arranged for Henry to wait in the conservatory for what seemed like an age, while Lady Jane donned a suitably splendid gown and adorned her hair with a band of pearls. When she appeared, she stood strategically framed against a riot of white jasmine before extended a lace-gloved hand towards him. Henry bowed low, noting as he did so the unmistakable flash of triumph in the bird-like eyes that so much resembled her mother's. But, whatever his misgivings, there was no going back. A stroll between the rose beds and the avenues of yew sealed his fate.

After a glass or two of claret and a serving of game pie and strawberries for lunch, his mood mellowed. He felt like an actor in someone else's play, reading lines that were not his own. But the time passed pleasantly enough until, after tea on the lawn, he kissed his future bride and assured her, as Lady chafed at the bit, that every moment away from her side would be more than he could bear. Lord Harrington, who had arrived late at the table and had viewed him with a strongly critical eye, was evidently impressed by this performance. He tapped the ground with his silver caned stick.

'We'll have an Easter wedding, young Henry.

Tell your father we must meet. We have lots to discuss.'

The deed was done. There was a certain amount of relief in that but it took the long ride back beneath the lengthening shadows to bring the reality home to Henry. What should have been the most joyous day of his life would in fact be a theatrical show to unite two ambitious families. It had little to do with his true feelings, which he had been in the habit of concealing with alcohol. Now all that had to stop, and the thought frightened him.

His resolve, however, remained firm as he plodded through the straggling village of Topcliffe towards the gates of Skellfield Hall. He passed the ale-house at the end of the long street without looking up and told himself afterwards that he wouldn't have turned back but for Lady picking up a stone in her shoe. Of course he could have dismounted and walked her home. But the perfect excuse for a cool beer in the setting sun while someone else attended to his mount was too good to miss. Besides, back at the hall, his life would be monitored. Didn't he deserve a final fling?

It was not an inn he had frequented before. Men with the soil and sweat of the day's work still ingrained in their faces were ill at ease with a gentleman's presence. For that reason, he secured the reins to a stable door and settled himself on a bench outside. A serving girl bearing a cracked earthenware jug set it down in front of a young man nearby.

'There you are, Master Jack.' She winked

impishly. 'Let me know if you need owt else.' Her manner changed abruptly when she saw Henry's polished boots obstructing her path and his disturbing blue eyes appraising her. She bobbed nervously, nodded and scurried indoors to do his bidding, leaving the two men to turn and stare at each other in mutual surprise.

'Jack, my dear fellow, just the man I need. Would you care to take a look at Lady's left fore?' He indicated the mare gingerly shifting her weight from leg to leg behind them. By the time the serving girl returned, Jack had deftly removed a sharp stone from the horn beneath the horse's iron shoe and calmed her with a handful of corn.

'Another beer for the coachman,' Henry insisted, ignoring Jack's protests and quickly relapsing into his old ways. 'Why, we must talk on an evening such as this. Unless,' he added, looking at him man to man, 'I'm interrupting a romance with that bonnie little wench.'

Jack laughed. 'She's a comely lass to be sure sir and a fine companion but I know nothing yet of romance. No doubt that will come in its own good time.'

The man was so assured considering his appalling past, Henry reflected. He almost envied him his steady methodical life, his obvious conviction that he could better himself and succeed. His own swagger and confidence was a cover for low self-esteem.

'You are happy here, are you not?' Henry quizzed him. 'D'you have any regrets?'

Jack whittled absently at a twig with the small knife he still held till the point was sharp.

'I would like to be able to write, sir – and to be able to read and be learned like yourself. One day I shall, you'll see.'

'And to what purpose would you put this skill?' Henry enquired, unaware that he was seeking answers for himself. Jack's dark eyes focused on the setting sun and glowed with a passion.

'Why, there are so many things I could do.'

'But what? What in particular?'

There was a long pause before Jack answered.

'There is a man I have heard speak in York. A man called Richard Oastler. I should like to be like him. I should like to change things.'

'Ah. I've heard talk of him. A Tory radical, a trouble-maker, I believe.' Henry returned to his ale. 'You should not associate with the likes of him.' He would have changed the subject but Jack persisted.

'Do you have any beliefs, sir? I mean no disrespect but do you have any thoughts for the people who work beyond your door? People such as Beth and I who, but for good fortune, might have perished in the mills like poor William. Some men think on such things and use their skills to persuade others.' He dropped his head suddenly and became silent, aware that he was overstepping the mark between master and servant. 'I speak too freely, sir,' he said at length. 'You must forgive me but I feel strongly about these matters.'

'Aye, that you certainly do – and I admire you for

it. You are loyal to your fellow man. But do you not remember the revolution and bloodshed in France? The aristocracy here still have much to fear.'

'They are right to be fearful,' Jack ventured quietly, 'if they oppress the people. They must learn to be wise and fair as Oastler is fair. Then the country will thrive.'

Henry buttoned his jacket and prepared to leave.

'You have quite a vision, young Jack, and I've enjoyed our talk.' He sighed deeply and supped the last of his liquor with relish. 'We both have our fortunes to follow. Why, I saw a gypsy today near Brampton Hall – a girl with just a black and white nag and a small potter's cart for a home. What different lives we all lead, eh? But that's how it has to be.'

He mounted and clattered out of the yard as Jack leapt to his feet.

'This girl – was she wearing a scarlet cape?'

'Aye. I believe she was,' the answer came back.

Chapter Twelve

The servants' hall buzzed with gossip as Jack hurried in and took his place at the table. He smiled across at Beth and her eyes lit up in response. She was growing in confidence, he decided, and even her plainness was diminished of late by a new vitality. Her shoulders no longer drooped and the little toss of her head, he observed now and then, showed a happy awareness that her hair had grown silky and strong. She could even cope firmly with Joe's coarse remarks and no longer shrank from the cut and thrust of everyday life. Her desire to be a cook was being quietly encouraged and her skills grew by the day under Mrs Bullen's watchful eye. She would always retain a certain reserve but Jack's heart was gladdened by the change in her.

The chatter came to a sudden halt as Mr Scott called for silence.

'I have news for you all that, judging from the unseemly talk around this table, you have already gleaned. I would remind you that it is not the business of this household to listen at doors or repeat confidences from upstairs to which you should not have been privy.'

Mrs Buchanan cast a reproving eye over the assembly as he continued.

'Now it is with great pleasure that I announce the forthcoming nuptials of Master Henry and Lady Jane Harrington. The wedding will take place at Easter next year and that of course will entail a great deal of work for us all. However, I am sure we all wish the happy couple well.'

Jack reached for his ale and joined in the unanimous cheer though Beth, he noticed, sipped her water thoughtfully instead. He drew her aside as the housemaids and footmen, whispering amongst themselves, filtered away to resume their chores.

'We don't have much time to talk any more,' he acknowledged sadly. 'I am to take Sir George and Lady Elizabeth to Brampton Hall after church tomorrow. I shall stay in their coachmen's quarters for a week until they return. Will you be alright?' He pinched her cheek playfully and lowered his voice. 'I shall expect to see a beautiful garden when I come back.'

'And so you shall!' A sparkle returned to her honey-coloured eyes. 'By Michaelmas t'will be full of late blossoms. You must find yourself a girl, Jack, a special girl, then I'll pick you a splendid bouquet.'

'Aye, I must,' he agreed, adding mysteriously, 'and when I do I want blue flowers, all blue.'

'Cornflower blue – like Master Henry's eyes?' Beth suggested dreamily.

'Aye, that's right. Or like bluebells.' His voice trailed away. The similarity between Henry and the girl hadn't occurred to him before.

'Jack?' Beth looked at him intently with a woman's intuition. 'Who is she?'

'Ah, that's another story,' he smiled, 'and I don't know who she is yet.'

Mrs Bullen interrupted their talk to reclaim her protégée.

'Now then, Beth. These dishes won't wash themselves. Look lively, girl. And your fanciful stories will have to wait,' she added, trying to look sternly at Jack. 'There'll be no time for dreaming with a wedding in the spring.' Her show of authority hid the very real pride she increasingly felt towards them. Ever since that night in the storm, if she were honest, when they had shivered by her range like two fledglings thrown from a nest, her life had been enriched. She wrapped a slice of cake in a piece of muslin and slipped it into Jack's pocket. 'There. Now be off with you. And mind you come back safe with the master next week.' She turned abruptly on her heel, followed meekly by Beth.

'T'aint fair,' Joe muttered to Annie as Jack disappeared. 'She don't give me no cake.'

'You're no coachman,' Annie retorted. 'Now if you was to be a coachman, 'well, I might sees fit to give you a treat too.' She was beginning to see Joe as a last hope of escape from her grinding daily toil. 'You should listen to Master Jack and learn to hold that temper of yours. Then you might learn something and we might – well you know – one day.'

Joe's florid features reddened still more as the implication dawned on his slow brain. 'You mean – you and me?' His voice trailed away in disbelief.

'I mean you and me, Joe,' Annie repeated firmly, 'but not till I see you in a smart green coat like Jack's.' She ran broken dirty finger nails across his unkempt head. 'It would suit you grand, you being red-haired an' all.'

It was all too much for Joe. He lunged towards her with brawny arms outstretched, a manoeuvre that earned him a resounding slap. He started to curse then backed away, grinning.

'I'll make you proud of me Annie, you'll see.'

Chapter Thirteen

As Sir George and Lady Elizabeth disappeared down the drive in their finest barouche for their visit to Brampton Hall, there was a general feeling of relief amongst the staff. If they thought life would be easier, however, they were much mistaken. Mr Scott and Mrs Buchanan made good use of the week to overhaul the downstairs rooms. Footmen, hoping to idle the time away, were directed to polish the floors with beeswax till they shone and to empty the cupboards so that housemaids could dust the shelves. Beth too was kept busy turning out the larder and restocking the jars with spices and herbs.

Henry spent his time on the estate, overseeing the crops and the livestock from the saddle of his horse and preferred, when he returned, to take his meals without fuss in his study away from the prying eyes of the servants. On the odd occasion it had fallen to Beth to deliver a tray, he had seemed aloof, preoccupied perhaps with his future plans. In fact, she had to admit to a certain sadness when he failed to acknowledge her presence at all. So this was the real Henry, she told herself firmly. The man destined to be master not just of Skellfield but of

Brampton too. His status was so far removed from her own that he would never be aware of the quite irrational joy she had felt when he had spun her in his arms with such apparent ease. It had been a momentary loss of reserve on his part, brought on by a goblet of wine. That was all. Now, on the orders of Sir George, no liquor was to be left on the drawing room table.

'This confounded pen. Tell Scott to bring me more ink.'

Beth, struggling with emotions she had never experienced before, scarcely heard what he said. She paused with her tray by the study door, unwilling to turn back for fear he should see her distress. When she did, he looked up.

'Is that a tear?' His unflinching gaze was disconcerting.

'No, no. Definitely not,' Beth protested in a panic. 'A bit of dust, sir, that's all. I shall wipe it away presently.'

'It is a tear,' Henry stated, in a tone that implied the matter was of no consequence. He turned back to his work and Beth was grateful. Her eyes lingered for a moment however on the golden hair and silk cream shirt reflected beneath the pool of light. When she left the room she couldn't explain either to a curious Annie or to herself, why more tears flowed.

By the last day of the week, the combination of stifling heat and sheer hard work had left the household dispirited and inclined to defy their superiors, a fact noted by Mr Scott as he settled himself at the table once more. He correctly judged that some praise was due and raised his hand to silence the chatter.

'I think we can all be proud when the master comes back on Sunday,' he began. 'You have all played your part and the house is a pleasure to behold as it should be. As a gesture of goodwill, some of you may take the day off while the weather holds; others will be granted some time tomorrow. There will be bread and cheese and a basket of fruit on the sideboard for your supper tonight so that Mrs Bullen too can enjoy a well-deserved rest.' He beamed at the plump starched figure to his left, causing her to blush slightly and adjust an imaginary hair behind her lace cap.

'That is all,' he concluded, tucking a serviette into his stock before tasting his portion of rich beef stew.

Beth excused herself quickly. She had longed all week for a glimpse of the cool river which was just visible through the wilderness of trees surrounding her tiny plot. She would take her cloak and lie down in the dappled shade and listen to its rhythm. The healing scent of lavender and camomile and newly emerging buds of sweetpea would surely calm her unquiet mind.

Declining Annie's excited suggestion that they visit the village, she slipped off unseen through a tradesman's door and ran with a light heart along the forbidden path that led down to the river until the tangled undergrowth once more snatched at her thin ankles and snagged her linen dress. With several backward glances she picked her way along their secret track until a canopy of white elder flowers parted to reveal a kaleidoscope of colour. Nature had fashioned her plants into a fine tapestry and she stood breathless to admire it.

'Why, it's beautiful!' she exclaimed out loud, as she sank to the ground and discarded her bonnet.

'Beautiful indeed!' a familiar male voice echoed.

Beth sat transfixed, her flaxen hair in disarray. Like the open-cupped blossoms around her, she had raised her face to the sun so that now she could see only the outline of Henry's languid figure. She stared, speechless, at the golden halo framing shadowed features.

'So this is your big secret,' the voice mocked, as Beth struggled to gauge his reaction. The slightly slurred, over-emphasised words alarmed her. This was the other Henry. The one that had to be hidden deep in a thicket like this. The one only she knew about. Would he tell the household? Would she and Jack be dismissed? He stumbled slightly as he moved away from the broad tree-trunk that supported him and she flinched as his feet crushed her carefully-tended plants. He was in the mood to hurt her, she could tell.

'The big secret,' he repeated laughing, not bothering to conceal the flask in his hand, 'a tangled patch of wild herbs and weeds. Why, is the walled garden not good enough for you? Or the bush roses between the avenue of yews?'

Beth's anger overcame her fear but she kept her voice steady.

'Those are your gardens,' she replied. 'Yours and your family's. This is William's garden – and my mam's,' she added quietly. She smoothed the two stone slabs, surrounded by lavender, that formed a focal point. On each she had put a single rose. They needed replacing from the small bush she had grown but Henry now threatened her private world and her future too.

She waited, watching him wide-eyed, as he absorbed what she said with apparent difficulty. Finally his flask was empty and the thought seemed uppermost in his mind. He forgot about Beth and her garden and moved suddenly towards the river and the track that led to the boathouse. He had further stocks there and he smiled to himself in anticipation as he lurched from tree to tree.

At first Beth was relieved to see him go but her sanctuary, like a fledgling's nest, had been violated and she knew already that nothing would restore its tranquillity. Instead of calm, she felt growing unease as she watched Henry's receding figure lunge through the long grasses along the river's edge. Suppose he lost his footing as his uncle must have done all those years before. The thought prompted her to rise to her feet and stand on tiptoe to observe his progress. Her anxiety did not end when she heard the boathouse door slam shut behind him. Images of the fast-flowing water and the loose boards inside, the possibility of him tripping in the semi-darkness, as she herself had done, left her no option but to follow.

It took several minutes for her small feet to

negotiate the same overgrown track and a further minute as her hand hesitated over the latch. Was this her duty? Or was Henry's life his own concern? After all she was a mere servant and she had not been summoned. The sound of cursing inside and the constant lapping of water against the boats emboldened her. The man was not himself and there was no one else here.

She slid inside without drawing his attention. He was far too intent on reaching the small rowing boat that bobbed on its moorings near the mouth of the building. Her heart missed a beat as he leant too far forward over the bubbling foam and she ran instinctively to the landing stage opposite.

'Don't do that! You'll fall.' But it was too late. Normally a sure-footed oarsman, Henry teetered as he withdrew a bottle from the stern of the craft, then crashed sidelong into the current and was swiftly submerged. Beth's fingers flew to her mouth and her eyes widened like saucers as she waited for him to re-surface. When he did, she didn't hesitate. Heedless of her own safety, she stretched out her hand to grasp him.

'I'm here, here!' she cried, but the flailing limbs were just too far away. She needed a boat hook but she couldn't see one and in any case there wasn't time. She reached out once more.

'Grab me, Henry. Here, here!' Just another six inches and their fingers would lock. It was six inches too far. In a trice, Beth found herself underwater, out of her depth and gasping for air in a twilight world. The situation was reversed now. A non-swimmer, she was the one who needed support. She caught a glimpse of Henry's startled eyes as she clung in terror to his solid torso. Together they were being swept from the safety of the boathouse into the hazardous waters outside. Whether he was aware of their plight, she couldn't tell, for her own consciousness was fading fast. Certainly the shock had revived his senses and prompted him to hold her tight. Too tight. She wanted to cry out, to draw breath – but the water engulfed her and suffocation seemed close. As she sank beneath the surface into an underworld of eerie muted sounds she felt her pulse race and then an intense throbbing in her head that brought with it a desire to cease the struggle. She could see William beckoning now, and her mother – and Jack staring at her with great sadness. And was that Henry's face too, wafting above her? He was shouting. Why was he shouting? She must go back to find out.

Gradually, Henry's face became clearer. Her fingers felt strangely disembodied as she traced the contours of his jaw and smoothed wet strands of flaxen hair across his brow. As consciousness returned she withdrew. This was no dream. Those features were real and they broke suddenly into a broad smile.

'I thought I'd lost you, Beth. I thought I'd lost you,' he murmured, with more feeling than she had imagined possible. He was not yet sober, she told herself, but all the same it was a genuine tear that coursed down his cheek. She was back in her garden, she discovered. She listened quietly as he told her of his struggle with the treacherous current. How he had grabbed the overhanging reeds and somehow managed to pull them both out. She was dressed only in her thin petticoat and wrapped for warmth in her cloak. Her smock hung with his own outer garments on the branch of a tree, where a gentle breeze and the afternoon sun would soon render them dry. All the same, Beth shivered.

'Delayed shock,' Henry commented. He took out a pocket flask that still contained a shot of brandy. 'I won't be needing this – intemperate fool that I am. But trust me, it will do you good.' His powers of persuasion were too much for Beth in her weakened state. She gasped as the unfamiliar fluid scorched a path down her throat. After a time however, she sank back amongst the camomile feeling languid and relaxed. Henry lay close to her, his hands behind his head, staring at the vault of blue above. She dozed fitfully, awaking at last to find his eyes fixed upon her, his face disconcertingly close.

'You're not beautiful, you know. Not even pretty.' Beth laughed, familiar now with his outrageous behaviour. She kept herself clean and tidy enough but she had long accepted that she would never be pretty. 'So why do I feel drawn to you?' he continued. Then as though answering his own question. 'There's a light behind your eyes like a small flickering candle – that's what draws me. I noticed it that night in the storm. I saw a kindred spirit.' His gaze unnerved her but she stared back at him with a new intimacy until there seemed to be nothing else in her world except those clear blue eyes.

'You love me, don't you?' he said at length.

Beth's glance faltered.

'How do you know?'

'Everyone does,' he laughed without a trace of arrogance. His face was much too close again and she knew he was going to kiss her.

'Don't you feel it?' he murmured. 'The elation of being alive when we might have been dead? I don't know when I last felt more alive.'

It was all so natural. Her past, and all the nightmares of her past, seemed erased when his lips glanced against hers, like a bee seeking nectar from a flower. He was right. She had never felt more alive and nothing else mattered except this moment. Nothing.

His hand ran gently over her wet petticoat, exploring the contours of her breasts and hips and thighs. He watched her face for signs of resistance but there was none. Beth arched her small frame in luxurious ecstasy as he slid across her, silencing her cries of rapture with an increasingly passionate embrace. A single cloud, like an omen, scudded across the universe as abandonment gripped them. Her petticoat tore as he plunged himself into her.

Afterwards, they lay in a state of animal lassitude with no need to talk as the afternoon waned. Henry fell into a deep sleep, his arms flung back, framing for once an untroubled face. Beth gathered her things in silence.

'Goodbye, my love,' she whispered. She had seized the moment and whatever the consequences she would never forget or regret it. A large tear escaped down her cheek as she turned to leave but whether born of joy or sorrow she couldn't tell. The two after all were bedfellows.

Chapter Fourteen

At Brampton Hall too, life was gathering pace. The Cunninghams, from the moment they arrived, were lavishly entertained by their hosts and it was plain that the union of the two great families was equally pleasing to both. The match between Henry and Jane seemed almost incidental as the two elder gentlemen strolled the long avenues in the afternoon or sat late into the night, sustained by brandy and cigars. They had much to discuss of mutual interest.

Since he never knew when the carriage would be required for yet another visit, Jack was constantly on call. Often he was obliged to stand for hours beneath the trees as Lady Harrington and her guests enjoyed a picnic in the park. Their finery impressed him, as did the elegance of their coiffured hair, their flawless skin and soft hands, so rare in his own circles.

Towards the end of the week, as the champagne flowed, their manner towards him relaxed. He was, after all, a fine-looking young man with a hint of mischief in his dark eyes that had not gone unnoticed. A slender arm, swathed in silk, extended itself limply towards him from beneath a parasol.

'Can you help me rise, Cartwright? I do declare I feel quite giddy. I need to take some air over there by the lake.'

Lady Jane glared at her sister as Jack stepped forward.

'Certainly, ma'am,' he replied as he stooped to assist her, noting, as no doubt she intended, the firm swell of her breasts and the long graceful curve of her neck. He bowed slightly then withdrew with feigned indifference.

'Why, Master Jack, you've worked so hard this week,' the young lady simpered, eager to retain his favour. 'You shall have an afternoon off tomorrow to do as you please. Won't he, Mama?' The older woman nodded curtly. Her daughter's behaviour was far too familiar.

'The air will do you good, my dear. The champagne has quite gone to your head, I believe,' she added with a meaningful glance.

For his part, Jack was pleased that it had. His gaze strayed to the distant hillside and the ribbon of water that wound between beech and willow. Didn't his lead horse need exercise? Tomorrow, he would ride out to look for the black and white cob that Henry had mentioned and the girl in the red cape. He touched the letter and the silver pendant that he kept always close to his heart and smiled. Was the gypsy, whose life ended on the gallows, guiding him from beyond the grave?

The weather turned sultry the next day so that his mount was flecked with foam after a good gallop across the estate. She tossed her ears and tail constantly to ward off the midges beneath the trees while Jack dismounted to loosen her girth. It was as he did so that he noticed a small glade close to the river. Surely an ideal place for a camp. Judging it wiser not to be seen, however, he secured his steaming horse behind a stout tree and approached on foot like a hunter. There was evidence of wagon wheels and the buried remains of a fire but no sign of travellers at all. At least, he thought not, until he heard the snap of twigs in a covert nearby.

'Who's there?' He parted the branches of a thick bush and peered through. 'I'll do you no harm.'

It occurred to him that he himself might be in danger, but curiosity overcame caution. He pushed forward until another small clearing revealed the source of the disturbance. A young black horse, head held high, stood motionless, one foot raised as though poised for flight. Jack whistled softly, taking in its perfect conformation at a glance. This was no draught horse. It was no riding horse either, he discovered, as four flying hooves lashed out at him.

'Steady there,' he soothed. 'You're just a baby aren't you?' Nevertheless he was careful to stand beyond the confines of its rope to admire its coltish action. This horse was a rare beauty, he decided. But why should the owner want to hide it away? Had it been stolen? Such things happened in the traveller's twilight world.

He retraced his steps towards his own thoroughbred mare, deep in thought. He was still on foot in the centre of the track when a fast-trotting black and white cob appeared. Behind it, a slip of a lad with an overlarge hat was urging it on from the edge of his cart. He made no attempt to pull up – in fact, just the reverse, and its pace increased to a canter. In sudden anger, Jack stood firm, held out his arms and caught at the reins as he passed.

'Hold it, my lad! Do you have no thought for other folks on the road? I've half a mind to use that whip on your breeches.' The youth bowed his head and sulked beneath the brim of his hat, wanting only to escape.

'Well, you can perhaps help me after all,' Jack continued. 'Do you know a young girl with a pony like this? A girl with very blue eyes. She's been seen in these parts.'

The large hat shook vigorously.

'Are you sure you don't know her?'

The hat shook again and the cob moved forward.

'Her father died on the scaffold in York. He gave me a letter to give her and I have her pendant here too.' He took them out of his pocket and displayed them on the palm of his hand, to emphasise his words.

The lad's downcast eyes lifted slightly. There was a pause, then strangely fine-boned fingers shot out and snatched both the letter and the silver charm.

'You rascal, you!' Jack roared as the whip cracked and the startled pony set off at a gallop. With both hands on the reins now, the boy's hat first wobbled then bounced off his head, releasing a cascade of nut brown hair. Jack was too stunned to react till the girl had disappeared in a cloud of dust.

'That's what I call a lass!' he declared at last, slapping his thighs and laughing out loud. Fate was with him. The gypsy's predictions were true. He had found her once. He would find her again.

Chapter Fifteen

J ack felt listless in the weeks that followed. He continued to earn his master's respect on their regular visits to York but his sharp brain absorbed more than a mere coachman's should. Sir George attended meetings now with the new capitalist manufacturing classes but his motive like theirs was one of self interest. From conversations overheard, Jack knew all too well that economic slavery still prevailed. If he remained behind Skellfield's iron gates for the rest of his life he could forget, as the aristocracy did, the suffering masses outside. But Oastler's campaigning speeches continued to stir him and he vowed he, too, would one day make himself heard.

For the present, however, he had a good master to serve and he would not burden Beth with his restless thoughts. She knew nothing, either, of the gypsy girl whose destiny he sensed was linked to his own. How could he explain such irrational desire? After all, Beth had no experience in matters of the heart. Her energies went, as she had promised, into repaying her benefactors with honest hard work. She had little time to devote to herself. He should take her to a fair one day, he decided, and made a mental note to suggest it at lunch.

She did not respond to his wink across the table, a gesture usually guaranteed to raise a smile. Instead her eyes remained steadfastly fixed on her pewter plate until Mr Scott, calling for silence, compelled her to look up.

'Master Henry, as you all know, has been away,' he began. 'He is now here in residence. He has just returned from Brampton Hall and would like his lunch in the library. Perhaps you would be so good, Beth, since you don't appear to be hungry today. Mrs Bullen has already prepared a tray. You'll find it on the shelf in the larder.'

Beth's face flushed and she sat for a moment, clutching her stomach, unable to move.

'Well, go on lass!' Mrs Bullen chuckled. 'Why, if I didn't know you better, I'd say you was pregnant.' A ripple of laughter at such an unlikely notion was quickly suppressed as Beth hurried out. Jack's glance followed her with mild concern. She needed a break and he would see that she got one.

Meanwhile, in the cool of the larder, Beth tried to steady her shaking hands. Taking a deep breath, she picked up the tray and walked as calmly as she could along the marble corridor that she had first admired as a barefoot child all those years ago. There was the domed roof under which she and Jack had waited in awe. She knocked on the library door.

'Come in,'

'I've brought your lunch, sir.' She had not seen Henry since their last dramatic encounter several weeks before and he seemed as taken aback as herself.

'Leave it there,' he said, with a nonchalant gesture towards the desk. She could tell however that his thoughts were in chaos like her own.

'You look bonnie. Genuinely bonnie,' he said at last.

Beth said nothing but set down the tray. She turned to meet his gaze and saw in his blue eyes all that she needed to know. On an impulse, she ran to him and pressed her lips against his with a passion that surprised them both. She was gone before he could react but his voice halted her as she fled down the servant's passage.

'The garden. I must see you, Beth. Be there this evening. I'll wait for you.' She heard him and wept but she didn't turn back.

Later in her room, she was physically sick. She splashed cold water on her tear-stained face and lay on her bed until the spasms of grief had passed and her heart had ceased to race. She opened her eyes, calmer now, and let her gaze rest on the crisp white apron and the starched cap that hung on the door. They were the symbol of her station and she wore them with pride. Her few possessions lay folded on the chest that she shared with Annie. It wouldn't take long. She would wait until dark, she decided. Her case would attract attention and she mustn't be seen. Her thoughts returned to Jack and the heart-break she would cause him. But better that than to wreck two lives. After a while he would forget her and after a while their shared past would fade and he would flourish here as he deserved. It was better this way. There was a hesitant knock on the door and her panic returned briefly.

'Who's there? Who is it?'

'It's me. Jack. I want to talk to you.' Such visits were forbidden and he had taken a chance. For fear of being caught, he let himself in before she could stop him and leant against the wall laughing, enjoying the challenge of his escapade. His humour vanished, however, as the significance of Beth's tear-stained face dawned on him. He picked up the small case she had just begun to pack and looked at her in disbelief.

'You were going to leave, weren't you, Beth?' He was so angry that his eyes blazed. 'You were going to leave without telling me, weren't you?' He shook her hard. 'Weren't you?'

Beth took the case from him.

'It's for the best Jack. There's no other way. You see, I'm with child.'

'I don't believe you Beth.' But he could see the signs now – a womanly curve to her girlish physique and a blossom in her cheeks that work usually dulled. Why hadn't he noticed before?

'I'll kill the bastard if......' He clenched his fists until the knuckles whitened.

'No, Jack! It wasn't like that,' she protested.

'Well then, who was it? I demand to know. Whoever it was, he's ruined your life. You know that, don't you?'

'My life, Jack. Not yours. That's why I'm leaving – as soon as it's dark.' She was quite serene, quite controlled.

'You little fool! Have you no idea how the world treats fallen women? How will you survive?' The reality of her situation hit him like a bolt as he spoke and he buried his face in his hands. 'At least tell me who,' he murmured. His voice was bereft of emotion now.

'That I can never tell you and you must never ask.'

There was long silence before Jack got up with sudden purpose. Perhaps this was all part of his strange destiny and Beth's too. He took her small sorrowful face in his hands.

'We'll both go. We'll both go tonight. But you must promise me one thing. That you won't leave without me.' His fingers slid down her thin neck. 'Promise.'

Beth blinked through tears at his anguished face.

'I promise,' she whispered. I promise.'

Chapter Sixteen

Beth closed her door silently for the last time, clutching her case and the delicate stems of a few fragrant sweetpeas. She would avoid the back stairs, where servants often stopped to gossip, and hurry instead to the main gallery. There at least she could take refuge in the empty rooms if anyone approached. Her decision proved right. She sped like a driven ghost along its length and on down the sweeping staircase to the great hall below. Only the passive eyes of long dead forebears witnessed her flight as she continued with many a backward glance towards the kitchen quarters and the tradesmen's door. Once through its stone portal she knew she could never return.

She thought of Mrs Bullen and stifled a sob. The old lady had nurtured two destitute children with a mother's pride and the sweetpeas Beth placed on her sitting-room table would do little to ease the pain of betrayal. Nevertheless, they were a token of her gratitude and love. Her final gesture accomplished, Beth wrestled with the bolts on the outer door. Now the house felt safe. She wanted nothing more than to slip back into her warm bed and to close her eyes to the sweeping flight of the bats outside. Instead, like a furtive nocturnal creature, she fled across the courtyard towards the wooded path that bordered the estate. There beneath a canopy of leaves and a full harvest moon, she sank to the ground to wait.

Jack, meanwhile, was closing the door on security too. He was dressed not in his smart uniform but in the clothes of a countryman – a loose multi-pocketed jacket, moleskin trousers and an old flat cap. He set down a bag that bulged at the seams as he stooped to shake a sleeping form.

'Wake up Joe! Wake up! I must talk to you.'

The snoring ceased and Joe stirred, rubbing his eyes with large red hands.

'I'm asleep. Let me be,' he protested but Jack ignored him.

'Joe, listen. You want to be a coachman, don't you? A coachman like me so that Annie will marry you? Well, now's your chance.' He continued slowly, emphasising every word. 'Beth and I must leave here tonight – for good. But I can't tell you why.' He had Joe's full attention now.

'Just get on with your work like I've taught you. You'll see – the job will be yours when they find out I've gone. I shall miss you and Annie and the horses too. I can't say no more. It's your chance. Make sure you take it.' He withdrew suddenly, leaving Joe too bemused to follow him down the rickety stairs. Lady, dozing in her stall below, merely flicked an ear as he whispered a choked farewell.

'I'll not forget you, lass.' He ran a hand along the warm back that had saved their lives that night in the storm. She had brought them good fortune. Who

116

could tell whether that would follow them now? He lingered in her stall, afraid for the moment to leave the life he knew and the people he valued. But he had no choice and this was no time for sentiment. He must hurry. Beth would be waiting beneath the trees.

She was still there, staring restlessly into the night. Her attention was focused on a thread of river that had caught the moonlight behind the hall. Would Henry still be waiting, too? Waiting in vain? She could picture him striding with growing impatience over the garden that nature had already reclaimed. She had only been back once since that fateful day. Her eyes glittered with tears as Jack approached.

'You must stay,' she insisted, rising to meet him. 'I can't let you do this. I've thought it through. I'll be alright. After all, I've learnt to cook and clean. I only waited to say goodbye proper....' Her voice trailed away, betraying her anguish. Jack responded by picking up her case and striding so fast along the track that she had to run to keep up. She tugged at his sleeve to no avail.

'Think about it, Jack. Don't throw away your life. I'll send you news when I'm settled, honest I will.'

'There's a hole in the hedge, if we can find it. We'll cut across the meadows, then over the bridge to the village.'

'Jack, wait!'

But it was no good. He was quite intent on his purpose now. He stumbled ahead of her through the undergrowth until he came across the gap he had often used after a night of carousing at the inn. He squeezed through and stepped away from the trees. The moon was bright enough to cast a silver mantle over the landscape beyond.

'Come on, Beth,' he said sharply. 'I shan't change my mind so you'd best keep up. Besides,' he added with a mischievous grin, 'it's beginning to feel like a whole new adventure. Hurry! We've no time to lose.'

Beth, aware of his stubborn nature, gave up and steadied herself on his arm as she, too, squeezed through. They skirted a chicken coop and the dark outline of the man who tended them. He was reputed to be mad because he paced his land and raved at the stars on nights such as this.

'Follow the hedgerow,' Jack instructed, watching him as they bobbed like rabbits through the ripening corn towards the crest of a hill. They were both breathless when they reached the top and what they saw beyond took a moment to absorb. 'Why, the gypsies have gathered,' Jack murmured. He could just make out the tents that had sprung up like mushrooms on the pasture below. Alongside the river, ponies were tethered and he could hear the faint sound of music and dance. 'Their annual fair must be due. I didn't know.' He kept his voice level but his pulse unaccountably quickened. He glanced at Beth but she had turned away and was looking back at the ramparts of the hall, rising black and majestic into the night sky.

'I'm afraid of the gypsies,' she whispered, crouching closer to the ground. 'They came to the house last year. They read our palms. Sir George and Lady Elizabeth's too. Jack, they told me I would be with child before Michaelmas came again. Of course we all laughed at the time.' Her voice trembled slightly as she continued. 'You know – when I knew, knew for certain, I prayed for a while that it wasn't true. That it would all go away. That I would be spared. And yet now...' She paused, staring at him intently. 'Now I'm not sorry at all. Can you understand that? In spite of all the pain I've caused and all the pain to come, I have no regrets. I want this child more than life itself.'

Jack stared at the bareback riders galloping along a make shift-track. They slithered snorting to a halt not far away.

'Aye,' he sighed, 'I can understand that.' No doubt one day she would confide in him but until then he knew she could no more explain the mysteries of her heart than he could his own. 'We're alike, you and I, Beth. We've both taken a chance but we'll not spend our lives wondering what might have been. For better or worse we will know. We mustn't look back.' As he spoke he scanned the scene below. The older women, their faces framed with shawls, sat near flickering fires on the fringe of the gathering, indifferent to the festivities. They had seen it all before. Beth thought they saw more. She became convinced of it when one of them stared long and hard in their direction. Hidden as they were, she and her dog seemed to know they were there.

'Let's go down to the road and be on our way, Jack. We mustn't let them see us.' Her fears were justified. These people were wary of strangers. Eager to move on, she crept through the long grass on their right towards the familiar track which wound through hawthorn trees to the village.

Jack followed, his sharp eyes fixed on the swaggering youths and their womenfolk, decked for the occasion in bright coloured dresses and adorned with flowers. He wanted to join them, to drink ale with the men and to seek out a girl with nut brown hair. Had gypsy sorcery in her father's final moments bound their fates, he wondered? If so, tonight it was not to be. Tonight Beth was his first concern.

A few sidelong glances were cast their way as they hurried on past that part of the meadow which bordered the road. Ponies were tethered on the verge – skewbalds, piebalds, chestnuts and greys – they were all there.

'What a sight,' Jack murmured, pausing to admire the abandoned dancing that accompanied a piper playing a reel. Further still along their way, a sweet echoing voice sang a mother's lament. The cradle song had a very low air, prompting Beth, too, to listen tearfully before tugging again at Jack's arm.

The haunting melody followed them as they left the fair. They trudged on in silence, straining to catch the last sounds, until a commotion behind them caused Jack to turn back. A youth, the worse for his ale, was attempting to ride an unbroken horse. The animal had rebelled with unusual spirit and the spectacle was causing a mixed response, the women protesting, the men, fuelled by alcohol, urging the rider on. He, however, was no match for the thrashing antics of a panicked horse. Bunching its muscles against the unaccustomed weight, it launched itself high then plunged down, flinging the man head-first to the ground. He lay quite still. Concern was centred around him and no one attempted to stop the bolting horse. It careered down the road, the whites of its eyes clearly visible as it sped past Beth and Jack before veering suddenly across an open field.

A figure started running towards them but Jack, acting instinctively, did not wait. He had recognised the colt as the one he had seen near Brampton Hall and, dropping his bag at Beth's feet, was soon sprinting in pursuit. When a fence at the far side of the meadow failed to check its stampede, his worst fears were realised. The river ran deceptively deep beyond. He was too late to prevent it. The colt was already thrashing against the current in a cloud of spray when he reached the bank. He watched in horror as it drifted downstream in the moon's half light. A shallow area on the far side was the animal's only hope of safety now. Jack's brain was racing. Behind him, a gypsy with a dog had caught up with Beth. She would be frightened but he had no choice.

'Meet me at the bridge downstream. Beth,' he called. 'I'm going in after him. Can you pick up my clothes?'

'Don't, Jack, for mercy's sake!' Her words were lost on him as he threw off his outer garments and tore at the laces of his heavy boots. There was no time to lose – if he didn't act fast it would be too late. The moon, reflected in the water, lit his way as he ran barefoot, dodging the trees along the overgrown bank. Then, when he judged he was level, he leapt into the path of the exhausted colt. After three attempts he managed to snatch at a broken rein. He jerked its head brutally upwards as he swam towards the opposite bank, injecting some life and with it some hope into the limp body.

'That's it, fella. Fight! – you're not done yet' he shouted, feeling the hooves beneath him begin to struggle for a foothold. He heard a cheer from Beth as he anchored the colt to the roots of a tree. In time it revived and allowed him to coax it out of the water and back onto the land. There, it coughed and shook itself repeatedly.

'You'll not go swimming again in a hurry, my lad,' Jack grinned. 'Now we've got to find a way to get you home.' He cupped his hands to call back to Beth who seemed quite at ease with the stranger beside her. 'Tell him if he wants his horse, I'll go down to the bridge. I'll meet you both there but it may take some time.' Beth was unlikely to come to any harm, he reasoned, while he had possession of such a fine colt. He fondled an ear and removed the offending metal bit.

'That was no way to treat a baby like you,' he soothed, twitching the lead rope gently. 'No way at all. Come now. Let's go.' He knew he had gained its trust when it followed him, unsteadily at first like a new born foal, along the river's winding course.

Further up stream, Henry got to his feet and smiled. So Beth had not come but he had plenty of time. The girl had spirit after all and there was always another day.

Chapter Seventeen

It took time, as Jack had predicted, to find a way down the river to meet Beth at the bridge. The colt, shocked by its ordeal, had stiffened up and seemed slightly lame. A quick check had revealed no lasting damage but there was nothing to be gained by hurrying back. He found Beth too breathless to speak when they met on the road that spanned the two banks.

'Ungrateful wretches!' he fumed when he saw her. 'Did no one offer to carry our bags?'

'It doesn't matter, Jack,' she gasped. 'Look, your teeth are chattering. Let me hold the colt while you put on your clothes.' Seeing the sense in this, he took off his dripping shirt and replaced it with his jacket.

'Does nobody want the horse I took the trouble to save?' he complained, forcing scratched feet back into lace-up boots. Beth rummaged in their bags, her back turned to him.

'Yes,' she soothed, pulling out a scarf, 'but be patient. She had to go back – she'll be along presently.' Jack wheeled round, pushing wet hair from his eyes.

'She? What do you mean – she?' Before Beth could

reply a black and white cob yoked to a cart emerged from the lane amid a deafening clatter of hoof beats and wheels. Jack stood in its path, transfixed. It was the girl, he felt sure. Who else would travel at such reckless speed? 'Hold on to that colt!' he called over his shoulder but Beth, still fearful of horses, had already hitched the rope to a rung on the wall. Now with feet astride and hands outstretched, he forced the speeding cob to an abrupt halt. The shafts swivelled chaotically from side to side and the cart swerved into the hedgerow. As the dust settled he could just make her out. His heart skipped a beat but his voice remained calm.

'In a hurry again are you?' he enquired of the wild eyed figure in the driving seat, who was still brandishing a whip. She wore a crimson cloak. Her hair was dishevelled and the full blown rose that secured it over her left shoulder had lost most of its petals. 'We're always meeting like this,' he taunted. 'A mite dangerous don't you think?' His sharp wit earned him no favour. A sullen silence followed as they assessed one another – he, her unflinching blue eyes and the stubborn tilt of her delicate nose – she, the mocking grin that played round his undeniably handsome face. Finally she looked beyond him towards the softly whinnying colt.

'Is Storm alright?'

Jack nodded.

'Well then, I thank you but you're right. I am in a hurry. I'm going to York. Tie him to the spread rail on this side, if you would.' She seemed reluctant to step down from her position of strength but

Jack's mind and emotions were playing for time. He untied the colt and fondled it gently. Where was her courtesy, her gratitude for what he had done? Was he going to tolerate her dismissive manner? Beth, aware now that the two of them had met before, looked bewildered.

'It seems to me,' Jack said firmly as he led the colt forward, 'it seems to me that one good turn deserves another. Now as it happens, this young lady and I are going to York. We could use a lift.'

'I'll think about it. Hitch up my horse,' the girl snapped with an arrogant toss of her tumbling curls.

'Suppose I don't trust you,' Jack continued. 'I have no reason to, after all. No. I suggest Beth joins you with the bags. I'll walk with Storm. If you value your horse, you won't travel far.'

'I must,' the girl protested. 'I must go tonight while the moon is high, while the fair is still on...' But the uneven rhythm of the colt's stride proved his point. Her voice faded slightly giving Jack a chance to seize the initiative. He bundled Beth into the seat beside her and threw their bags on top of the cart. A dog yelped in the back. 'Mind Kip,' the girl scowled as he led Storm forward and grasped the cob's reins.

'Aye, I'll mind you all tonight,' he said, guiding the animals onto the road, 'but we'll travel at my pace if you don't mind.' He waited for a retort and grinned beneath his cap when it didn't come. He adjusted it to a jaunty angle. Gypsy sorcery this might be, he reflected, but he wasn't complaining.

He set off towards the village, turning south at its boundary without hesitation. He knew every rut of the road to York, every twist and turn, but his days of riding high above a coach and four were already in the past. The stable lads would wake to find him gone at sunrise – just a few hours from now. How would Sir George react? Surprise certainly, that such a trusted servant should have let him down. Then anger perhaps at his apparent ingratitude – and Beth's too. Mrs Bullen alone, shedding silent tears, might perceive the truth. He wondered for a moment if they would send out a search party as the overseers had done at the mill. Sadness, regret, even uncertainty weighed in his mind against the strange lure of following his destiny, of being his own master. He could go where he wished now, make his own decisions – like the gypsy girl sitting disdainfully behind him.

Beth's polite enquiries and his own light-hearted banter had so far been met with resolute silence. It would take time to gain her trust he decided, resolving to treat her in the same off-hand manner. For that reason, when he judged that Storm had walked far enough, he turned the horses into a small clearing, without referring to his sullen host. As he unharnessed and tethered the cob, she tossed their bags to the ground with a flourish before setting up her own sleeping space in the back of the cart. Soon a canvas bow-top roof obscured her and she disappeared inside, calling softly to the dog.

'Well, it's a warm night, Beth,' Jack shrugged. 'We'd best just bed ourselves down.' He picked a spot a little distance away, where the ground was flat and the turf thick. 'Put the blanket there and make a pillow with your bag,' he instructed. 'I'll manage on the grass.'

Tired, both by the emotional turmoil of the day and her physical state, Beth lay down and tried to sleep. Jack sat up longer, looking at the small trusting face turned heavenward and the moonlight silvering her loosened hair. He could just see the slight rounding of her belly beneath the calico smock and wondered again what calamitous events had led her to throw away her safe, regulated life for an uncertain future. Beth, sensing his eyes upon her from behind closed lids, spoke without stirring.

'You want to know, don't you?' she murmured in a voice bereft of sentiment. 'Indeed you have a right to know if you must sacrifice all you have gained on my account. I didn't intend this – nor, I believe, did Master Henry. At first when our paths crossed, I was afraid of him. I would avoid him at all costs. But then one day I sneezed, sneezed behind the drawing room curtain. That was all. It amused him to find me hiding there and he spun me around like a top with such ease that I quite lost my senses. Perhaps I never regained them. I do know my heart leapt after that whenever I saw Master Henry.'

She went on to explain how she had become aware of his clandestine drinking. Of her concern for him and the dilemma she had been in on that day in the boathouse.

'Do you mean to say,' Jack interrupted incredulously, 'that Master Henry is the father of your child?'

A single tear escaped down her cheek as she nodded in response.

'He is a lonely man, Jack, in spite of his privilege and wealth and in spite of his friends. I think he needed me, in his own way. You must see now that I couldn't stay there – but I shall always love him and I shall treasure this infant more than life itself.'

She clasped both hands round her stomach and let her tears flow unrestrained. Too dumbfounded to reply, Jack simply reached out to comfort her. How strange life was, he mused. His gaze strayed back to the canvas-covered cart. Wasn't he too in thrall to feelings he couldn't explain? But more than ever Beth would need his protection now. He sank back, listening to the rhythmic champing of the horses in the darkness. Eventually the sound lulled him into a fitful sleep.

Chapter Eighteen

Jack was awakened in the early hours by approaching hoof-beats, followed by an exchange of angry voices. He could just make out a swarthy figure dragging the girl from her bed behind the drapes of the bow-topped cart. She was fighting like a wild cat but he hesitated. This was clearly a gypsy matter. Would she welcome his interference or should he lie low? He put a finger to his lips, as Beth sat up, her eyes widening like saucers as the shouting continued.

'I'll not! I'll not come back with you, Franco!' the girl shrieked. 'I know a man who'll take care of me.' She reached for the whip but the lean dark-skinned youth had a strength far beyond her own. He wrenched it from her and bound the leather thong round her slim waist in one easy movement.

'You will come with me.' His voice was full of menace. 'You'll come with me and you'll marry me – like was always agreed. I'll learn you some manners – and Storm too.'

'Ha!' the girl scoffed. 'Storm left you for dead last night. He was my father's horse. By rights he's mine.' The man jolted the whip, causing her to wince. Her eyes blazed with defiance. 'I'll not come with you! I'm going back to Michael. I'll work on the farm. He said I could. He always said I could.'

The youth responded by throwing her to the ground and tying her wrists with swift, practised knots as though hobbling a horse. She spat in his face and he slapped her in return. That was too much for Jack.

'If you do that once more, I'll lay you flat on the ground.' The steady voice from the shadows surprised the intruder, giving the girl a chance to leap to her feet. 'I repeat. Strike her once more and I'll flatten you. Let the girl go,' he said evenly, sizing up his opponent as he stepped forward to confront him. Gypsies, in spite of their slight build, were deceptively good fighters. He himself was out of touch but he could defend himself against a lightning jab and used his brain to advantage.

'You take on me – the mighty Franco?' the youth sneered scornfully. 'Why, ask Ramona here. She'll tell you. No one beats Franco. No one.'

He lunged at him with such speed that Jack was caught off balance and ducked only just in time. The cross-bred lurcher leapt from the cart, barking and nipping at their heels as the two adversaries clashed again. This time, Jack was not so lucky and Beth's hands flew to her mouth as his lip started to bleed and the gypsy taunted him with a succession of well-timed blows. Jack was getting the worst of it and he knew it. Yet strength was his asset. If he could just land a punch on the point of the jaw! Blood streamed down his chin and onto his jacket. He struggled to contain his anger, to channel it into one crushing, decisive blow.

Then his opportunity came. The dog was focusing its attention on Franco, causing him to lower a fist to brush the animal away. It was all Jack needed. His right arm struck not the jaw but the body with all the force he could muster. The dark-skinned youth crumpled and lay gasping on the ground.

'Not so mighty now, Franco,' Jack jeered. 'I got you right in the stomach.' He let out a victorious roar as he grabbed the lapels of the gypsy's torn coat and bundled him back onto his trembling horse. Franco, struggling to regain his breath and his dignity, gathered the reins and pulled himself upright. He fixed Ramona with a malicious stare.

'You're not one of us anyway. Not a true Romany.' He took a crumpled piece of paper from his pocket and tossed it contemptuously in the air. 'We asked a man in the ale house to read it. Your real father was a gorgio. Edward Cunningham. Everyone knows. I'm the only one that would have you now.' He paused again to catch his breath. 'Your mother was cursed from the day you were born. That's why she died. Go to your simple farmer, if you must. But you'll be back. He'll have married some country wench – you'll see.'

'That was my letter. You had no right to read it!' Ramona cried, as Jack slapped the rump of Franco's horse and sent it cantering briskly back down the road. The hoof beats faded, leaving the three of them stunned and silent in the emerging dawn.

Jack dusted down his clothes and took his time to unshackle the girl's slim wrists. So she was called Ramona. And the blue eyes that had seemed so familiar on that day in York were the eyes of a Cunningham – Sir George's dead brother, Edward. That was what the letter had revealed and why she had been so keen to escape. These people closed ranks against outside blood. Whatever the reason for that strange liaison all those years ago, the man she had believed to be her father must have kept it a secret till his final hours. Then he had judged she had a right to know.

As he released the last knot, she darted forward to retrieve the crumpled page. The words made no sense to her and clearly frustrated, she thrust it into Jack's bruised and bleeding hand.

'You read it. Read it again,' she demanded.

'But Jack can't read and neither can I,' Beth said matter-of-factly as she dabbed his wounded face

'That's right,' Jack admitted. 'But one day I intend to learn.' Ramona's lip trembled as he passed the letter back. For a moment he thought she would burst into tears. His arm hovered around her waist but the mask of toughness returned in a trice.

'I thought you was a learned gentleman,' she snapped as she turned on her heel. Jack's colour rose. Her behaviour was intolerable. He had risked his neck to protect her from Franco – for what? He glowered at the nonchalant figure moving swiftly about her chores as he rubbed an aching limb.

'Come on, Beth. We'll be on our way. I don't much care for this lady's company.' Still smarting with anger, he gathered their bags and strode ahead of her down the road. 'We'll stop at the inn for some bread and milk.'

'But Jack,' Beth protested, 'Ramona needs us. She needs our help.'

'Not that lass,' he retorted. 'That lass knows how to look after herself.' Gradually, the still morning air and the steady exercise calmed him. Perhaps he had been hasty. After all he, too, was coping with a major change. He may not have reacted as well as he might. When they approached the inn, he set down their bags on a bench outside and ordered milk fresh from the cows in the byre. 'Drink it all – it will do you good,' he told Beth, aware that she, like him, was straining her ears for the sound of a cart.

Ramona. Damn the girl, he thought. She had hurt his precious pride with her dismissive remark. But it was the truth. He would never amount to much because he couldn't read and write. Smart he may be but he was no learned gentleman. He had known that even as he listened enthralled to men like Oastler who so much inspired him. How could he, a mere mill boy, hope to make a difference? If he was honest, even his prospects of a job were slim without Sir George to vouch for his character.

Beth looked up suddenly and smiled. Ramona's horses had pulled up at the trough and were drinking noisily.

'The poor girl must be hungry, Jack. I shall give her some bread, whatever you say.' Jack sulked with his back to them as Beth's gentle nature worked its magic on the girl. He caught snatches of conversation. It seemed she was going not to York but a farm near Scarborough. She would turn east towards Malton soon.

The coast. She was going to the coast. Hadn't he always been drawn to the sea? No, he reasoned, they must stick to York where he and Beth might just find work. But he knew already his heart was set on another course. A young girl was not safe on these roads – not even one dressed as a lad. Burkers, snatching bodies for research, roamed the woods at night along with all manner of unsavoury men. And she, like them, was an outcast now. He walked slowly across to the cart, put their bags in the back and offered Ramona the remains of his milk.

'We'll come with you to the coast,' he said simply.

A trace of a smile flickered across her face, before she cracked the whip over the pony's tail.

Chapter Nineteen

S ummer was coming to an end. An even layer of leaves stretched far into the morning mist, rustling beneath the horses' hooves. Jack had plenty of time to think as he strode along beside them. Their progress would be slow and there was no knowing if he and Beth would find work when they reached the coast. He must eke out his meagre savings as best he could. Ramona was quick to spot the rosehips and berries in the hedgerow. No doubt she could teach them how gypsies survived, he reasoned, watching as Beth, too, slipped gingerly down from the cart.

By late afternoon their baskets were overflowing with ripe fruit which Ramona stored quickly out of sight. Her sharp ears had caught the rumble of a coach approaching and she instinctively drew up her hood and twitched the reins to the left, away from the rutted track and towards a stream. She still spoke little. Her hair was drawn back into a thick plait which she drew over her shoulder and fingered pensively from time to time. When her eyes caught Jack's, she looked away, concealing her thoughts behind feigned antipathy.

Tilly, the cob, swished her tail revealing a temperament as stubborn as her mistress. She was jaded by the long day's drive. Lathers of thick sweat frothed round her harness and she shook her head, demanding to be unyoked to taste the sweetness of the grass and the running water.

'Whoa,' Jack murmured, restraining her as a carriage he did not recognise swept past. They had not been seen, nor had they been followed, he noted with relief. He tethered Storm to a stake and returned to release Tilly, who moved very slowly out of the shafts.

'She's an old lady, isn't she?' Beth looked up at Ramona. 'Can't we stop by the stream to give her a rest?'

The girl nodded, her face impassive, her eyes grave. She had learned to remain aloof from strangers and those who did not share her culture. But she knew, too, the dangers of travelling alone. She looked up at the sky, studying the clouds and the strength and direction of the wind which blew a little brisker now from the north. The evenings were drawing in. It was a good place to stop, she decided. The shallow stream would provide for their needs and the horses could graze till the following day on the lush vegetation that grew nearby. Jack had already removed a large square of turf, marking the spot where they would build a fire. Ramona merely busied herself collecting wood in the folds of her crimson skirt. It fitted tightly round her waist and Jack was aware of the copious white underskirts that peeked from beneath and the yoke of lace that encircled her slender neck.

A scuffle in the undergrowth distracted him. Kip

had scented a pheasant and the bird was making a bid to escape.

'Go on, Kip,' Ramona urged, looking first right, then left, then behind her. They had all seen the signs depicting the gallows, warning of the penalty for roadside trespass. Beth dropped her bundle of twigs and drew back towards Jack. A high pitched squawk ceased abruptly, and shortly afterwards Kip reappeared, bedraggled but with a limp corpse in his mouth, which he dropped with pride at Ramona's feet. He sat panting, saliva dripping from his jowl, as she deftly retrieved it and dropped it into an iron pot.

'Isn't that stealing?' Beth began, blanching with fear. 'Weren't you taught not to steal?' She would rather not eat than risk the awful consequences that she had heard talk of at the Hall. Why, she knew of a man who had been transported far across the sea to a distant land. She shuddered at the thought but Ramona was defiant.

'We don't get caught,' she said scornfully. 'These creatures belong to us all and we have a right to eat, same as you. How else do you think we live?'

She turned towards the stream, to collect water Beth supposed. But instead she filled the pot with handfuls of sand, quickly covering the bird until there was no sign of its feathers at all. Beneath the pot she positioned large sticks like the spokes of a wheel, then on top of these placed twigs and leaves and bark and finally a dry log. 'I can light a fire anywhere. Can a gorgio make flame from two bits of wood?' she challenged Jack suddenly.

Responding in the same contemptuous manner, he reached into his sack and withdrew a small metal box. In no time he had kindled the tinder with the flint it contained. He transferred the blaze to her pyramid of twigs and fanned the flames with his cap, repressing a smile as her blue eyes widened with curiosity. When he looked up she turned away, pretending disinterest in his shiny box.

'What is a gorgio?' he asked, watching equally intrigued as she hung the pot on an iron rod and continued to feed the flames.

'A gorgio is what we call a non-gypsy like yourself – and Beth,' she added. As the sand heated, she stuck a few lengths of ash and willow in the top but offered no explanation. The reason only became clear later when a farmer chanced by and peered without a word into the iron pot. Ramona withdrew a willow stick. The end had softened so that it could now be bent to form a handle.

'Would you like to buy a walking stick, kind sir?' she purred, sashaying her wasp-like figure towards him. 'Special price for you, sir.'

'I want you off my land now!' he growled, immune to her charms. He was accustomed to moving gypsies on and aware of their pilfering habits. He turned towards Jack, pushing his weather-beaten face close to his. 'And if you've been stealing my game, you'll find yourself in a cell, that you will.'

Beth's fear transformed suddenly into presence of mind.

'Why, kind sir, we would have continued our journey but this poor colt is lame. Come and see for yourself. His fetlock is swollen.' She seized the cane from a startled Ramona. 'And take this as a gift for yourself. We'll be gone by tomorrow – honest we will, sir.' Her contrite manner and gentle, beseeching eyes swayed him where Ramona's ploys had failed.

'I'll not expect to see you here at dawn,' he said, kicking the fire viciously with his heavy boots before stomping through the trees with the willow stick clasped in his fist. The ashes were scattered but the embers were hot enough to cook the bird to perfection. Not much was said as Ramona peeled the scorched feathers and skin from its frame and threw them onto the fire. But as she stripped the flesh and passed it round, each was aware of a mutual respect that might yet unite their different worlds.

Chapter Twenty

Beth did not sleep well that night. She longed for her narrow attic bed and the reassuring sound of Annie's snores. Instead she tossed listlessly on the hard earth, not quite awake enough to banish harrowing nightmares from the past. She was back in the mill once more, watching helpless children writhe against the whip, their cries muted by the ceaseless grind of cogs and wheels, their small lungs choked by dust and gas and fetid air.

William drifted through these scenes, unaware of her wraithlike presence, and her small hand stretched out in vain towards him. She woke to find herself calling out his name aloud beneath the sailing moon. There was no response – only the haunting cry of an owl as it took wing from the great oak above.

Beth shivered and drew her cloak more tightly round her. It was as though she had never known a happy interlude. Why could she not dream of Henry and sink peacefully into oblivion within the comfort of his arms? Would he, too, be awake she wondered, as she watched the clouds scudding against the black, increasingly skeletal trees? Would he suffer as she was suffering, when he heard the news of their departure? He had never declared his feelings for her. After a while it would be of little importance. It would be a matter of curiosity and gossip – that was all – amidst the preparations for his forthcoming Easter wedding. He must never be burdened by the consequences of his brief attraction or with the intensity of her love for him.

Dawn brought welcome relief from the sweeping flight of the bats and the sinister shadows, and the ghosts receded further as Beth splashed her eyes with cold water in the stream. Ramona was already washing her hands and feet and rubbing her face till it glowed but she neither looked up nor offered a greeting. She did not hesitate, however, when Beth felt suddenly faint and began to retch. She reached her in the nick of time and guided her towards the bank.

'I'll be alright, presently,' Beth murmured, glancing at the perceptive blue eyes that so reminded her of Henry. 'It's happened before. It will pass.'

Jack hurried towards them, pulling on his boots. After the long walk the previous day, he at least had slept well.

'What is it, Beth? What's wrong?' His concern increased as she continued to retch.

Its significance however was not lost on Ramona.

'It's the morning sickness. Your cousin is with child, isn't she? She must sleep under cover tonight.' It was a statement not a question and Jack did not bother to explain or deny it. He had no experience of women's problems and was grateful for Ramona's calm reassurance. Together they helped her back to the cart and settled her in the rear with Kip to keep her warm, a morsel of bread and a herbal drink.

'Sip it slowly. It will settle your stomach,' she urged.

Jack eased Tilly between the shafts and busied himself with her harness. Risking a rebuff, he swung Ramona with effortless grace onto the trap and passed her the reins. His eyes held hers for a long moment before his hand slipped away from her waist. The morning's events had softened her reserve. Beneath that hard veneer beat a heart that might yet succumb to his masculine charm.

For the present, however, it was not to be. Pigeons clattered suddenly out of the wood, jinking in flight and voicing their alarm – clear signs to Ramona that a stranger approached. She cracked the whip over Tilly's rump. The pony obliged with its characteristic gallop, leaving Jack, cursing softly, to untether Storm and gather their bags. He had just time to cover their ashes with turf and slip out of sight before the farmer appeared.

A mile down the track, Ramona waited with her usual nonchalance. She brushed her chestnut hair and braided it over her shoulder before pulling up the hood of her scarlet cloak. Within its folds she was safe to mourn the life she had lost – safe from the outside world and the people she had been taught from birth to distrust.

'You must ride with us on the cart today, Jack,' Beth said firmly, rearranging the bags. One glance at the firm set of his jaw however told her he would not.

'Nay. It'll suit me just fine to walk with the horses,' he snapped, striding ahead with Storm. An uneasy wind stirred the leaves. He pulled his cap down hard against the first spots of rain. He wouldn't think of Ramona. The east beckoned and a whole new life lay ahead. But it was no good. He was all too aware of the capricious girl sitting silently behind.

Chapter Twenty-One

Ramona's aloofness persisted for the next three days. Out of concern for Beth, however, she collected sapling sticks each evening and showed her how to create a shelter using canvas strips. Jack simply placed a piece of sail cloth over the wet earth close to the fire and stared moodily into the flames. There was no story telling, no exchange of intimacies, no discussion of the future. They were simply three fellow travellers whose paths would separate when they reached their destination.

It was mid afternoon when Tilly's ears pricked and her steady plodding stride quickened. Jack followed her gaze to a cluster of stone buildings set in an exposed position on the hillside ahead. She had evidently spent time there in the past, perhaps enjoyed warm shelter and a good feed. He glanced at Ramona who had thrown back her hood to scan the landscape. 'For whom?' he wondered. The farmer's son who had offered her sanctuary – even captured her heart? He felt a stab of something close to jealousy as he watched her, poised like a young gazelle scenting the air. A sudden burst of sunshine burnished her hair and, and if this was to be his parting image, he knew he would not forget it. A signpost nearby indicated that Scarborough was no more than four miles. Would she hand them their bags and bid them farewell?

To his surprise, she seemed suddenly diffident – aware perhaps of the mud from the wayside on the hem of her dress and the smudges of blackberry on her hands and face. She needed a stream and knew exactly where to find one.

'This way. I know a good place to spend the night,' she announced without explanation, seeming keen now to keep the horses out of sight. She guided Tilly down a track to where a beck tinkled invitingly over flat stones. Relieved at this turn of events, Jack watered and tethered the horses before flopping on the grass next to Kip. After days of tramping through penetrating rain, it was good to close his eyes and relax. The autumn warmth had even enticed the bees from their hives, seeking late flowers amongst the seed heads. It was a welcome scene and Beth's spirits revived too.

'Are there fish in this stream?' she asked Ramona as she soaked her feet and drank from her cupped hands. Ramona, discarding her cloak, laughed with rare delight and placed a finger to her lips.

'Sit there and watch. I'll show you something presently.' She was aware of Jack opening an eye to watch her and eager to demonstrate her skill. Hitching her petticoats to reveal trim ankles, she waded to the far bank and crouched for several minutes over a gully that ran between two large stones. Using one hand to block an escape, she slid the other below the rocks until her fingers traced the sleek shape of the trout concealed beneath. Holding her breath, she stroked its belly upwards towards the gills. In a trice she had scooped it out of the water, high into the air and sent it arcing into the long grass

Jack let out a whoop of triumph and leapt up to retrieve the twisting fish, laughing with abandon for the first time in days and giving Ramona a spontaneous hug.

'You're a clever girl indeed,' he said with genuine admiration. 'Will you not show a mere city boy how to do that?' He watched her sombre eyes waver then light up with impish humour. She responded to flattery, he noted, as she grasped his hand and led him upstream. They peered together at the likely haunts on the edge of the beck.

'There,' Ramona whispered pointing out a shady spot. 'Place one hand over this end first.' Her slender fingers guided him towards the fish which she knew would be lurking beneath the stones. 'Just touch his belly gently. He won't move. Then scoop him out but don't grab him. He'll be gone if you do.' Her eyes met his and both for a moment felt the shock of intimacy distracting their purpose. There was a flurry of spray as the trout disappeared and, in the same instant, Jack lost his footing so that the two fell backwards into the stream, drenching their clothes. As Ramona's laughter echoed into the blue sky, Jack made no attempt to release her. Savouring their last moments together, he smoothed a tendril of hair from her forehead and cradled her elfin face against his chest.

'You're a fairy's child,' he whispered. 'I could swear you are.' On an impulse, he brushed his lips against hers. They parted, though whether in surprise or invitation he couldn't tell – all he knew was that he was powerless to prevent the passionate kiss that followed. Both pretended afterwards that nothing had happened. They were silent and bemused so that Beth, observing them later, saw only their customary reserve.

'Well, that's no way to catch a fish, Jack,' she teased, as she helped them out of their wet clothes. 'It serves you right, the both of you. You shouldn't steal.'

'This land belongs to Hilldene farm. 'Twill belong to Michael when his father dies,' Ramona informed them with a hint of pride. So this little domain would be hers one day, Jack reasoned. Was that the attraction of a farmer's son? Or was she in love? The thought tormented him as he built up the fire and watched Ramona, swathed in her cloak, deftly cook the trout on a heated stone. Behind her, Beth had strung out their freshly washed clothes to dry and they billowed in the breeze like a ship's sails, causing Storm to prance skittishly at the end of his rope. Jack walked towards him and ran a practised hand over the damaged fetlock. The swelling had gone and his stride had regained its youthful spring but the horse stood calmly, soothed by his voice and his touch. Ramona looked up and cupped her chin.

'He'll miss you. He trusts you,' she observed, aware of the uncanny rapport between man and beast. 'What will you do when you get to Scarborough?'

'Jack was a coachman at the Hall. One of the best,' Beth declared proudly. 'He'll soon find work.' Her voice trailed off however, betraying her lack of conviction. They were strangers here and had no one to recommend them, after all.

'Aye. We'll walk on the shore first and breathe the salt air.' He filled his lungs, anticipating the pleasure. 'I believe in fate,' he added, staring so boldly into Ramona's blue eyes that she turned away. Kip nuzzled his nose into the folds of her cape and she stroked him absently.

'There's a barn at the farm with a small attic space above. I slept in the straw when we helped with the harvest. It's warm. You could lodge there for a day or two.'

'Why, that's a grand idea! And who knows – there might even be work on the farm.' Beth beamed with relief as she took her portion of sizzling fish from the stone. 'You've brought us good luck, Ramona, and we're grateful to you, aren't we Jack? You said yourself you believe in fate.'

Ramona let her smile fade and did not reply. The Lockwoods eked out a living from a few acres on a bleak hillside. They were in no position to employ extra hands for a smallholding that relied on their own hard work. But she would not dash their hopes tonight. She would leave that to Michael's father tomorrow.

Chapter Twenty-Two

Hilldene farm was in mourning when they turned in through its crumbling gates the next day. A ploughboy astride a draught horse tipped his cap and then, recognising Ramona, paused to tell her the news; old Mr Lockwood had died the week before and the house had been in turmoil while the funeral took place.

'Master Michael's the governor now. I'm to do the top meadow with Bonnie. I ain't never ploughed on my own before,' Nathan called back as the huge animal beneath him ambled on its way, unperturbed by his ineffectual jabs on the rein. Jack grinned as he watched him depart, then steered Tilly and Storm through the scrawny hens in the yard towards the dairy at the back. The stalls were filled with cows still waiting to be milked.

Ramona allowed him to help her step down from the cart and guide her round the puddles to the solid front door. There she dismissed him, smoothed her skirts and her hair and banged the tarnished knocker firmly. A maid, looking harassed with her mob cap askew, admitted her after a brief conversation, and she disappeared inside, leaving Jack to guess at her reception. After an hour strolling between manure heaps, wheelbarrows and rusty tools, he had exhausted his curiosity and was becoming impatient. They should leave with their pride intact, he decided, starting to unload their bags. But as they did so, the maid re-appeared, a middle-aged woman who moved quickly in spite of her large size and shortness of breath.

'This way, this way,' she wheezed. 'I'll show you the barn. Well I never! Fancy young Ramona coming back after all! He's quite a ladies' man you know – our Michael – quite sought after, he is. He certainly took a shine to that lass, mind you. It was when they came to help with the harvest,' she explained. 'Like a couple of love birds they were – but her father didn't approve. He took her away. She says he died on the gallows, poor man – for killing the scoundrel who stole his favourite mare. As honest a fellow as I ever met, he was.' Her strong arms pushed open the rotting barn doors and she pointed to the ladder that led up to the loft.

'Take care – there's a loose rung but you'll be warm enough there and the horses can go in the paddock at the back.' She turned towards them, straightening her wayward cap and lowered her voice. 'You know the old man, bless his soul, was not one for feeding an extra mouth. But if it's work you're after, it's my guess Michael will need all the help he can get. Come to the kitchen for soup later on.' She winked and bustled off talking to herself.

Beth let out a deep sigh, giggled and smiled up at Jack.

'Didn't I tell you Ramona has brought us luck?'

'Aye, you did too,' he agreed but his mind was full of conflicting emotions. He had no doubt now of Ramona's purpose. She had come back to rekindle a forbidden love. He was confronted by his rival as soon as he and Beth entered the house and accepted a place at the long kitchen table. Ramona sat unusually stiffly at the far end, unsure for once how to conduct herself. She turned constantly to Michael for reassurance. He was taller than Jack, with a farmer's strong physique and the confident stance of a man who likes to dominate. There was a hint of menace in the granite eyes set deep beneath a rugged brow. He swished a crop against his fustian leggings and surveyed the room.

'Well, Ramona, what am I to do with these travelling companions of yours?' He pointed the whip at Jack. 'Can you use a plough?'

'Aye, I've worked on the land.'

'And the lass – can she milk a cow?'

'Aye, sir,' Beth lied, with her fingers crossed in her smock to absolve herself of the sin. 'I can milk a cow.'

'That's settled, then. You can sleep in the barn and earn your keep here for a week or two.' He winked at Ramona. 'And you – you shall have my father's room – next to mine.'

Ramona flinched and the colour rose in her cheeks.

'That would not be proper, Michael,' she insisted, showing a flash of her old spirit. 'I shall sleep in my own bed in the barn and earn my keep, too. If you wish, I could milk the cows and look after the hens and Beth could help Agatha in the kitchen instead.'

Beth shot her a grateful look and took up her proposition.

'Aye, sir. I've worked in service and I can cook, too.'

Michael regarded her for a moment, as though assessing the condition of one of his beasts.

'Is that so?' he said slowly but did not voice his suspicions. He would use her until she became big with child. If he was right, she would be thankful enough for a meal each day. As for her companion, he was in no position to barter for a wage as the labourers did at the Martinmas fair. He sensed an equal in Jack, with a competitive nature like his own but he would not keep him long enough to threaten his own authority. He had only just escaped from his father's iron will and he intended to enjoy his long-awaited freedom by stamping if necessary on his fellow man.

His intuitive roving eye came to rest on Ramona. He could bend her to his will now that her father was gone. It was sweet revenge indeed, he thought, that the man who had cursed him for trifling with his daughter should end his days on the gallows. He would bide his time to crush her stubborn pride but he had no doubt at all they would marry. Easter perhaps – or a little earlier to suit the farm. The decision would be his. He would dress her in fine suiting and his young wife would be much admired for her good looks on the town's promenade.

If Beth and Ramona felt relief as they arranged

their few possessions to afford themselves some privacy, Jack felt unease but he did not speak of it. After all he told himself, whatever his forebodings about Ramona's future, they had a roof over their heads and an opportunity to work. They must take each day as it came and count their blessings.

He released the two horses in the paddock and grinned as they shook their heads, rolled in the grass and savoured their freedom by galloping crazily from end to end. He whistled under his breath as Storm's long fine limbs ate up the ground like a true thoroughbred. His dam had escaped during a storm, Ramona had told him, and no one had any idea where her offspring had been sired. Only careful nurturing had pulled him through when the mare was stolen. Now the colt needed firm handling and he had Ramona's permission to break him in – a task he would relish.

He turned to scan the landscape towards the coast, eager to smell the sea air. Four miles would be an effortless walk to see a sight he had dreamed of since his youth and there were no demands on him today.

'Can I come with you?' Ramona stood behind him, reading his thoughts with a gypsy's intuition. Her grave blue eyes recognised the turmoil in his face as he looked back at her but gave no hint of her own feelings. 'Beth wants to rest. The work will be hard tomorrow.' Anticipating his reply, she set off in front of him along a track rutted by the regular passage of coaches. They ran from the Bell Inn in Scarborough to the staging posts in Pickering and

Malton and beyond. Seeking to distract him from his thoughts, she pointed out the scenery that was familiar to her from past visits.

'That is a race course on top of the hill. I've seen fine horses run there,' she added, knowing he would be interested, 'and yonder is Seamer where my people meet for a fair every year.' Her voice faltered and Jack, glancing at her, knew that she was suddenly close to tears. They were no longer her people. She had chosen to reject them and she must live with that decision.

'Come on, lass,' he smiled, grasping her hand and leading the way eastward. 'Today, we are going to enjoy ourselves – you'll see.' Their carefree laughter echoed on the wind as they spotted a thin line of blue on the skyline. Jack put an arm round her shoulder, wanting to share the moment. 'There it is – the sea at last,' he sighed. He wanted to kiss her, too, but Michael's shadow had fallen between them. She was not his to kiss.

Chapter Twenty-Three

Four months had passed. Jack guided Storm through the wooded ravine that led to the shore. He smiled with satisfaction as the horse chafed gently at the bit, awaiting the signal to toss his mane in the salt air and gallop along the broad sweep of wet sand.

'Off you go, then,!' he laughed, revelling in the sudden burst of speed and sea spray against his face. It was the highlight of his week – this trip into Scarborough – to deliver mail for the master and collect provisions for the farm. This included fish sold straight from the cobles on the beach. Sam was there, as usual near the pier.

'You've done well with that horse,' he commented, as Jack pulled up to a disciplined halt near the harbour wall. Herring gulls swooped like driven ghosts over the fisherman's catch but their black-tipped wings provoked no reaction from Storm.

'Aye,' Jack responded proudly, stroking his neck. 'He needs the right handling but he's coming on fine.'

'Now, what's it to be?' Sam continued without removing his pipe. 'A bit of skate for a groat? Or can ye afford something better? He pulled out cod, plaice, whiting and haddock from the silvery heap in the stern of his boat. The purchase completed and the fish secured with a cord through the gills, he relit his pipe and resumed his preferred role as a sea-going sage. 'There's no good will come of that westerly wind. See that bank of cloud? There'll be quite a storm tonight, that I can tell thee.' He narrowed his blue eyes towards the horizon. Following his gaze, Jack could just make out the bold outline of a three-masted square rigger. A whaler, no doubt, on its way from Hull to the Arctic. They were often to be seen in late March but seldom came close to the shore. This one, however, had set course for the harbour. Already it rose high on each crest and sank deep in the troughs.

'You mean, it's coming into the bay?' Jack exclaimed with a jubilant punch of his fist. He liked nothing more than to enjoy an ale at the Mariner's Inn and hear a whaler talk of his exploits in the pack ice of the frozen north. The townsfolk revered these hardy glamorous men, even though they no longer sent any ships of their own. The smell of blubber on the quayside perhaps didn't complement the attractions of the newly-promoted health-giving spa.

Sam glanced at the flag on the lighthouse tower.

'Still ten foot of water there. She'll have to be sharp to catch the tide or she'll not find shelter tonight.'

The unfolding drama appealed to Jack but he must return home before darkness fell. Reluctantly, he bid Sam farewell and rode slowly past the busy ship-building slipways that lined the shore. Perhaps he would find an excuse to return, he thought, without much hope, as Storm reached Mill Beck and broke into a canter down the valley.

He felt unsettled on the journey back. The image of the ship stayed with him, almost as his first sight of Ramona had done on that day at the gallows in York. Once again, he sensed it would play some part in his life. His old yearning for adventure had been almost extinguished by his need to protect the women in his life. He had sacrificed his ambitions in their best interests and would always do so. But was it necessary? Beth's figure had begun to thicken yet still she worked gratefully from dawn till long after dusk in exchange for a place to sleep and some nourishment for herself and her unborn child.

His thoughts turned to Ramona. She still held him hopelessly in thrall, he acknowledged – the more so since she had acquired a Cunningham taste for the finer things in life. Michael seemed content for the present to indulge her, knowing that Jack without a wage had nothing to offer and no way to compete. While enjoying being spoiled she seemed quite unaware of the nature of the man she would wed in the spring. Jack, however, sensed the dangerous bully that lurked beneath and feared for her safety. He resolved to confront her with his feelings on the matter before it was too late.

The opportunity came sooner than he intended. It was almost dusk when he led Storm into the cow-shed to rub him down with a handful of straw.

Ramona had finished milking and was carrying the pails to the dairy. She returned with a small lamp and leaned against the rough stone wall to watch him with her characteristically grave blue eyes. She still made his heart beat faster but gave away nothing of her feelings towards him. He remained silent, allowing his pent-up emotions to dissipate in the rhythmic grooming of the horse. Occasionally he stole a sidelong glance. How he yearned to caress the girl's elfin features and her lustrous tresses of nut-brown hair.

'I'm to marry soon, you know,' she said at length.

'Aye, I know.'

'Aren't you pleased for me?' She tilted her head, coquettishly, childishly, Jack thought. She was playing with him like the cats in the barn played with the mice. But she was playing with fire. He moved towards her, unable to curb his anger, frustration and pain. He set the lamp on the ground and watched her eyes widen in surprise as he pinned her slender wrists to the wall.

'Nay, I'm not pleased you're to marry. How could I be? You're my girl and you always will be. How can you marry a man you don't love? And you don't love him do you?' he insisted. 'For all the fine clothes and fancy hats. He'll destroy you. Your father knew that when he cursed him.'

Ramona struggled to escape as all attempts at restraint deserted Jack.

'Kiss me!' he commanded. 'You know you want to. Kiss me.' He crushed the breath from her body in his anguish and lowered his mouth onto hers with such raw passion that her protests were reduced to a whimper and finally a soft moan. For one brief moment she surrendered; her eyes closed and her lips melted against his, telling him more than words ever could. Neither saw Michael's shadow approach but both heard his voice bellow like an enraged ox through the open shed door. He seized the cuff of Ramona's smock and flung her like a rag doll into the night.

'Go to my room, woman, and wait for me there. If any man can have you, it may as well be me. As for you, Mr Cartwright,' he snarled, 'you've grown a bit too big for your boots at my expense.' He thrust him back into a stall with a pitchfork intent on revenge but wavered when Jack raised his fists. There was no need to brawl with a farm hand when a few words could destroy him. 'You will leave here tonight. I don't expect to see you in my house again.'

As he turned on his heel and strode towards the house, Jack wiped his mouth on the edge of his sleeve How had he allowed this to happen? How had he become the aggressor? He, who seldom lost his composure. Would Ramona suffer for his folly? Or would it shock her into changing her course and escaping with him while she could? He had no way of knowing. Because of his actions they would all, including Beth, have their own decisions to make.

Storm nudged him impatiently and Jack blinked away a tear as he scooped grain from a bin in the corner. The shock of dismissal had numbed him so that his hands shook as he tipped the feed in a trough and stroked the horse's fine ebony coat. Michael with his steel-spurred boots and heavy fists would ride him in future.

'Bye, lad. Good luck,' he whispered hoarsely as he closed the half door and stumbled with the flickering lamp towards the house. He would not leave Ramona to her fate. She was sitting ashen-faced at the table as he approached from the hall and Michael, brandishing a whip, did not immediately see him. Something of Jack's old caution returned and he paused in the shadows to listen.

'You'll not lay a finger on me till I'm wed, Michael,' Ramona was saying. 'Not till I'm wed. I'll not go to your room and no whip will make me.'

'You with your fine airs,' Michael mocked her. 'Fine airs that I have given you, I might add. You forget your place, my dear. But of course, you have no place any more. Isn't that right? Well, there'll be no white wedding for you. You'll be up at five tomorrow and ready for a long ride. By nightfall you'll be my wife and that should settle the matter of where you sleep and who takes liberties with you in future.'

Ramona stared long and hard at Michael's granite features while Jack waited with his heart in his mouth for her response. Would the farm and a life that offered a few luxuries influence her choice as it would many women in a harsh world?

'I'll marry you on one condition,' she said at length. 'You've dismissed Jack. I accept that, after the way he behaved. But Beth has not wronged you and she must be allowed to stay as long as she wishes. Have I your word?'

Michael nodded curtly.

'Be up at dawn and wear your grey riding habit. You will sleep in the parlour tonight and on no account will you see Mr Cartwright.' He flicked the whip in an unmistakeably menacing gesture. 'Is that clear?'

Ramona didn't respond but lowered her gaze. The beginnings of submission, Jack noted bitterly, ashamed that he had brought about these events by his own reckless behaviour. There was nothing to be gained now from a confrontation. Ramona's decision was made and Beth at least would be safe in her care. With a heavy heart he turned back towards the door and slipped into the chill of the night. He must pack, say farewell to Beth for the present and seek his fortune elsewhere.

Chapter Twenty-Four

Jack was cold, dispirited and wet when he trudged back down the muddy leafless track into Scarborough that night. Beth had been tearful, as he might have expected, at the sudden turn of events and had at first insisted on leaving too. He had only managed to dissuade her by promising to keep her well informed. She must seek out the serving girl at the Mariner's Inn on her visits to the town and Nelly would know his movements, he assured her. Once he was established he would quickly send word. If only his hopes of employment were as high as he had led her to believe, he thought, as his mind scrolled over the last few months. There was no one to vouch for him now – and the fault was his own for allowing his heart to rule his head.

He lowered his sack to the ground to examine the coins in his pocket. There were precious few. Resisting the bright lights of the Bell Inn with its constant clatter of carriage horses, he slithered instead down the steep Bland's Cliff and made his way to Quay Street below. He needed an ale and he would spend what he had at the Mariners where he could hear the sea lapping close by and perhaps even find a bed for the night. In fact there were eight or more inns and lodging houses in the narrow thoroughfare but the Mariners, a place of character and colour, was his favourite. It was the pulse of the town, surrounded by timber merchants' attics, boat-yards and berths where the clinker-built cobles were hammered into shape. Whispered talk of smugglers and secret passages beneath, abruptly halting when a customs man approached, lent an air of intrigue to the low beamed rooms.

Jack entered and nodded at Nelly behind the bar without his usual buoyant smile. Favouring him above the crush of rough seafaring men, she poured an ale and pushed it towards him

'There you are, Jack. Has the cat got your tongue tonight?' He placed a coin on the counter.

'Aye, that it has,' he sighed as he made his way to a bench in the corner from where he could observe without being jostled by his fellow men. He needed time to unwind, to think, to adjust but most of all right now he needed to numb the pain of his loss.

He drank the first pint fast and was about to beckon for another when a whaler man pushed through the door – a captain, Jack surmised, by the way men stood up to allow him to pass. The distraction from his heartache and reeling emotions was welcome. How he envied him his life of liberty on the waves, at this moment, free from female enslavement, with only raw courage and the conquest of the elements to fire his blood. Grey eyes full of far-sighted wisdom shone from the chiselled, bearded face as he glanced half smiling round the smoke-filled room. They lingered for a moment on

Jack, leaving him once more with the notion that destiny had intervened. The feeling was so strong that he wove his way back to the bar to order a flagon of ale and, emboldened by drink, approached the captain.

'I hear you are set for Greenland, sir. Might I ask when you sail?'

'On the tide at first light, lad,' he responded, downing his own earthenware pot with finality and wiping the dregs from his well-trimmed moustache. He turned away to leave, ending the conversation, until Jack called after him with an audacity born of despair.

'Can you use another man, sir? I can turn my hand to anything.'

The captain turned slowly towards him before his solid muscular frame rocked with laughter.

'You smell of horses, lad. You don't have the salt of the sea in your veins. Seafarers are born to it and believe me it's a hard life – not one you could stomach.'

'Who's to say I couldn't?' Jack countered, flushed with alcohol and indignation. 'I'm as strong as an ox. See those muscles.' He bared a forearm, raising a ripple of mirth among the drinkers at the bar. Nelly, sensing something was wrong, looked puzzled by his boorish behaviour.

'Nay, lad,' the captain smiled good-naturedly, 'I have a full complement.' He glanced once more round the room as though taking in the scene to recall on the hard days ahead. 'I bid you all good night and farewell.'

'And here's to your safe return!' the cry went up, prompting everyone to raise their tankards. 'Aye, we'll all drink to that.'

Jack picked up his flagon under Nelly's disapproving eye and returned morosely to his corner. Things were not going well. He drank steadily into the night until he fell into a dull stupor, allowing his head to droop, then to sink onto the table.

Some time later, consciousness returned, and his eyes swivelled unsteadily round the room. The logs in the grate had been reduced to ash, emitting only an occasional shower of sparks when the wind gusted down the chimney. Sam had been right about the storm. The small casement windows rattled around him and the doors slammed shut behind drinkers departing to the sanctuary of their homes. Thoughts of his own forlorn situation prompted him to raise his hand for more ale before self-disgust restrained him. In any case Nelly was occupied, he noted. A youth, sporting a sealskin jacket and the overlarge boots of a Greenland fisherman, was attempting to pluck a ribbon from her chestnut hair. Succeeding at last, he raised it aloft.

'You shall be my sweetheart, Nelly,' he cried, 'and this shall be nailed to the mast when we sail. Will you be my girl when I return?'

Jack, absorbed in his own wretchedness, watched with indifference, all too aware of what would happen next. Jimmy Gordon, her current paramour and not a man to harness his temper, stepped out of the shadows.

'We'll see about that, you varmint!' He pushed

his face to within an inch of the young seaman's, who, delighting at the chance to demonstrate his skills, gave no quarter.

'No, Jimmy!' Nellie protested. 'Let him be. He meant no harm.'

But it was too late. The two disappeared in a flurry of fists as the cry went up – 'A fight! A fight!' – and beer sodden men rose to their feet to jeer or cheer the challengers on. Some even placed wagers and Jack, too, lurched towards the circle to watch, until, catching sight of Nelly's distress, he tried to intervene. He was roughly pushed back, however, as the baying pack demanded a victor. This was a fight to the finish and the best man would win. Both were bruised and bloodied already as bare knuckles bore into bone and flesh, matching punch for punch. Neither would yield, it seemed, as they grappled and wrestled amongst tables and chairs. Then it happened. An audible crack that left the seaman's arm dangling uselessly and put an end to the contest as swiftly as it had begun.

Jack's wits returned in a trice. A broken bone would take weeks to heal and the whaler would sail with an incomplete crew. In the mayhem that followed, he gathered his sack and elbowed his way towards the door. A doctor had been summoned and Nellie was berating both men equally as she tended their wounds.

'I'm going to tell the Captain,' he called to her above the fray. 'Be sure to tell Beth if I don't come back.' With that he hurried out and picked his way with sudden purpose through the ebbing tide. The

a

167

swaying masts of the whaler towered above the harbour walls, firing him with his old thirst for danger and challenge. Neither chill wind nor the sting of salt spray could deter him now. He groped his way along a slippery gangplank onto the deck.

'Who goes there?' a stout figure demanded from behind the bulwark.

'Jack Cartwright, sir. I wish to see the Captain.'

'An' why should you see the Captain, might I ask?' the man hollered back.

'I have news for him, sir – regarding one of his crew.'

The seaman approached with a lantern, examined him for a moment and apparently satisfied his visit was genuine, led him to the officers' quarters in the stern. The Captain, breaking off a conversation, emerged from his cabin to see who had the nerve to demand an audience.

'What the devil are you doing here?' he exclaimed, recognising Jack immediately. 'Have you no sense? Have I not told you I need no extra hands?'

'With respect, sir, I bring bad news.' Jack removed his cap and awaited permission to continue.

'Well?'

'A lad called Ginger, sir. He's broken his arm in a fight. Over a lass, it was.'

The Captain's brow furrowed and he struck the door with the flat of his hand.

'Will that lad never learn?' he fumed, talking half to himself, half to his colleague. 'Well, we'll sail without him. I'll pick up a Shetlander when we stop in Lerwick. Thanks for your trouble, young man.

That will be all.'

Jack twisted his cap in his hands and cleared his throat.

'Could you not find a use for me, sir? Like I said, I can turn my hand to anything... anything at all.'

'Be off with you! I've had enough of your impertinence.'

'But, sir..'

'No 'but' about it.' His face softened briefly. 'But you're a determined beggar. I'll give you that.'

A long legged figure, cramped in the cabin behind, leant forward to study the intruder.

'Why, if it isn't Jack Cartwright!' he declared. 'Well I'll be damned! Take him on, Ross. The lad's a survivor. He'll do you no harm.'

The Captain's indignation at this waiving of his authority was evident. Henry Cunningham stood up, stooping beneath a swaying pewter lamp.

'He worked for my father as a coachman. I can vouch for him.'

The Captain responded by drawing himself up to his full height.

'Your father may own this ship, Cunningham, but let us be quite clear, I am her master and what befalls her on this trip will be my responsibility.'

Jack's delighted surprise turned to despondency as a deck hand was summoned to escort him ashore but he had not allowed for a change of heart.

'Take him below, McBride. Give him Ginger's bunk.' He stretched out a firm hand. 'Welcome aboard the Polestar – and pray God you return because many do not.'

Chapter Twenty-Five

Few members of the crew suffered from sleeplessness and, thanks to his consumption of ale, Jack was no exception. He was to learn quickly however that short interrupted periods were the norm aboard ship and that the cry, 'All hands on deck!' required an instant response. Rudely awakened in the early hours, he grabbed his jacket and followed the general stampede up the forecastle hatchway to the deck. Sobered by the half light of dawn and a fresh breeze, he looked around him at his new companions, gazed with disbelief into the harbour's murky depths and up at the rigging with its sails still tightly furled. The storm had abated and the shoreline was shrouded in mist, lending a dreamlike quality to the remarkable events of the night. He struggled to take stock, to assess the outcome of his actions on Beth and Ramona. There was still time to jump ship but a stroke of good fortune, he felt sure, had led him here and he must trust to it now.

'Go for'ard, lad. Spring to!' McBride bawled at him, as he dithered near the bulwark. 'Man the windlass and heave!'

He was thankful there was no more time for

thought and threw himself like the other men into his allotted task.

'Shoulder to it, lad! You can do better than that.' Gasping for breath, Jack heaved until he thought his back would break, sinking down exhausted only when the ship had weighed anchor. There were no mighty engines here, only winches and chains and the sweat and toil of seasoned muscular limbs to counter the elements. But already he felt better as he watched the daring expertise of men teeming up the mast heads and shinning the yard-arms. This would be a fine adventure.

'Stand by to square the yards!' the first mate hollered and, eager to prove his worth, Jack seized a halyard and helped to hoist and secure a sail. He stared in wonder as the huge canvas billowed above him and the ship glided gently forward towards the open sea. It was only when they turned north into the wind and headed up the coast that he gave thought to his clothes. They were quite inadequate, he soon discovered, but he masked his discomfort, reluctant to show weakness amongst these cool-nerved men.

Captain Ross's keen eye took note, however, as he stood on the quarter deck surveying his crew. Satisfied with the trim of his ship, he set the watch, then summoned the cook, who saluted him respectfully.

'Take the new lad to the slop chest, Isaac. See that he is equipped with more suitable attire.' He turned to Jack. 'This is no gift, boy. If the trip is a good one, it will come from your wage. If we

171

come back clean, the debt will be yours. Do you understand?'

'Aye, aye, sir,' Jack responded, attempting a salute. He understood all too well, from his visits to the Mariner's Inn, the gambling nature of the whaling business. A good trip meant returning with the blubber of ten or more whales safely casked in the hold. A good trip meant a wage that would support each member of the crew through the following winter. But a clean ship with no fish caught meant no pay, and hardship for all.

He followed the cook to the 'tween deck which housed a blacksmith's forge and working quarters for the carpenter, cooper and sailmakers. Two youths sat picking oakum in the corner and Jack was soon the butt of their coarse wit as he pulled on worsted stockings, striped flannel shirts and layers of wool. He exchanged his moleskin coat for a waterproof jacket and his cap for a lambs-wool wig.

'You'll need mittens, too,' Isaac advised him, 'or your fingers will drop off when we get further north.' He was a stout, ruddy-faced man, better suited to the business of preparing meals than clambering up ropes. He doubled as a doctor when required, on the basis of his flimsy medicinal skill. 'When you've stowed that away, come back to the galley. I can use you there. Be sharp, lad.'

Jack ran to do his bidding and returned to find the cook heaving cauldrons onto a massive iron stove. Potatoes were heaped on one side and a paring knife lay ready. Jack set about them diligently but his heart sank. Was he to be a mere kitchen hand after all, while this gallant ship ploughed a furrow through the world's seas? He resigned himself to the task, however, reasoning that at least he was warm and had time to reflect. Isaac, his face growing redder as he stirred his broth before clamping down the lid, wanted to know more than Jack was willing to tell him about his past.

Taking advantage of his talkative companion, Jack ventured to enquire after Henry Cunningham and why he had embarked on such a perilous voyage.

'Ah, it's in the nature of the man, d'you see?' Isaac replied, emphasising his words with a dripping ladle. 'His father owns most of the shares in this ship but he's a wild one, all right. Ran away from a wedding, it seems. He's been seasick since we left Hull,' he laughed with no trace of sympathy. 'He'll not make a sailor, that's for sure!'

The ship heeled in a heavy swell and the combination of boiling animal fat and agitated bilge water emanating from below left Jack wondering if he too would fall victim to sickness. The opportunity to question Isaac further passed as he gulped back the contents of his stomach. A galley boy appeared, carrying more supplies of coal. It was his job, he explained, to keep the galley fire burning till the end of the trip.

'You're to go up on deck and report to the third mate,' he told Jack who, desperate to get some fresh air in his lungs, took his leave of Isaac and scrambled up the forehatch.

The Captain had already retired to his quarters, leaving the third mate, Thomas Hewson, to superintend his watch. The two-day voyage to the Shetlands required nothing like the skill and vigilance that sailing amongst the pack ice of the polar seas would demand. Jack approached the lantern-jawed Hewson and saluted in the manner he supposed appropriate.

'Jack Cartwright, sir. Reporting for duty,' he added, trying to gain control of his churning stomach. The older man glowered at him from beneath the peak of an officer's cap. He wore it firmly clamped down to contain an otherwise unruly thatch of grey hair. His disdain for landsmen was evident and sensing it, Jack, perhaps unwisely, raised his chin a fraction and coolly returned his stare.

'Stand straight, lad. Feet together. That's no way to salute a senior officer,' he snarled. 'You've a high opinion of yourself, I see. Well, lad, you'll soon find out. On board ship, it's my opinion that matters. There's more than thirty sails up there. Do you know the name of even one of them?'

'No, sir,' Jack mumbled.

'Speak up lad.'

'No sir!' Jack shouted.

Hewson strode ahead of him towards the bowsprit. 'What's this mast called?'

Jack shook his head but his brain was racing.

'I know the middle mast is the mainmast, sir.'

'This is the foremast, lad, and this, the shroud – the rope that supports it.' He swung himself round abruptly and strode towards the stern. Grabbing the lower shroud to steady himself as the ship heeled, he stabbed a finger into Jack's chest. 'This, the mizzenmast. Now, starting from the top, you have the mizzen skysail, the mizzen royal, then the top-gallant and below that the topsail. Here at the bottom, the foresail, the mainsail, the spencer and the spanker. That's a seaman's life up there, lad, but you're only a landsman. You'll work in the waist, splicing rope, cleaning decks and mending sails.' He turned towards him with a challenging, triumphant smile. To his surprise however, Jack gazed upwards at the canvas vault above and carefully repeated all that he had said.

'Well, now.' Hewson had been about to dismiss him to his menial duties but, impressed by his sharpness of mind, he hesitated. 'Want to work aloft then, do you?' Again he paused, checking that the ship's sails were filled and that her course was correct. 'Very well, lad. Let's see what you can do.'

'What now, sir?' Jack, still finding his sea legs, was taken aback but if this was a test he would not be found wanting.

'Right now, lad,' Hewson replied, leading him to the rigging at the base of the mainmast. Jack's heart pounded as adrenaline coursed through his veins. He placed a tentative toe on the tarred rope and was surprised how it gave beneath his weight. The rungs swayed as he took a further step up.

'You're not a wench, lad! Use the ball of your foot if you don't want to slip!'

Stung by his remark, he clambered higher and higher until he was beyond earshot and could hear only the steady ~~breathing of a benign~~ wind caressing the sails. Looking resolutely upwards, he pressed on – beyond the mainsail to the topsail rigging before stopping and holding fast to a yard-arm. The masthead lookout was a stage further up but one glance down from his eyrie at the remote figure of the third mate stifled his ambition to reach it. This was far enough. He mustn't look down again, he resolved, as he savoured the extraordinary view.

To the east on their starboard, a weak sun was painting the folds of the sea with pastel colours which rippled like a child's kaleidoscope. Up here in the elements, he was alone with his thoughts yet somehow far removed from Ramona and the emotional pain she had caused him. He must let time pass and trust to fate. At least with luck he would return in late summer with the means to support Beth and her infant child.

He sang a sea shanty to boost his courage on his slow descent but jumped to attention as he sprang onto the deck, flushed and exhilarated.

Hewson studied him thoughtfully.

'You'll do. You'll need practice but you'll do,' he commented shortly. 'Every man on my watch must know the ropes and be ready for anything. Tell me. D'you still feel sea-sick, lad?'

'Sea-sick? Why no, sir,' Jack responded ~~and indeed~~ he did not. Hewson nodded, clasped his hands behind his back and turned towards the helm. 'Scare 'em to death,' Jack heard him confide to the quartermaster on the wheel. 'Make 'em think. Cures the sickness every time.'

Chapter Twenty-Six

The Polestar made good speed over the next two days, covering the four hundred miles to the Shetland Isles without incident. The short voyage gave Jack a useful insight into how the ship was manned, how the watches were split and the significance of the eight bells and four bells which summoned the crew to their duties.

The death watch from twelve until four, he learned, was so called because it commenced and was handed over during the darkest hours. The first mate presided over the four until eight period while he himself remained on the Captain's watch from eight until twelve both morning and night. As he scrambled from his bunk another weary seaman would collapse into it, the small sea chest beneath, which acted as table, seat and closet, being his only personal sanctuary.

The confined space, however, fostered a team spirit, even a kind of equality, born of awareness that their safe return home depended on unity. He was enjoying the comradeship of these hardy people, he decided, as he sprang up and down the ratlines with increasing confidence.

'You're not a seaman yet, boy,' Isaac assured him

as he slopped oatmeal into his bowl at daybreak. 'Two thousand miles it is to the Davis Straits. Two thousand miles west across the Atlantic to Cape Farewell. And that didn't get its name for nothing, I can tell thee.' He traced an arc in the air with his ladle. 'Then a thousand-mile trip up the west coast of Greenland and back through the ice fields of Baffin Bay.'

'Aye,' Charlie McBride continued between mouthfuls as they seated themselves elbow to elbow in the galley. 'There's bergs big as mountains up there and many a ship gets crushed or stuck fast.' He glanced with grim cheeriness at Jack, pondering no doubt why a man not bred with a passion like his for ice and wind and sea would want to subject himself to such dangers. Far from being deterred however, Jack found himself intoxicated by talk of this wild frontier where men pitted their wits against fifty-foot creatures weighing sixty-five tons. Such an extraordinary adventure was worth the risk.

Sensing Jack's resolve and satisfied that he had a heart stout enough for the voyage, McBride scooped up the last of his porridge, got to his feet and ducked his broad back beneath the bulkhead.

'We'll be anchored in Lerwick, soon' he called over his shoulder. 'After we've stowed the hold and shortened the masts, we should get leave to go ashore – so jump to it, lad.'

Against a dark grey sky and sea, the solid stone houses of Lerwick seemed to merge timelessly with the land from which they were hewn. Set off against treeless purple hills, they gave the impression from the harbour of antiquity and strength. It was only when Jack ambled through the refuse-strewn streets that the level of poverty in the town became clear. Miserable dwellings with mud floors and peat fires served as shelters for both humans and livestock. Even the whisky houses where, despite the filth, the sailors gathered, were pitch-black dens without windows or chimneys.

Lured reluctantly by the drone of a bagpipe from one of these places, Jack stooped through the smoke that made a lazy escape through the door. With smarting eyes he scarcely noticed at first the troop of crones on either side – all keen to relieve him of what coppers he possessed. He had just cursed the foul-tasting noggin they urged him to drink when his attention was drawn to a tall blonde man engaged in a reel with a dark-eyed girl.

Astonished to see Sir George's son in such a place, Jack sank back into the blackest corner of the den. A woman, as broad as she was tall, pestered to tell his fortune but, having no wish to hear her devilries, he pushed her aside and continued to observe Henry. After days confined to his cabin he was as wildly drunk as any of the sailors mortgaging the voyage to pay for their fun. A lost man indeed, like his Uncle Edward, Jack thought sadly. No wonder he had fled his former life. Was he seeking self destruction in the polar seas?

The piper upped his tempo suddenly and Henry, caught off balance, staggered sideways. Cackles of laughter followed as he struggled to remain on his feet before crashing spectacularly to the ground. Such things were commonplace amongst the tough Greenland whaler men but Jack noticed with growing concern that Henry did not rise. He held back however, having no wish to reveal his presence. Still Henry did not stir. Tentatively at first, Jack moved towards him through the crush of revellers. Then on an impulse, he grabbed his jacket and dragged him away from the suffocating smoke to the fresh Shetland air outside. Within minutes he had revived and Jack, suggesting that a couple of tars take him back to the ship, melted discreetly away.

A small kirk further up the hillside seemed the only refuge from the wrinkled hands that constantly proffered their knitting and lace work. Without the means to barter or even the skill to deter them, he stepped inside. Its damp prison-like walls offered no more comfort than the whisky dens below, but seeking peace and solitude he settled in a pew at least slightly warmed by a shaft of light. His thoughts turned inexplicably to that last wretched day in the mill, to William's emaciated face close to his and his last whispered words. 'It's up to you, Jack.'

Had he let him down, he wondered? He wanted so much to succeed, to make something of himself; to protest to the world at its inequalities. His thoughts turned, too, to Henry's squandered life. Here was a man, an educated man, who could have made a difference. If only he himself could read and write as Henry did with such assurance. If only he was eloquent enough to stir the hearts of men.

He looked up. A small bird seeking a nesting site in the beams had become trapped. It fluttered with increasing panic around the enclosed space, battering its fragile body against each stone wall in turn. He found himself willing it to escape through the only gap in the roof that emitted light. Instead its tiny feathers spiralled downwards as it continued its frenzied flight. The spectacle reminded him of Ramona. She would be back at Hilldene now, wife to Michael and mistress of her own home. Overwhelmed by the notion of such a man possessing her, he stumbled towards the door. Outside, he released his collar and took several deep gulps of fresh air. He must count his blessings. Beth, after all, was safe and here he had an opportunity to provide for them both.

The bird swept suddenly through the open door and soared joyously skyward. In spite of his resolve Jack wept soundlessly as he watched it go.

Chapter Twenty-Seven

At the end of March, a month after Jack's dismissal, Michael took his new wife on a trip to York. Beth watched as they boarded the yellow bounder that passed the gates of Hilldene once a day. She waved until Ramona's feathered hat disappeared inside, then turned away suppressing a tear. Storm stood motionless, head lowered, as she walked back through the yard and on an impulse she slipped into his stall. She soothed him with gentle words as she knew Jack would have done while she bathed a seeping wound on his flank. The horse had been ridden too hard against seasoned steeplechasers and Michael's spurs had raked into his flesh.

'Don't fret now. T'will soon heal,' she murmured, emboldened by his lack of spirit. But she was in no doubt it would happen again. Jack had been proved right. Michael was ruthless and, as Ramona would soon find out, not a man of his word. Agatha shuffled past on her way to the dairy for milk.

'Come on, girl. Ain't no time for that horse. We've got work to do with the master away. He'll expect the house right when he gets back tomorrow. You'd best get those sheets aired.'

'Aggie?' Beth stepped from the stall, wiping her wet hands on the hem of her apron. 'I have something I must tell you.'

'Well, be quick about it, girl. We haven't all day.' A permanently amiable smile belied her sharp words as she turned back with plump arms folded. 'What is it? What have you to say?' Beth smoothed the calico smock that already stretched tight over her swelling girth.

'The master came to see me just before he left. Said I was to leave before he returned. Me being with child an' all, I suppose. So I won't be seeing Ramona again.' Her voice cracked and she paused to collect her emotions. 'I won't be seeing you no more either, Aggie. I shall miss you both dreadful.' Seeing the older woman's hands fly to her mouth at this unexpected news, Beth drew herself up. 'I shall be all right, mind. I shall go and find Jack.'

'We'll see about that, my dear!' Aggie declared, taking her hand and steering her into the parlour. Indeed, we'll see about that." Ever practical, she brewed a pot of tea and stirred it vigorously. 'Miss Ramona would never have that. Never. Why, the man has broken his promise. And you with a babe to consider.' She shook her head in disbelief. Beth however was determined too.

'I'll not cause trouble for Ramona. It's best I go and let her get on with her married life. I've got a few coins. I'll go down to the Mariners Inn tomorrow. Jack and I – we've always been lucky. You'll see, no harm will come to us.' She was adamant, despite Aggie's outrage. 'I'll prepare Ramona's room before

I go. And I'll find some bluebells down by the beck. She likes woodland flowers. You will tell her, won't you, how sad I was to leave?'

'Aye lass. I'll tell her alright. I'll tell the master too. He shall know how I feel about the matter, make no mistake. Why, I believe I'd leave with you if I was a younger woman – but I'd miss this place and there's Mistress Ramona to think of now. She's going to need me, poor girl.'

The two women completed their chores and then sat long into the night until the embers in the range had almost died. Reluctant to end this phase of her life but knowing she must, Beth sighed as the last log crumbled into the grate. She must get some sleep before the first light came and with it the ordeal of walking down the road on her own.

Dawn revealed a cool grey morning with a hint of rain and it was hard to maintain her breezy optimism once Aggie's weeping figure was out of sight. She clutched her basket of fresh farm food and stepped daintily along the track to preserve the hem of her laundered smock.

She would go to see Sam first, she decided, and if he had no news of Jack, she would venture into the Mariners Inn. She could imagine the curious stares of the locals. A woman in her condition was shunned. Without her cousin's support, she might well have been obliged to seek out the workhouse. How fortunate she was to know that her son would be spared that fate. Once he was born, she would work so hard to ensure that he thrived.

There was no doubt in her mind that the child

was a boy and that he would grow up with a halo of gold like his father. This positive image brought a smile to her drawn face and put a spring in her step as she descended the hillside towards the white-capped waves in the bay. The future looked good. Suddenly she felt sure of it.

She followed the wooded course of the beck until it spilled onto the shore and she could sit at last on the sand to rub her tired feet. The sea, ebbing and flowing in timeless symmetry, calmed and delighted her as it had done on her visits here with Jack. This morning it was the colour of pewter, like the servants' plates at Skellfield Hall. In the distance she could see Sam setting out his stall, but she would not hurry, she decided. She would eat Aggie's fruit cake first.

At length, she got up, swept the crumbs from the folds of her dress and continued on her way, humming a cradle song remembered from childhood. Perhaps her unborn son would hear it and be soothed, she mused, as she felt a small kick in her belly. Sam looked up as she approached but his smile seemed tinged with unease.

'Why Sam, is trade not so good?' Beth laughed. 'I'll buy a skate from you as a present for Jack. I'm hoping you can tell me where he is.'

Sam's far sighted blue eyes returned to the horizon, avoiding hers.

'Aye lass, I can tell thee – but I'm not sure as you'll want to know. It's just as well thee has a place at the farm.'

Alarm quickly replaced Beth's good humour. Her

hands dropped instinctively over her taut belly.

'What is it, Sam? Where has he gone?'

'Calm yourself, lass. You'll be proud of him when he comes back in the autumn. He's quite a lad, that Jack of yours. Had a chance to sail on the morning tide with the Polestar. Gone whaling, he has. Ah, if I was a younger man...' He gazed wistfully out to sea, chewing on his pipe. 'I'd be out there with him.' Lost in his fantasies, he didn't see Beth's face turn to chalk but he heard her turn away to retch. 'It'll be smell of t'fish in your condition,' he observed knowingly. 'Now, you take care of yourself,' he called as she took advantage of his assumption to hurry away.

Beth could only think that she must not tell him of her own dismissal. He would want to help, even though his wife was old and frail. But what on earth was she to do? She had neither money nor friends in this town. She retraced her footsteps along the shore and sank to the ground on the spot where earlier she had been so full of hope. Her tears fell soundlessly as she stared at the waves – waves that already seemed alien. They had carried Jack away when she needed him most.

At length, she closed her eyes. Henry was laying by her side again amongst the tendrils of sweetpeas and lavender in her riverside garden. She remembered the ecstasy of his touch as he explored her body, the irrelevance of everything else in life except that moment of intimacy. The moment she would never regret but which had led her down this path to an uncertain future. Would joy always bring her an equal measure of sorrow? she wondered as, many miles away, Jack was wondering too. She bowed her head and wept at last as though her heart would break.

Chapter Twenty-Eight

L ulled by the soft lapping of the waves, Beth sank into a fitful sleep. She awoke, purged of her grief but emotionally spent, to find the sea snaking up the beach on all sides. The sky had cleared and barefoot children ran past, eager to clamber over the rocks and splash in the newly formed pools. She watched pensively, imagining her own son romping in the surging tide. She could almost hear his cries of delight, almost see his hair glinting like Henry's in the sun's rays but she must steel herself for the present to cold reality. It was almost April. By the end of May her pregnancy would have run its course. She had no choice but to submit herself to the hardships of the workhouse until, God willing, Jack returned.

Somewhere above the harbour near the castle walls, she heard a church bell toll. She would find shelter up there, she decided, and say a prayer for Jack before her ordeal began. The climb up the staithes left her breathless and in need of rest so she settled herself in a south-facing corner of the churchyard to enjoy the slight warmth of the afternoon sun. She ate the last of her provisions later in the day and watched the first curls of smoke rise from the chimneys below. Her legs felt unsteady when she got to her feet. A cheerful smile at a passing priest met with no response as she made her way bravely towards the town to face the grim prospect of what lay ahead.

The workhouse was in Newborough on Waterhouse Lane. She remembered catching sight of it once – a straggling brick building on a cramped unwholesome site. Her mind filled with images of the conditions within so that her fear was at its height when the solid black doors came into view. She found herself gasping for breath. Perhaps that was why she didn't see a carriage approach, or hear the shout of warning as she stepped into the road. What happened next was a blur. The coachman helped her to her feet and, satisfied she had merely fainted, called to the refined lady in the four-wheeled barouche.

'One for the workhouse, no doubt, ma'am. Don't concern yourself. I'll see her inside.' His hands gripped Beth like a vice and propelled her hurriedly towards the doors.

'Wait, driver. Wait!' The lady withdrew a lorgnette from a small black velvet bag and scrutinized Beth from head to toe. 'The wretch is clean, at least,' she murmured as the coachman's hand hovered impatiently over the latch.

Beth forced herself upright, letting her pleading honey-coloured eyes speak for her. The sea breeze had given her cheeks an unaccustomed glow and she had braided her hair neatly an hour before.

'Quite presentable, too' the woman observed, as though assessing the good and bad qualities of a horse. She replaced the lorgnette in her bag and snapped it shut. 'Help the girl into my carriage, Harvey.'

'But, ma'am – look at her condition! Are you sure this is wise? What would the master think?'

'When the master is away, it is what I think that matters, Harvey. Stop dithering, man. Do as I say and be quick about it.' Still dazed but elated by this turn of events, Beth found herself shuffled with slightly more respect into the leather seats opposite her benefactress. The woman smoothed her silk-gloved hands and smiled – a smile which did not quite reach her eyes. She seemed lost in thought as she instructed the coachman without once glancing away from Beth.

'Put up the hood, Harvey. Forget the promenade. It's grown quite chill anyway. Take me back home instead.' She patted Beth's knee. 'You'll like Oxpasture House, my dear. You can tell me all about yourself there.'

Beth nodded bemused then found her voice.

'Thank you, ma'am. You are most kind but I don't wish to be a trouble to you.'

The horses sprang forward and were soon trotting eagerly northwards through leafy lanes into open countryside. Where they were bound, Beth had no idea but whatever her fate it could not be worse than the horrors of the workhouse. Perhaps the woman was lonely, she reasoned, and required a companion. She would be only too happy to fulfil that role. This conclusion was bolstered by the continuing concern the woman showed for her welfare, even passing her a wrap to keep her shoulders warm.

They turned left into thick woodland. A small lake flashed by. Then the horses slowed to manoeuvre down a track almost hidden by overhanging trees. Beth clutched her basket wide-eyed until the jolting carriage finally emerged onto lush pastureland. Ahead, a stone house with noble features and carefully manicured lawns slumbered under the last rays of the sun.

'There you are, my dear. Harvey, help me down and take this young woman'... she paused. 'We're to call you Beth are we? Take Beth to the kitchen and ask Grace to show her to the servants' quarters. I'm tired now, We'll talk later.' With that she raised her skirts, revealing thin ankles and swept indoors, leaving the coachman unsure how to react to his new protégée. He took off his hat and wiped his sleeve against his forehead. Women! He wished the master was here.

'You'd best come this way,' he said gruffly, striding pointedly ahead so that she was forced to run to keep up.

Events took on the unreality of a dream as Beth was shown to her room and then, later, to the polished dining table for tea. The lady of the house, Mrs Ruston, she learned, joined her and encouraged her to eat as much as she wished of Grace's fine produce. Grace was a strangely silent older woman, interested only in doing her mistress's bidding. As far as Beth could see, she was the only other servant in the house.

There was a touch of mystery about Mrs Ruston, too, despite her effusive manner. Without the concealment of a fashionable hat, her features, though striking, looked well past the first flush of youth. She dabbed her small, carefully-defined lips with a serviette and lowered her voice.

'I suppose that was a mistake.' Her deceptively soft brown eyes rested on Beth's swollen girth. The remark was made nonchalantly but there was no disguising her sharp interest. Beth blushed and nodded.

'Does the father know?' She asked

Again Beth shook her head.

'Just as I thought. No one to support you, then.' She folded her napkin, apparently satisfied and got up to leave the room. 'Well, you're in good hands. I know all about confinement and I'd like to help. You shall rest here and do some light work around the house. After that, if you show willing and my husband agrees, we'll see about a job.' She turned at the door, again with studied nonchalance. 'One thing. When do you think the child is due?'

'When May is out, I think, ma'am.' Mrs Ruston smiled and closed the door quietly behind her. Beth smiled too when she had gone. Her prayers had been answered. If Jack was also protected from harm, she need have no fear, for the present.

Chapter Twenty-Nine

Many miles north, unaware of Beth's prayers or of her change of circumstance, Jack was finding the sea a hard taskmaster. As the Polestar ploughed across the Atlantic towards Cape Farewell and the Davis Straits, he was made daily aware of its perils. Stamina and strength were as much required as skill and experience, and in none of these areas could he match the seasoned whalers. After all, he was a mere landlubber with a taste for adventure. His muscles, though strong, seemed puny in the face of heavy swells and gale-force winds as he ran from lever to pulley and pulley to capstan in response to the captain's barked orders.

The layers of clothes and the sealskin jacket, needed now to protect against the intensity of the cold, weighed him down so that he sometimes missed his footing on the ratlines or his grasp on the yard-arm. More than once he had feared he would be pitched astern into the tossing sea where, he had been told, he would be out of reach in seconds. To avoid this fate, he had rashly abandoned his mittens on his last ascent, to find that his fingers quickly became as straight and white as candles. Only brisk rubbing with snow from the deck and the endurance of great pain had saved them from frostbite.

So he was learning fast that discomfort and danger were withstood cheerfully by these mariners, that the swagger in their walk back at home was deserved. They suffered the privations and the long hours of toil because the wild elements tested their courage and favoured the brave.

Jack had also become aware of how much the voyage depended on the captain's skill. His vigilance in the crow's nest and his ability to navigate through tortuous passages as they approached the ice was often all that stood between the ship and disaster. He had to be cautious and daring at the same time, to instil confidence in his crew when all might seem lost. Besides being well versed in all the tasks on board, he had to be a keen observer of how each man performed.

On May Day the Polestar reached the Straits and the customary celebrations began with the hoisting of a garland of ribbons up the top-gallant stay. The atmosphere relaxed and Jack was pleased to receive an approving word as Captain Ross handed each man his tot of rum. Henry, lured from his cabin by the lively shanties and the calm but freezing sea, tested his legs on the quarterdeck. He drank a measure of spirit from his own silver flask and gazed in wonder at the grand scenery that greeted him.

No one could fail to find the icebergs gleaming in the warm glow of Arctic sun a source of delight. As water cascaded from the summits, prisms of light showed every gradation of colour from emerald to blue and deepest purple, in a land where rainbows, mirages and the strange flashing brilliance of the Aurora Borealis illuminated the sky.

'Quite a sight, is it not, young Jack?' Henry breathed, scanning the horizon from north to south and from east to west. 'Quite a sight, don't you think?' Jack cleared his throat, wondering if this seemingly light conversation would lead to the inevitable question of why he was here and why he and Beth had fled.

'Aye, sir, it is that,' he muttered, pulling his cap down firmly over his eyes but volunteering no more.

After a pause, Henry, reading his thoughts, continued.

'No doubt you had your reasons, same as I. Whatever they were, fate seems determined to throw us together. Indeed I have a job to escape you,' he laughed, 'so let's drink to our renewed acquaintance.'

Relieved, Jack grinned up at the wayward blue eyes that had so captivated Beth. The man was charismatic for all his faults.

'Let us hope, sir, that this ship, like Lady, will bear us both home safely.'

Henry clapped him on the shoulder good-naturedly.

'If that's what you want, I wish it for you too. As for myself, I do believe it would be quite a fine way to perish – here, amongst all this majesty. Oh, I jest lad! 'Tis merely the ramblings of a blackguard. One must look to the future.' He sighed and returned his gaze to the cliffs and gorges of Greenland, ending the conversation before mention of Beth became necessary.

Jack tipped his cap and moved down the deck to the waist. Here the roughest of seamen were gathered to enjoy a brief period of abandon before the season began. The captain moved amongst them stiff-backed, his moustached mouth smiling slightly but his eyes as ever alert. He drew Jack aside to the gunwale and looked down at the blue-green depths and the floating splinters of thin white ice.

'You know Henry Cunningham from the past, I gather. Worked for the family. Is that right?'

'Yes, sir,' Jack responded reluctantly.

Captain Ross stroked his chin.

'He's with us as a special privilege. His father owns most of the shares in this ship, as you know. Henry's a nice enough fellow. A bon viveur with a taste for adventure. But I have a responsibility to get him home. Frankly, the man's a liability and I would not have permitted him aboard had I known. I want you to keep a discreet eye on him, to use your influence, if you can, to curb his habit – which I fear has already marked him as a lost man. Would you not agree with my assessment?'

'The Cunninghams have been good to me sir. I could not possibly comment.'

Captain Ross straightened up.

'Loyalty is a fine thing lad but it will not save him. Adversity might, if it doesn't kill him first. I've seen a need to drink wreck men before. He lacks any sense of discipline.'

'Or purpose, perhaps?' Jack ventured quietly.

'I see you have insight, lad, and that's always a good thing' the captain called as he hauled himself back to the quarterdeck and joined the first mate at the helm. Jack downed his rum and sought out Isaac who was struggling to place his unsteady feet in the rigging.

'Come on, lad. It's bad luck to miss this – follow my leader up the main mast and round the deck. Keep your head, mind. Some fool jumped in the sea last year.'

'What does 'insight' mean, Isaac?' Jack panted as he scrambled behind him up the ratlines.

'It means you think too much, lad. We're simple folk, you and I, and we always will be. You'll not change that.'

Chapter Thirty

Beth's delight with her chance encounter with Mrs Ruston was still evident a fortnight later as she poured her gratitude into polishing the pans till they gleamed. Mrs Bullen would have been proud of her, she thought, as she replaced the last one on its hook by the range. Grace popped her flat expressionless face round the door and nodded approval but did not smile. She never did, and Beth frequently wondered what sadness had occasioned her brusque manner.

'I'll be gone now with the mistress. She has some shopping to do in the town. Mind you light the fire before we return.'

Eager to please, Beth nodded vigorously before venturing to ask a question that had been on her mind.

'Do you think I might go into the town one day soon? I have a friend, you see, and she will be wondering where I am.'

Mrs Ruston swept in from behind before Grace could reply.

'Good gracious, girl! I can't allow that in your condition. Have you no shame? Confinement is just that, my dear. You must consider my position.

Do you not think I have been more than generous already?'

Beth stuttered an apology, regretting her request immediately. 'I don't want you beyond the gateposts of this house until the child is born. Your friend must wait for news. Is that understood?' The autocratic voice softened suddenly. 'Take some air now, then have a rest. You look tired, my dear. Come, Grace. Harvey will be waiting.'

Beth watched through the mullioned window as the horses clattered out of sight. She sighed and was about to turn away when a small shabbily-clad girl caught her eye and drew her towards the open door. Apart from Grace and a gardener who never looked up from the soil, she had seen no other folk at all. The child peered back through matted strands of mousy hair, before judging it safe to approach.

'Please, miss,' she whispered, stepping crabwise across the flagstoned yard, 'I've lost my ball.' Her voice faded as she pointed back towards the walled garden.

Beth bent down to hear her better.

'Can you not go in and fetch it?'

The child shook her head and chewed her fingers. 'No one's allowed in there. It's locked. The key's up there,' she added more boldly, sensing Beth's gentle nature.

'What's your name? Where do you come from?' Beth asked, asserting herself, as she pondered what to do.

'I'm Daisy. My papa does the garden here on Fridays. I come with him sometimes. The key's up there,' she repeated, pointing to the mantel. 'Can I lend it?'

'Borrow it!' Beth corrected laughing. 'You can borrow it but only if I come with you and we are very quick. Now where is this garden?' The child's face danced with joy and she skipped ahead, obliging Beth to keep up in spite of her full-term size. But Beth enjoyed weaving through the overgrown shrubs towards the solid iron gate. For a moment she was back in her own secret garden again and emotions she had learned to conceal threatened to overwhelm her.

'There, there it is. I can see my ball!' the child cried, pressing her face to the bars as Beth struggled to turn the key.

'Quick! Fetch it,' Beth ordered, 'and come out directly.' Hugging the precious toy against her ragged dress, Daisy returned beaming. Evidently keen to repay such a favour, she paused impishly inside the garden.

'Shall I show you a secret?' she whispered, her eyes widening with excitement. 'Come. Come with me.'

'No, child! I'll do no such thing. Come back!'

Daisy however had disappeared through a tangle of old damask roses and was not to be seen anywhere. Anxious and angry now, Beth followed. She would seize the child's hand and confiscate the ball, if this was how she behaved towards an adult. Daisy, when she found her, was in a small clearing free of weeds and well stocked with spring flowers. In the centre was a small headstone and its resemblance to poor William's plaque stunned Beth for a moment.

'It's Mrs Ruston's baby,' Daisy whispered conspiratorially. 'He died on New Year's Eve.'

In spite of her exasperation, Beth kneeled to study the small, as yet unworn, inscription.

'I know what it says,' Daisy announced. 'My papa told me. It says: Robert Ruston. Beloved only son of Frances and John. Born 1st December 1837.'

Beth blinked back a tear, imagining the pain her benefactress must have felt. The child had lived barely a month before he was snatched away. How unbearable the agony must have been. Feeling suddenly ashamed of this intimate knowledge that was not intended for her, she snatched Daisy's sleeve and bundled her down the winding stone path to the gate. Only when she had once more turned the key in the latch did her heart cease to race and questions crowd into her mind.

Still elated, Daisy seemed keen to confide.

'Mrs Ruston was so sad that she didn't go out for a long time. Grace is sad, too, because the press gang took her husband away. So they look after each other, you see – while Mr Ruston's abroad.'

'That's enough tittle-tattle, child,' Beth scolded. 'Run along and play with your ball, now. I have things I must do. If you're good, I'll help you to get on the swing next week.'

Beth listened as Daisy's carefree laughter receded, and massaged her belly thoughtfully. What a joy children were. But pain was a part of pleasure and she must endure the agonies of childbirth soon with all the risks she knew it entailed. God willing, Henry's son would be born without mishap. She would try not to think about the girls whose hips were distorted by working in the mills. She wouldn't think about the stories she had heard of how they suffered. Life was good and all would be well, she told herself firmly, as she laid the coals in the drawing room grate.

Chapter Thirty-One

'A fall! A fall!' The by now familiar cry, alerting the crew to the sighting of a whale, rang through the early morning air and echoed round the cramped berths in the forecastle. Jack's response was instant. Grabbing a bundle of clothes prepared for the purpose he joined the stampede to the hatch. The single-mindedness that united every man on board fired him with strength as he ran towards the davits. His job was to lower the boats with the greatest speed possible so that the harpooners, the rowers and boat steerers could leap to their places and skim across the sea. The craft rocked as half clad figures scrambled onto seats. Only when the oars were in motion would each in turn continue to dress. Not a moment must be lost.

'Come on, lads! Are ye a bunch of old women? D'you wish to be last away? ' the steerer goaded. 'Where's Ishmael? Ishmael, where are you?' he bellowed over Jack's shoulder.

There was a pause before a man enveloped in a hooded coat stepped forward and took up his place. Captain Ross brought his hand down sharply on the bulwark.

'Right, men. Undo the lashings. Easy does it. Lower them down.'

A gentle swell lapped against the hull as it reached the surface. As it did so, a wild-eyed seaman appeared alongside the captain, clutching his bundle of clothes.

'Why, they've gone without me, sir!' Ishmael protested. 'Who's that gone in my stead? I'm a wee bit sick, I'll admit, but I won't have any man take my place.'

'Henry, damn it! Henry Cunningham is that you down there sir?' the captain demanded.

'I can row as well as any man, Ross – and I'll not go home without knowing what it is to hunt a whale.' Henry's face remained defiantly concealed behind the hood as he took up an oar and tested the water. Captain Ross cursed under his breath. Ishmael was plainly ill and shivering from fever as well as cold. He glanced at Jack.

'Can you shin down that rope, d' you think?'

Jack's face lit up. Like Henry, he longed to experience the thrill of the chase.

'Aye, sir. Of course, sir.'

'Look after him, lad. That harpoon line goes out like an arrow. It can cut a man in two if he's not alert.'

'He'll come to no harm. I promise you,' Jack called, already halfway down the swaying rope. Impatient hands pulled him aboard. Soon the oars were dipping in unison, the long powerful strokes of the rowers skimming them across the sea. He caught Henry's eye and saw that he, too, was delighting in the sensation of speed and the spice of danger. For a moment, they were equals sharing boyish secret grins as the Shetland men pulled grimly onward, their minds sternly set on the task ahead.

By chance, the black bulk of the whale surfaced close to them to take in new air and to expel the old through the blow hole in the top of its head.

Careful to approach from behind, the steerer skulled to within eight yards of its neck. In a trice, the harpooner's weapon had found its mark and, with a line attached, the chase began. The boat jolted as the startled mammal, terrified and in pain, lurched forward. A hundred and twenty fathoms of rope ran out with such speed that another soon had to be fastened.

'Douse the bollard with water!' the steerer ordered as the friction produced smoke which threatened to ignite. Jack reached for a bucket to do as he was bid as they shot helplessly along in the victim's wake. The crewmen's purpose was to get close enough to the weakened creature to plunge their lances into its flesh. Henry's aristocratic blood was up – though whether through alcohol, concealed at all times in his flask, or his own natural taste for risk was hard to say. He had always been to the fore in the hunting field and saw no reason to be different now.

Ignoring the strict code of behaviour between the men, he dropped his oar, stumbled forward towards the bow and seized a lance from its mounting. At that moment, the huge arched back of the whale appeared beneath them, lifting the boat like so much matchwood from the waves. Before Jack could restrain him, Henry had thrown back his hood, let out a battle cry and hurled his weapon deep into the animal's inch-thick flesh.

The scene that followed was chaotic as the whale's twenty-foot tail flukes pounded the sea and blood spurted and frothed over the cursing men. By sheer good fortune their boat was not smashed. The harpooner's remaining lances struck home in the mayhem.

'Pull away, pull away!' the boat steerer roared as the flukes continued to batter the sea and the panicked whale rolled in its tangle of lines. 'Grab an oar, Jack, and row.' But Jack's concern was elsewhere. There was no sign of Henry where he had last seen him on the prow. Had he overbalanced and fallen foul of the whale's most lethal defence – its ton weight of tail? Then for just a moment in the sea of blood, he caught a glimpse of yellow hair. The man was unconscious, face down in the water.

'Row lads, I tell you row!' the boat steerer bellowed above the fray.

'I cannot, sir. Master Henry's overboard. I cannot leave him.'

'Would you have us all dead, boy? She's on a line. We must leave her to tire or she'll sink us for sure.'

'But what of Henry, sir? We must help him.'

'I have no time for the man. He broke the rules. Let him be, I say. Row! That's an order, lads.'

The whale's frantic attempts to escape were turning the sea into a cauldron, but amongst the spume Jack spotted Henry's tossing body for perhaps the last time and knew he must act. Bracing himself to face the cold, he launched himself over the stern. The boat steerer hesitated, loath to see the boy perish too.

'Wait, men. Throw the lad a line, Thomas.'

His action was life-saving. Jack, a poor swimmer, reached Henry but was too numb with cold to return and could only manoeuvre him onto his back and hold his head aloft in the turbulence. He grasped the rope gratefully and somehow held on till the steel-sinewed oarsmen hauled them both in. Their strong arms pummelled Henry's chest until, after several tense minutes, he coughed and retched and spluttered back to life. The boat steerer, a Yorkshireman, took off Jack's coat and handed him his own.

'You're a good man to sail with, Jack. You're a better man than I,' he said quietly.

The whale, they now noticed, had ceased to stir and a cheer went up that was heard on the Polestar as its life blood seeped into a suddenly calm sea. The men would be toiling for many more hours, towing it back and stowing its flesh in the hold but the benefits would be shared by them all. Jack's teeth chattered as he grinned at Henry's ashen face. They had survived and that was victory enough for him.

Chapter Thirty-Two

J ack's elation soon wore off. No one escaped from an Arctic sea without a degree of frostbite and both he and Henry were chalk white with cold by the time their boat was winched aboard the Polestar. As he tumbled onto the deck, Henry was bundled down to the galley, groaning with pain from a dangling lower limb.

'Place him on here,' Isaac ordered wiping ship-biscuit crumbs with his sleeve from the surface of an oak table. 'Hang an oil lamp overhead.' His medical skills were as basic as his cookery but as self-assured. 'Warm some flannel clothes by the stove,' he instructed as he stripped off Henry's sodden garments and loosened his boots. 'Tell the carpenter to come. I'll need splints for this leg and calico to bind them.' He turned to Jack, who had gravitated instinctively towards the fire and was trying to undress with rigid fingers. 'You must heat yourself slowly, lad. Get yourself dry and then run round the deck.'

'I'll not do that, Isaac. I can't feel my legs,' he protested, moving closer to the warmth.

'If you want that blood of yours to flow again, you'll do as I say and do it until I tell you to stop,' Isaac

/ there are no carpenters on a

208 ship

growled, rolling up his cuffs as he bent over Henry's protruding broken bone. Not wishing to witness his pain as the limb was re-aligned and bandaged, Jack did as he was bid. When he returned, the galley smelt of eucalyptus and pungent antiseptics instead of greasy boiling soup. Henry was unconscious and about to be stretchered to his cabin when Captain Ross ducked under the bulkhead. He bent forward to examine the splint and the face as pale as marble beneath the flickering light. Even with life almost sucked from him, Henry's profile resembled that of a Greek god.

'I want him confined to his quarters. I'll not have my authority questioned on my own ship. Jack, you said you would turn your hand to anything. I want you to stay with him and see to his needs from now on. He'll be bedridden for at least six weeks with that leg. Is that clear?'

Jack choked back his indignation. It was true he had volunteered to do anything at all. But to be relegated to nursemaid an over-indulgent man, even a gentleman such as Henry, was a bitter disappointment.

'Isaac, have a hammock set up in Henry's cabin and see that they both get their meals in there.'

Captain Ross swept off to prepare for the flensing of the dead whale, leaving Jack, grumbling aloud, to follow the stretcher bearers to the deck above. Henry was laid gently on his wooden bunk and covered sparingly with warm flannel sheets. There was just enough room for a small desk and chair, a shelf of books, a metal jug and bowl and, on top of a cupboard, Henry's personal effects. Opposite was the captain's cabin and adjacent, a small study which served as a dining room for the officers. To his relief, Jack was told he could use this room and wait upon the men at mealtimes. With its small square windows, it afforded him a view from the stern of the ship.

For the present, however, he settled back in the chair at Henry's desk, aware that he must maintain a strict vigil until consciousness returned to his charge. No doubt he would be expected to pick oakum from old rope like the other apprentices when his fingers regained their strength. He listened to the slapping of the waves against the hull, accustomed now, after three months at sea, to gauging an increase in the swell or the presence of ice. After the previous bad year, it had been a good season, he was told, with eight whales caught, amounting to almost ninety tons of oil.

Away from the constant noise and companionship of the galley, Jack found himself unable to blank out the past. Painful and pleasurable thoughts returned. Visions of Ramona with her mane of chestnut hair and scarlet cloak, her carefree laughter as they stumbled in the stream, the spontaneous kiss they had shared. And always the shadow of Michael which would never go away.

Beth. He must think of Beth instead. She would have given birth to her child by now. Ramona and Aggie would have cared for her far better than he himself could have done, and he would return with some hope of a future for them both. Should he tell

Henry he had fathered a child? He looked at the sleeping form and the strangely peaceful face that, awake, was so tormented by his family's demons. Would Beth be at risk of losing what she valued most? No, he decided. It was not his place to tell him.

Henry stirred, lifting his head slightly and opening his eyes wide before dropping back on his pillow. He squeezed them tight shut as pain surged once more through his aching body.

'I'll be damned,' he muttered 'if it isn't the same leg I've broken. And the same lad here to tend me,' he added with a wry glance at Jack. 'Make yourself useful, would you. There's a flagon of brandy in the drawer.'

'I'm afraid there isn't, sir. Bad for the frostbite, Isaac says. Captain Ross took it away.'

Henry grimaced and attempted unsuccessfully to get out of his bunk.

'We'll see about that! Fetch Ross, this minute.'

'He's busy, sir. Bringing up the casks for that whale you struck. That was quite a strike – just behind the head,' Jack placated him. 'You'd make a good harpooner.'

'Harpooner, be damned! Am I to lie here groaning like an old man for want of a drink? I'll not have it, I tell you!.'

'You can have gruel and warm tea – that's what Isaac says.'

'That's what Isaac says!' Henry mimicked. 'You listen to what I say or I'll see you suffer when we get home. There's a barrel of rum in the store. Take

Ross's key from his cabin and get me some of that. And be quick about it.'

Jack left the room without a word and returned with a mug of warm tea. Henry's shaking hands, anticipating liquor, reached out for it then flung it away in disgust, splattering the walls and floor. Anger replaced respect as Jack mopped the mess from his breeches.

'I risked my life for you out there,' he cried, 'and you ain't worth it! You ain't worth nothing!'

To his surprise, Henry sank back, crushed, and lay with his eyes closed for several minutes.

'Aye. You're right, Jack. I'm a worthless fool,' he said at length. 'Twice you've saved my life. You deserve something in return. Tell me. What can I do for you?'

Stunned by this suddenly penitent Henry, Jack stared at the worn wooden desk in front of him with its anchored pot of royal blue ink. An idea occurred to him as he stared. An idea that would occupy their time and benefit them both.

'Would you teach me to read and write, sir – while you're lying there with nothing to do?'

Henry, still wincing with pain, looked at him thoughtfully.

'Why not, indeed? You're a bright lad. I'll teach you to read and write like a gentleman.'

Jack's face glowed. How strange life was. Some good had come of a bad situation.

'I'll get you more tea, sir. Perhaps you'll drink it this time,' he grinned.

Chapter Thirty-Three

Henry rose to the challenge Jack had set him. He prepared work painstakingly, watched his pupil's first faltering attempts to write and took genuine pride in his progress. But, his own demons were never far away. By night, as well as day, hallucinations plagued him so that he cried out, wide-eyed with terror, and shrank more than once into Jack's sturdy, steadying arms. Not once, however, as he battled his craving did he ask again for the return of his flask. In spite of sickness, fever and sleeplessness he showed a rare determination to repay his debt.

After three weeks, he emerged from his drink-fuelled existence a quieter, more pensive man, content to listen for hours to Jack's halting words and to watch his resolute hand labour across a page. After three more weeks a rapport which bridged the social divide grew between them, perhaps even a dependence on the part of Henry – a realisation too that being of service to others was helping him survive.

Jack was now official cabin boy to the officers on board, a job he did not relish but could perform while his head teemed with the exciting world of books that Henry had made accessible.

As the Polestar sailed south down the Davis Straits however, on the last leg of her journey home, her fortunes changed. Narrow passages of water opened up in the pack ice, only to close again minutes later, threatening to crush the ship's hull like the shell of a walnut. Captain Ross hurried between stem and stern and crow's nest, barking orders to the crew. Wiping frost from the windows, Jack pressed his face against the panes. What he saw sent adrenaline coursing through his veins. A berg was approaching at about three knots. The force of its progress on the field of ice was pushing the ship before it to what seemed like certain destruction. Not waiting to be summoned, Jack raced up on deck and sought the first mate.

'What shall I do, sir? Tell me what to do!' His words were lost amid the deafening roar of advancing ice but he heard the bellowed reply.

'Hoist the jib and the stay sail on the top mast. Help the men, lad. Hurry! Hurry!'

Jack needed no further exhortation. The huge white mountain bearing down on them had sent the crew into a frenzy of activity and some, anticipating disaster, had even run with provisions to the boats. The prayers of the devout were answered, however, and even the godless amongst them muttered their thanks to the Lord as the sails filled and the captain was able to cast the ship between the berg and the broken-up floe. Words could not describe Jack's feelings as the majestic monster glided by.

But danger was still present. The splintered floes, forced out of its path, were now being compressed into a solid mass. The Polestar was beset, immobile in a white wilderness that stretched as far as the eye could see.

Captain Ross paced the ship boards, peering over the bulwarks to gauge the safest place to cut a dock.

'I shall set the watch and we'll saw round the clock,' he announced. This entailed the men slicing through ice sometimes seven feet thick to create a refuge, but they would be at risk until the work was done. Jack volunteered to take his turn.

In Henry's cabin, the very walls creaked ominously and the door no longer closed in its frame. He himself had limped to the adjoining room to view the scene from the small square windows in the stern. Although his leg had healed, there was no strength in it. He would be a burden to others if they had to take refuge on the ice. He was weary now of his Arctic adventure. The men were unwashed, their hair and beards encrusted with smoke and rancid oil, and the galley stank like a fox's lair.

That night, conditions worsened, the cold increased and the ship's deck tilted as the vice-like jaws lifted her several feet out of the water. There was no way of knowing if she was doomed until the ice released her. Captain Ross ordered the men on deck with basic supplies to await their fate. Henry too, he decided, must be helped upstairs away from the risk of collapsing timbers.

'You must be ready, sir, in case she goes under,' Jack explained quickly, as he packed his master's possessions in a wooden box bearing the family crest. Henry sank into the captain's leather chair, his face quite calm, his voice when he spoke, unruffled.

'No. You must be ready, Jack, and you must take my things. I should like that. With your good fortune, you will survive. As for me – I shall stay down here. It's of no great consequence whether I live or die.'

'I don't have luck. I have purpose, sir. And so should you. Your life is of value,' Jack responded, his anger returning.

'Of value to whom, I wonder,' Henry mused, his eyes drawn now to a tankard of ale left in a hurry by one of the men. He stared for a moment at the golden fluid that he had not tasted for over six weeks, swirled it gently then lifted it towards his lips.

'Of value to your child, sir,' Jack cried, before he could stop himself.

It had the desired effect. The tankard was replaced with a thump on the table. 'What child, Jack? I have no child. This is no time for games.'

'You do have a child, sir,' Jack repeated quietly.

'That's a lie, Jack! Drink has rendered me impotent. The night you came across me in the storm, I was returning from a woman I had no wish to wed. She claimed I had fathered her child but we both knew it wasn't true. She died of a fever when I left her, it seems.'

'No sir. I refer to Beth. She had no wish to compromise you. This child could only have been yours.'

Henry leant forward in his chair, suddenly taking in every word.

'Beth? By Jove, I do believe you. That is why she left. Me, a father? Well I'm.... I'm delighted!' He slapped Jack on the shoulder. 'My little moorland waif! Who would have thought it?' His voice was transformed with excitement. 'Take my box upstairs, Jack, and anything else that will keep us warm. You and I are going to survive!'

Under a leaden sky in that desolate landscape, the seamen sharing a common peril huddled together on the deck. They talked of loved ones, murmured comforting melodies and sometimes hymns, aware that the boards beneath were all that stood between them and a watery grave.

Good fortune prevailed. The next day a dock was completed and the ship remained safe from destruction for a full week before a heavy swell broke up the floe. Passages began to appear so that the Polestar could be towed and warped, tracked and heaved towards good sailing water. The exhausted men, led by Henry, expressed their joy with three loud cheers which echoed for miles across their saviour, the North Atlantic sea.

Chapter Thirty-Four

Higher! Higher!' Daisy pleaded as the swing soared towards the last remaining blossoms on the apple tree.

'Hush, child. That's enough. My back aches from pushing you,' Beth protested, lifting the slight figure with difficulty back onto the ground. 'Find your papa now. I must go and rest.'

Daisy's impish grin disappeared as quickly as the spring sunshine behind the moving pockets of cloud.

'Papa's not coming back next week. Mrs Ruston don't want him no more.'

She looked down, blinked away a tear and kicked the tip of her almost soleless shoe against the turf.

Surprised by this news but seeking to reassure her, Beth drew the child close.

'I shall miss you too, Daisy. But the mistress must have her reasons. And your papa grows his own vegetables, does he not?' Daisy wiped her nose on her sleeve and nodded doubtfully. 'Well then, you must help him. Perhaps one day I'll visit your home and take you to the beach for a treat. Off you go, now.'

Beth watched as Daisy dawdled out of sight with a final wave. It was strange that no one had mentioned the gardener's dismissal. A definite twinge in her belly distracted her from the matter, however. Had her exertions brought about the first stage of labour? After all, her time was due and she had been aware since morning of a feverish energy and an unusually high colour in her cheeks. Childbirth was an intense drama in any woman's life. She was all too aware that what should be a joyous event could so easily become an unbearable disaster.

As she ambled back towards the house, the griping pain returned, radiating now from her back to her groin and down the inside of her thighs. She rested against a broad oak, breathed deeply and closed her eyes. For some reason her thoughts scrolled back to the Sunday service at Skellfield, to the day she had dropped her prayer book in the aisle; how Henry had paused with his escort and winked at her as he gathered up the pages and the broken spine and replaced them in her trembling hands. Dear Henry! She loved him so – but he would never know the outcome of his brief unwise liaison. It would be forgotten, like all the other episodes in his chaotic, self-destructive life.

As the pain receded, a new confidence swept over her. This child was meant to be. Why else would good fortune have brought her here to this house, to a benefactress who had fed her and allowed her to rest and grow strong? She would be attended by Grace, whose coarse hands she had been assured were adept at ushering infants into the world. Why should she be fearful when she might have been compelled to give birth in the workhouse?

Forcing herself to stroll across the courtyard and through the pleasant, lilac-scented rooms of the house, she found Grace knitting by the kitchen range. The older woman showed no emotion, in fact went on knitting as a further contraction caused Beth to gasp.

'Relax, child. The clock's scarce struck five. There'll be no bairn before sunrise tomorrow, I can assure you of that.' Even so, she put aside her needles to griddle ash from the grate and stoke the embers with a fresh supply of coal. 'Get me some pans. We'll need hot water. Lots of it. Ewers, basins ... and three-ply linen thread from the sewing drawer.'

Keen to keep moving, Beth busied herself with errands, pausing only to glance at the fingers on the clock at the start of each seizure.

'Ten minutes between,' Grace muttered, twisting and knotting the thread to form ligatures before dropping each one in a boiling pan. Mrs Ruston, hearing the clatter from below, emerged from her room and peered over the landing with her hair in disarray.

'The child is to be born this night, is it not, Grace? Oh, the excitement of it! Bring me my salts or I shall surely faint. Take the girl to my chamber and see that she has a bath.'

This was a new experience for Beth. Sighing with pleasure, she submerged her swollen body in the porcelain tub, enveloping herself in its womblike warmth. When she emerged, smelling faintly of lavender, Grace had lit a fire in her room and placed brown paper and fresh sheets on the bed. A small frame stood near the hearth and on it already hung an infant's clothes. Beth picked them up, one by one, with shining eyes.

'They're so tiny,' she marvelled. 'Oh Grace, I'm so happy! You are all so kind.'

Grace appeared not to have heard and bustled on with her tasks. There was no cradle as yet but a basket with a flock pad and a winding sheet lay on the dresser. Next to it was a tray containing scissors and bowls. She indicated, somewhat impatiently, that Beth should sit down by the window and keep out of her way.

'But I wish to help,' Beth insisted, feeling quite unable to remain still.

'If you want to help, you'll sit down and do as you're told without question,' Grace retorted. 'You've a long night ahead.'

Subdued, Beth turned her gaze towards the sky outside the mullioned panes. Gashes of red seeped through a veil of distant cloud, casting a pink tinge on the riot of blossoms in the garden. It would be a fine day tomorrow. Soon her baby would lie under the boughs, listening to the soft breeze, watching petals fall at this most beautiful time of year. She brushed away a tear as another contraction gripped her, stronger this time, catching at her breath and lasting longer than before. As Grace had predicted, it would be a long night.

By two in the morning, all three women were tired. No one could sleep. The drawing room was littered with weak cups of tea as Mrs Ruston paced its polished floor in a velvet robe, as though she herself were being delivered of a child.

'Still in the first stage,' Grace informed her as she passed the door with another shuttle of coal.

Beth moaned as the spasm abated once more but anticipation of the next left beads of sweat on her forehead. Still ten minutes between. Was she making no progress at all? Grace knitted silently in the corner, apparently resigned to this state of affairs.

By four, when Beth had scarce recovered from one bout of pain before another began, Grace put away her wool and washed her hands. The intensity increased till Beth knew not how to endure it and cried out for Jack, in spite of herself. Her eyes fixed upon the oil lamp, impervious now to everything except the need to expel her child. Mrs Ruston, with a handkerchief held to her face, put her head round the door.

'T will be born within the hour,' Grace informed her, 'if all goes well.'

'Give Beth some laudanum afterwards, Grace. It will make her sleep.'

Beth shook her head.

'No, Grace. I don't want to sleep. I want to see my child.' Agony enveloped her once more, unceasing, permeating every nerve. She cried out for help from the Almighty between clenched teeth. Several minutes passed, every second of which was excruciating, before the pain slowly ceased, leaving her sobbing with relief and joy and gratitude as her son was born. He was here at last. She need endure no more. A thin puling wail told her that the child Grace was separating from her with linen thread was alive and well. She watched her deftly wipe the lolling head and the frail body with a warm towel.

'Let me hold him!' She smiled weakly with outstretched arms but Grace was not listening or, in fact, attending to her at all. 'My son, let me hold my son!' A slow, seeping haemorrhage was stealing her strength so that her voice was barely audible. Without a word, Grace bound the infant in a winding sheet, placed him in the basket and carried him away.

Beth's eyes widened in horror. Her vision clouded. The room, with its litter of soiled instruments and blood-stained sheets, faded like a bad dream into dancing shadow. She wanted to crawl out of bed, to scream for her son but she was too feeble to move.

'Let her be,' she heard Mrs Ruston say. 'She won't survive. If she does, I know a place that takes women such as her. It's no less than she deserves. But this child is mine. I shall call him Robert.'

Chapter Thirty-Five

Henry clambered with difficulty into the boat that had been launched to take himself and Jack ashore. The familiar sweep of Scarborough's bay lay ahead, basking under an early morning August sun.

'Take care, Ross' he called as they drew away and the Polestar weighed anchor. 'My father's lost ships before on the last leg home.' Lured by the sight of green cliffs after months in the north, the unwary could be swept onto rocks in a sudden squall.

'Aye,' the Captain shouted back. 'There's a graveyard of wrecks between here and Hull but, rest assured, I'll not be one of them'.

Jack saluted, with gratitude and respect, an outstanding whaling master. What an adventure it had been. Even on a diet of ship's biscuit and salt meat, he seemed to have acquired a maturity and strength unique to these seafaring men.

Only when the crew waving from the rigging became indistinct did Jack's thoughts turn to the life he had left behind. So many questions now remained to be answered. Beth was in good hands but how would she react to Henry's undoubted interest in her child? And how would Michael receive them when they appeared at the farm? Emotions that had lain dormant in the Arctic for nearly half a year began to emerge. His pulse quickened as he scanned the people and horses going about their business along the beach. In reality he knew that neither Ramona nor Storm would be there to greet him but as their craft rolled in on the surf he saw a familiar figure setting out fish near the harbour wall.

'Over there – it's old Sam,' he told Henry as they waded across the silvered sand. Two seamen carried their boxes to the quayside and smiled their thanks as Henry bestowed a shilling on each of them. The voyage had been rewarding. They would be free from hardship until the spring. When they had gone Jack pushed back his cap, removed his tight moleskin jacket, and prepared to lift Henry's possessions onto his broad back.

'I'll leave them with Sam and collect them later,' he explained. 'Can you walk up the cliff to the Bell Inn, sir? They have carriages there that run through to York.'

'You're a good man. I shall do as you suggest and exercise this leg of mine,' Henry replied, showing some of his old high spirits. 'And I shall order a splendid breakfast for the two of us.'

Sam did not recognise Jack at first. This was no boy who stood legs astride and hands on hips before him but a man deeply bronzed by the Arctic sun. Muscles rippled beneath his braces as he set down his boxes and extended a firm hand. The old man paused, then grasped it with surprised delight, reluctant to let go. As soon as Jack pressed him for news, however, he seemed ill at ease and turned away.

'What is it, Sam? Is it Beth? Is something wrong?' He moved round to confront him, seeking the truth behind his troubled eyes. 'Tell me, my friend. You must tell me.'

'Aye. It's about Beth, Jack.' He sat down wearily and took out his pipe. 'Soon after you'd gone, it seems, Michael turned her out. She came down here. Said nothing of this to me. The last time I saw her she was walking up the cliff towards the church. Me and the missus would have taken her in. But it was too late, you see. We didn't know what had happened. Ramona, poor lass, came looking for her the very next day. Asked everywhere, she did, but there's been no word of her since.' He lit his pipe slowly and blew a cloud of smoke before looking up. 'I'm glad you're back, mind. You're the only one who might find her now.'

Jack was quite speechless with shock. Remorse and fear for Beth's safety overwhelmed him. He should never have left her. He should have known better than to trust a man like Michael. Not even for his wife could he keep his word but Ramona was wed to him now. Her fate was sealed. Beth, on the other hand, was adrift in a friendless world. Jack found his voice at last and punched a fist in the air.

'By God, I'll find her! I'll find her somehow!'

Sam shook his head sadly.

'Not at the workhouse, you won't. And she's left

no word with Nell. You could try the coachmen in the town, I suppose.' Jack ran up the steep cobbled track to the Bell, dodging carriage horses as they swept round the tight corner of the yard. It was market day and farmers and traders had congregated there to drink coffee and tea and eat slices of ham. Jack spotted Henry enjoying the plentiful supply of food by an open window but ordered an ale for himself. He drank half its contents before mingling instead with the post boys and coachmen. His urgent enquiries about a woman with child raised eyebrows and blank stares but that was all. No one had seen her. He would have to tell Henry, he decided, as he pushed past a man in a soiled waistcoat to reach the only remaining vacant chair.

'Have a coffee, my dear fellow. It's delicious. The best for six months.' Henry's aristocratic voice carried across the room, bending eyes and ears towards him. His reaction when he heard the bad news, however, was the same as Jack's.

'She must be found. That is all there is to it. Someone must have seen a woman in her condition.'

The countryman at the next table shifted slightly and rubbed his mud-ingrained fingers together.

'What's it worth to you?' he muttered, like a ferret on the scent of its prey.

'A lot,' Henry stated emphatically, 'if you can help us. If what you say is true.' He took some coins from his pocket and placed a sovereign in front of him. 'Start talking, my friend.'

The man lowered his voice further.

'I'm a gardener, see. About May it would have been, the mistress arrived home with a girl in her carriage such as you describe. I remember I was surprised because she was big with child. Well, I keeps myself to myself. I don't ask no questions. But that girl was still there when the mistress paid me off, sudden like, at the end of May.'

Convinced his story was genuine, Jack's patience ran out.

'Who is this lady? Where does she live?' he demanded.

A flicker of the weasel eyes towards Henry indicated that another coin was required. Apparently satisfied, he slipped the shilling in his waistcoat, then stooped towards them as he got up to leave.

'Mrs Ruston. Oxpasture House in Raincliffe woods. That's all I can tell thee. Good day.'

'What a stroke of good fortune,' Henry breathed, handing Jack a roll with a dish of fresh prawns. 'Eat up. We'll find a carriage directly.'

Soon they were following the route that Beth had taken, through tree-lined avenues into country lanes. They turned into woodland, past a lake and, after some debate with the locals, found the secluded track which no longer bore the name of the Ruston's house.

'Our Beth has done well for herself, it would seem,' Henry commented as the horses pulled up outside an elegant porch. The bell brought no response but Jack's urgent knocking brought a reluctant maid to the door. She ushered them into a drawing room where they waited for a very long time, hearing only whispers and scurrying feet. Eventually, the mistress of the house appeared and humoured them with apologies.

'Servants, you know. You can't keep them out here and it's not easy when your husband's away. Do take a seat. I'm Mrs Ruston. Now what can I do for you gentlemen?' She sat very upright with hands interlaced in her lap as Jack explained the purpose of their visit. If it was a shock to her, she did not show it. Instead she feigned grief with a dramatic flourish of her handkerchief.

'I wish with all my heart it was not my sad duty to tell you – but tell you I must – that your cousin died in childbirth.'

Jack's throat constricted. He couldn't breathe or speak.

'My God, no!' Henry gasped. 'And the child too?'

'She had the very best care here but her son died also. They are buried in the garden. You must visit the grave before you go. I'm really so very sorry. She was always frail, you know. We found her collapsed on the street and I wanted to help her. Believe me, I did. But it was just not to be.'

She took them to the walled garden, unlocked the gate and led them to the bed of well-tended roses where Robert Ruston's tiny plaque had been. A recently inscribed stone bearing the simple words 'Beth Cartwright and son. Rest in Peace' had replaced it.

Jack gazed until the letters blurred at this stark, irrefutable proof. Beth was dead and so too was the child she had longed for. He turned on his heel and strode quickly away. Behind him, Henry remained with head bowed by the grave, shedding unashamed tears.

Chapter Thirty-Six

Henry and Jack said little as the horses, tossing their heads in the heat, trotted briskly back to the Bell. The richness of colour in the hedgerow and the chatter of bird song, which should have stirred their senses after months at sea, flashed by unobserved. Both, stricken with guilt and remorse, sat lost in their own thoughts until the carriage pulled up in the cobble-stoned yard. Was this the point at which they would go their separate ways, Jack wondered, each carrying their grief with them? He offered his hand in farewell. But a valued friendship, based on mutual respect, prompted Henry to suggest an alternative.

'I need a manservant and you need a job, do you not? You must come back to Skellfield with me.'

Jack's normally sharp brain had deserted him. He stared uncomprehending, at the stable lads and tradesmen going about their business, feeling removed from their world and unreal, as though only his substance remained. Without waiting for a response, Henry called to a passing footman.

'Has the mail coach left, young man?'

'Aye, sir. There won't be another till dawn tomorrow.'

'Then we'll take the stage to York,' he announced, pointing to a carriage already groaning beneath the weight of its passengers.

'You won't like that, sir,' the lad replied. 'Pack 'em tight they do – and there's no guard on board.'

But Henry was not in a mood to be idle. Still resolved to change, he wanted to be away from the lure of the ale-house, to return ~~quickly~~ home and to make amends at last to his long-suffering family.

'Get our boxes, Jack, or they'll be gone without us.' Henry was already clambering up the steps to claim a seat inside. The decision taken from him, Jack did as he was bid. There was just enough time to secure their baggage and a place for himself on the roof before the coach rumbled forward. His legs dangled precariously over the side but the position offered him a view and the breeze, he found, soothed his turbulent thoughts. As the horses toiled up Racecourse hill, he leapt down to relieve them until they reached the brow. From the summit, it seemed, he saw nothing but sadness. Behind him was the sea whose once-beckoning waves now filled him with guilt; far to the right, in a walled garden, lay Beth's final resting place and ahead, just coming into view, Hilldene – and Michael's wife, the girl he could not erase from his mind. There was still time, he thought, to abandon his journey and appeal once more to Ramona's free spirit. But the moment passed and the carriage rumbled on, bearing him away from her life forever. He did not look back.

It was five long hours before the coach arrived at the George in York. Henry emerged stiff from the cramped seats inside to find himself jostled by people in the street. On enquiry he soon discovered why.

'Richard Oastler, sir,' a merchant informed him. 'The factory king, they call him. A fine speaker! Always guaranteed to draw a crowd. Down at the Knavesmire, you'll find him.'

'A crowd, be damned!' Henry muttered. 'It's a public disturbance. It shouldn't be allowed. Hire a hansom cab to get us to Skellfield, Jack. Offer over the odds if you have to. I shall wait in the hall.'

The landlord, spotting Sir George's son, stooping beneath the beams, bore down upon him with hand outstretched.

'Well, if it isn't Sir Henry!' he exclaimed.

'Not Sir, merely Master,' Henry corrected him.

The obsequious smile faltered as did the outstretched hand.

'You mean, you don't know?' the dapper figure stammered, extending a protective arm instead. 'I think you had better come this way. My wife will explain.'

What it was that Henry didn't know, Jack was left to ponder as he set off to order a two-horse cab. He paused to watch the tide of humanity sweeping towards the Knavesmire, wishing that he too could join the procession to hear Mr Oastler's stirring words. He owed it to Beth and William to support their cause and if Henry's patronage could help him do so, his future might yet have a purpose. The thought raised his spirits slightly. That indeed would be a fit tribute to his cousins.

When he returned with a cab and a driver to the forecourt of the hostelry, Henry was waiting and bounded inside without a word. He offered no explanation for his silence as the horses threaded their way north, past the elegant theatre and the inspiring ramparts of the Minster. It was only when they slowed at the lodge and swung between the iron gates of Skellfield Hall that he turned to Jack with desolation in his eyes.

'It seems you must call me Sir Henry, now. My father died a month since, while we were at sea.'

Chapter Thirty-Seven

Ramona edged her way upstream with a gypsy's stealth, her dainty lace petticoat and fine riding-skirt hitched above her knees. She would be lucky to catch a trout in the full glare of the sun and the heat of the afternoon but she liked to remind Aggie of her countrywoman's skills. She had spotted a dark shape lurking under a stone and now her hand slipped with practised ease beneath its belly. In a trice she had scooped it onto the bank, just as she had with Jack almost a year before.

She removed her bonnet and lay back, allowing her coiffeured hair to spill out onto the long grass. Jack and Beth. They had passed so briefly through her life and only now did she realise how much they had meant to her. Jack had been right about Michael. He was not a man of his word. She would never forgive him for dismissing Beth. She had lost all contact with both of them in spite of her persistent enquiries in the town and vague stories of Jack having gone to sea. He had told her he believed in fate. Was this then her fate? Had she not married Michael simply because her father had forbidden it? Had her stubbornness guided her rather than wisdom? Or was it his last revelation on the gallows that Edward Cunningham was her father, not he, that had left her wilful and angry?

She sighed. Whatever her reasons she was Mrs Lockwood now. Mistress of Hilldene – but increasingly subject to Michael's will.

Tilly stopped grazing and tossed her head up suddenly. A coach was passing by on the road above and she whinnied softly to the horses. Shading her eyes, Ramona stared at it with little interest. The stages rumbled by several times a day. A young man with a cap pulled low over his eyes sat dangling his legs from the roof. He reminded her of Jack but he was too muscular, too bronzed and he was not looking back at Hilldene as Jack surely would have done, she thought wistfully. A tear trickled down her cheek as she remembered their embrace in this very stream. His tenderness and strength, his understanding and resolve – all qualities she had been too proud to value until he had gone.

She gathered herself up abruptly, placed the trout in a pack on the saddle and led Tilly forward up the steep incline. She had made her bed and she must lie on it and that was an end to the matter. When she reached the track that led back to Hilldene, the cob pricked her ears again as a horse approached at full gallop. It was Storm responding to the stab of Michael's spurs. The two pulled up in a cloud of dust.

'I thought you'd be all day at the market, Michael,' Ramona said evenly, returning his disapproving stare.

'Aye, I see that you did' he snapped. 'I buy you a stylish bonnet and you walk about like a common peasant when my back is turned. I want my wife to look like a lady.' He dismounted, approached her and tugged her dishevelled nut-brown hair hard to lift her chin upwards. 'Do you understand, Mrs Lockwood?' He caught sight of the trout and his eyes swept down to her soiled wet petticoat. 'You've been up to your gypsy ways again. I'll not have it, I tell you. Those clothes are the finest in the county. There's many a woman I could name would envy you.'

Storm, drawn to the sparkling water below, pushed suddenly past with flanks heaving and did not stop until he had dipped his foaming nostrils in the stream. Michael pulled Ramona down the bank and pinioned her against a tree, lifting her skirts roughly as he did so.

'But since you're no lady, I needn't treat you like one, need I, my dear?'

Ramona submitted to his assault, for that was what it was, because her spirit was broken and she could not face a life alone, alienated from her own people. She could rely on Aggie for comfort and Hilldene for security. That must be enough. Her eyes remained closed, her body motionless, her voice mute as he thrust himself against her in a frenzy of sexual excitement. There was no intimacy on her part, and his seemed confined to bodily need. When he had gained relief he simply dropped her skirts and walked away.

Ramona wiped her mouth on the back of her

hand as she watched him go. No wonder her father had cursed him. How naïve she had been! It was true, many finer women had set their sights on Michael. Yet she, a mere gypsy girl at Hilldene to help with the harvest, had caught his eye with her wild good looks. He had wanted to tame her, to cage her, a creature to be admired. She in turn had been flattered. It was her own fault if her conquest was proving hollow. But the cornflower-blue eyes that had dazzled Jack were developing a new steeliness. There would be no child unless she willed it. Her gypsy ways would see to that.

Chapter Thirty-Eight

The servants' hall, since Sir George's death a place of whispered confidences, was unusually noisy as the household gathered for their midday meal. News of Henry and Jack's return to Skellfield the previous day had given rise to a wealth of rumours. Annie's voice, as always, rose above the rest.

'Consumption. That's what my Joe heard. Beth had consumption and Jack took her away – so as to be no trouble. Died of a fever, she did.' She rolled her eyes for dramatic effect. 'That's why Jack went to sea. Broken-hearted, he was.'

Across the table, Mrs Bullen, still in mourning for Sir George, pressed a black lace kerchief against her swollen face and moaned softly into its folds. It was all too much. There had been nothing but misfortune since Jack and Beth had left and Henry had abandoned his bride at the altar. The house was not as it was. Lady Elizabeth had taken to her bed and the estate was falling into disrepair. They must be thankful for Henry's return but what good was a wastrel son with no thought but to amuse himself? She sniffed and drew herself upright as Mr Scott entered the room and assumed his place at the head of the table. At least Jack had returned. She smiled through her tears at the memory of the ragged mill child she had nurtured by her kitchen range. It had been a blessed storm that had delivered him here that night.

Mr Scott raised his hands, orchestrating silence with a mere glance of disapproval.

'Shame on you all. Have you no respect for your late master?' As heads bowed, he interlaced his fingers and spoke with carefully chosen words. 'You will all have your own thoughts on recent events but I want no more talk of it in this household. We have a duty to our employers at this sad time and that is not to indulge in tittle-tattle about what does not concern us. Is that understood? All you need to know is that the new Sir Henry is proving a great comfort to his mother and we can only hope that she will rally. As for Jack, I gather he is valued by his master and will continue as his manservant for the foreseeable future. He will take residence in one of the cottages and will be known as Mr Cartwright in recognition of his role.'

'Now, I'm sure you would all wish to join me in a prayer for the one person who is absent from this room, and alas from this life, for reasons we may never know. Beth Cartwright.'

Mrs Bullen buried herself once more in her kerchief, while Annie snivelled loudly until Joe, now her proud husband, placed his big red arms around her.

Several days passed before it became obvious that Henry had returned a very different man. At first it was assumed the shock of his father's death and the inevitable burden of responsibility this placed on him had taken its toll. But gradually it became clear that there was a much more profound change. The servants risked a scolding if they gossiped in the dark corridors of the house about the reclusive figure in the library who received his meals on a tray with a mere nod of acknowledgement. He seemed scarcely aware of their shadowy presence. A lacklustre pensiveness had replaced the old flamboyance. It was as though his resolute decision to reject alcohol had left him bereft of interest in other people or their lives.

His leg, weakened now by two accidents, had left him disinclined to ride or inspect the estate. Even his mother, in whose eyes he could do no wrong, preferred his youthful, drink-fuelled behaviour to this quiet acquiescent son who no longer teased and flattered her. There was no doubt that guilt and the knowledge that he could never make amends to either Beth or his father had deeply subdued him.

Only from Jack did he seem able to take comfort, encouraging him to join him by the fire of an evening to read and write as he had done aboard ship. On one occasion he had felt drawn to walk with a heavy heart through the tangle of briers to Beth's long-overgrown garden. There he had found Jack too, contemplating the small tapestry of plants that had given his cousin so much pleasure. They had sat in companionable silence, listening to the steady murmur of the river and the sharp calls of a blackbird marshalling its young. The poignancy of a single fast-fading rose was not lost on them. On the way back, Henry had paused to rest on his stick.

'I've been thinking, Jack. You've a sharp brain and you've proved that you can learn quickly. How would you like to manage the estate? I would teach you, of course, and oversee the finances. But I have no appetite to deal with the tenants and their petty complaints. That would be your concern. In time you would earn a good living, I believe. And the cottage in the courtyard would be yours to do with as you wish.'

If Jack, too, had not been wrestling with his own grief, he would have responded to the offer with open delight. It was, after all, a major achievement for a lad who had arrived here in fear of the workhouse. But that lad had matured into a wise and reflective young man.

'Well?' Henry prompted. 'What is your answer?'

Jack's concern was for his master. Would he not sink further into apathy, without obligations to attend to each day?

'I would be honoured, sir,' he answered shrewdly, 'but I fear your faith in me is more than I deserve. I should need a great deal of help from you.'

'That's settled, then,' Henry said with satisfaction. 'And you may still join me in the evenings to continue your studies. You shall succeed where I have failed, my friend, and I shall be content with that.'

'Nonsense, Sir Henry. When your strength and your spirits return, you will burn a path like a meteor across the heavens. As this single rose is my witness, I predict it,' he laughed with something of the old sparkle in his dark eyes. Henry laughed too but they both fell silent as the pale petals dropped one by one amongst the briers.

Chapter Thirty-Nine

Henry's spirits did not return over the following months. Fine carriages no longer rumbled down the long drive and liveried footmen were seldom seen ushering guests inside. A melancholic spell seemed to have fallen over the household as Christmas approached. Jack, grateful for his new responsibilities, threw himself into his work and allowed himself little introspection. His energies became focused on the new mood of reform that was sweeping through the counties. A few enlightened men were beginning to make themselves heard both on the streets and in Parliament. Men such as William Wilberforce, Titus Salt and Richard Oastler who saw the injustice in society and refused to accept it. Fate had given him the opportunity to better himself. Why should he, too, not set his sights high and join them in their valiant crusade?

To this end, he began to seek out the meeting houses in the towns and villages where reformers gathered and to speak up with increasing confidence. He became recognised as a passionate and convincing orator, treated with respect by those of his own persuasion but with suspicion by others.

On the estate, he brought a new urgency to the practical matters of the cottagers. Their roofs and windows were repaired, their children greeted by name and encouraged to visit him. When time allowed, he would even teach some how to write their names and smiled at their bright eyed delight as they chalked their letters on an old slate board. He even talked of setting up a school but this suggestion made to Henry one evening met with a sharp rebuff and a reminder that his job was to maintain the productivity of the land.

Jack checked his urge to use his powers of persuasion, merely agreeing with his master that he was right. After all, Christmas was almost upon them. He had no wish to jeopardise the generous bonuses being paid to the staff – bonuses he himself had negotiated during their quiet evenings together.

Tonight, Henry pushed away the books, lit a cigar and invited Jack to pour himself a drink.

'Don't refuse on my account,' he ordered with a tetchiness that Jack had learned to overlook. 'Damn it, have a drink if you want one.' It was evident he had not found serenity behind the quiet closed door of his study. His demons, even in sobriety, still plagued him every day. In an effort to distract him, Jack pointed to the portrait of his father on a sleek grey horse. The pooled light from a card table caught the proud aquiline nose and penetrating blue eyes that so resembled Henry's. His face dominated the panelled room, casting a permanently reproachful gaze on his son.

'Fine uniform, isn't it?' Henry mused, almost to himself. 'He was a fine man, my father. Fought at Waterloo, you know, alongside Wellington. I'm writing it all down in a journal. All his achievements so that the family will never forget. It's the least I can do for him now. That is what you must remember, Jack. You and I will always respect each other but we will always be different. I have a tradition to uphold, a centuries-old way of life to protect. One that could so easily be destroyed by your misguided ideas. Give the people a voice and power and they will overthrow you as the French overthrew their monarchy. And I shall never allow that to happen here.'

His eyes misted over in the firelight's glow as, lost in his own thoughts, he exhaled a column of smoke. Its distinctive aroma permeated the room. Jack allowed the silence to lengthen until Henry looked up, as though suddenly reminded of his presence.

'What about the wenches, Jack? he said, changing the subject. 'A young man like you should have a sweetheart, even a spouse. It would take your mind off the weighty matters that threaten to turn you into a dull companion.'

Jack paused for a moment, wondering how much of the truth to reveal. He had never told Henry about Ramona but as he looked at the familiar blue Cunningham eyes, a thought struck him like a bolt.

'My God, of course! She's your cousin!' he exclaimed.

'What the devil are you talking about, Jack? Has the brandy gone to your brain? I have no cousin that I'm aware of.'

'But you have,' Jack breathed, replacing his goblet with a firm thump on Henry's mahogany desk. 'Your father's ill-fated brother, Edward. It was Christmas, just as it is now. They were partying when a gypsy woman called at the hall. It appears she wanted to tell fortunes in return for a small piece of silver. Edward, the worse for drink, took a shine to her. Days later he drowned in the river, just as she had foretold.'

'How can you know all this, Jack? Why should I believe you?'

'I believe it,' Jack said simply, 'and you would too if you could see the gypsy girl with the bluest of eyes who bewitched my heart. I shall never be free of her. I know that now. I have tried to forget, to learn to love again but there is only ice in my veins and no amount of sweetness or beauty can penetrate it.'

'You believe it but how do you know it?' Henry persisted, riveted now by Jack's story.

'Because her father died on the gallows. I was drawn to Ramona as though by a thread but she ran away in terror and he fixed his black gaze on me, a total stranger. He threw me a sealed letter, insisting that he knew my future and that I alone should take it to her. It revealed that Edward Cunningham was her true father, not he, the man she adored, who had raised her since her mother died. She did not take kindly to this news and turned her back on the gypsy folk. By chance, that night we left Skellfield, she travelled with us on the road to Scarborough. I knew then I loved her but she was already set on another course. She's wed now to a farmer who I believe will destroy her.'

Jack retrieved his glass and drained its contents. 'So you see, I have not been blessed in matters of the heart,' he concluded wryly. 'But I have a purpose and you cannot dissuade me from that, my friend.'

Henry either disregarded this last remark or, being in reflective mood, did not hear it. His thoughts dwelt instead on Edward Cunningham's untimely death. A veil of silence had protected the family from the shame of it for the past seventeen years. Now the lead coffin buried deep in a secluded part of the churchyard was revealing its secrets, reminding Henry how closely his own behaviour had mirrored that of his uncle. A cinder rustled in the grate, producing a shower of sparks, and his eyes turned to rest on it as his mind scrolled back to the previous summer.

'I was drinking too, you know. In the boathouse, just like Edward. I loved the place. Had done since I was a boy. It was out of bounds, of course, but that was its attraction. That and the menace of the river thundering beneath the rotting boards. I stumbled upon Beth's garden by chance that afternoon. And I mean stumbled. Quite shocked her, I believe. But if she hadn't followed me out of concern, well who knows what might have happened? I remember being unsteady when I stepped into the boat. That's where I kept my liquor and I needed more. Beth stretched out her hand to catch me but instead we both fell. Of course she couldn't swim and soon lost

248

her strength. When my senses returned, I swear I heard Edward, urging me to let go, to let the river take me. But Beth was limp in my arms and I could not let it claim her too. I fought then for her life and mine. So you see, in a way, she saved me.' The small flame died and Henry paused to throw another log on the bed of ash and to draw on his cigar.

'Somehow, I caught the cleft of a tree and hauled us inch by inch out of that torrent. I gave her brandy from my flask. It revived her – brought her colour back – and suddenly the return of her little flickering life brought me more joy than I had ever known. We lay as in a dream under that afternoon sun and when I took her it seemed the most natural thing in the world. That is when my ill-fated son was conceived. In spite of the pain I cannot regret it and nor, I believe, would she.'

Preoccupied, Jack reached for the brandy and refilled his glass without reference to Henry. He swirled it gently round the bowl before he replied.

'You said so yourself, sir. We are different. Worlds apart. Beth would not have changed anything but she knew there was no future with you. She had a short sad life but she touched the stars briefly. Perhaps that's all any of us can hope for.'

Henry felt his throat tighten and turned away to hide a tear.

'Aye,' he whispered hoarsely. 'May she and my son rest in peace.'

'Come. We have purged out souls enough for one night.' Jack emptied his glass with an appreciative sigh, stood up and smiled at his host. 'And I must

take my leave before I develop a taste for your
Cognac. I bid you goodnight, sir.'

Chapter Forty

Snow fell gently over Skellfield on Christmas morning and lay virginal upon the long drive and rolling pastureland. Still no carriages came or went from the Cunningham household and the horses dozed in their stalls, enjoying an unaccustomed rest. Only Jack stirred amongst them as he saddled up Lady and led her outside. He attached a pack to the pommel, pulled his cap down low and set off at a brisk walk to tour the estate. He would do his round early, he decided, to ensure he was not late for the family's festive lunch. It would only be a small gathering: Henry, his wheelchair-bound mother, his sister Nell and her husband and their two young daughters, but Jack was honoured indeed to have been included. He was looking forward to the fat goose that Mrs Bullen had prepared with pride the night before.

'Good morning, Bess,' he called as he approached the first of the cottages and pulled up outside the rickety fence. A red-haired girl, struggling to usher the family's pig back into its pen, looked up and flushed when she saw Jack. His robust features and dark penetrating eyes had long fed her fantasies.

'Mornin' Mr Cartwright, sir,' she stammered, for some reason bobbing a curtsy.

'Can you catch a small package?' Jack grinned, delving into his oilskin bag.

'Oh, aye. That I can,' she said, darting to intercept the gift that was arcing towards her.

'It's some candy from Mrs Tuke's shop in York. There's a piece for you all.'

Her father, Ned Hutton, emerged from the open front door, beckoning.

'A Merry Christmas, Mr Cartwright. My missus has a high opinion of you. She bids you come in for some ale and a slice of her cake.'

'Another time, Ned,' Jack responded gathering his reins, then, seeing his daughter's crestfallen face, added kindly. 'The lasses will be jealous of your bonnie red hair.' The girl bridled with pleasure as she waved farewell. 'The sheep will need hay this evening, Ned,' Jack called back as Lady plodded on through the deepening snow. He would check the drifts and ditches himself for any that were trapped. Excited children had gathered near the lake. He paused to watch their scuffling limbs as they fought for a place on a makeshift sleigh, yet felt strangely saddened by the scene. Beth should have been here to absorb their laughter, to see the sun glinting through the threadbare trees.

When Jack, freshly changed, hurried into the great hall at midday to join the family, the same sense of mourning prevailed. Indeed Lady Elizabeth was still swathed from head to toe in black and merely nodded a greeting as he took his place at the table. The conversation was low key as the servants placed an array of festive dishes before them.

'Was there ice on the lake, Mr Cartwright?' the girls wanted to know, evidently longing to discard their bows and smocked dresses and to join in the fun.

'Indeed there was, Miss Alice, and on the water troughs too. But the sheep were sheltering under the trees.' He addressed his last remark to Henry, omitting to tell him that a gypsy boy had darted over the wall with a barely concealed rabbit beneath his coat. The incident had perturbed him. Was he poacher or gamekeeper now? His life was changing and his loyalties were constantly challenged.

Life at Skellfield had changed too, he observed. Since Henry's reckless rejection of Lady Jane Harrington on their wedding day, local society had closed its doors on the Cunninghams. No doubt this had contributed to Sir George's death and to his wife's weakened state. Jack did his best to lift their spirits with amusing tales but there was no disguising the cheerless mood.

Henry, all too aware of this, wanted the meal to be over so that he could retire to his private room. He sat with a fixed smile as the plum pudding arrived and the children clapped. Under Mr Scott's supervision, a blue flame engulfed it, consuming the brandy and blackening the holly and its crimson berries. No sooner had the crackling ceased, than Mrs Buchanan entered the room, glided in her usual silent manner up to Henry's chair and whispered mysteriously into his ear. He shook his head firmly and dismissed her with a movement of his hand.

'What is it, dear? What did she say?' his mother

demanded to know. She had not talked throughout the meal but her eyes and ears were alert to what took place.

'Nothing, Mother. A gypsy woman at the door, that's all. The usual thing. Wanting silver in return for mischievous talk. I've sent her away.'

'Then I shall see her, Henry. Mrs Buchanan, will you show her in? It's bad luck to send a gypsy away.' Lady Elizabeth had become autocratic of late and Henry judged it best to appease her.

'I shall take no part in this, Mother. But if you must, you may speak to her by the fire.'

Her wheelchair was placed near the hearth and a rug arranged over her lap. A dark-skinned woman, no great beauty, was presently ushered in and in spite of themselves the diners listened. Lady Elizabeth proffered her small white palm and looked intently at the cloaked figure before her.

'Tell me what you see, old woman, and you shall have a sovereign.'

There was a silence in the room for a full minute as the wrinkled, berry-stained hand encased Lady Elizabeth's and examined the lines. The children, their eyes wide as saucers, watched, transfixed by this unexpected drama. Candles that had thrown benign shadows moments before, seemed suddenly to produce fearful images. At length the gypsy women looked up.

'Fire. That's all I can tell you. I smell it. I feel it. A fire that will change lives.'

'Not here at Skellfield, surely,' Nell ventured to ask from across the table.

'That I can't tell you. I see only flames and panic and people running.'

Henry stood up, pushing his chair from under him with such force that it fell backwards.

'Pay her and take her away, Scott. I'll not have this nonsense spoken in my house.'

'Will my son have an heir?' But it was too late. The woman had gone. Lady Elizabeth's poignant question echoed unanswered round the great hall.

Chapter Forty-One

Daisy stopped on her way through Raincliffe woods and set down her baskets of freshly picked fruit. The midges here always vexed her. She swatted them with her battered straw hat, knowing the gesture was futile. Soon she would be away from the trees, she consoled herself, ~~and~~ enjoying the sea breeze on the road to the market. She was about to move on when a crackle of twigs in the bushes distracted her. A rabbit or squirrel, no doubt. Intrigued, she crouched down, waiting for whatever it was to break cover.

It seemed to be within the hedgerow of Oxpasture House. Five summers had passed since she had played there in the gardens while her father pruned the roses and dug the beds. Now the place was neglected and overgrown and few people knew what went on behind its handsome stone walls. Mrs Ruston had died the year before and been quietly laid to rest by the local priest. Her attempts to salvage her marriage by adopting a child had failed. In truth her husband had already transferred his affections elsewhere, a fact that his wife had known but tried not to believe. Always nervous and erratic, she had alternated between lavishing love on her son and retiring to bed with unexplained pains for days on end while her husband ignored the young blonde intruder. Village gossip concluded that the strain had finally broken her heart.

Daisy grew impatient.

'I know you're there' she said, creeping a step closer. The leaves first quivered then parted and two very blue eyes confronted her. Not a creature but a small boy.

'Bless my soul!' she exclaimed, knowing immediately who he was. 'You must be Robert. I've heard talk about you.' In fact, talk was all anybody had heard. Nobody had seen the child growing up in the confines of the Ruston estate.

He nodded gravely and stood up undaunted. Daisy stared at him as though she had discovered a rare bird in the undergrowth. He was golden-haired, robust and of average height for a five-year-old but seemed to her mature for his years. His voice when he spoke was precociously firm.

'I'm Robert and I live here. This is my house,' he announced, pointing behind him through the trees.

'I know,' Daisy said softly, 'and you have a swing under an apple tree.'

'How do you know that?' he demanded, and then in the same breath. 'Will you push me? Please come and push me. Please.' He was already heading down the drive, entreating her to follow.

'I can't come in here,' Daisy protested, picking up her baskets and looking from right to left, as she nevertheless trailed after him. 'You'll have me in trouble, young Robert, that you will,' she grumbled as she settled the smiling child on the swing.

'How did you know it was here?' he repeated, as he thrust his young limbs to and fro and gained height with Daisy's assistance. 'Whee! Look at me! Look at me!' he cried as he soared towards the ripening apples.

'Beth used to push me when I was your age.'

When the swing had slowed down and come to a halt, the boy turned his unflinching blue gaze towards her.

'Who was Beth?' he asked, this time waiting without distraction for her reply.

'Why, don't you know child? Beth was your mother.'

'My mother's gone to heaven. That's what Grace says.' Evidently he did not know the truth of his birth. Daisy, never one to curb her tongue, saw no reason why he should not.

'No, Robert. Beth was your mother. Truly she was. And a nice kind lady she was too.'

'You tell lies.' Suddenly, he was gone, his blonde hair bobbing in the sunshine as he loped like a deer through the long grass. Daisy watched dismayed as he disappeared indoors. Gathering her crumpled skirts and her baskets she headed towards the drive. She had better disappear too and quickly, before someone came out to scold her.

Arriving breathless in the dining room, Robert found he was almost late for lunch. His father had already taken his seat at the head of the table and he slid into his own opposite Grace, expecting a reprimand. But the two were deep in conversation, and seemed indifferent to his presence. In fact they had been discussing his future and their own. Grace had just informed Mr Ruston that her husband had escaped from the press gang after many years at sea. She must tender her notice so that they could flee inland, away from the threat of re-capture. Leaving her employer to digest this news, she retired to the kitchen without further comment.

John Ruston settled his stout frame back into his chair and glowered at Robert. His large hands gripped the carved wooden arms. This boy with his finely drawn features and shock of blonde hair bore no resemblance to himself at all. Why should he feel kinship to a waif born of a mill girl because his wife had wanted a child at any price?

It was true that his trips to Flanders to trade in cloth had destroyed his marriage. It was also true, too, that his devotion to the fairer sex had left him vulnerable to the charms of a Flemish woman he had met in the Guildhalls of Bruges. Now he wished to remarry and there was no place in his life for this cuckoo in his silk-lined nest.

Robert, unaware of his father's thoughts, stirred circles in his soup as he recalled his morning's encounter. He was unused to strangers apart from old Mr Parsons who came when it suited to teach him his letters. Since Mrs Ruston had died, Grace had ignored him, leaving him to wander alone round the house and the grounds. He found his own amusement and, knowing no different, was content but he was a thinker and his fertile mind demanded answers.

'Papa. Who was Beth?' he asked suddenly, continuing to swirl his soup.

'Who the devil mentioned Beth?' John Ruston growled, before gaining a grip on himself. 'I have no idea, Robert. Why should you ask?' Nevertheless, his dark eyes watched his son's like a hawk.

'A nasty lady in the lane told me Beth was my mother. I told her Mama had gone to heaven. Why did she say that, Papa?'

His father's face deepened in colour but he said nothing as he scooped up his soup, then wiped the bowl dry with a piece of bread. Already the boy was inquisitive and there were things he must never know. Robert unwisely persisted. 'Papa, Beth wasn't my mother, was she?'

'Damn it! Stop your questions! Leave the table and eat your bread in the kitchen. Tell Grace to come back. I've matters to discuss.'

'I wish I had got another Mama,' the boy thought as he stomped defiantly out of the room. His father was always cold and angry now and no one cuddled him anymore. He would seek out the kittens in the garden shed. They at least welcomed him with his saucer of milk and he could brush their soft fur against his cheek.

Grace put her flat expressionless face round the dining room door a few minutes later.

'Did you want me, sir?'

'Yes. Come in, Grace. We understand each other, you and I. You know my situation. The boy is already asking questions and I have a reputation to uphold.

Madame Van de Berg cannot be expected to share her future home with another man's bastard.' He dusted imaginary specks from his fine worsted jacket and straightened his stock before leaning his bulk towards her. Flattered, a glimmer of a smile crossed her habitually dour features as she too leant forward like a conspirator.

'I've been thinking,' he continued. 'Can you take the boy with you when you go? I shall not be ungenerous if you can find him a home. An orphanage perhaps, in the West Riding.'

Grace tapped her nose and raised another smile. She had always resented Beth and her offspring's unwarranted place in the household.

'You leave it to me, sir. I know just the place. The mill. Beth told me about it. Back where she came from. Now what could be fairer than that?'

Chapter Forty-Two

John Ruston was conveniently away a month later when Grace took up the reins of a small covered wagon drawn by a stout mare and left Oxpasture House for the last time. Beneath the canvas, amongst the boxes and bags that represented her life, sat her fugitive husband, Tom, and a wide-eyed Robert clutching a black kitten from which he had staunchly refused to be parted. The child was both excited and afraid and sought reassurance from the shadowy figure beside him.

'Where is Grace taking me? When will she bring me back home?'

The man, reeking of cheap ale, pressed his dark bearded face within an inch of his own..

'You're no little lord now, boy. There's nowt grand about you any more. So keep your mouth shut unless I tells thee to speak.' Robert shrank back in alarm as the wagon lurched forward under Grace's unskilled guidance.

'Let me drive the nag for pity's sake, woman!' Tom called from the rear but his wife, equally robust in strength and will, pushed him back firmly out of sight. No press-gang was going to seize her man again. She made a clicking noise and flicked the whip over the animal's haunches until it sped along at a satisfactory pace.

At the top of Racecourse hill, however, the mare trembled to a halt, exhausted. Grace was obliged to coax her off the road to a plantation of trees that bordered the heath. By chance, people had converged on the moor that day to watch horses race on a disused track. Knowing the rogues that frequented these events and the attraction a wager held for her husband, Grace cursed this stroke of bad luck. Everywhere small booths had been erected, beneath which thimble-riggers and card sharps were plying their trade, using sleight of hand to empty the pockets of simple folk. The lure was too great for Tom. Grace could only watch vexed as he pulled down the brim of his hat and slipped into the crowd.

Robert had never in his short life witnessed such a scene and, forgetting his fear, he peered open-mouthed through a gap in the canvas. The purple heath stretched under a blue summer sky to the sea. He watched as distant specks became shapes and the drumming of hooves became louder. Then a black horse thundered by in a cloud of dust, and all around, men cheered or jeered the favourite home. Huntsmen in scarlet and farmers on feather-hoofed mounts joined the general stampede past the post. When the noise and the feting subsided, his attention wandered.

On the far side, he could see ladies in carriages with parasols and felt suddenly forlorn. That was where he should be. His mama would never have allowed him on a wagon such as this. Tears welled but before they could fall, his eye met the gaze of a woman nearby. She sat quite motionless on a black and white cob. Her glossy hair, the colour of earth, was gathered at the nape and gleamed in the sun's rays. She alone had observed him and he felt consoled. He would slip out of the wagon and tell her he wished to go home, he decided, securing his kitten in a wooden box.

Her smile encouraged him as he approached but words would not come as he stared up at her striking blue eyes. He was looking at a mirror of his own. His heart gave a leap of joy. Perhaps this beautiful lady was his Mama. The one Daisy had told him about. She wore an elegant suit of silver grey which emphasised her trim shape. He put down his box as she bent low and extended a gloved hand.

'Good day to you, young man.'

He was about to respond when Grace's shadow fell between them.

'Pardon me, madam. My boy should know better than to wander off. Lord knows what might happen at a place like this.' The lady patted her cob thoughtfully as Robert withdrew.

'Then you shall have some white heather,' she insisted, unclipping a sprig from her silk lapel. 'Keep it, child, and it will bring you luck.' Her fingers brushed his cheek in a gentle caress before his guardian whisked him away.

'You'll give me no more trouble, either of you,' Grace fumed, passing the struggling child to Tom who, deprived of a sovereign on the thimble tables, was now disillusioned and willing to leave. She pushed them into the wagon and drew the canvas tight. As the mare jolted forward under pressure from the whip, Robert leapt to his feet.

'Wait! I've left my kitten. Let me go! Let me go!'

Tom's iron fist restrained his flailing limbs but his shrieks could be heard long after they had gone.

Too late, Ramona saw the small wooden box on the ground. The kitten spat at her when she lifted the lid and she closed it again with a sigh. She would take it back to Hilldene and keep it safe. Why she had been drawn to the boy and he to her, she couldn't explain. Perhaps the gypsy in her blood had sensed his distress. Or thoughts of Beth and her growing child had prompted her interest.

Where was she now, she wondered, and where was Jack? There had been no news of either for five long years. Five very long years as the chattel of a man devoid of any sensitivity towards her beyond that of seeing her clothed to his taste and responsive to his will. As she turned, preoccupied, to remount Tilly, a stranger gripped her arm. She sprang back like a wild creature before recognising the man's swarthy features.

'Aye, it's me – Franco,' he murmured, darting his eyes round the crowd before fixing them on her. 'What a fine lady you are, to be sure,' he sneered, 'with your buttons and bows and your high-falutin' hat. But it ain't you and it never will be. Leave him, lass. Come back to your own kind. I'll be at Seamer fair till the end of the week.'

Ramona did not respond with her past youthful

spirit. She had matured into a calm and reflective young woman and she chose to speak gently to her childhood friend.

'I shall always think fondly of you, Franco. But I've made my bed and I must lie on it. I'm neither one of you nor a fine lady. Truly, I don't know where I belong.' Franco's dark eyes narrowed and he drew back, jealousy curling his lip.

'I see it now. You can't deny it, can you? Your heart belongs to Jack. It's him you should have married.' His grip tightened on her arm. 'I'm right aren't I?'

'Aye,' Ramona replied wistfully. 'I dare say you are.' It was the first time she had acknowledged the fact, even to herself. A horse was approaching, its mouth flecked with foam and Ramona saw that it was Storm. Michael sat astride him, laughing, with a celebratory flagon of port in his hand.

'Go quickly, Franco,' she whispered. 'I wish you all the luck in the world but you must forget about me and find yourself a wife.' She touched his lips in farewell then turned quickly away to face her spouse.

Michael dismounted and tossed her the reins without a glance, addressing his entourage rather than her.

'Come. Let's collect my wager from these rogues. Didn't I tell you my horse would win? That was a fine race, was it not?'

When the jocular group had gone, Ramona looked in dismay at Storm's blood-stained flesh. He had been ridden too hard. Jack would have given him a good rub down but Michael left such matters to others. How she hated the constricting clothes that prevented her doing this simple task.

As she waited impatiently for his return a cry went up.

'Welshers! Welshers!' and several horns sounded from the centre of a mob. Suddenly booths were toppling as ruffians wielding table legs battled against the punters who were charging at them like enraged bulls. Deprived of his winnings, Michael too was flushed with anger and an excess of port.

Stumbling back to Storm, he heaved himself with difficulty into the saddle and raked the animal's flanks with his spurs.

'No, Michael! The horse isn't fit!' Ramona protested in vain. Everywhere farmers with clubs and huntsmen with whips were pursuing the thieves as though they were prey. Racing was abandoned in favour of the chase and Storm had soon galloped far out of sight.

Distressed at the plight of her beloved horse, Ramona turned away in disgust. Now all she could do was wait. Her husband would return as usual in his own time. She would go back to Hilldene, put on her dairy smock and help Nathan with the cows. As Tilly plodded back through the lengthening shadows, she could see him herding them in from the fields. The plough boy had grown into a thick-set young man as devoted to her as the dog that sniffed at her heels when her dainty boots slid to the ground. She hurried indoors to release herself from her tight-boned dress, then, relaxed at last, picked her way through the hens to the dairy.

She sat on her stool in quiet harmony with Nathan, hearing only the chewing of the cows and the rhythm of milk flowing into the pails. The monotony of the task left her mind free to wander and it was not until she stood up to wipe her brow against the heat of the afternoon that she became aware of the passing of time. At that moment she heard the irregular clatter of hooves in the yard and, stepping outside, saw a riderless Storm. Broken reins touched the ground and a stirrup was missing. So too was Michael. It was several hours before his body was found beneath a solid stone wall, ~~finally~~ fulfilling a gypsy's curse.

Chapter Forty-Three

It was known as the cooler but this time Beth was beyond terror as a nurse hustled her through the basement to the green-painted door. This time she did not protest. She was familiar with the windowless room and its single bed.

Beth sank onto it, looking at nothing, thinking of nothing, feeling nothing. After five years of confinement she was finally spent. She knew now neither pleading nor anger nor bribery nor reason could gain her release from this godless asylum. She would never be free. Never see her child. Rage and the wild fits to which she was prone, like the other inmates, were subdued by punishment; cold baths and tranquillising draughts and, as a final resort – isolation. The nurse thrust a goblet in front of her.

'Drink up!' she snapped, jangling her keys impatiently. 'I ain't got all night to wait on the likes of you.'

With a cunning she had learned, Beth tipped the vile liquid onto the floor. Soon after, the door slammed shut. She was unaware of the passage of time as the night wore on. The room became hot, the air fetid and her head ached as she tossed first one way, then the other on her narrow bed. The light, directly above, caught her red-rimmed eyes, denying her sleep and release from her misery. Somewhere on the ward above, the women with whom she shared her life could turn away from the night nurse's lamp. Here she was tormented by its yellow glow. Henry, Jack, Ramona and the infant son that had been snatched from her were at last receding from her conscious mind into some dim recess. She might just as well be dead. The thought had not crossed her mind before but it did now and she wondered dully how she could achieve it.

It was then, in her deepest moment of despair, that the idea came to her. An idea that gave her hope. She gazed upwards, seeing salvation suddenly in the oil lamp's flickering flame. There was after all no one here to watch her. Tearing the sheet from her bed, she knotted it loosely, then cupped it in her hand like a ball of wool. It was a reckless plan but she did not falter. Taking careful aim she threw the cloth high into the air. It soared over the glass funnel that contained the flame but her fevered brain was set on its purpose. She leapt onto the mattress, steadied herself and aimed again. Still the threadbare fabric would not settle on the light. At the sixth attempt she succeeded and gazed up ecstatic as a small singe grew into a large brown hole.

'Burn! Burn!' she breathed with an almost demonic grin. 'Please God. Let it burn!'

It was many months since she had appealed to God but, as she watched, a tiny spark grew into a flame, producing a column of smoke which curled along the ceiling. A soft rushing noise followed as the fire grew, enveloping the entire length of the sheet and kindling the mattress below. Beth, alert to its movements and oblivious to her own safety, pushed the bed head against the wall, watching in delight as the red glow advanced towards overhead beams. Only when the fire was well alight and the air so thick with acrid smoke that she choked, did she pound on the bolted door.

In the nick of time, she heard footsteps running, people cursing, keys turning in panic. The cry went up, 'Fire! Fire!' Then the door flew open and she stumbled out. The chaos that followed was complete as the crackling and snapping of flames continued. Soon everyone was coughing and no one could see beyond their own hands.

Beth could scarcely believe her luck. Crouched low beneath the smoke she felt her way along the wainscot. Without being challenged she glided as in a dream through doors that miraculously opened and gates that were no longer barred. All except, to her dismay, the main gate that gave access to the outside world. Stifling a sob, she shrank into foliage. To be denied freedom by two metal bolts was more than she could bear. Shivering in the chill night air of autumn, she watched as the commotion grew and people ran back and forth shouting for water, ladders and keys. Flames were playing up the building's grim façade. Somewhere a window exploded, showering shards of glass onto the gravel drive. After what seemed an age, bells and heavy rumbling wheels could be heard. Beth recoiled further and held her breath.

'Open up!' someone called. 'Open up! Let the fire wagon in.'

This was her chance and she seized it, darting perilously close to the horses hooves'as they sped through the gates. But the gateman saw her.

'Who goes there? Stop I say!' She did not and he launched himself at her, bringing her to the ground like a bird smothering its prey. Beth was powerless beneath his weight. The horror of her experience in the mill returned, rendering her suddenly as mad as any of the deranged people spilling out of the cramped wards. Her fingers, pressing frantically against the gravel, closed upon a shard of glass. The man rolled her over towards him so that his ugly misshapen nose was an inch from her own.

'You'll not escape,' he growled. 'You'll never escape from here. This is where folks like you ...' His voice faltered as Beth's piece of glass found its mark in his torso. He slumped with a surprised look on his face and Beth tore herself free. For a moment she stood with legs trembling, too stunned to move as she scanned the scene; the great blaze she had started that was now engulfing the roof – and the damning evidence of a man's blood on her gown.

Then, as though unleashed from a bad dream, she stumbled through the gates into darkness and ran and ran and ran until her sides hurt and she could find no more breath. Instinct carried her on towards distant lights. All else was a blur. She fell and got up and fell again, scuffing her knees but feeling no pain. Briers and roots tugged at her thin smock but she pressed on, clawing at branches, until the tangled undergrowth gave way to a path. The path gave way to a track, its ruts just visible under a harvest moon. Ahead lay a village, offering comfort and danger in equal measure.

Beth hesitated. No one could be trusted. No one. At dawn she would follow the sun to the east. But what if she was seen? She remembered with a stab of panic the blood still wet on her bodice. Her mind raced. Somehow she must conceal it. A lantern swayed above an ale-house door and after looking about for several minutes, she crept soundlessly towards it. There was no sign of life apart from the occasional shuffle of hooves in the stable behind. Through the small panes of a window, Beth judged that the hour must be late. A weary barmaid was collecting pots in a manner calculated to awaken her last remaining customer – a man slumped over a table with his back to the door. What Beth saw however, was not the drunkard but the cape he had tossed on the back of his chair.

Courage born of desperation guided her towards the entrance and her fingers towards the latch. Through an inch wide gap, she gazed round-eyed at the prize, waiting for the moment, the right moment. An inner door swung to. The room was briefly empty but for the sleeping figure. In a trice she had seized the hood and melted once more into the night. As her small feet sped, fast and hard under the moon's rays, Beth knew she had paid dearly for her freedom. Her actions had condemned her. She would never be the same.

Chapter Forty-Four

The moon cast a trance-like spell over Beth. Her legs seemed blessed with supernatural strength but as dawn broke through the overhead trees, will power alone could not sustain her. She stumbled, her rhythm broke and she found herself suddenly in a ditch full of leaves. At first she lay exhausted, listening to the thumping of her own heart, savouring the smell of wet earth and the sheer joy of freedom. Her teeth chattered and her body shook. She must not, could not stop she told herself. But to no avail – sleep intervened.

She awoke to the sound of a coach's wheels and shrank back in fright as four horses passed by. It was the mail coach. She had often waved to it from the gates of Hilldene and the post boy had sounded his horn in response. This happy reminder of the world she had known renewed her courage. She must think of her child. Henry must know what had befallen his son. She must find the strength to reach Hilldene before she was called to account for her crimes.

Suddenly her brain was alert. She must find the river and follow its course to the east as Jack would have done. No one would notice her there as they would on the road and the dogs, if they pursued her, would quickly lose her scent. She hurried on, hoping the small winding stream that had crossed her path would soon join the river. She had no food and no way of knowing how far she must walk but her heart was steadfast. She must succeed.

Beth struggled on for several hours through reeds and wet turf until the stream first widened, then burst upon a broad ribbon of water that meandered across pastureland dotted with cows. The River Derwent. Her judgement had proved right, she thought, quickening her stride. It would lead her to the very place where Jack had caught trout on the borders of Hilldene. The cows turned large impassive eyes towards her as she circled round them towards the bank but the sight of a man gathering cress from a seed bed set her shivering with fear. It was the start of a distrust of her own kind that would continue to plague her. Only when the man moved away and the birds sang again with full-throated ease did she dare to continue.

The noon sun gave way to cloud and the river soon reflected a pewter sky. Rain dimpled its surface as the day wore on. Beth became aware of a pain in her chest and a cough that became more persistent. Her head throbbed and she felt hot in spite of the chill wind. For the first time she wondered if her strength would prevail. Many miles, she felt sure, lay ahead. Nightfall, at least, would protect her from the real or imagined eyes that she feared. She had no desire to eat – in fact a plump apple she had found beneath a bough had caused her to retch.

Once more the moon rose, casting its pale image on the water and lighting the riverside track more brightly than she had thought possible. There was nothing to hinder her but her own fragile body. She heard the midnight hour strike on a church clock and trudged on with painfully blistered feet. She mumbled incoherently as different images from her past hovered disembodied in the gloom, sometimes fading, sometimes extending a hand which held no substance when she tried to grasp it.

She was not aware of the last few miles of her journey. Some instinct guided her faltering step to her goal. As the cock crowed in the farmyard, she pushed through the gate to the bottom field. Beneath lids half-closed by exhaustion, she saw the weathered stone house hewn into the landscape and the barns to the side, just as she remembered. Hilldene! Hilldene and Ramona and help at last. She tried to walk on but instead pitched forward into darkness and lay quite still.

Nathan unleashed the dog, whistling, as he set off for the bottom field.

'Come on, lass. Lets have those cows in,' he called as he swung open the gate.

The collie paused, scented the wind, sniffed the ground then scented again.

'What's up wi' ye this morning? Get on with it,' Joe called sternly.

The dog whimpered, distracted, looking first at his master then into a distant corner of the field. Nathan narrowed his eyes and followed her gaze. There was no cow in trouble down there but he could just make out a sack of some sort on the ground. No doubt a poacher had been disturbed. Serve him right too, he thought. He would pick it up later when the work was done.

'Nay, lass. Leave it! Leave it,' he repeated, prodding a cow's rump with his stick. 'Bring 'em in. There's a good girl.'

Encouraged by his voice, the dog settled to her task and obeyed.

Chapter Forty-Five

It was well past noon before Nathan remembered the sack in the corner of the field. Even then, with his tendency to daydream as he went about his tasks, he would have forgotten if Tilly had not been grazing there. As he slipped a halter over her head, he narrowed his eyes against the autumn sun. Was that not a human limb he could see? He looked again and his jaw dropped. Abandoning Tilly, he began first to walk and then to run towards the motionless form.

'God forgive me,' he murmured, as he drew back the wet cloak. 'A slip of a lass and I left her out here in the cold.'

There was a large bruise on her left temple and she lay face down against the stubble. Her skin and hair were caked in mud concealing her identity so that some moments passed before the truth dawned on Nathan.

'Why, if it ain't Beth Cartwright!' he exclaimed out loud. His shocked senses at first refused to function. Should he lift her? Should he fetch Tilly or call Ramona? Her body was chilled to the core. Had she already perished? No. He was sure he could see her chest move. Hope galvanised him. He must get her to warmth without delay. Scooping up the limp, weightless body, he sped across the field, through the crumbling gateposts and the mud of the farmyard and kicked open the front door with none of his usual servility.

He was met by an indignant Ramona. She was dressed in sombre mourning garb as befitted a widow. It was only four weeks since Michael's funeral cortege had passed from the house on its way to the church. Before she could chastise him, however, he burst past her to the kitchen and placed Beth near the range, just as he would have done an ailing lamb.

'Found her in the bottom field. It's Beth. Beth Cartwright!' He was breathless and his eyes did not leave her for a moment. 'I'll not forgive myself if she passes away.' He tried to tear, with urgency rather than tenderness, at her sodden outer garments. Ramona's hands flew to her face. She too was stunned by this turn of events. Behind her Aggie stood open-mouthed, her hat askew as usual. Quickly taking charge of her kitchen however, she pushed Nathan aside and turned to her mistress.

'You'll be wanting her in the spare room, I dare say. We'll need warming pans and hot water.'

'Yes, yes. That's right, Aggie.' Ramona struggled to compose herself. 'Poor, poor girl. What could have befallen her? Look. There's blood on her smock and her feet are blistered to the bone.' She placed an ear close to the stained bodice.

'Her heart beats still. We must hurry but treat her gently. Fetch blankets and dry clothes. Nathan, light the fire next door and another upstairs.'

Soon, firm caring hands were bearing Beth to a small back room. Logs, piled high in the hearth, crackled with vigour as her dripping rags were replaced with warm flannel sheets. She, however, was unaware of this as pneumonia tightened its grip. She was unaware for three whole days.

When consciousness returned, the concerned faces that hovered above her prompted no reaction. She saw a pleasant view through the ivy-framed window, and cows, like a child's cut-outs, on a *nd* green field beyond. She felt warm and cared for and enjoyed the thin gruel that trickled at intervals down her throat. Beyond that her world was a blank.

'It's me, Aggie. Don't you recognise me, child?' The cook withdrew in despair shaking her head.

Ramona stepped forward again to mop the fevered brow and returned Beth's blank stare thoughtfully

'We mustn't press her. She'll speak to us in time. I'll collect honey and rosehips,' she added, adjusting her scarlet cape over the foot of the bed like a gypsy's charm.

'Aye. I dare say you're right. Your country ways have done more for her than any doctor I know. I wouldn't have given a fig for her chances two days ago. We'll have her strong again yet.'

Little by little, Beth did gain strength and was carried downstairs to sit in the inglenook by the hearth. The peat fire cast a pleasant glow over the simple furnishings and she appeared to relax, listening to the ticking of the clock and the sound of the women going about their chores. The antics of a kitten with a ball of wool produced a wan smile which did not go unnoticed. Not once, however, did Beth show any recognition of her old friends or any awareness of past events. Gentle probing produced only a furrowed brow. She would fold her arms tight and rock the chair faster. All she remembered was an old cradle song which she hummed constantly as though it held the key to her shattered mind.

As days turned to weeks it became clear that Beth, though fit enough to perform simple tasks, had no recollection of who she was or where she had come from. Whether shock or concussion had induced it, her memory of facts and sense of identity showed no signs of returning as the evenings drew in. Ramona herself, striving to adjust to a new life, knew she must make decisions before the first snows fell. She must take Beth back to Skellfield. Surely someone there could unravel her past. Had she not talked of Henry Cunningham with a warmth that belied mere friendship? Could he have been the father of her child?

Ramona sighed and swept her long free-flowing hair into a band over her left shoulder. If only Jack was here. If only she knew where to find him. But he was gone from her life and would be too proud to return, however much her heart leapt when she answered a knock at the door. Over supper one evening, she announced her intention to Aggie and Joe.

'I'll take Tilly and the covered wagon and travel by the route I know. I'll go along slowly. Perhaps the fresh air will do Beth good. She's too much indoors. Too much afraid of the world outside.'

'Aye. And so should you be,' Nathan interrupted manfully. 'I'll not let you go on your own.'

'You will stay here, Nathan,' Ramona replied evenly. 'I'm the mistress of Hilldene and I need you to run it. Aggie can't manage on her own. Besides,' she added by way of encouragement. 'They don't talk to me in the village since Michael died. I need you to find some farm hands to help me.'

There was some truth in this. She was an interloper in the eyes of her late husband's family and friends. However, knowing Ramona's strong self-will when her mind was made up, Nathan acquiesced and promised to ensure that the wagon was safe and the pony sound.

'When will you go, then?' Aggie asked in a resigned tone. She could see the logic of the plan. 'If you ask me, the sooner the better while the tracks are still dry.'

Ramona got up and gathered some clothes from the rack overhead. She was focused now on what she must do.

'We'll leave at dawn tomorrow,' she declared, folding a clean woollen wrap. 'I'll explain to Beth as best I can. She'll need a suitable dress if we're to be received at Skellfield. And we'll take plenty of broth and fresh milk.' She put a delicate hand round the old woman's ample waist. 'You're a treasure, Aggie. This journey is right for all of us. Some good will come of it. I know it. I feel it. Trust me.'

'You and your gypsy soul,' Aggie laughed. Jack

had been right. She did have eyes the colour of bluebells in spring.

Chapter Forty-Six

J ack, looking very much the gentleman since his elevation to stewardship of Skellfield, pushed forward through the wildly applauding crowd. A closely buttoned coat, white neckerchief and shirt frills, displayed his manly figure to advantage. Smoothing his dark hair over his collar, he waded resolutely towards the man he had not seen for fourteen years but who, he knew, had fought tirelessly to expose the cruelties in the mills. Richard Oastler's mistake had been to threaten the owners with sabotage and strikes. Today however, after three years in Fleet prison, he was back in the North, campaigning once more and the supporters who had raised the funds to release him were ecstatic.

Jack was among this number. Improving the lot of the factory workers had become his crusade. A means of making sense of Beth's short life – perhaps too, of filling an emotional vacuum that Henry's continued friendship only partially satisfied. He had attended countless committees and arranged functions to boost the liberation fund. He had spoken passionately whenever he could in favour of the Ten Hours Bill which would limit the exploitation of children. But in spite of his obvious skills as a speaker, he was frustrated by his lack of gentry status. The nation was ruled by squires, parsons and wealthy landowners. Only recently had the new middle classes of industry and business been given a more just share of power in the House of Commons. Henry, who was careful not to encourage the reformers for fear they would rock the aristocracy as they had done in France, could so easily have become a Member of Parliament. Jack on the other hand, for all his fervour, could never hope to attain such influence.

Such was the throng around Oastler that no one but his henchmen could approach him. Jack positioned himself near the exit and waited in the portico of the town hall for his chance. When the powerfully built six-foot figure emerged, he thrust a hand firmly forward.

'A very good day to you, sir,' he smiled. When it was grasped in return, his smile broadened and he added. 'It is a privilege indeed to shake the hand of such a great man.'

Oastler paused, raised a dark eyebrow and surveyed Jack with instinctive interest.

'Have I met you before?' he enquired. The voice that resonated from his broad chest held a commanding presence.

'I doubt that you would remember, sir, but I do,' Jack replied.

'Tell me where, young man.' He showed no urge to move on until he had heard Jack's response.

'It was early one winter's morning – about fourteen years ago. 1830, I believe. I was with my cousins walking to the mill. You stopped your carriage and questioned us about our work. I'm sure you wouldn't recall such a small event, sir,' he added humbly.

'You think not, do you?' Oastler replied slowly. 'Then be assured. It was providence that brought you into my life that morning. Indeed I remember it well. That meeting with you and your two companions is etched on my heart. And to see you in such evidently improved circumstances confirms my faith in the human spirit. Everything is possible, young man. Everything, If we but persist. Wouldn't you agree?' He tapped Jack's shoulder with the tip of his cane. 'Keep up the good fight. We will succeed.'

He was gone, swept on by his entourage before Jack could find the right words to thank him. His throat felt tight and a tear threatened to slip from the corner of his eye. They had made a difference. He and Beth and William had made a difference. Stumbling into a cab, he sat misty-eyed, composing himself, before instructing the driver to return him to an inn on the outskirts of town. The journey took far longer due to the large swell of people cheering Oastler home. For that reason Jack did not stop for his usual refreshments with the genial innkeeper but went straight to the stables where his horse had been well fed and rested. With luck, he would be back at Skellfield before dusk and his duties there would not have been neglected.

His bay mare cantered easily over long stretches of leafy track but he checked her and rode on a loose rein for the last few miles to allow her to cool.

It allowed his mind to wander, too, and gave him time to appreciate the rich colours of autumn now glowing in the copses and hedgerows along the way. Was he not fortunate to live in such a place? Why, then, did sadness still drag at his soul? He glimpsed a black and white pony amongst the trees on the skyline and felt a stab of pain. Were the memories it evoked not connected with his listlessness? Why could he not find peace and happiness with any one of the pretty wenches that set their cap at him?

His thoughts turned to Henry and the quiet comradeship they shared. Their experiences would always unite them but his employer remained withdrawn and purposeless, content to let Jack take control of his life. He read literature for hours in his study and talked with belated admiration of his father's military campaigns. But any attempt on Jack's part to interest him in the cruelties in the mills met with a firm rebuttal and a reminder of who was master. The landowners had their own affairs to protect.

It was unusual therefore that when Jack joined him for supper that evening, he should have enquired, with perhaps more self-interest than altruism, about the scenes in Bradford that day. After all, this reforming zeal, however unwelcome, was touching his own doorstep.

'You met the great Oastler himself then, did you?' he asked with a mocking smile. 'Did he impress you?'

Jack took a sip of his brandy and strolled towards the window.

'The man is a gifted orator with a vision of a fairer world. I have the greatest respect for him. Peaceful persuasion can achieve a great deal.' He waited, resigned, with his back to Henry, for his customary lecture on the French revolution and the dangers of the rabble overstepping their station. His eyes were only half focused on the lodge at the end of the drive as a small covered wagon turned in. Suddenly, he was no longer listening to Henry. The wagon was drawn by a black and white cob.

The next chapter should
carry on here

Chapter Forty-Seven

Sensing his conversation was falling on deaf ears, Henry looked up at Jack who still stood transfixed by the window. Though his protégé did not sport the embroidered waistcoats and fripperies of his own class, he looked a man of distinction. The plain buff jacket that he had changed into after his long ride complemented his dark looks and, in profile against the light, it struck Henry that he had matured into a very handsome young man.

'What's caught your eye out there?' he laughed at last. 'Some wench, I suppose.'

There was a long pause before Jack responded.

'Some wench indeed,' he breathed, scarcely daring to believe what his eyes could now plainly see. 'By God, it is sir! It's Ramona. It's my Ramona!' Forgetting his usual courtesies, he bounded from the study, along the marbled corridor to the gallery of portraits in the great hall and beyond to the imposing front doors. It was not an entrance he would normally use but he did not hesitate.

By the time the covered wagon approached, he was standing astride the steps that swept down to the drive, his attention fixed on the cloaked figure behind the reins. Her hair was swept back at the nape into a black ribbon which served to accentuate her fine features and the extraordinary blue of her eyes – eyes which now met his with the same unspoken intensity. He stepped down to hold the pony's head without breaking his gaze. She was here, here in the flesh before him yet he could not find words to express his delight. Ramona too was speechless, overwhelmed by the suddenness of this reunion with the man she thought she had lost.

'What's going on, Jack? Who is this lady?' Henry's voice broke into their bemused silence as he strode onto the forecourt adjusting his jacket to the chill of autumn. 'By Jove, man! She is a pretty wench. I'll grant you that. But where are your manners? Aren't you going to help her down? Come on, my dear, come on.' Extending a hand like a footman assisting a lady from a crested coach, he guided Ramona from her humble farm cart with an air of gentle mockery. Then he stood back with hands on hips to regard her, revealing as he did so, his gold-stitched waistcoat. She could be in no doubt that he was master of the house.

'You two are acquainted, I gather,' he continued. 'Well then, whatever the reasons for your visit, the sun is low, You will need a bed for the night. Come, Jack. What is the matter with you? Take the pony round to the back. I'll escort the girl inside.'

Ramona, dressed in black from head to toe with a neat lace trimming round her neck, bobbed a curtsy before agreeing to this arrangement.

'Please, sir, I'm most grateful but as I shall

explain, I am here for a purpose. And we shall need two beds not one. You see Beth Cartwright is with me.'

Henry turned abruptly to Jack.

'This wench of yours plays tricks, does she not? And not very nice ones at that. Why, I've half a mind to turn her away. Does she not know that Beth's death was a great source of grief to us both?' Ramona drew her slight frame up straight and projected her chin out firmly in a manner that Jack remembered.

'I can assure you, sir, that Beth Cartwright is not dead though neither is she well. That is why I am here.' It was hard to say who was the more stunned by this news, Jack or Henry, but both moved instinctively towards the rear of the wagon. Ramona raised her hands and stood firm. 'The journey has tired her, sir. It would be an indignity to disturb her before she is ready to receive you. Let her sleep in a quiet room tonight and tomorrow you will see for yourselves how she is.'

Momentarily forgetting his humbler status, Jack clapped an arm round Henry's shoulder.

'Was there ever such good news, sir? Tonight I am doubly blessed. Beth alive after all! Is it not a miracle?' His eyes returned to Ramona with a fervour that he knew had never really died. But his joy was laced with sadness already. Would she be gone again tomorrow? Back to her own life?

Henry too blinked away a tear, unable to speak for the tightness of his chest. At length his breathing and his pulse steadied.

'Come. Come with me, my dear' he murmured. 'We must talk. You must tell me all you know. Jack will attend to Beth and the wagon if that is what you wish and I shall try to be patient.' As his wits returned he called over his shoulder. 'Find Mrs Bullen. She'll know what to do. And Mr Scott too. We may need a doctor.'

Jack paused only to watch Ramona's trim ankles ascend the steps. For the first time he wondered about her solemn black clothes. She had always favoured scarlet – the colour of life and passion. As soon as the door closed behind them, Jack could contain himself no longer. Whatever Beth's state, she would be cheered by his presence and they knew each other too well to stand on ceremony. His fingers trembled as he released the ripcords and tore open the canvas. She lay, semi-reclined, enveloped in a red cloak. Her face was pale, leaner than he remembered but unmistakably Beth. She stared pensively around and Jack, smiling broadly, gave her time to absorb his features. Instead she withdrew like a frightened child within the folds of the cloak.

'Hey, it's alright, Beth. It's Jack. Don't you remember me?' He stretched out a hand to reassure her but she recoiled even further until only her honey-coloured eyes stared wildly back at him. 'You're not hurt, are you?' he asked puzzled, thinking of the maimed creatures he sometimes found in the woods, too stunned to react to capture. Still she did not reply, nor show any hint of recognition.

'Dear Beth. Whatever's befallen you, you're safe

now. Do you understand? I shan't leave you again. Ever. I promise.' He waited for a response but there was none. She began to hum a cradle song, one that he remembered, in a faster and faster tempo reflecting her growing anxiety. So this is what Ramona had meant. It was her mind not her body that had been scarred by the past five years. And what of the baby? Did that hold the key to her suffering? One thing was certain. She did need rest in a quiet room and Mrs Bullen's maternal touch would surely reassure her.

By the time he had driven the wagon in some agitation round to the courtyard, Mrs Bullen had been alerted and was waiting, flushed with emotion, for the arrival of her prodigal child. Perhaps not her own but she had mourned her departure from Skellfield as much as any mother. Now, like Henry and Jack, her joy knew no bounds. Indeed, a small administration of brandy had been necessary to ensure that she did not have a fainting attack.

'Bring the poor dear in, Jack. Into my sitting room while Mrs Buchanan prepares a bed. Let me catch a sight of her for goodness sake! Is it really Beth?'

Jack lowered the slight, shivering form in his arms for Mrs Bullen to inspect. He was hurt by the fearful look on Beth's face and at a loss to know what to do. His instinct was to hold her, to surround her with affection but this was precisely what she seemed to resist. She trusted no one. Mrs Bullen's gentle tears and kind words met with the same reaction so that she, too, was reduced to dabbing her nose in dismay.

'We mustn't lose heart,' she wept, taking a clean kerchief from a drawer. 'When we know what she's been through, we'll be able to reach her. Won't we?' she whispered.

Jack enveloped her in a consoling hug.

'Aye, we will' he assured her, as they contemplated Beth's small frame curled up tight as a kitten by the fire. 'And if anyone can do it, you can. She is alive. For now, that is all that matters to me.

Chapter Forty-Eight

For the past five years, the servants had been unused to much activity at Skellfield. They were thrown into some confusion by Ramona's arrival and by the master's return to his old autocratic self. Henry rang bells and summoned maids, ordered rooms to be opened, fires to be lit and tea to be served, as though the news of Beth's survival had restored his reason for living – which indeed it had. There was a new energy in his stride as he escorted Ramona into the faded splendour of the drawing room, took her cloak and tossed it to a flustered footman. Seating himself next to her, he was struck by the similarity of their remarkable blue eyes, forgetting for the moment the accident of birth which linked them.

'Now, my dear lady, I can wait no longer to hear your good news. Take a sip of tea if you wish – then spare me no details. I want to know everything that has happened to Beth and how you came to be part of her life.'

Ramona picked up her delicate china cup and savoured the pale fluid as she returned his gaze over the rim. So this dashing golden-haired man was her cousin, Edward Cunningham's nephew. She replaced the cup in its saucer with care as Henry leant forward.

'I cannot tell you a great deal, sir,' she began. 'Only that she worked at Hilldene, near Scarborough that is, until she became heavy with child. Then Michael, my husband, told her she must leave I could never forgive him for that. I searched the town but there was no trace of her anywhere and with Jack gone to sea – well, what could I do?'

She glanced down and smoothed her black taffeta skirt, unable to continue. She had endured five years of misery as Michael's wife.

'Drink your tea. Take your time,' Henry instructed.

She drew a long breath and sighed.

'About a month ago, our ploughman, Nathan, found her lying in the bottom field. She was wet. She must have travelled all night. Heaven knows from where. There was a bruise here on her forehead.' Ramona pushed back her thick tresses to point out the spot. 'Perhaps she fell and was stunned. At any rate she has told us nothing about her life from that day to this – or what became of the child.'

Henry threw his weight back in his gold carved chair causing it to creak.

'Mrs Ruston!' he exclaimed. 'That woman must have lied. Why, she showed us Beth's grave Buried, she said, with her infant son – my son! And if she lied about Beth...' Hope illuminated his face. 'Then she could have lied about the child,' he finished triumphantly.

'Who is this woman you talk of, sir?' Ramona

asked, leaning forward herself now. 'I know of no Mrs Ruston.'

'Oxpasture House, my dear. Beth was taken to Oxpasture House in Raincliffe woods.' Henry was not concentrating on her now but pacing the room, voicing his thoughts aloud. 'The child has been snatched. That's obvious. And I'll not rest for a moment until I find him. Where's Jack? Where is he?' Before he could reach for the bell, Jack appeared at the door.

'Come in, man, come in. Tell me, how is Beth? No, don't tell me. I shall see for myself. Stay here. I'll be damned if I'll wait till morning.'

Jack stepped aside as Henry swept through the door, leaving himself and Ramona alone. Showing all of his old impulsiveness, he shut it firmly and bounded across the room. These precious moments may be all that he had before she went back to her life on the farm. He drew her to her feet until his waistcoat buttons touched the firm swell of her breasts. A woman's breasts now, no longer a girl's. His eyes were an inch from hers as he wrestled with the question he was too afraid to ask. 'Tell me,' he murmured at last. 'Tell me that your black gown means what I think?'

She had barely time to nod before his mouth encompassed hers in a frenzy of desire. He traced the well-loved curves of her body with strong familiar hands, pressing her against him, until her lips parted and her whole being melted into his. Tears of relief trickled down her cheeks.

'What a fool I've been, Jack. Can you ever forgive

me?' she whispered. Radiant with joy, they were scarcely aware of footsteps approaching until the handle turned on the drawing room door. Ramona tore herself away but Jack, ignoring the intrusion of an embarrassed maid, refused to let go. The girl coughed discreetly and her cheeks coloured. She had harboured her own hopes of winning Jack's affection.

'Please, miss. The housekeeper says your room is ready and she'll bring you hot water if you want it now. Says you'll be tired after your journey. I can show you upstairs if you wish.'

Ramona smoothed her hair, nodded and slipped gratefully from the room, leaving Jack to regain his composure. She was too spent to risk another glance at the smouldering passion in her lover's eyes. Equally overwhelmed, Jack sank into a chair. He could scarcely believe the events of the night. His hands were still shaking when Henry returned.

'Damn it, man. Help yourself to a drink. That lass has bewitched you, has she not? Well, your great romance will have to wait. I need you, Jack. We must leave at dawn and ride like the devil for the coast. Mrs Ruston will account to me before tomorrow is out.' He walked to the sash window and stared, his thoughts elsewhere, at the broad expanse of lake reflecting the rising moon. He wished the night would pass.

'Beth is sleeping but, if what Mrs Bullen has told me is true, her recovery lies in the return of that child – and perhaps mine too,' he added with a flicker of insight.

'I've never told you, my friend, but I was more maimed by that cursed Arctic whale than you think. It's unlikely I'll father a child again. Can you imagine what this news means to me? Who would have thought little Beth, a mere mill girl, could bring me such joy?'

Jack nodded and downed his empty glass. 'Indeed fate has favoured us both tonight, sir. But how will you ride a horse after all this time. What about your leg?'

'Nothing wrong with my leg,' Henry declared, discarding his cane. 'Nothing at all. We'll take the two bays. Make sure they are saddled and a packed lunch prepared. Ramona must stay here to look after Beth.' He glanced at Jack's pensive expression. 'What's bothering you now?' he demanded impatiently.

'I shall be delighted if you find your son. Delighted for you and for Beth. But you must bear in mind that he may yet be dead or the pain will be insufferable.'

'You have my interests at heart, Jack, and I thank you for that. But this boy is a Cunningham.' Henry's eyes flashed with pride. 'He's alive. I know it.' He placed a hand on his silk waistcoat over the region of his heart. 'I know it in here. And I will find him.'

Chapter Forty-Nine

Henry and Jack had already skirted the Howardian hills and were approaching the Vale of Pickering before sunshine broke through an autumnal mist which had persisted till noon. The two bays, jibbing at the reins, had cantered steadily through a succession of sleepy villages, their hooves echoing on cobbles as country folk unshuttered windows and unbolted doors. Now they hung heavier on the bit. Flat pastureland gave way to a patchwork of fields on either side of the winding river Derwent. Then, marking their progress, the square clock-tower of Malton came into sight.

Hearing it strike the hour of two, Jack, without instruction, drew up his horse and dismounted.

'We all need a rest,' he stated firmly, loosening the girth of his steaming mount, 'and these two need water before we ride on.' Henry followed suit without dissent, grimacing slightly as he slid to the ground and stooped to massage his weakened leg. Jack, quietly alert to his master's needs, threw his waterproof cape on the grass, providing him with a place to recline. The horses were already snatching at the rich turf and drinking from the river through mouths flecked with foam.

'Aye Jack, you're right. We'll have an ale and a portion of Mrs Bullen's cake. But when the clock strikes the quarter, we must be on our way. I swear I shall not sleep until I have unravelled the truth of Beth's lost years and discovered the fate of my son.'

Jack completed his chores in silence before seating himself on a log nearby.

'And what then, sir?' he asked quietly.

Henry's blue eyes settled on the surrounding hills and the domed tower of a distant estate. It rose majestically above ancient cedars and oaks. For miles around the trees were shot through with the russets and golds of autumn. No traveller could pass this place without a sense of pride in his English heritage.

'My father revered the Harringtons, you know. Their family is steeped in history. I don't think he ever forgave me for bolting when the possibility of a union with them was within his grasp. They no longer receive the Cunninghams. Sir George died an unhappy man and my mother lives out her days with no hope and no purpose. The fault is mine, of course. But then, which of us is happy? The die is cast when we are born, don't you think?'

Jack did not reply. Perhaps he was fortunate after all to be free of the social strictures which bound the gentry. Nothing would stop him from following his heart. As soon as Ramona felt able to consent he would make her his wife. He smiled at the memory of that day in York when he had first glimpsed her cascading nut-brown hair. He remembered the strange intimacy he had felt as her eyes caught his when the crowds surged towards the gallows – the certainty that their destiny was somehow connected.

'And what about you, Jack? Your mind is distracted. I can tell. It's that confounded girl again, isn't it? Will I get no more sense out of you?'

'Possibly not, sir,' Jack grinned, 'until we are safely wed. I trust you will have no objection to that?'

'I can see no one will stand in your path,' Henry chortled with a deep-throated laugh. 'And I grant you she is uncommonly pretty. But what do you know of her? I mean, really know?'

Jack plucked a long grass and twisted it aimlessly.

'Do you recall me telling you of your Uncle Edward's liaison with a gypsy? Around Christmas time when they tended to visit the great halls to beg and sell lace. You would have been a boy then, and the gossip was hushed but the servants still talk of it behind closed doors. The gypsy woman disappeared in the spring but she bore a child. I told you that child was Ramona, though your family heard no word of it. So you see, my future wife is your cousin.'

Henry sat up and straightened his stock.

'My dear fellow! You claim this but you have no proof. Why, gypsies are known for their trickery.'

'No, sir, I have not and it is of no importance to me. But the proof is in her eyes. Did you not feel when you met her that you were staring into your own soul?'

Henry got up and busied himself with his horse before allowing Jack to help him into the saddle.

'Damn it, she's a bonnie girl,' he conceded as he dug his heels into the bay. 'I dare say my uncle would have been proud.'

Taking the lead along the deeply-rutted road to the east, he settled into a brisk canter. His jaw was set and his face preoccupied so that Jack knew any advice to slow down would fall on deaf ears. He was relieved, therefore, when the horses pulled up, exhausted but unscathed, at Oxpasture House. It was almost dusk and the gate had been closed as though the occupants discouraged contact with those outside. Some force was required to open it.

Overblown roses still flourished around the imposing front door, scenting the air and lending charm to the crumbling sandstone walls. There was a hint of neglect about the place and Jack worried that, after their long ride, no one would answer their call.

Henry, throwing him his reins, strode towards the bell, pulled it hard several times, then stood back, hands on hips, waiting for a sound from within. Barely a minute passed before he beat upon the panels with his crop.

'Hello there! Open up if you would. I must speak to the owner,' he cried. Still there was no response. Birds, uttering distress calls, flew out of the ivy as he rapped loudly on a mullioned window.

'I think it's Mr Ruston, sir. He's at the door,' Jack

called, still standing at the horses' heads.

A stout figure emerged onto the steps.

'Indeed it is Mr Ruston. And who the dickens are you to disturb a gentleman at this time of day? I rarely receive visitors and certainly not when my wife is away.'

Henry positioned himself close to the door and stood his ground with a look of rare determination on his face.

'A gentleman are you, Mr Ruston?' he said softly. 'Then perhaps you would care to explain why your wife showed us the grave of a young girl and why that same young girl recently turned up at my house. Perhaps you can recall a Miss Beth Cartwright?'

John Ruston was momentarily taken aback. He attempted to close the door but anticipating his actions, Henry swiftly pushed his shoulder into the divide.

'Not so fast, sir. I will have an answer one way or another. Believe me.' There was a note of threat in his voice that was not lost on the older man.

'You speak of my first wife,' he growled. She died some time ago. I am not responsible for her unstable mind. I can tell you nothing.'

The horses' heads shot up, startled, as Henry lunged towards Ruston, gripping his bull neck until his eyes bulged. Jack was impotent to help or intervene.

'Have a care, sir! He'll be no good to you dead,' he warned as the red face grew purple. But Henry's blood was up.

'You will be dead, I promise you. Unless you talk when I release these murderous hands of mine.' A further minute passed as Ruston struggled against his vice like grip. Only when he sensed submission did Henry let go of his throat and reach instead for his velvet lapels. But Ruston, coughing and gasping for breath, had already surrendered. His soft hands, used only for smoothing and measuring cloth, were no match for Henry's. He fluttered his kerchief like a white flag before wiping the foam from his mouth.

'It was all my wife's fault,' he whimpered. 'She was childless you see. This girl Beth you talk of stumbled in front of her carriage. The idea must have occurred to her then. What life would she have had in the workhouse after all? She was due to give birth.'

Henry pressed Ruston's shoulders hard against the porch.

'What happened to Beth and that child? Tell me – and it had better be the truth.'

'Mrs Ruston, my first wife that is,' Ruston stammered, 'sent Beth to an asylum. A suitable place for such women. It was in Rillington – owned by an acquaintance of hers. Robert grew up here until his mother died. When my new wife took over the household, it wasn't convenient to have him around. You understand as a gentleman, surely?' he simpered.

'That boy is my son. Now where is he?'

Ruston flinched at this news but Henry's face was an inch from his own.

'Alright, alright. Give my poor brain a chance to

think! I've not been the same since Camille left. She went back to Flanders. Didn't settle over here. Ah, it's been a bad time for me, a very bad time.'

His play for sympathy was wasted on Henry.

'Perhaps this will concentrate your brain,' he snarled, pounding his head against the wall. 'And this! And this!' Ruston's skull rebounded like a rag doll's until he cried out for mercy.

'Tell us what you know!' Jack called, trying to judge whether intervention was necessary. 'Tell us what you know and you won't get hurt.'

Ruston sank to the ground as his legs folded.

'I paid the housekeeper. She took him back to West Yorkshire. Back where his mother came from. There's a mill there that takes children, I believe. He'll be well looked after.' He did not raise his eyes however to meet theirs.

Jack's face blanched.

'My God, sir! The mill! He won't survive that. We must find him without delay.'

Chapter Fifty

Henry and Jack left Oxpasture House without a backward glance, leaving John Ruston to seek help as best he could. They had extracted from him what they needed to know and had but one purpose. Jack's brain was already planning the practicalities of their trip to West Yorkshire. They must stop briefly at Skellfield; then he would take the reins of the carriage and four so that Beth's son when they found him could return with his father in privacy and comfort.

For now, however, their progress was slow. The horses, too tired to be spooked by the screech of owls, picked their way with heads low through the darkness of Raincliffe Woods. An hour passed before they emerged onto Seamer Moor. Seeing the lights still flickering at Hilldene, Jack turned in his saddle and pointed out the buildings set amongst trees slanted against the north wind.

'With respect, sir, I suggest that we stay at Ramona's farm. It's just yonder. Not far from the track. The housekeeper is a hospitable woman and she'll welcome news of her mistress.'

Henry took little persuading. His leg was aching persistently now.

'Lead on, my good man. If they can provide simple fare and a clean bed I shall be content. With the horses rested and fed, we can still make a good start tomorrow.'

Aggie responded timidly at first to Jack's urgent knocking on the farmhouse door. After all, the hour was late and there was only herself and Joe to confront intruders. Such was her joy at seeing Jack after all these years, however, that she flung her arms round his neck, dislodging as usual her precarious cap. When Henry, too, emerged from the night, she became flustered and unsure whether to curtsy or retrieve her wayward hat from the mud.

'Please, sir. This way, sir. It's an honour, sir,' she gushed, breathless with shock and excitement.

'Come come, my dear woman,' Henry interrupted, ushering her with a firm hand into her own kitchen. He lifted the lid from a simmering pot of pungent soup. 'Is that not the most delicious smell when one is tired and hungry, Jack?'

Jack did not hear him as he led their two mounts away to the stalls. He must attend to their needs before his own. Despite his weariness, he stripped off his jacket, rubbed them both down and measured two feeds from a barrel of grain.

When he had finished he paused to glance into the loose-box next door. There was no sign of Storm, he noted with disappointment. No doubt he was kept out at grass. He thought no more about it until he had enjoyed a robust evening meal and a tankard of ale with Henry and Aggie and Nathan. The news concerning Beth had been exchanged for Aggie's account of Michael's death. There was general agreement that no effort must be spared, no time lost, not even one day, in rescuing Henry's son from his plight. It was only as they retired with their oil lamps up the rickety stairs that Jack's chance comment caught Nathan's ear.

'But Storm is in the stables,' the farm hand countered. 'I gave him a feed not an hour ago.'

Jack yawned and made his way on up to bed. There would be some explanation. At dawn, however, when he and Henry, refreshed after a night's sleep, were mounting the two bays, Nathan approached them with disturbing news. Storm was nowhere to be found. He had vanished, it seemed, into the night.

'I'll find him,' the lad vowed vehemently. 'You'd best not tell the mistress. I'll wager it's that gypsy, Franco. He's a dark one, he is. He's been skulking round here since Michael died – wanting to know Ramona's plans. He'd do owt to draw her back to his way of life. The man's not to be trusted.'

'Look after the farm and Aggie, Nathan,' Jack called as Henry cantered impatiently ahead. 'They are your first responsibility, just as Ramona and Beth and Robert are ours. Only when they are safe will we think about Storm.'

But as his horse lengthened its stride in Henry's wake, his mature reaction gave way to doubts. What did he really know of Ramona? He knew that she sent his pulse soaring in a way that no other woman ever had. That he was aware of a void when she was not present in his life. Yet Franco also had these feelings and presumably believed that no outsider could win her gypsy soul. After all, her brief attraction for Michael had not made her happy. Was he, ~~Jack,~~ so sure that he could? Would she settle for a steady way of life on Henry's estate? Was she Cunningham or Romany? He had yet to find out.

His thoughts returned to Henry's son, Robert, and the horrors the child would be suffering in the mill. Horrors that he remembered all too well. His personal life must not deflect him, he decided, from the pledges he had made. Like Oastler he had another passion, ~~too;~~ his resolve to improve the factory children's lot. For a fleeting moment he was a frightened eleven year old boy again holding a flickering candle in a draughty room as poor William breathed his last. His cousin's fate must never be forgotten.

Fired with energy after learning of his son's existence, Henry sprang from his horse at the end of the long ride home and lost no time in seeking out Mrs Bullen to enquire after Beth.

'There's been no change, sir. No change at all,' she said sadly as she led the way round the gallery and tentatively opened a bed-chamber door. Curtains billowed gently on each side of an open window framing the last rays of the sun which reflected in the lake its final burst of splendour. The scene could hardly fail to catch the eye. But the small figure lying motionless between crisp white sheets showed no reaction to either this or Henry's entrance. Undaunted, he moved forward, pulled up a chair and took her limp hand in his.

'My dear Beth. I have news that I hope will give you as much joy as it does me. We have a son, you and I. A son who is in danger at this present moment. But soon I shall return with him and you shall see the boy for yourself.' He paused, willing her to respond to the fervour in his voice and the import of his words.

'You see, sir? Nothing. It's as though she has lost her very soul. What am I to do?' Mrs Bullen dabbed her nose with a kerchief. 'She takes a little soup from time to time but only then with a lot of encouragement.'

Henry studied the blank honey-coloured eyes that had so captivated him with their warmth and sincerity. Now they stared uncomprehending into his. Still not a pretty face he thought wryly, but the delicate fine-boned features were precious to him.

'My poor moorland waif,' he murmured, as Mrs Bullen sniffed away tears. 'What pain you must have suffered to reduce you to this.' The sunset fell across her pillow, gilding the neat plait of hair that a maid had arranged on the crown of her head. Her kissed her brow and then, on impulse, her bloodless lips. Mrs Bullen held her breath, ignoring the lapse of protocol. Surely such a bold demonstration of his feelings would provoke a response? But apart from pulling the sheet right up to her chin Beth remained quite impassive.

Henry stood up, deep in thought. 'We must let time be her healer. She must continue to rest until I find our child – and may I find him soon.'

'Indeed, sir. My prayers will be with you in church

on the Sabbath and with...' Mrs Bullen's voice petered out as the master placed a comforting arm round her waist. She was too fond of the man to be judgmental. Beneath his wayward behaviour she sensed a heart as genuine as her own.

'We shall leave at first light. Have a basket prepared for Jack and myself – and a small hungry boy,' Henry added, scanning Beth's face for a flicker of sentiment.

Mrs Bullen pulled herself together, resuming her maternal role as she guided him gently towards the door.

'Don't distress yourself, sir. She'll be well looked after while you're away and you need some rest. Why, you must be exhausted.'

Outside in the yard, Jack struggled to focus on his duties. He longed to seek out the Ramona he had known during their journey to Scarborough. To hear her laughter in the breeze as she waded upstream, heedless of her wet petticoats. Here, propriety demanded restraint. He could not simply run in to embrace her as he so much wished. He found Joe polishing brasses in the harness room.

'We'll need the carriage with four fresh horses at dawn, my friend,' he warned him. 'Can you manage that?'

'Aye. Anything for you, Jack. You've been a good friend. Me and the missus are doing well. Annie's right proud of me and our two little bairns.'

They discussed the horses and their relative fitness, the stiffness in Lady's ageing limbs and how it might be eased. Jack's thoughts returned to Storm and the matter of his strange disappearance.

'We think he was snatched by a gypsy from Ramona's past life. I shall deal with the fellow when I come back.'

Joe grinned. He still relished a fight but sensed this was a personal matter.

'Aye. I can see you will,' he said, noting the sudden flash of anger, or was it jealousy, in his friend's dark eyes.

At dinner that night, Jack could only converse with Ramona between the formal candlesticks on the Georgian table. Their eyes locked frequently as they dined, saying far more than their seemingly meaningless words, but any hope of intimacy was dashed when Henry insisted that they all retire early. They must be fresh for the challenge that lay ahead.

Jack's opportunity came, however, in the brief moment when he bade her goodnight. He pressed his lips against her cheek, longing as he did so to tear away her stiff starched collar and the net that contained her radiant hair.

'Marry me!' he whispered. 'Say nothing now but give me your answer when I return.'

Chapter Fifty-One

Dawn the next morning found Joe and a stable hand hauling a carriage from the coach house and assembling a team of fresh horses. Thirty miles away behind the unforgiving soot-ingrained walls of a Bradford mill, young Robert Ruston was being roughly dragged from his straw pallet. Half asleep, he stumbled between the narrow beds in the apprentice shed. Indentured here until the age of twenty-one he had no choice but to submit in all things to the will of his masters. For almost two months his noisy protests had been quelled by the whip. Now one fearful glance at the raised knotted thong was enough to silence him as it did the other infants who filed into the yard.

There, a pig trough, chilled by the approach of winter, served as a crude washtub. After a snatched bowl of gruel with his fellow sufferers, Robert waited, shivering in his tattered smock, for the locked gates of their dormitory to open. The six-storey mill with its forty windows on each level and on each aspect, emerged slowly from the lingering night, its chimneys belching black smoke as the furnaces in the bowels of the building gained heat. The great machines within, the pride of the new industrial revolution, required a constant supply of expendable children to produce more and more cloth and hence more and more wealth for the mill owners.

Already Robert, denied hope, was becoming a spiritless wretch aware only of his body's capacity for pain. He dreamt constantly of escape, dreamt of it daily as he mounted the steep stairwells and entered the vast dusty halls. Dreamt of it when he toiled almost beyond endurance to keep pace with the clanking gears and whirling spindles which would not cease again till nightfall. As a scavenger, he was required to crawl under the moving rods and pistons to collect fragments of thread – a process fraught with danger and frequent accidents.

This morning he proved to be the luckless one. Weakened by fever, he was slow to flatten his trembling limbs as the hissing contraption passed overhead. A glancing blow rendered him briefly unconscious. Since the whip would not rouse him, he was dragged to a corner and left to recover on a sack of wool. As his senses returned, Robert felt the soft fur of a kitten rub against him and remembering the comfort of his lost pet, he reached out to embrace it. In a trice it had slipped from his grasp and through a gap in the door.

There was no plan, no thought in his dazed mind beyond that of seeking the kitten yet amazingly none of the overseers saw him crawl after it or indeed even thought him capable. Scarcely aware of his actions, he slid down the stairs to the floor below and then down again to where he could just glimpse the fleeing kitten. Each time he drew close enough to catch it, it fled again until Robert was brought up sharp by the sight of the sleeping porter in the entrance hall.

The man was a giant and quite terrifying enough to send him scurrying back up the stairwell. But still his dulled brain was transfixed by the small wild creature imprisoned in the mill to contain the rats. It too sought escape from the ceaseless noise and the fetid air. No ventilation was allowed to disturb the manufacturing process, no matter what discomfort this caused but the porter had broken the management's rule. Behind him, a small window was slightly ajar and the kitten was quick to spot it. Robert watched open mouthed as it disappeared, then returned his gaze to the shuddering red face of the door keeper. All he needed was the courage to tiptoe past. Fate had given him a chance and his headstrong spirit was returning fast.

He waited until the man's snoring subsided into a gentle slumber then could not believe how easy it was to slither through the aperture and drop onto the wasteland outside. At first his feet would not run but remained rooted to the spot, beyond his control like the nightmare from which he regularly awoke sobbing for comfort.

'I'm free!' he whispered – then louder, 'I'm free. I'm free!' The spell was broken and suddenly he was running in long loping strides as fast as he had ever done in his whole life. Past horses and places and people who thankfully showed no interest in him. He was safe again amongst human beings he could trust and approach. He had escaped from the hateful place where Grace had left him so friendless and alone.

When weakness overcame his euphoria, his pace slackened and he paused to gaze with rapture at the shiny fruits on a market stall. It was daybreak and others were producing coins to purchase it. Coins that he did not have, nor did the sharp-eyed barrow boy look likely to be charitable. He moved on, drawn now by the smell of a bakery opposite. After fidgeting in the doorway and studying the shopkeeper's pleasant pink face and snow-white moustache, he sidled inside.

'Please sir,' he began, 'I'm hungry. Mightn't I have a piece of bread?'

The baker dusted his floured hands on his apron and leaned forward to look at the bold blue eyes peering at him from beneath the counter.

'Away with you, lad. Do you think I work to feed beggars like you?' His attention was already back on a tray of cakes. Robert, briefly discouraged, stared at his own image in the window. It bore no resemblance to the Robert Ruston who had been taken away from Oxpasture House at the end of the summer. His blonde hair was an unruly matted mud colour, his cheeks hollow and the limbs protruding from his filthy mill clothes, white and stick-thin. He scratched his head and then an armpit.

'Cook always gave me bread when I was hungry' he murmured. 'Sometimes she gave me a biscuit too.'

'Oh, aye. What cook was that?' the baker replied, continuing to stock his shelves.

'The cook at my house. Before Grace took me away.' The man turned back and placed his hands on his hips, giving Robert his full attention.

'An orphan, are you?' he said, narrowing his eyes, as though some thought had occurred to him.

'I think so, sir. I think I'm one of them,' Robert replied doubtfully, keen to maintain his interest.

'Alright, lad. You shall have some bread and milk in the back room until I thinks what to do with thee. You touch owt mind, and you'll feel the back of my hand.'

Robert's face lit up as he was led inside to a windowless room where a cat lay sleeping by the hearth. Its belly was swollen with its evidently rich diet of mice.

'I'll not move, honest, sir, I won't. I'll just sit here with the cat.' He was already on his haunches fondling its fur and basking in the warmth from the fire. When the baker closed the door, he smiled and pulled a brown crumpled twig from the pocket of his smock. 'It's lucky,' he told his feline companion. 'A nice lady said I must keep it.' Moments later he was asleep, his face no longer etched with pain but serene and full of hope.

Chapter Fifty-Two

A steady drizzle made the prospect of a forty mile drive to Bradford more gruelling for the coachman than the passenger. Realising this, Henry sent last minute instructions that a recently promoted groom should take the reins and Jack should join him in the comfortably padded interior.

'You are the estate manager, not a liveried servant,' he declared. 'We have both ridden hard for the last two days and I, for one, am quite spent.' He clambered inside, gritting his teeth as he dragged his leg up the steps.

'Besides, I shall need good company to pass the time. We'll be lucky to arrive before dusk if this weather persists.'

In fact, Jack would have preferred the task of guiding the horses around the fallen branches which littered the road. Unduly strong winds had made the trip hazardous. His master, however, was in talkative mood and, as the journey began, they were soon in deep debate about their firmly held political views. Being out of favour with the local gentry, Henry was perhaps more open to the ideas of the new Yorkshire reformers whose voices were being increasingly heard in Parliament. Yet he was still wary of the forces which might weaken the established bonds of his own society – a legacy he had inherited from history.

Jack's association with Skellfield had equally infiltrated his own thinking. He admired the rural institutions with their emphasis on continuity, loyalty and the natural order of people and things. He considered himself a humanitarian Tory, like Oastler, whose name regularly sprinkled his conversation.

'Why, you worship the man!' Henry laughed. 'You are becoming something of an orator yourself in his defence.'

'You will, too, before the day is out, I promise you,' Jack replied, leaning back in his seat. Outside, the landscape was changing. They had already passed Harrogate. Ahead lay the Pennines and the very track along which he and Beth had first escaped from the mill. The same reflection must have occurred to Henry.

'It was an auspicious night which brought us together in that storm. I owe a great deal to you and Beth. I shall never forget it. And soon my son shall sit here beside me to share our joy.' His eyes, lost now in private thought, focused on the distant gritstone peaks.

Jack felt a tightening of his stomach. He could not eat Mrs Bullen's carefully prepared lunch. He was remembering again what life was really like in that satanic building beyond the outcrops of weathered rock. How the little ones would scramble with their bony fingers for a morsel of this cake. How their sunken, half-closed eyes would plead for liberation when he entered. Could he face the ordeal? Somehow, he must. Only if Henry saw first hand the cruelty mere infants endured, would he understand why he himself was committed to their cause.

As Henry had predicted, it was late afternoon before the coach lumbered down a steep slope and gave them their first grim view of the town. A pall of smoke had settled under low cloud so that the air became increasingly acrid as they descended. Jack scanned the blackened roofs until his eye came to rest on a cluster of chimneys amongst the many on the far side of the valley.

'That's it,' he said bitterly. 'That's Scrimshaws. All six storeys of it, just as it was when we left.' He called up to the driver. 'Take the horses to the right when the road divides and pull into the forecourt when you reach the mill. You'll see wagons of wool unloading there.'

Henry said nothing until the horses drew to a halt but he missed nothing either. His face became more and more grave as he looked left and right and upward at the stark brick walls – then around him at the people young and old with strangely bent spines who moved silently about. Most of the workers were still imprisoned within. The noise of the spinning and weaving machines was muted by windows stuck fast in their frames. Dust and oil and the perspiration from hundreds of labouring lungs obscured them from the outside world.

Jack knocked boldly on the porter's door with his cane then withdrew. It would require Henry's status and authority to gain admittance. The porter, however, after the escape of one of his inmates that morning, was doubly vigilant.

'How do I know you are Sir Henry Cunningham?' he grumbled. 'I can't let you in without permission from the governor.'

'You will soon find out that I am if you don't,' Henry shot back. 'I've no time to wait. My son is in this place and I intend to find him. Come on, Jack.' Henry pushed past the nonplussed porter and strode two steps at a time up the stairs to a landing. He pushed open the door to the first factory hall and staggered back within minutes to cover his mouth. The stench of gas and sweat and human breath was nauseating. Through the dusty particles he could scarcely make out the little people moving like ghosts along the rows. The clanking of gears and the whirling of a thousand spindles assaulted his senses to such an extent that he withdrew to the landing, indicating to Jack that he should follow. 'How can a man survive in there!' he spluttered between coughs, trying without success to open a window.

'They are not men. They are children, sir – and they don't survive. They wear out and are replaced by others like my poor cousin William and orphans like myself and your son.'

Henry lost no time. He swept downstairs to confront the porter, shaking him by the lapels of his jacket until the keys jangled on his thick belt.

'Robert Ruston. He was brought to this confounded place two months ago. You are going to tell me where he is.'

The giant of a man visibly crumbled and quickly adopted a fawning manner.

'I don't know the lad's names, sir, but the overseers do. I'll ask them.' He slid away, grateful to escape Henry's fury. 'You just wait here. Sit down on my chair if you will. I'll not be long.'

Neither Henry and Jack did sit down but paced the floor impatiently until a weasel-faced overseer appeared. His harsh lined features broke into an unnatural obsequious smile.

'No lad here by the name of Robert Ruston, sir. I'm afraid you've had a wasted journey.'

'Have you asked on the other floors?' Henry demanded, aware the man had not been gone long.

'Aye. No lad of that name.'

'We shall check this, Jack. We shall go into every hall and see for ourselves what goes on in this place. If he is here I will find him.' He knew the child was strikingly blonde and blue-eyed like all the Cunninghams. Steeling himself to enter the second hall with Jack, it quickly became clear, however, that every child's hair was so encrusted with dirt that the colour was a uniform brown. Each time they asked an overseer to identify Robert the response was the same. No child of that name.

By the time they had completed a tour of the top floor, Henry was speechless with horror at what he was witnessing. It was true what was being said.

This was no less than slavery on their own doorstep. As he turned to leave, a commotion developed at the far end of the hall, bringing a spark of hope. Was his own son risking punishment to make himself known?

'You must leave now, sir,' the overseer shouted above the din. 'You have no business here.'

Henry stood rooted to the spot as a girl resembling a rag doll was transported by. Her arm was severed and swung grotesquely as it bled. Overcome with nausea, Henry allowed Jack to usher him out.

'Come, sir. This is no place for a gentleman. You have seen enough and you need the fresh air.'

Holding a scarf to his face Henry had no choice but to leave. Once out of the building he was sick in the yard. He sat afterwards on a barrel with his head in his hands while Jack pondered what to do next.

'Your son is not here, sir. We must try another mill. Try them all if necessary.' He pointed to a blackened shed opposite. That is where the indentured children are housed. If you have the strength left, sir, we could ask in there. The caretaker may know something,'

'Aye,' Henry replied vehemently. 'I'll not leave a stone unturned to save my son from this hell.'

Chapter Fifty-Three

The dilapidated door to the apprentice house was slightly ajar. Jack and Henry pushed through it to find themselves confronted by the apprentice master's wife. Though small in stature, she quickly made it clear that this was her domain.

'No one's permitted in here, sir. Order of the governor. Besides.' She swivelled her sharp eyes towards the ceiling and grinned, revealing black teeth. 'You wouldn't want to catch the fever would you? They're two abed up there in the sick bay.'

Henry, profoundly appalled by what he had already seen, ignored her.

'Show me, Jack. Show me where these children live.'

'I shall have to fetch my husband, sir,' the woman intervened. 'I can't take it upon myself to let you in there.' She attempted to bar the passage with her sinewy arms but Henry was having none of it and brushed her aside. She trailed after the two men, her authority for once overruled, as they entered a long low-ceilinged dormitory. Human filth covered the floors and walls and the straw beds reeked of every kind of excrement.

'Does Robert Ruston live in this pig sty?' Henry asked in a deceptively quiet voice.

'There's fifty sleeps in here, sir. How would I know all their names? We get new 'uns every day. You can't expect an old lady like me to keep tabs on 'em all. They have numbers, see. That's easier.'

A quick glance up and down the empty pallets that lined the room with barely a gap between confirmed that no child had been allowed to linger here. The only sounds, plaintive cries for help, came from the sick bay above.

'Won't do you no good to go up there, sir. Nobody goes up there 'less they want to get the fever. There's only the good Lord as can help 'em now.'

'Or a good lady,' Henry retorted. 'You can make yourself useful by escorting us.' He pushed her up the attic stairs and limped less nimbly behind as she grumbled her way to the top. There, wasted hollow-eyed children lay everywhere in different stages of decline and Henry could only stare in disbelief at their misery. Stooping beneath the blackened rafters, he could just make out their outlines in the semi-darkness. It was like a scene from hell. The stench of ammonia from stale urine and vomit was suffocating. He could taste it on his lips, feel it stinging his eyes and penetrating his lungs as hands coated in untouchable filth stretched out to him. He withdrew, choking with revulsion. Jack, too, stood back, numbed by anger and impotence as his past became reality again.

'Water. Water please, sir,' a child little more than a skeleton beseeched Henry. He responded by reaching for a metal jug in the corner. The contents smelt tainted.

'Fetch them fresh water, woman,' he ordered, 'and be quick about it. Don't you know that children with fever need fluids?' When she had gone, he raised his voice. 'Does anyone here answer to the name of Robert? Robert Ruston?' There was no response, even from the ones that were capable. 'Does anyone know him?' Still there was no answer, no recognition of the name at all. With a heavy heart Henry led the way downstairs and walked uninvited into a more comfortable chamber. The apprentice master's wife had just returned from the pump and she thumped the jug onto the table with a sigh.

'Them stairs will be the death of me,' she moaned. Henry looked at her coldly and pulled a purse from inside his jacket.

'Would a sovereign ensure that you tend to the sick?' Her eyes darted to the coin on the table and widened when he placed another beside it. 'That,' he said 'is to provide a meat-based gruel. If it is not given to those poor souls, I shall see that you are dismissed. You may be sure of that.'

The woman said nothing but nodded, shame-faced, as she slid the coins into the folds of her apron. She seemed keen to conclude the deal before he could change his mind and encouraged him to leave by opening the door. Henry, however, chanced to look once more into the grim dormitory as though to impress the image on his stupefied mind. An insistent tapping noise seemed to be coming from the far end.

'What's that?' he said, inclining his head towards it.

'Rats. We get rats everywhere in this place.'

'That's no rat,' Henry persisted, walking closer. This time he could just catch a faint human voice. He strode the length of the hall with renewed energy to pinpoint the source which proved to be a locked and bolted door in the wall. Pressing his ear to the frame, he could just make out a child's plaintive cries. 'Can you explain this, woman?' he called back, flushed with fresh indignation.

'Aye, sir. There's some as have to be punished, you see. As an example to the others. This little varmint tried to get away. They never succeed, of course, because decent folk spot 'em and the management makes it – shall we say gainful – to bring 'em back. A baker turned him in. He'll not do it again after the thrashing he got and a few more days in there.' She cackled triumphantly. 'I remember that one alright. Ben Cartwright. More trouble than most. But he'll learn. They all do in the end.'

Jack was galvanised by the mention of his name.

'That's it, Henry! That's your son. Grace would have called him Ben Cartwright after Beth.' Colour flooded into Henry's ashen face.

'Get the key!' he stormed. When the old woman still stood rooted to the spot, he shook her thin shoulders. 'Get the key! Now! This minute! And be damned quick about it.'

'I ain't sure about this,' she murmured but sensing Henry's outrage, she slipped one off the ring that was chained to her waist. He snatched it from her, slid back the bolts and unlocked the door. The moment the child fell out of his dark tomb and gazed at his liberators, Henry knew. Without a shadow of a doubt, this boy was his. Cunningham eyes stared straight back at him. In a spontaneous gesture of delight, he reached out to embrace him.

'I'm your father, Robert,' he said gently. 'Come to take you away from this place.'

Robert however, recoiled. Life had taught him that he could trust no one and four hours in that solitary cell had left him almost mute with terror. With what power he could muster in his bony arms, he fended off any attempts to approach him. He hid himself instead behind a pallet of straw. Sensing that Henry was at a loss and overcome with emotion, Jack knelt down until he was level with Robert's bruised and tearstained face. It seemed to be mere skin stretched over bone but the contours were noble.

'Listen to me, Robert. Have you heard of a lady called Beth? Beth is your real mother and she needs you. Now you can stay here if that is what you wish. Or you can walk through that door and look for a carriage drawn by four fine horses. You can return to where you belong. The choice is yours. We'll be waiting outside.' With that Jack ushered Henry from the room. He opened the carriage door, helped him inside and joined the coachman in the driving seat. A minute passed before Robert tottered unsteadily over the wet cobbles and accepted Henry's extended hand. He clambered aboard and the steps were quickly folded away. It was almost dark and gaslights cast shadows across the yard.

'Which road should I take, sir?' the coachman asked gruffly.

Jack was too choked to respond. Instead he took the reins and startled the horses with an uncharacteristically harsh lash of the whip. They leapt forward, showing the whites of their eyes.

'Let's get out of here. Let's go home,' he said hoarsely. He was aware of the tightness in his throat that always seized him when tears threatened.

Chapter Fifty-Four

Ramona was surprised to find Lady Elizabeth at Beth's bed side when she entered her room after breakfast. She curtsied with instinctive grace and Henry's mother responded with a nod of approval. Shunned by society since her son's rejection of Lady Jane Harrington and paralysed with grief by Sir George's death, she had confined herself to her chamber for many months. Now, transformed by the news of a grandson, she felt sure she could help the stricken Beth.

'Come in, my dear,' she said softly, extending a frail hand from the folds of her robe. 'Come and sit down and let me look at you.' Ramona returned her frank gaze and the two women examined each other with interest.

'Yes,' she said at length. 'You are Edward's child. I have no doubt of it. My husband would never have acknowledged you but his brother for all his faults was a fine-looking man. You, my dear, resemble him.' She turned her attention back to Beth who was still languishing beneath the sheets.

'Blood is so important, you see. Young Robert is all that matters to me now. When he is found, Beth will recover as I have done. I know it. I shall teach her our ways and she and Henry must marry. Skellfield will then have a legitimate heir and I will die content. In time, the world will move on and forget. In time our honour will be restored.' She dabbed her eyes with a lace kerchief and seemed lost for a moment in her own thoughts.

Not wishing to intrude on the old lady's vigil, Ramona excused herself quietly and left the room. Without Jack, she felt unsure of her place in the household and sought refuge, not by the fire in the morning room but in the magnificent grounds outside. Used to the wild beauty of the countryside, she could only marvel at the vast areas of manicured lawns which stretched down to the lake. To the sides of the house, however, avenues of topiaried yew harboured rose beds and sculptures, and secluded garden seats. It was on one of these that she chose to sit and reflect, though, in fact, she had already made her decision. She would happily accept Jack's proposal of marriage. Life had given her a second chance in spite of the mistakes of her youth. Now she could face the future boldly with the man she loved by her side. She would support his cause and prove a wife worthy of him. She was startled by the sound of heavy boots approaching. Joe was equally surprised to find her there.

'Why, you must be Jack's girl,' he laughed. 'Eyes the colour of bluebells in spring and I'll be damned if he's not right. You're a bonny lass to be sure.' He took off his cap, wiped a rough hand on his jacket and introduced himself. 'I'm Joe. From the stables.'

'Pleased to meet you, Joe,' Ramona responded warmly. 'I've heard about you and your wife Annie. I hope to meet her and your children soon.' An idea occurred to her. 'Can I walk with you to the stables, d'you suppose? I can't go unescorted but I do love horses, so.'

Joe proffered his arm with pride.

'It would be an honour, miss. And I shall take you to see Tilly. Jack was telling me that Storm had been stolen by a gypsy friend of yours. I wouldn't fancy being that man when Jack catches up with him.'

Ramona stopped abruptly in her tracks.

'When did Jack tell you this Joe?'

'Why last night, miss. When he came to arrange a carriage for this morning. Didn't he tell you?'

'He didn't get chance.' Her mind raced and she pulled her wool wrap tighter round her. 'He musn't go, Joe. He would get hurt. Franco is a jealous man. He is not to be trusted.' Her old spirit returned with such force that Joe was taken aback. 'I must go. Now. Before it's too late. Have Tilly harnessed to my cart and have her ready in the yard. I'll be back in a few minutes. Go. Go and do as I tell you. I have no time to waste.'

She was running lightly towards the house before Joe could stutter a response. What should he do? 'Women!' he muttered to himself as he turned towards the coach house. 'She's a feisty one, alright. Just like Annie. They're all the same.' Nevertheless, he hurried on to do her bidding and had the pony harnessed before she returned.

'You must lend me your cap, Joe,' she said,

seizing it from his head without his consent and bundling her thick hair inside. 'See, I look like a farm boy now. No one will notice me.' Wrapped in her scarlet cape, she settled herself on the driver's seat and took up the reins and the whip. 'Tell Lady Cunningham I had urgent matters to see to at Hilldene – and on no account tell Jack I have gone to find Storm.'

'How long will you be, miss?' Joe asked bemused, scratching his bare head. But she had already disappeared at a spanking pace down the drive.

Chapter Fifty-Five

It was only when one of the team stumbled as they strained to pull the carriage uphill that Jack's usual concern for the horses returned. He jumped down and when they reached the top ran a reassuring hand over their heaving flanks. Far below, smoke still belched into the night, reminding him of the hundreds of enslaved children labouring on in the stifling mills. He sighed. He felt angry and impotent. Robert at least had been saved but when would Oastler's reforms succeed? He heard the carriage window drop as Henry released the strap and peered out at the dark hazardous track ahead. REPEATED too much

'Two miles on, Jack. Stop at the Lord Nelson, I noticed it on the way. We'll take rooms for the night and the horses can rest.'

Relieved, Jack led the team on at a steady pace until the lights of a large posthouse came into view. He remembered it now. Not a humble inn but an imposing establishment that he himself would have considered extravagant. Such places offered comfort and space to the more discerning. Henry, cradling his sleeping son in his arms, was surprised therefore when the elderly patron ushered him to his room through a crowded bar.

'We have a meeting here tonight, sir,' he explained apologetically as he turned the key. 'I hope you won't be disturbed. Your companion can take the adjoining room and the coachman's quarters are round at the back.' The old man watched with discreet curiosity as Henry lowered Robert onto a feather bed. He could hardly fail to notice his filthy state and tattered clothes. 'Forgive me, sir, but the lad looks as though he needs a wash. Would you like the maid to attend him?'

'Let him sleep now,' Henry murmured, tracing a finger around the boy's face with a tenderness that brought a tear to Jack's eye.

The innkeeper stroked his white whiskers, uncertain whether to voice his thoughts. Finally he asked with a sidelong glance, 'Are you one of the reformers, sir? A committee member perhaps?'

Henry responded with a wry smile and shook his head.

'Perhaps I should introduce myself. I'm Sir Henry Cunningham. And no, sir. I've never been one for committees. Now my friend Jack here – he is,' he added. 'Why do you ask?'

'Oh, no matter, sir. I was wrong. It was just the boy, you see. He looks like a mill child. I wondered if...'

'You wondered what?' Henry's interest was aroused.

'I wondered if you had brought him along to give evidence, so to speak.'

'This meeting,' Jack intervened. 'Does it concern the Ten Hours Bill?' The patron nodded

'What is all this, Jack? What is the Ten Hours Bill?'

'It's what Oastler is fighting for in Parliament, sir. A Bill to shorten the hours of the factory children. There are meetings all over Yorkshire now and in Lancashire too. Short Time Committees they call them.'

'You're not a mill owner then, sir?' the innkeeper asked warily.

'Most certainly, I am not,' Henry responded fiercely. 'Today, I have seen the hell children suffer behind those brick walls and I shall never forget it. This boy, I have discovered, is my own flesh and blood. He was taken to Scrimshaws against his will. We were fortunate to find him and by God I swear I shall seek election myself if it helps their cause.' The innkeeper extended an enthusiastic hand.

'My name is Matthew Turner, sir, and I'm at your service. What a happy coincidence brought you here tonight. We need men like yourself and your friend who share our outrage at these horrors but we have to proceed carefully. There are many who do not think as we do and want only to acquire wealth.' He glanced at the prostrate child. 'He is fortunate indeed. Will you not take refreshment downstairs while he sleeps?'

Henry removed his cloak and hat and rubbed his hands by the freshly kindled fire.

'I shall not leave my son's side tonight. A platter of beef and a pot of coffee is all I require. But my companion I'm sure would enjoy an ale and a good debate with your members. And you have my permission, Jack, to arrange such meetings at Skellfield. You can be sure I will attend.'

When the two men had gone, Henry turned to look at the face framed by flung-back arms and dirty flaxen hair. It was a troubled face. Would it melt in laughter when the morning came or would his experience have maimed him too? As though in answer, Robert cried out suddenly and sat upright rubbing his eyes. Henry moved swiftly to restrain and comfort him.

'Let me go! It's dark! It's too dark! Let me go!'

Seizing the lamp, Henry turned up the wick so that the pleasant floral furnishings of the room came into focus.

'Look at me, Robert. I won't touch you. I'm your father and you're safe now. Why, don't you see, we have the same blue eyes?'

Still fearful, Robert scanned the room before allowing himself to meet Henry's steady gaze. He looked away, then back again as though mesmerised by a mirror. Finally he lifted a dirt-ingrained hand and touched his father's distinctive blonde hair. With fingers as light as a feather, he followed the contours of his brow and aquiline nose to the stubble on his chin.

'Do you believe I'm your father?' Henry asked gently.

The boy nodded, somewhat awed.

'Are you a nice man?' he whispered.

Henry felt a lump in his throat and swallowed hard before replying.

'I hope to be one day, Robert. I hope one day you will be proud of me.'

Chapter Fifty-Six

The horses pricked their ears as they turned through the gates of Skellfield in the late afternoon. Jack, sharing their impatience to be home and anticipating the excitement that would ripple through the household, allowed them to canter down the long drive. When the carriage drew up at the main steps, he leapt down to open the door.

'Help my son first,' Henry instructed. 'He's as weak as a kitten.'

The pale child that emerged was unsteady when Jack set him on the ground on stick-thin legs. He had been thoroughly scrubbed, however, and bore some resemblance to the confident boy he had once been. Plain country clothes, hastily bought from a village shop, had replaced his rags. His hair, curling beneath an over-large cap, had been stripped of dirt and lice by the innkeeper's maid so that it, too, shone like his father's in the afternoon light. He stared open-mouthed at the magnificent ramparts above.

Henry stepped down behind him.

'Welcome to your new home, Master Cunningham. Do you think you will like it here?'

unlikely

For answer Robert simply grinned from ear to ear and continued to gaze at the building. At an upstairs window Lady Elizabeth clasped her hands to her breast and wept unashamedly. Her prayer had been answered. It was a time for rejoicing at last. She rang the bell in a fever of excitement and reached for her salts. When the housekeeper appeared she had gathered her composure.

'Ah, Mrs Buchanan. You will have heard, I'm sure, that we have a new arrival. I want you to see that Beth is dressed this evening as befits the mother of my grandson. We shall meet him by the fire in the drawing room and we shall take tea. And ask Mrs Bullen to provide a special cake.'

'Of course, my Lady,' the housekeeper nodded, but hesitated to leave.

'Oh, what is it, Mrs Buchanan? Have you something to say?'

'With respect, my Lady, I wonder if that is wise. After all, Beth is scarcely aware of the people around her and has not yet been out of her room.'

'Then it is high time she was, Mrs Buchanan. And what better occasion than when there's good news. Now do as I ask and send me my maid. I shall wear a silk dress,' she declared, opening her closet wide. 'I feel a new life lies ahead for the first time since my poor husband died. All will be well when Beth sees her child. You'll see.'

Mrs Buchanan left the room with a barely concealed sigh. She must comply with her mistress but she could not share her optimism. Beth was a lost soul in the view of many downstairs. The staff, however, sped about their tasks with renewed vigour, exchanging snatches of gossip as they crossed paths on the stairs with buckets of coal, and lit fires and aired beds for their master's triumphant return.

The drawing room met with Lady Elizabeth's approval. She settled herself under the soft light of a candelabra which caught the rich sheen of her dress. A servant placed a bouquet of pleasantly scented flowers on a table nearby. Another applied the bellows to the first yellow strips of flame until they leapt from the coals providing welcome warmth.

'Come and sit down, my dear,' Lady Elizabeth murmured as Beth was ushered in.' She patted a satin cushion beside her. 'How delightful you look in that pink and cream gown. And how exciting this is, is it not? To see your son for the first time after five long years.'

Beth did indeed look elegant. Her hair had been braided high at the crown and teased into small curls round her forehead, lending an altogether softer look to her usually plain face. The emphasis fell instead on her hazel eyes, delicate neck with its collar of pearls and slender waif-like body. She stared, however, without comprehension at the people around who persuaded her firmly to take a seat.

'There now. That wasn't so bad, was it?' Lady Elizabeth encouraged, taking her hand. The room fell suddenly silent and the servants melted into the shadows as Henry entered with a protective arm round his son. He guided him forward gently. Jack followed at a discreet distance, his attention fixed on Beth. Would she respond to this longed-for reunion?

'Robert. I would like you to meet my mother, Lady Elizabeth,' Henry announced proudly.

Robert, without any prompting, shook her proffered hand then returned his fingers swiftly to his father's palm.

'Dear boy, how much you resemble each other. I am so pleased you are here with the Cunninghams where you belong.' Tears coursed down her powdered cheeks and further words failed her as Henry moved on to stand before Beth.

'And this lady is very precious to me. This is your mother. Do you not think she is pretty?' he smiled, voicing aloud his surprise at her transformation.

Robert nodded slowly and with a child's directness asked.

'Are you really my mama?' He waited, they all waited but there was no response. Beth's eyes wandered listlessly from face to face, recognising none, like a sleep-walker trapped in a never-ending dream. She simply wanted her bed and oblivion.

Recognising her mistake, Lady Elizabeth took control and rang the bell.

'Take Beth to her room and bring in the tea for my guests. We'll have a slice of Mrs Bullen's cake. Your mother has not been well, Robert. She needs rest, just like you. You can help each other, can't you?'

'Perhaps she doesn't want me,' Robert said sadly. 'My last mama didn't want me. Daisy told me she'd gone to heaven. They sent me away after that.' He sniffed and wiped his nose on the cuff of his new jacket.

'Your mother wants you, child – more than you know. And no one is going to send you away. Now.' Lady Elizabeth caressed his hollow cheeks and drew him onto the vacant seat beside her. 'What will you have to eat, dear boy?' The array of rich food was too much for Robert. Like a starved kitten he had once tried to feed, he could only retch at the sight of it.

'Might I have some milk and a piece of bread, Ma'am?'

Henry, plainly disappointed that the joy of their homecoming could not be shared by Beth, nevertheless watched his son's every movement with wonder. The child he feared he would never have would grow strong and fit in his care. Together they would find a way to reach Beth's tormented soul.

His thoughts turned to the hell he had seen the previous day. The images had left him tossing in his sleep. Small, prematurely aged faces moving through clouds of dust haunted him still. He began to understand why men of honour such as Oastler had taken up the cause of the mill children. Could he not use his wealth and privilege to fight for them too? Robert turned towards him at that moment and Henry saw that his eyes bore witness to his suffering but also a hint of his old precocity. He had been rescued just in time. There were thousands of others who would never know freedom.

When the conversation faltered Jack ventured to ask when Ramona would join them. He could scarcely contain his impatience to see her.

'Ah, Ramona.' Lady Elizabeth replaced her china cup in its saucer and dusted imaginary crumbs from her gown. 'She's a rather impulsive young lady, isn't she? You'll have to ask Joe. He came up from the stables with some garbled message that she had matters to attend to at Hilldene. At any rate, she's gone Jack. Taken the pony and disappeared, it seems. Perhaps she didn't like it here,' she added rather vaguely.

Jack had heard enough. Abandoning protocol, he leapt to his feet and asked to be excused. He wasted no time in seeking out Joe who was whistling tunelessly in Lady's stall. He continued to groom the mare with long rhythmic strokes as Jack burst in and tugged at his sleeve.

'What's this about Ramona, Joe? Has she taken the cart? Is she travelling alone?' For once Joe was reticent. 'There's something wrong, isn't there? Something you're not telling me,' Jack persisted, seizing the brush. Joe scratched his red hair and moved awkwardly from one foot to the other. 'You told her, Joe, didn't you? Told her about Storm. Tell me or by God I'll....' He raised his fists, leaving the groom in no doubt of his intentions.

'I wasn't to tell you, see,' Joe said helplessly. 'Anyway she don't want you to go.'

'Go where?'

'She's gone looking for Storm. I don't know where,' Joe sulked, picking up another brush. 'I suppose that means you'll go after the lass.' He raised an eyebrow. It was a question rather than a statement.

344

Jack didn't answer but punched his fist against the wall. Lady Elizabeth was right. The girl was impulsive. Well, if she thought he would follow, she was mistaken.

'No,' he said brusquely. 'She must make her own decisions. I'll not beg. She knows where I am.' He kicked the mud from his boots and turned on his heel.

Joe watched him go with a wry smile as he moved his brush absently over Lady's withers.

'Our Jack is jealous' he confided to the mare. 'He'll not admit it. Too proud for that. But there'll not be another. That girl has bewitched him.'

Chapter Fifty-Seven

Ramona pulled Joe's cap low over her eyes as she approached the outskirts of York. The flat scrubland studded with copses had for years been the haunt of Romany folk in the winter months. She scanned the scene with the keen sight of a born gypsy woman but there was no sign of Storm amongst the tethered horses. Nor were any of the wagons amongst the trees familiar to her.

She sighed and drew her cloak tighter against the chill of the late afternoon. Had she been impulsive to attempt this trip on her own? If she was recognised at all, she could expect only silence from these most tight-knit of people. She had been a 'gorgio,' an outsider, since her father had revealed her accident of birth on the gallows. From that moment only Franco, her childhood companion, had pursued her. Not, as she would have wished, with the true affection of a trusted friend but with a passion that scared her. She longed suddenly for Jack's protective presence yet knew that his courage and strength would be no match for Franco's sleight of hand with a knife. She pictured his deft fingers skinning and skewering a rabbit for the fire, and shivered. Her instincts were right. She must deal with this alone and seek to soothe his tempestuous spirit. His kin would have left Malton at Michaelmas, she reasoned, so it was likely she would find him in one of the clearings along the way. Tilly was tired but she would urge the cob on until dusk.

Turning away from the distant spires of the Minster, she followed the well-worn track to the east. It was her gypsy roots not her aristocratic ones, however, that she recalled as her small cart rumbled on. How her paternal grandmother with her hardy character and robust health had trained her in country lore so that she could instinctively read nature and learn from its signs. Bird song cut short or the sudden jinking in flight of pigeons and crows, the various alarm calls of blackbirds and wrens – all were a language she understood. How to see without looking and hear without listening; how to observe people in order to know more of their inner souls.

When the old lady had died and been buried in a favourite churchyard, Ramona had felt a vacuum in her life that her taciturn father could never quite fill. The Romanies bowed to religious authority to procure respect. They were often married, baptised or buried in the Christian faith, but at heart they remained loyal to their ancient ways. She remembered lying prostrate in the grass, staring with wonder at the wide dome above and imagining a stairway stretching up to the stars. Sometimes she and Franco would gaze into the velvety darkness as though into a crystal ball, creating faces and shapes and omens in the clouds. Now the magical childhood they had shared had been wrecked by his insane jealousy.

The sound of a post-horn from a carriage behind brought Ramona back to the present. A clearing lay ahead where she could pull away safely from the galloping team.

'Come on, Tilly,' she urged, flicking the whip over the sturdy piebald's rump. 'Out of the way before it runs us down.'

Such accidents were not uncommon after sunset and having reached the glade in the nick of time, she decided they had travelled far enough. She led the pony from the shafts and allowed her to graze in the covert nearby. Meanwhile she prepared a bed for herself between the seats of the cart. The night would soon pass and she intended to be on her way at first light.

She slept like a child until the early hours when a snapping of twigs deeper in the wood caused Tilly to throw up her head and scent the breeze. Following the direction of her pricked ears, Ramona crept towards the disturbance until she could just make out the silhouette of a horse. Behind her, Tilly was whinnying in clear recognition. Was it possible she had stumbled upon Storm in the night?

'Whoa there,' she murmured, as her hands slid down the withers to feel for the raised edge of a scar on the foreleg. It was there. The horse nuzzled her in the darkness without fear. 'Why, it is you, Storm,' she whispered, her pulse racing at this stroke of good fortune. There was no sign of Franco, though a bag and a poaching net hooked to the saddle told her that he was up to his old tricks. The horse was ready to ride. Was Franco hoping to make a quick getaway if the keepers appeared? He had eluded them for years so that now the challenge of catching him red-handed was a sport. She decided to harness Tilly without delay and secure Storm with a leading rein to the rear of the cart. He had after all been stolen from her, his rightful owner. Her father had been unjustly hanged for no less a crime.

Busying herself with this plan, she did not hear Franco's stealthy approach until he dashed towards her from a few yards away. He gripped her arms so tight that it hurt. His voice when he spoke was heavy with menace.

'I knew you'd come back. You'll not cheat me this time. I'll not let you go!' He pinned her with ease against the cart and reached for the snare wire he kept coiled round the buttons of his wide-pocketed coat. Ramona fought like a trapped animal and cried out in alarm, to no avail. Sensing gentleness might calm him where anger would not, she pressed her lips lightly against his cheek.

'I came to talk to you, Franco. To seek your blessing,' she began. She quickly realised the folly of her visit. This man would never see reason.

'Ha! My blessing,' he sneered. 'My blessing to destroy your life again. I can't let you do that. I won't let you. You belong to me – not your precious Jack. I'll take you to Ireland if I have to. He'll not find you there and you'll soon forget.'

The horses jostled and the cart swayed as Ramona fought to break free, so that neither heard the rattle of a jay or the chatter of magpies over the wood that might have warned them. Too late, a keeper in the velveteen suit of his trade burst upon the scene, blowing his whistle in triumph. Soon others arrived to encircle them.

'We've bagged a brace here, mi' lads,' the first one chortled, 'and I'd swear that's the gypsy we've been after for years. It'll be transportation for you I shouldn't wonder,' he gloated with a hugely satisfied grin.

Franco made no attempt to discard the rabbits that swung limp from his belt. His usual cunning had deserted him. One thought seemed to offer him hope. He snatched the cloth cap from Ramona's head, allowing her hair to cascade down her back.

'Then the girl goes too. She was in it all along. You'll find a poaching net on her horse,' he lied as they clapped him in irons and dragged him away. Ramona's protests fell on deaf ears as she too was arrested. In desperation she fought her captors until she had no strength left.

'Cunning little minx! Dressed as a boy, too. Guilty as hell, if you ask me.' The men nudged each other, enjoying the moment. 'Fine-looking woman, mind and a fine-looking animal,' the keeper observed with a covetous glance at Storm. 'I'd best stable the horses – until the law takes its course, you understand,' he added cautiously.

Chapter Fifty-Eight

Two days after Robert's arrival at Skellfield, the seasons changed suddenly. A light dusting of snow settled over the estate, transforming the trees and pastureland into a virginal expanse of white. Jack stared at the scene in dismay when he emerged from his cottage at dawn. Its grandeur was lost on him. He saw only an obstacle to Ramona's return – if indeed she did return, he thought moodily. He had allowed himself to imagine their future together, had agreed to Henry's suggestion that he set up home in the lodge with his new bride. He could just make out the steep slate roof on the far side of the lake and the wooden stalls that would house a suitable horse for Ramona and one for himself. In time, he had mused, his son or daughter would be raised there and he would ensure that the rustic hearth was always supplied with aromatic pine.

Why was happiness so elusive, he pondered as he set off on his morning chores. Why was even Robert's homecoming marred by Beth's continuing decline? He smiled wryly as he checked a fence and made a mental note that it needed repair. At least the child would not want for love and affection.

Already he scampered happily between Henry's study, Lady Elizabeth's boudoir and Mrs Bullen's kitchen with its two sleepy cats.

Towards midday, the snow gave way to slush and Jack's thoughts turned to the meeting he had arranged for the late afternoon when his work was completed. It would be the first Ten Hours assembly to be held at Skellfield and it would need his full attention. He must block out his own emotional turmoil and encourage Henry to throw his weight behind the factory movement. Whether Ramona returned or not was up to her. In the meantime, he must not waste this precious opportunity to make a difference.

Jack was surprised to find Henry taking the air as he approached the main house. Robert was by his side, clapping his gloved hands in delight as he rolled together pockets of shrinking snow. He did not say much but the wide smile that split his bony features warmed Henry's heart as little else had done in the past.

'I shall take this young man to see his mother now. We must make every effort to find a way through. You, too, must visit her Jack. She knows you best of all. We can only hope that one day she will respond.'

'I speak to her all the time, about the past. Even about her brother William. I see no improvement at all. Is there nothing more we can do?' Jack asked. 'No doctor she could see?'

'They suggest only rest and more rest,' Henry sighed. 'No excitement. No exertion at all. I swear she grows paler each day in that confounded room. But we must not lose faith. We must wait.' He changed the subject abruptly. 'Come to the library, Jack, when you've seen to the men. We must discuss the agenda for this afternoon. I shall need to know who all these would-be reformers are.'

It was decided that the meeting would take place in the suitably male surroundings of the smoking room. Sufficient chairs were placed round a rectangular table to accommodate all the names on Jack's list. Amongst them were lawyers, clergymen, editors, medical practitioners, masters of industry and members of the aristocracy as well as plain-spoken working men. All were united not by class, creed or politics but by their radical view that government should be based on liberty and equality.

When his guests had introduced themselves and taken their places, Henry invited them to speak, content merely to listen at first and form his own views. He knew that outside the walls of his own estate, a downturn in the economy was causing hardship, that when the price of bread fluctuated there was no longer a parish relief to cushion the starving. The unpopular Poor Law, introduced a decade ago, simply condemned the destitute to the harsh regime of the expanding workhouses. He himself had been brought up to accept that poverty was a natural device to keep the population down. Yet here in his house was a new breed of nonconformists who had a broader Christian view. A belief that anarchy and revolution would result if the right of ordinary people to a decent life was not respected.

John Fielden, a mill owner with a seat in parliament who had long supported the Ten Hours cause, rose first to address the committee.

'My honourable friends,' he began. 'No doubt you will be greatly encouraged to learn that our efforts to secure the release of the Factory King have proved fruitful. Enough money was raised, I am delighted to inform you, to free Richard Oastler from Fleet Prison – a full four years after his confinement there. The debts incurred by his ceaseless campaigning will finally have been paid, thanks to the contributions of his loyal supporters. And from my visits I can tell you that he is still a man who sees only the suffering of others and cannot forget what he has seen. Let us be ready to receive him. Let us be prepared to throw our last ounce of strength behind the Ten Hours Bill.'

By the time the meeting closed Henry was speaking with as much fervour as Jack and his many new acquaintances.

'Gentlemen,' he concluded, 'I have seldom been as moved as I have been tonight by what I have heard. Through an accident of fate, my eyes have been opened to the horrors that are daily perpetrated in our mills. Whatever influence I have, I shall use to support your worthy cause. If parliament is within my reach rather than yours, I shall put myself forward as a candidate. I shall fight on the hustings with my heart and my head on your behalf. And with God's help and that of men like Oastler, we shall surely succeed.'

Matthew Turner stood up and raised his glass of claret towards Henry and Jack.

'Our cause, it seems, attracts the finest of men. I speak for us all when I say we would be honoured if you would attend our next meeting in York at the end of the month. To your very good health, sirs, and God bless you both.'

Chapter Fifty-Nine

enry's experiences, perhaps even his father's death, had done more than sober him. They had profoundly altered his attitude to life. The youthful self-indulgence that had brought shame to his family was being replaced by real conviction and moral courage. He discovered he was a natural orator and used this skill to promote the interests of the oppressed mill workers. Jack was never far from his side on these occasions and the two of them became a respected and familiar team.

By the end of the month, however, it was clear that a happy conclusion to their other relationships was to be denied them. Hope was beginning to waver in the case of Beth's mental state. She seemed as deeply entrenched as ever in her shadowy world of secrets and fears. And any mention of Ramona to Jack was met by a wall of silence. The hurt of her disappearance was still too raw for him to contemplate.

It was on their way back from a meeting in York that the sight of some gypsies on Clifton Moor prompted Henry to confront his friend. Dismounting, he pointed to a woman gathering wood for kindling in the folds of her skirt.

'I'll look after the horses. Let's settle this matter once and for all. Offer her a piece of silver. They can all be bought. She'll tell you what she knows.'

Jack shook his head stubbornly.

'Don't waste your time, sir. I don't give the wench a thought any more,' he lied.

But Henry would not be deterred.

'Then I shall go. Confound your churlish pride, Jack Cartwright,' he muttered as he threw him the reins and strode away. The woman tried to make off towards her camp but paused when Henry hailed her with a promise of reward. 'A shilling for you, my good woman. More if you can tell me what I need to know.'

The weathered old eyes narrowed but darted covetously towards the coin Henry tossed in his palm. She listened as he talked of Ramona, her pony and trap, the theft of Storm and Franco's part in it. When he had finished, she looked at him with a triumphant toothless smile. If she had intended to keep silent, the temptation to talk was too great.

'Aye. I know the pair,' she cackled. Got their just deserts. Locked up, they are. There's talk they'll be transported beyond the seas. Poaching, see. Not like Franco to get caught. Gorgio women bring bad luck. Good riddance I say.'

Stunned by this news, Henry produced more coins.

'What else do you know, old woman? Where are they now?'

'Far as I know in Ripon gaol. Till the magistrates' court meets again.' She snatched the money from his hand and melted quickly out of sight, fearing she had said too much already. It was not their way to talk to strangers. Jack was adjusting the saddles with studied disinterest when Henry returned but he soon sensed there was news of Ramona. He, too, listened in disbelief as the reasons for her absence became clear.

'What a fool I am! What a heartless fool! My god, has my stupid pride cost her her freedom, even her life? I must do something, Henry. I must do something now.' He leapt into the saddle, startling his horse.

'Steady, Jack. You must let me take care of this.' Henry glanced up at the clouds and paused to assess the strength of the wind. They had spent the night in York and the horses were relatively fresh. 'We could be in Ripon by mid afternoon. We'll stay at the Unicorn. I can make enquiries there and tomorrow I'll speak to the landowner concerned. Believe me, my friend. Most men can be bought at a price.'

'I am indebted to you, sir, for so many things but never more than now,' Jack called as the two settled down to a steady gallop. There was greater activity than usual in Ripon when their spent horses drew up in the Market Square before threading their way to the Unicorn Inn. The courtyard here, too, was packed with carriages, the reason for which would prove a stroke of good fortune. It was the afternoon preceding the quarterly sessions when the Justices met for their customary dinner at three o'clock. The guests included many who would take part in the parade from the Town Hall to the court-house the following day. This was a fine spectacle attended by the Mayor, the High Constable and a number of the local dignitaries. During his reclusive years Henry had shown little interest in matters outside his estate but he had no illusions about these often pretentious and corruptible men.

'Take the horses quickly, Jack. I see an opportunity here.' Henry's eye was fixed on a robust figure stepping down from a coach.

'Sir James Oxley if I'm not mistaken,' he announced, intercepting him swiftly with outstretched hand. 'May I suggest that I buy you an ale? It's a coincidence indeed that I should be lodging here too.'

Sir James turned, holding his velvet lapels in a judicial manner as he regarded Henry for a moment.

'Cunningham's son, aren't you? Why yes, I always have time for a fellow landowner. We must stick together the likes of you and I. You have something you wish to discuss, I suspect. We'll meet in the snug before dinner is served.' Lifting his hat and followed by his entourage, Sir James disappeared inside. Jack returned hurriedly from the stables with no thought in his mind but to seek out Ramona.

'I suggest you take some refreshment first,' Henry advised to no avail.

'I can neither rest nor eat, sir, until she is at least aware that we know of her fate and are doing our best to get her released.'

'Offer comfort by all means, Jack. She will be heartened by your single-mindedness. But I can be of more use to you here. My authority is your best hope. Any dissent or disorder on your part may be used against her. Remember that.' A wagon, driven too fast, caused Jack to move smartly aside. 'You'll find the Liberty prison in St Marygate,' Henry called. 'Keep your composure, my friend.'

The patron of the Unicorn discreetly reorganised his guests to ensure that Henry had a suitable room overlooking the square – a privilege he always accorded the gentry. When Henry, washed and refreshed, came downstairs, he was waiting to usher him through the crowded lounge to a private bay at the back. There, Sir James had already settled with a bottle of sherry and two large glasses.

'Thank you, no. I don't,' Henry said firmly. 'I'll have coffee instead.'

Sir James raised an eyebrow and surveyed him over the rim of his glass.

'So it's true. You don't drink any more. Can't be easy. Not in our society. Your father would be proud of you, my boy. Well, what is it that you want to talk to me about?'

Henry outlined as briefly as he could the circumstances surrounding Ramona's life and her foolhardy attempt to deal with Franco alone. She had no interest in poaching and indeed no reason to steal. Could the matter not be resolved by the payment of a fine? Sir James slapped a jovial hand on Henry's shoulder.

'Well, I'll be damned if I'm not the injured party. It

360

was my land, you see. I know this fellow. He's a sly one alright and he deserves to be punished. Darned nuisance, he is.' He paused to savour his sherry and reflect. 'I accept your word as a gentleman, however, about the girl. I'll see that she's discreetly released tomorrow and her horses returned. To keep the matter quiet, we'll discharge Franco, too, on payment of a fine to keep the clerics happy. Mark you, Henry. He must be told. One more offence, and no question. He'll be transported across the seas for at least seven years.'

Henry sank back in his chair, relaxed at last.

'My estate manager is a good man, Sir James, and you have just made him a very happy one too. He plans to marry the woman he loves before any more disasters befall them.' He laughed softly. 'There must be something in that mixed blood of hers that drives a man wild.'

'I'm glad I could be of service to you, Henry,' Sir James replied. 'Your Uncle Edward has left his own legacy it seems. These things happen of course. We all know it but it's not talked about in polite society, is it?' He leant forward conspiratorially, his eyes sparkling with alcohol now. 'Why, even my own son sired an illegitimate child, you know!' He winked at Henry and his robust chest shook with laughter.

Henry sipped his coffee, unable to share his mirth.

'It happens sir, as you say. But it is too often a tragedy for the offspring. Forgive me, but I've heard gossip amongst the servants about the foundlings in the workhouse. One I believe is the result of your son's liaison with a kitchen maid. We are careless of what suffering we cause, are we not? I speak as one who knows.'

'Why, what a serious fellow you've become, to be sure.' Slightly discomfited, Sir James poured another sherry with a flourish. Perhaps you should not have given up the vine after all.'

'I don't intend to be serious, sir. Life has made me so. I have seen things that I chose to ignore in the past. I have seen sights in the mills that still haunt me and will do so until their cruel practices cease. Do you realise sir, that the very same blood that flows in your veins, flows in that poor foundling? And that child is very likely to suffer the horrors I have seen.'

'Henry, my boy. You must not betray your class. The aristocracy cannot afford to weaken now. You have only to look to France to see what happens if we lose control.'

'You speak as I once did, sir – not so long ago. I challenge you to come with me and see such a place for yourself. If you have no compassion afterwards then you have no heart – and without a heart a country cannot thrive.'

'It is not my business to visit mills. It is my business to support the establishment.'

'You dare not, sir. That is the truth. You wish to remain blind to what is going on.'

'Are you questioning my integrity, sir?'

'Exactly that,' Henry replied evenly.

'Then, damn you, I shall come to your mill. You shall name the day and I shall come with you. Now, if you'll excuse me, I have duties to perform as Justice of the Peace.'

'I have been too harsh, sir. I meant no disrespect and I admire your courage. Please accept my apology and my genuine thanks. I hope very much to see you again.'

Chapter Sixty

The next day, when the court-house opened for its quarterly sessions, Ramona's case was dealt with swiftly. She emerged pale and subdued from the confines of her cell but stood before the bench with dignified composure. No shapeless prison garb could disguise the perfectly formed figure beneath nor could its drabness detract from her natural beauty. Sir James Oxley looked over his spectacles to view her fine Cunningham features before signing the sheet in front of him.

'No charge. Dismiss. Next one,' he announced laconically, lowering his eyes to the dainty ankles that stepped down from the dock.

Once out through the stone portico, however, Ramona's show of strength crumbled. She melted into Jack's waiting arms and allowed him to carry her to a nearby yard where he laid her gently in the rear of the cart. She watched, shivering slightly beneath her wrap, as he harnessed Tilly with the fumbling hands of a lovesick youth.

'I'll send a lad to collect the horses,' he called to the bewildered ostler, urging the cob forward and onto the road at a spanking trot. He said nothing to Ramona. There was no need. The unspoken words

mixed blood would survive well in a prison for one

between them required an unspoken response. 'Would the confounded meadows never give way to woodland where a man might find privacy?' Jack thought, as he passed a wagon at speed. His impatience earned him an angry riposte but he sped on regardless. At last his objective came into sight and he guided Tilly deep into a forest of pines. Before the pony's hooves had drawn to a halt, he had abandoned the reins and clambered over his seat to Ramona's side.

They lay motionless, anticipating the ecstasy that would follow, their breathing synchronised, their eyes reflecting each other's joy. At last Jack lowered his lips over hers. He kissed her gently at first until they parted like a bee-sucked flower, allowing his tongue to explore. The pain of thwarted love exploded into pleasure beyond any they had known so that Ramona gasped, afraid suddenly of its intensity. Then she gave herself up to desire, moaning as he kissed her hair, her neck, her breasts, her very being. The exquisiteness when he loosened her smock to reach her small rounded abdomen made her weep and cry out. Their love might well have been consummated in a moment of wild abandon if Tilly had not been startled at that point by a bird. Jack leapt forward, cursing, to restrain her.

'Whoa there! Whoa,' he soothed but the pony fought against the bit as she cantered wide-eyed towards the open road. Behind him, Ramona drew her cloak tight and laughed softly.

'My Tilly is wiser than I, is she not?' she sighed,

wiping away tears. 'Your son must not be born out of wedlock, Jack Cartwright. This must not happen again. Not until we are man and wife.' She tilted her head and smiled coyly at his broad back but he did not turn round. Several minutes passed before he felt calm enough to respond.

'Aye,' he said finally, his voice hoarse with emotion. 'Aye, we'll be wed.' He pulled his cap down, squared his shoulders and set Tilly on a straight course. Ramona was to be his at last. Next time it would be different. Next time their love would be lawful and serene and would mellow into a life of fulfilment. But he knew this moment would never be surpassed.

Like a creature tasting freedom, Ramona felt strong enough now to sit by his side. He slung a possessive arm around her.

'You smell of carbolic soap,' he murmured laughing, caressing her hair as the wind swept through it. 'Not like the gypsy woman I love.' She snuggled her head in his shoulder. Each time he glanced down her eyes shone back at him so that he scarcely noticed the journey at all. When they passed through the gates of Skellfield, however, he pointed out the lodge.

'That is where you and I shall live. We must marry before Christmas. I can wait no longer. And you shall ride Storm whenever you wish. Does that thought please you, Mrs Cartwright?' he grinned.

She kissed his cheek tenderly.

'Aye. That thought delights me, Jack.' She looked up in wonder at the solid stone walls of their future home. In the summer, roses festooned the doors and windows, and rhododendrons bloomed in the garden.

'And Tilly – can I keep Tilly too?' The pony's ears flicked back.

'Aye. Tilly's your family, part of your past.'

'What will I do with Hilldene?' she asked as an afterthought.

'We'll find you a tenant. You'll be free to go back if you choose.'

'I shan't choose, Jack. The love and the life that I have is yours now till the day I die.'

Chapter Sixty-One

B eth reached for the herb-scented cushion that had slipped from her grasp onto the bedside table and pressed it against her cheek. It reminded her of a meadow fragrant with wild flowers, a scene etched in her mind since childhood. Indeed, at one time she would have known this delightful place was close to the cottage where she and her brother were born. It was where her mother had spun thread and her father woven yarn while she and William spread the colourful warps along the hedgerows to dry. As the mill towns expanded, their simple livelihood had been swept away.

But Beth could remember none of this – only the pasture, bright with buttercups and heavy with the scent of summer. She clung to the image now, as though it held the key to the wasteland in her mind. Recently, a garden pungent with lavender, sweetpeas, roses and foxgloves had infiltrated her thoughts but she had no idea why.

She sighed and stared at the lady in a peach-coloured gown who sat by her side, pulling silk thread through a tapestry. She felt comfortable in her presence, even reassured by it. Were they both wanderers in the same twilight world? Was she, too, lost? Not knowing which path she had travelled nor where it led? Or had she found a way out? Their eyes met and exchanged a smile. At the same moment, the door opened a crack and a small boy with blonde hair peeped through.

'You may come in, Robert, and say hello to Beth but you mustn't tire her. She needs rest. Don't you my dear?' Lady Elizabeth soothed. She put aside her needlework. 'Come and sit here beside your grandmother.' Her smile broadened as the child snuggled himself happily into her arms.

'Now, Beth,' she continued. 'This fine-looking boy is your son. You know that, don't you?'

Beth transferred her gaze slowly to the newcomer. He had the same clear blue eyes as the tall man who came daily to visit her. But she had no son that she knew of. She sank back against her pillow, drawing the floral coverlet up to her chin. Where did she belong? Who were all these people? And why did they talk of things that perplexed her? She liked the boy's face. He even made her laugh but his attempts to remind her of Oxpasture House left her bewildered and fearful.

'But you must remember,' Robert persisted. 'There was an enormous apple tree in the garden.' He demonstrated its size with his still-emaciated arms. 'My swing was underneath it. Daisy used to push me. I gave my kitten a ride once.' His face clouded suddenly and the impish grin vanished as the loss of his pet and the horror of his time in the mill returned to haunt him. His voice dropped to a

have me not? permeates though? Her look

whisper. 'Grace took me away. Why did you let Grace take me away? Why didn't you come? I don't like you. You're not my mama.' Before Lady Cunningham could restrain him, he had slipped from her lap and run out through the door.

'I'm so sorry, my dear,' she said, brushing aside a tear. 'We have all suffered, have we not? You mustn't blame the boy. He is still so young. I must go to him and try to explain. I shall pray for both of you.'

Beth fell asleep after she had gone, and dreamt once more that she was alone in a vast mansion. It was a recurring dream in which she moved soundlessly down sweeping staircases and up servants' back stairs, through a maze of corridors lined with closed and locked doors. Somewhere behind one of these were her few possessions, in effect her past life, but which? Her search was always in vain. Always she awoke lost and crying out in despair.

On this occasion she was rescued from her torment by a firm hand on her brow. It belonged to the tall man with blonde hair who came to see her each day. He had pulled up a chair and was talking to her softly.

'My poor moorland waif. You don't know me, do you? Or our fine son. Nor even your cousin, Jack, who brought you into my life all those years ago. Well, I shall tell you the good news all the same. Jack and Ramona are to marry – just a week before Christmas and I want you to be there to see them wed. You have a month to grow strong, Beth.' He leant closer, willing her to listen. 'Look at me. You must do it, my dear, for Robert's sake and for mine.' He would have kissed her but Beth withdrew instinctively from his embrace. Men hurt her. Men were not to be trusted. This much she knew.

'That confounded mill,' Henry muttered to himself. Whatever happened there had maimed her for life. Had their brief liaison been the only window in her sad life, her only experience of joy? If so, she would be better dead than in her present hell, he thought bitterly. All the same he would encourage her to walk in the grounds and perhaps take the air in a carriage with Jack. He would try everything in his power to rekindle what they had. Though what that was, even he could not define. Love? No. There had not been time for such a passion to develop. Empathy, yes – and an awareness that together they formed a whole. That this fragile damaged women, rather than any of the titled beauties he had known, could offer him peace and freedom from his demons. He held her small limp hand between his own, seeking to infuse her with his own strength.

'I will not lose you, Beth. I cannot. I shall never give up. Mary will make you a suitable gown and you will come to Jack's wedding. I promise you.'

Much later, when the drapes had been drawn and the room was in shadow, Robert reappeared at her bedside. So soundless was his approach that she reached out to touch him. Was he a figment of her dream world? Her fingers traced the contours of his face with a mother's tenderness, perhaps aware at some level of a bond between them. He struggled to maintain a sombre expression as a kitten wriggled beneath his jerkin.

'Grandmama has sent me to say I'm sorry. She says one day you will know who I am.' His duty performed, he glanced at the door and then back at Beth. 'Joe's going to drown them,' he confided, whispering so close to her ear that she felt his hot breath on her cheek. 'Will you hide this one and give him some milk? See – he's so soft – you must stroke him,' he insisted. Their hands touched as they caressed the velvety fur and Beth laughed. The fledgling relationship of mother and son might have progressed further had a maid not entered the room. Robert pushed the kitten beneath the covers and melted quickly away.

Chapter Sixty-Two

Mrs Bullen rubbed her aching back and sank into her sitting-room chair with a sigh. It was up to the other servants now to attend to the guests. She had cooked all day to provide for Henry's increasing band of political friends. Whigs, Tories, Radicals, even bishops and factory operatives were gathered in the great reception room above. Who would have thought that Henry of all people would take up the cause of his fellow man with such fervour, she mused. His self-indulgent youth had hardly been an indicator of what would follow. Yet such was his influence now that she would be very surprised if he was not elected Member of Parliament for Ripon. Had not Sir James Oxley himself joined the factory movement after seeing the cruelties practised in the mills?

Tonight Lord Ashley, fresh from Westminster with the latest developments on the Ten Hour Bill, was to be guest of honour. Mrs Bullen smiled to herself as an unusually flustered Mr Scott rapped out orders to the footmen. She heard him mutter an oath as a glass shattered on the marble floor. Like herself, the butler was unused to such sustained activity. With Ramona's wedding to think about

373

too, the household would have its work cut out till Christmas and beyond.

She closed her eyes as she sipped a cocoa and allowed herself, as she often did of late, to revisit the past. All that was happening now could be traced back to that night in the storm. To the arrival at her kitchen door of two destitute children. She had taken them to her heart, watched them flourish at Skellfield and prayed for their return when fate snatched them away. Now, nothing gave her greater pleasure than the prospect of Jack settling on the estate with the woman he loved.

But what of Beth? Mrs Bullen's old heart beat erratically and her face crumpled in sorrow. If she could give her life for that gentlest of souls she would do so, but there had been no improvement. She sensed with her deep insight into Henry's troubled life that he would settle for no other woman. Beth was the mother of his child. She and Robert were his family. Perhaps it was a blessing he could commit himself with such energy to a worthy cause. Quite what his militant father would have made of it, she could only guess, but times were changing. Henry's brand of courage could improve the lives of thousands. She was disturbed by a slight shuffling noise. Her eyes half opened.

'Why, if it isn't my Robert,' she beamed. 'And you can't fool me. There's another kitten in that waistcoat of yours.' She shook her head in mock disapproval as she gathered him onto her lap. 'Joe still hasn't found the black one. Now where could it possibly be?'

'I gave it to my mama,' Robert said, lowering his voice conspiratorially. 'She's going to hide it for me.'

The fact that he called her his mother was not lost on Mrs Bullen. It must surely be good for Beth. They sat for a while in companionable silence watching the firelight play on the walls. He was still just young enough to enjoy the comfort of her ample bosom.

'Time for bed, my little man,' she said at last. 'You may say goodnight to your father but that is all. He has a meeting to attend.'

'I know ~~that~~,' Robert said, reverting to his old precocious manner. 'Papa wants me to go to the meeting. He wants me to tell them things. Things about....'

Mrs Bullen interrupted.

'You must have a wash and a clean shirt then, child. I'll ring for Annie. But remember. You needn't talk if you don't want to.'

'But I do!' Robert protested, wide-eyed. 'Papa says it will help my friends. Papa says I will speak one day in a big House with lots of important people.'

'You're still a boy, Robert. You must do as you choose when you grow up.' Mrs Bullen caressed his blonde head thoughtfully. 'No doubt I shall be in the churchyard by then but I shall be watching over you.'

Upstairs meanwhile, the assembled guests were moving to their seats around a large table. Lord Ashley took pride of place at the top, flanked on either side by Henry and Lord Oxley. Next to them, on hand to ensure the proceedings ran smoothly, sat Jack and to his right, a robust county landowner called William Ferrand. The latter had campaigned tirelessly in London, soliciting eminent people night after night to secure the release of Oastler from Fleet prison. At last the liberation fund had made the discharge of his debts possible and there was every hope that he would rekindle his campaign in the north in the new year. Henry rose first to introduce each man by name and to express their general delight at this news.

'Gentlemen,' he continued, 'I am honoured to be host tonight to so many distinguished members of our cause. Indeed as a recent convert, I feel I am the least distinguished in terms of achievement but I intend to be of service in any way I can. If I may, however, I would like to digress for a moment. There are those of you here who know me of old. Perhaps, with justification, you look at me with a sceptical eye and think, again with justification, how long before I revert to my past self-indulgent ways?' He glanced up at an imposing portrait of the Duke of Wellington which dominated the far end of the room and allowed time for every head to turn towards it.

'There we have a noble and courageous man whom Englishmen the length and breadth of the country are proud to display on their walls. My father was such a man and I admired him, too. There seemed to be no way I could equal him. But times move on and perhaps through fate, and a mentor in the form of a less privileged man, Jack Cartwright here, I have learnt that the power of words and conviction is equal to the sword. And that there are many injustices in our new industrialised world.' He placed a hand on Jack's shoulder and continued. 'He is a very remarkable person, gentleman, who as a mere child trusted to providence and led his cousin Beth away from the mills in search of a better life. It is thanks to both of them that I am here today and that I now have a purpose in mine. Many of you will be aware of what they suffered from our previous discussions but I would like you to meet a more recent victim. None other than my own son, Robert.'

Jack, responding to a nod, ushered the freshly groomed child from the care of a maid to his father's side. Robert, unfazed, stared at the many faces that turned towards him.

'He's a Cunningham, alright,' a vaguely amused Lord Oxley murmured to Henry. 'You say you found him in Scrimshaw's mill?'

'Will they help Smudge, father? You promised.'

'Who is Smudge, Robert?' Lord Ashley asked gently.

'He was my friend. He slept next to me but he got sick and they took him away.'

'We want to help all the children, Robert. That is why we are here. Your father hopes to sit beside me in the House of Lords. Perhaps one day you will join him.'

Henry took Robert's hand and held it firmly. 'Would you show Lord Ashley the scars on your back before our meeting begins?' There were mutters of disgust around the table as Jack helped him roll up his shirt. It was evident his thin ribcage had been scored like a piece of meat by the merciless use of a whip. Jack felt compelled to intervene.

'They do that to keep them awake. There are not enough inspectors, Lord Ashley. In spite of all our efforts, children as young as five are still working from six in the morning until anything up to ten at night.'

Lord Ashley nodded soberly before turning back to Robert.

'Thank you for your help, young sir – and we'll see what we can do for your friend Smudge.'

Henry placed a proprietorial arm round Robert's undernourished frame.

'This fine boy was rescued from his fate in the nick of time. He is my son and heir, gentlemen. When her health permits, I intend to make his mother, Beth, my lawful wife.'

After the maid had escorted her charge from the room, Henry sat down. He had declared his intentions in spite of the social mores of his class. Would they accept him on his own terms? He invited Lord Ashley to speak. The strong-featured eldest son of the Earl of Shaftesbury was a softly spoken man who had taken an early interest in reducing the hours of the factory children. He, along with others, would see the Ten Hours Bill finally enacted in 1847.

'We should all strive to become good men and good women and useful members of society. I for one am moved by your humility, compassion and courage, Henry. How you came by these qualities is no concern of ours. All that matters is that I believe you are sincere and capable of great things as a future Member of Parliament for Ripon. And now, my honourable friends, to the subject of greatest importance – The Ten Hours Bill. We have no time to waste. We must campaign, print leaflets and publish our views by any means we can. We must all be ready to support the Factory King.'

Chapter Sixty-Three

Taking time off from her dairy chores, Aggie crossed the yard to the barn. The doors were open wide. Inside, Nathan was threshing sheaves laid out in layers on a wooden floor. He swung the flail with great skill, never missing his aim, but it was back-breaking work. Soon it would be her turn to sweep up the corn and the chaff with a broom and after that, to separate the grain. She sighed, removed her cap and pushed unruly strands of damp hair from her face. Hilldene was a small farmstead but she was getting too old to cope here on her own. Why, it was almost the end of November. A whole month had passed and still Ramona had not returned. She recalled her last words ruefully.

'Aggie,' she had said as she set off in the trap with Beth, 'some good will come of this journey. I know it. Trust me.' And she had. But that trust was wavering now. Perhaps some misfortune had befallen them on the way. Perhaps they had never arrived at Skellfield to tell Jack and Henry their extraordinary news. Nathan shook the dust from his clothes and sat down, equally exhausted but blessed with the optimism of youth. He had a chance to prove himself and no work was too hard. He was making mistakes but he was learning fast, how to foresee problems, how to manage a farm. With Michael gone, he need tip his cap to no one but he shared Aggie's concern for Ramona. A woman on her own, even a seasoned traveller, was always at risk on the well-worn tracks across the county. As mistress of Hilldene however, she had re-asserted her past independence and did much as she pleased.

'You need a break too, lad. Come back to the house for a slice of my cake and some ale,' Aggie suggested. 'We'll put our two heads together and see what's to be done. We can't go on like this. We must have another pair of hands about the place.' She wheezed noisily as they picked their way through the acrid-smelling slurry which seeped from the cowshed at this time of year.

Nathan glanced up as he always did when a stagecoach halted on the road above. It was a Yellow Bounder, a carriage which ran daily between York and Scarborough and prided itself on keeping to time. He should have persuaded Ramona to use it, he thought, as he watched with indifference a man and two children descend. To his surprise, when the coach departed, they walked not towards the village but to the rickety gate which led to the farm. He shaded his eyes.

'Why, Aggie. I believe that's Jack! I'd recognise his walk anywhere.'

Hampered by poor vision, Aggie could only wait, breathless with excitement, until he came into focus.

'Bless my soul, so it is – and with some little 'uns too,' she exclaimed and, fumbling for a clip to replace her cap, she hobbled after Nathan to greet them. The children, a pale emaciated boy and a girl almost too weak to walk, held Jack's hands as though their lives depended on it. Which indeed they did, as Jack, when he sat down at the kitchen table, explained.

'I'll tell you all that's happened over a cup of tea, Aggie,' he said, undoing the tight buttons of his buff jacket and releasing his stock. 'First I want you to meet these two young mill workers, Smudge and his sister Meg. They are friends of young Robert, who is thankfully back where he belongs at Skellfield. Henry promised his son he would help them and indeed he has – by paying off the indentures that bound them to their master. As you can see they are too sick to work but he wants you to help them grow strong again, Aggie. Strong enough to become useful hands around the farm. Do you think you can do that?'

Aggie enveloped the pair in her heaving bosom and gave each a hug before removing the lid from a constantly simmering cauldron of soup.

'My broth is the best in the county' she declared, stirring it proudly with a wooden spoon. The children's eyes closed as they savoured the smell.

Jack smiled at Smudge when he opened them again.

'And when you're fit, young man, Nathan will teach you ploughing, hedging, ditching – even sheep-shearing – while Meg, why little Meg will make jam and butter, and milk cows and look after Aggie when she grows old.' He winked at them and then at the housekeeper. Laughter echoed round the room as Jack put forward Ramona's proposals. That she should be absentee owner and place the tenancy in Nathan's young but reliable hands. That initially financial help would be available to hire labour from the mills. As time went on, however, he would be expected to support the small holding and its workforce and to make of it what he could.

The news of Jack and Ramona's planned wedding at Christmas was cause for more celebration and a fresh jug of ale. The jollity died, however, when Aggie ventured to ask after Beth's state of mind. Jack fell silent, looking for an answer in the depths of his tankard.

'Beth wants for nothing. She is surrounded by those who care for her.' He downed his ale in one movement and wiped his mouth before continuing. 'But she knows none of us. It's as though she is trapped in another world and cannot escape. It breaks my heart to see young Robert trying to reach her. I fear she will never recover. Yet Henry will not give up. She has been measured for a gown to go to our wedding and he insists she accompany him to the church. I am instructed to take her out daily in the carriage but I see only fear in her eyes when I do. Though perhaps recently it is more bewilderment than fear. She has courage and resolve – I know that from the past – but those qualities can't help her now, it seems.'

'God bless the poor soul,' Aggie murmured

quietly, 'and God bless Henry too. May his faith be rewarded.'

Chapter Sixty-Four

The prayers of both Aggie and the Cunningham household did not go unanswered as the day of the wedding approached. Though silent and unresponsive, Beth became accustomed to her outings in the park with Lady between the shafts and Jack at the reins. The sharp air brought colour to her cheeks and encouraged an appetite. Occasionally a smile flickered across her face like a shaft of sunlight breaking through cloud. Had the old mare's tossing black mane triggered a memory?

On the very morning of the nuptials, however, she withdrew unaccountably into her shadowy world. Perhaps sensing the activity in the house and the pressure from the maids to wash and dress her more forcefully than usual, she pulled the quilt firmly up to her chin and turned her face to the wall. Henry, anxious that the day should be one of celebration, perhaps also overwhelmed her with his jovial manner.

'You must not let us down today, Beth. I shall escort you to the church and it will mark a new beginning for all of us. Simply hold my hand and allow me to lead you. I can save you from your demons, my dear, but only if you, too, reach out as you did in the boathouse that day. Do you not remember? When you risked your life to save mine?' He whispered the words close to her ear but there was no response and still no recognition. He stood up, perplexed, and ran a hand through his tousled blonde hair. A dress of palest green silk billowed gently near the window, catching the winter light. Nearby, too, lay the string of pearls and the pink corsage that he had chosen to complement her porcelain skin. A maid entered the room, uncertain what to do. Henry glanced at his father's watch then replaced it in his waistcoat.

'Let her sleep now,' he instructed. 'There is time for her to rest. The ceremony begins at three o'clock. I expect to see Beth dressed an hour before. I shall come back to accompany her then. Do your best, my dear.' He winked at the girl with a hint of his old high spirits before sweeping from the room to prepare for the wedding.

Everywhere servants were scurrying to complete their tasks: to put the finishing touches to the dining table in the great hall; to furnish the many hearths with baskets of pine and scuttles of coal; to place festive arrangements in all the rooms so that the spirit of Christmas would enhance the happy event. Garlands of holly, ivy and mistletoe festooned the gallery and the sweeping staircase while the displays of white roses and lilies that Jack had requested, wafted their perfume throughout the house.

When Henry reappeared, resplendent in morning dress, he found the bridegroom admiring the effect from the far end of the oak-lined hall.

'It will be a splendid backdrop for the evening's celebrations, will it not?' he smiled, clapping a hand on his friend's shoulder. Jack turned towards him, his eyes bright with excitement. He looked flustered and unusually nervous.

'I have a decanter of brandy in the drawing room, Jack, for just such occasions as this. It's a good one and you at least can savour it on your special day. Come, we must spend some time together, you and I, before you move into your marital home.'

Jack allowed himself to be ushered into an adjacent room which was generally only used to receive special guests. Aware, however, of Henry's continued abstinence, he had no wish to drink in his company. When Henry moved to the dresser to pour one, he raised a hand.

'With respect, sir, I'll not partake. I have waited too long for this day and I want nothing to detract from it now.'

'Nonsense, my boy.' Henry had already measured the brandy into a glass and was studying it against the light. He walked towards Jack who had settled himself in a damask chair. 'It will calm you. Besides I've poured it already and it's too good a vintage to waste.' Still Jack declined so that Henry gave up, placed it on the mantelpiece and strolled thoughtfully towards the window.

'You and Beth have played a big part in my life. You have earned your good fortune, Jack, and nobody could be happier for you that you have found true love. It defies all reason, does it not? But it is what makes our lives worth living. Who could explain why Beth holds the key to my heart?' He glanced at the long velvet curtains that fell in folds round the mullioned window and laughed without humour.

'She hid behind this, you know. Too timid to leave the room when my family entered and confronted me – about my bad behaviour, you understand. She sneezed after they had gone and gave herself away. How I enjoyed that moment,' he recalled. 'She was light as a feather and I picked her up and twirled her round and round and then set her down. She was transformed briefly from a maid to a woman in love. Oh yes, she loved me then even if she doesn't now. I saw it in her eyes.' He returned his gaze to the parkland and the lake which reflected a pewter sky. 'It will snow later,' he said laconically. Then, determined not to dampen Jack's spirits, he clasped his hands behind him and strode back to the hearth. 'But we shall have a grand day. And Beth will be there to witness it. You'll see.'

Remembering his duties, Jack searched his pockets for a sprig of crushed white heather.

'Would you do Ramona the honour of wearing this? She was most particular about it. I have one, too, and so has Robert.'

'Anything to please your beautiful bride, Jack. No doubt she has her reasons. And who knows that her gypsy ways are not wiser than ours?'

The two reminisced quietly as the minutes ticked by, until the scheduled carriages, adorned with more flowers, drew up at the steps. Joe, as best man, sat stiffly in the first. Jack stood up and adjusted his stock. His hair was groomed until it shone, its mahogany lights accentuating his dark eyes and good looks. The butler, smiling broadly, appeared at the door to escort him. Henry extended a suede-gloved hand.

'Well, my friend, the time has come at last. Good luck and congratulations. Nothing must delay this wedding. Your marriage must take place at three o'clock whatever the weather,' he added, glancing at the first flakes of snow on the sill.

After they had left, Robert ran into the room, his feet clattering noisily in his new buckled shoes.

'Whoa there!' Henry chided him. 'You must learn to walk with dignity in front of the servants.'

'Yes, Papa. But I've been looking for you everywhere.'

He emphasized the words between breaths. 'Beth won't get up, Papa, and you promised she would come to the church today. Why won't she talk to me? I gave her my kitten and now she won't talk.'

'Calm down, child. I shall see that she dresses presently. You have a duty today to accompany Lady Elizabeth. Had you forgotten?'

Robert shook his head vigorously. 'No sir. But Mama will not get up. You'll see. I don't like my Mama today.' He ran off before his father could scold him again.

Henry sighed and walked up to the mantel. Catching sight of himself in the gilt mirror, he stared, bereft of emotion, at his own image. The reflection was caught by a mirror on the far wall so that his blank expression was multiplied.

'Which one?' he murmured aloud. 'Which one is me? I am no longer sure.' The brandy glass was multiplied too, and the irony of it was not lost on him. One sip of that would necessitate another until no amount would be enough. He knew where that path led. But did it not also lead to relief from pain and disappointment?

He knew suddenly that he was being tempted as he had not been tempted in months. His thoughts veered recklessly out of control. Did he want to spoil Jack's special day? He was wafting the brandy beneath his nostrils now and old resentments began to surface. Why could Jack not have drunk the damned brandy? He should not have refrained, to protect him. It emphasized his weakness. He had been blessed with a son, it was true, the only child he was likely to sire, but why should he not also be blessed with a wife?

Soon, rational sense disappeared. Life was not fair. Why should Jack be fulfilled and not he? And why did Beth torment him so? To hell with abstinence, he decided, justifying himself with such thoughts. A man needed a drink. Just the one would not hurt. He watched his own image as he tipped the wide bowl towards his lips. It tasted like nectar, better even than he remembered. The rest he drank in a trice and, already devious, wiped the rim of the glass with his kerchief and replaced it on the tray. When Mr Scott re-entered the room, he turned away to hide the sudden colour in his cheeks.

'It's time to leave, sir, or you risk being late to

and met again

give the bride away,' the butler reminded him. 'With respect, what should we do about Miss Beth?'

Pretending to be absorbed by the scene outside, Henry called over his shoulder.

'I will see to Beth. Send the maid away to join the servants in church. And Scott?' He paused, choosing his words carefully. 'If anything should happen, if Beth refuses to come, you will take my place. Is that understood? The marriage must proceed at all costs.'

'God forbid, sir. There is no need for that. I will leave a maid to attend her.'

'Just do as I say, Scott, there's a good fellow.' Henry's sharp tone implied the conversation had ended and the butler, wiping his brow, withdrew.

Henry waited until his footsteps receded and then, as though drawn by a thread, approached first the dresser and then the small silver tray at one end. The decanter of brandy was almost full. He did not bother to use a glass.

Chapter Sixty Five

Beth, meanwhile, was not aware of the events unfolding outside her room. The servants had filtered away, hoping to find pews at the back of the church. Even her own maid had slipped off to join them, leaving her to rest as Henry had instructed. Her hair, however, had been braided and coiled and interlaced with pearls to match the single strand that encircled her neck. Her cheeks had been subtly rouged and her body encased in a corset. Only the dress, still hanging by the window, was needed to complete her attire.

She lay stiffly on her bed like a fragile porcelain doll. Perhaps it was not surprising that sleep, when it came, was fitful; not surprising that her most disturbing dream should return and that she should find herself once more running soundlessly through a vast mansion, along corridors which allowed no access to its many rooms. Again and again she tried the doors but all were locked. Again she sped up stairwells and down, along galleries and through halls, with a rising sense of panic.

This time she was saved from her terror by the very real sound of her own chamber door being thrust back on its hinge as a dishevelled figure burst into her room. Her eyes opened in fright. She was not accustomed to anything but gentleness. For weeks no one had spoken harshly to her for fear of worsening her condition. A man with very blue eyes towered over her, as she shrank behind a light coverlet.

'Get up,' he commanded. Her response was to recoil still further but Henry was having none of it. 'Get up!' he repeated in a slurred voice. He leant forward, so close that she could smell his breath. It smelt like something she knew. Yes, it smelt like the little leather flask she had taken from a saddle once – in a snow storm. The man smelt of brandy.

'Get up!' This time the order was accompanied by a rough tug on her arm and Beth found herself standing on shaking legs before him. She tried to pull away, to find somewhere to hide but he was much stronger than she was. He hauled her across the floor towards the green silk dress.

'You'll put it on and you'll go to Jack's wedding, my girl. I've had enough of your dreams and your fears. I want a wife and my son needs a mother.'

Too shocked to protest, Beth stood motionless as he seized the silk dress and dropped it over her head and her delicate frame. He cursed softly as he fumbled with the fastenings, before pointing to her heeled satin shoes. 'Put them on!' His voice still held menace so that Beth silently obeyed.

When he attempted to propel her from the room, however, she transformed into an alley cat, fighting tooth and claw to resist. She bit his fingers and scratched his face. Startled by her violence, Henry staggered back. Letting her go, he reached instead for the flask in his jacket, supporting himself on the panelled walls as he slurped its contents.

'Well, quite the little tigress again,' he laughed, examining his finger. 'You actually drew blood this time, my dear.' Briefly at a loss, he surveyed her with the eye of an old connoisseur. 'Damn it! What have you got that I want?' he mused aloud. 'I could have anybody. Don't you see that? Why, Lady Jane has still not recovered from my refusal to marry her. Yet you – a mere waif – you fight to escape me.'

Beth sank onto a chair, for once firmly focussed on him but with her mind in turmoil. Her head was spinning with images from her past life. If only she knew how to put the pieces together. This man was beginning to sound familiar. But why? And who was he?

Henry's reflective mood changed suddenly, as it often did in the grip of alcohol. Anger prevailed now and Beth withdrew to a recess in the corner of the room.

'You promised Robert you would be there and you will,' he declared, bundling her into a fur-hooded cloak He was slurring his words but his strength was not compromised. He pushed her hard towards the door. Too hard. A kitten shot out from under the bed, catching Beth's heeled satin shoe so that she fell heavily on the polished floor. Henry watched bemused as she raised a hand to her left temple. He was no longer rational and showed no concern. Finding his flask empty, he headed towards the door.

'Well, I shall return to my old solace. There's plenty more in the boathouse, you know. I dare say it's still there. You remember the boathouse, don't you? No, you don't,' he added bitterly. 'How could you? You don't remember anything.'

His parting words left their mark on Beth. Mildly concussed, she got up, knowing only one thing. She must follow him. That was all. It was imperative that she follow him. In her trance-like state, she was back in her dream again. But this time someone was with her. Someone was showing her the way. Wrapping her fur cloak tight, she approached the door and stepped boldly onto the gallery. It was deserted apart from the man with distinctive blonde hair who had just reached the foot of the stairs.

'Wait! Wait for me!' she wanted to call but, as in her dream, no sound would come from her lips. By the time she reached the hall, his footsteps were receding down a marble passage. 'Henry, wait!' she found herself mouthing, without knowing why she recalled his name. Not a soul crossed her path as she sped after him towards the courtyard door. He had left it ajar and she found her feet suddenly sinking into light snow. There was no sign now of the man she pursued but his footsteps, however disorderly, were clearly visible. With hope in her heart, she followed the precious imprints away from the house towards the mossy paths that led down to the river. The sound of its mighty current grew louder and louder, ringing alarm bells in her rapidly expanding world. She sensed danger now.

'Wait, Henry! Wait for me!' she repeated. Her voice

was a mere whisper but it was there, it was real. This was no dream. She stepped with renewed optimism from the main path into tangled undergrowth. The trees were bare at this time of year so that she could just see the boathouse sunk low against the bank. It was camouflaged now by many years' growth of ivy and evergreen. Brambles tore at her dress as she fought her way towards it. She had lost sight of Henry and his tracks, but instinct was leading her on. Her satin shoes were wet, her feet cold and her fur hood coated with frosty snow but none of this mattered. She was almost there. She was almost home, she thought, as she sought the steps that led down to the old green door. Nature had almost obscured it but Henry had stripped tendrils away from the latch. Beth paused, suddenly fearful. This was the door to her life but would it be locked? With trembling fingers, she lifted it and pushed. It opened. She stepped inside. A tall man with blonde hair was attempting to reach a boat.

'No, Henry! You'll fall!' she warned. Her voice had returned, strong and purposeful. Henry looked up, so surprised that he reeled backwards onto the splintered boards of the jetty.

'Are you flesh and blood, Beth?' he pondered aloud. 'I'm damned if I've seen an apparition before.'

'Come and find out!' Beth challenged, distracting him from his purpose. 'Come and hold me.'

'Sorceress!' Henry muttered. 'How do I know what you are? I met you in a snow storm. For all I know, you bewitch people like me.'

'Henry, you've saved me! Don't you see? The pieces have all come together. I've found my way home!'

'You mean you can remember, at last?' Henry asked. 'All that has happened?' He struggled to get up and stumble towards her. 'Why my moorland waif, you are real!' he declared, grasping her chilled hands. Stunned by this sudden turn of events, he was sobering fast.

'Well, I'll be damned,' he exclaimed, guiding her back towards the door.

'Where are we going, Henry?' Beth wanted to know, but he said nothing, only led her on through the wood a short distance to where a small stone slab was still visible.

'What is that?' he asked quietly.

Beth stooped to scoop snow from the surface. There beneath were the letters Jack had inscribed for her. She knew what they said. 'In loving memory of William Cartwright.' She stood up smiling. 'That was for my brother, William, was it not? And this is my garden. The one Jack made for me.'

'And do you remember...' Henry paused and looked down, as though fearing her reply. 'Do you remember all that happened here?' He turned back and fixed her with his very blue eyes.

'Aye, sir. How could I forget the most memorable day of my life? That day sustained me through so much pain. That and my love for you and my precious child.' She gazed up at him, radiant with joy. Awareness, however, was returning fast and with it came the horror of her terrible loss. Her hands went to her mouth as the truth dawned. 'They stole my child, Henry!' she wept. 'That's what I had to tell you. They've taken our son!'

'Our son is safe, Beth. Our son is safe. Robert is here at Skellfield where he belongs. Are we not blessed after all, you and I?' Henry wanted to embrace her – at least to hold her in his arms – but shame held him back. Instead he shed unrestrained tears. 'Jack and Ramona are, at this very moment, being wed and I, wretch that I am, have let my friend down. In truth I could not witness their union without feeling bitter about my own despair. I thought I had lost you. I allowed my weakness to dominate.'

Henry looked up and met her gaze with unflinching resolve.

'I cannot claim to be worthy of you Beth, but I can promise you this.' He withdrew a flask from beneath his cape. 'If you are by my side, I shall never again seek solace in a bottle.' With a strong thrust of his right arm, he sent the silver vessel spiralling skyward. They watched, hand in hand, as it formed a glittering arc over the river, before disappearing, like a mythical sword, beneath the surface.

A moment passed – a moment each would hold dear for a lifetime – as the ripples faded and wedding bells pealed through the falling snow.

Good ending

Richard Oastler died in 1861. The Leeds Mercury recorded the unveiling of his statue on the 15 May 1869:

'A statue in memory of Richard Oastler was inaugurated on Saturday, at Bradford, the centre from which the 'King of the Factory Children' directed his agitation in favour of the Ten Hours Bill. The Earl of Shaftesbury took the most prominent part in the ceremony and was assisted by the RightHon.

W.E. Forster M.P., Lord F. Cavendish M.P., Mr Miall M.P., Mr W. Ferrand, the Mayor and a large number of the principal inhabitants of Bradford. A vast procession, composed for the most part of factory operatives, met Lord Shaftesbury in the Peel Park and accompanied him to the site of the statue opposite the Midland Railway Station. The proceedings at the inauguration were brief but, the weather being fine, they were witnessed by an immense crowd of spectators who manifested the greatest enthusiasm. In the evening a largely attended public meeting was held in St George's Hall where Lord Shaftesbury and most of the Members of Parliament already named delivered addresses.'